Inclusions

Inclusions

by Emily Duvall

Cover Artist: Susan Krupp
Editor: Dave Field
Printed in the United States of America

Published by
WHISKEY CREEK PRESS
Whiskey Creek Press
PO Box 51052
Casper, WY 82605-1052
Whiskeycreekpress.com

Copyright © 2015 by: Emily Duvall

Warning: The unauthorized reproduction or distribution of this copyrighted work is illegal. Criminal copyright infringement, including infringement without monetary gain, is investigated by the FBI and is punishable by up to 5 (five) years in federal prison and a fine of $250,000.

Names, characters and incidents depicted in this book are products of the author's imagination or are used fictitiously. Any resemblance to actual events, locales, organizations, or persons, living or dead, is entirely coincidental and beyond the intent of the author or the publisher.

No part of this book may be reproduced or transmitted in any form or by any means, electronic or mechanical, including photocopying, recording, or by any information storage and retrieval system, without permission in writing from the publisher.

Print ISBN: 978-1-68146-135-9

Other Works by Emily Duvall available at www.whiskeycreekpress.com

Back to You
When We Were Perfect

Dedication

To Sonal Patel, for raising the bar

Acknowledgements

A huge thank you goes to my family: Ann Marie and David Bezayiff; Nathan Bezayiff, for motivating me, and also for supplying the coffee. To my in-laws, Dottie and Glenn Duvall for their effortless support. With each book I am most grateful for the encouragement and friendship from Jamie Kenny, Kim Menyhart, and Erin Niemi—I'm so lucky to have you ladies in my corner. A special mention goes to Lorraine Bukilica, Speech Pathologist and dear family friend for her input; Vincent Lash, certified Gemologist who took the time to talk with me; and Dave Field for the time and attention to detail of editing this book. For my husband Brian, my sounding board and my biggest fan, and to Nolan and Abby, for pushing me to keep writing.

Chapter 1

The cell phone rang from under a pile of laundry. Melanie Cahill thrust her hand under the clean clothes, grabbed the phone, and glanced at the screen. The telephone number sent prickles up her arms. One quick swipe of the screen and she answered with the same mixed emotion she always did when taking Mark's phone call. "Hello?" she said to her brother. The sudden sound of a neighbor's lawnmower propelled Melanie off her bed and over to a corner further away from the window. "Are you there?"

"I can hear you," Mark said, from somewhere inside the Corcoran prison. The clock ticked and their fifteen minutes began. "You sound quiet."

She slanted the phone and spoke with her lips touching the phone. "What about now?"

"Much better; I'll make this quick."

"Take your time." Melanie slid down the wall. She'd grown accustomed to the rush in his voice during their calls. She pictured Mark sitting in a cold room with paint the color of nothing, metal tables, uncomfortable chairs, and some prison guard watching his every move from a few feet away. Basic human rights like privacy didn't exist in her brother's world. Seven years Melanie and her family had been at the mercy of these random, short-lived phone calls. Their catch-up time was reduced to a few minutes. She didn't blame him for speaking fast enough to shove the last several weeks into a few minutes. If the tables were turned, she would talk fast too, or not call at all.

"There's a rumor," he spoke low and fast. "I've got good reason to think I'll be up early for parole. I'm talking soon, within the next six months. Six years earlier than my original sentence isn't bad."

Melanie hit the wall with an excited hand. "This is great news."

"I'm trying not to think too far ahead. I'm relying on my sources."

The alleged sources of such good information weren't worth Melanie asking about. The intricate workings of prison spun like a delicate spider web: invisible, full of layers, potentially a trap. Mark had been on the inside long enough to know how to get what he wanted from the outside. The bartering, the pecking orders and rivalries, loyalties, they all worked for or against an inmate and thankfully, her brother had made allies. She didn't ask what he did in return and Mark wouldn't elaborate. They both knew his life wasn't easy. "Do you want the rest of the family to know?"

"Keep this to yourself for now. Don't tell Mom or Jessie. I'm counting on your discretion. Those parole board members are nothing more than derelicts on a power trip. My source is confident I'll be receiving notice from my lawyer in early September. Three more months and I might have my freedom." Mark breathed heavily. "This place is the underside of a dump. I can't spend another day for a crime I didn't commit. Each day I wake up here's a day I lose a piece of my life. I'll rot in this place if this doesn't come through. Luke's responsible for this hell. I won't ever see him other than as a leach. However, as much I dislike the bastard, I find myself in a dilemma."

Luke Harrison. The name alone made Melanie's mouth go dry. "Go on," she said cautiously.

"Harrison will work against any personal progress I've made doing my time. His influence is far-reaching and he's known to be friends with members of the parole board. So I need him on my side, which means, I also need your help."

The warmth in her cheeks turned chilly. "I can't."

"You have to talk to him."

"I won't."

"Go see him. Tell him about the possibility of parole, be honest with him. I don't want him blindsided when he receives a letter from the California Prison System that I'm up for early release. I need this time to convince him how sorry I am. The two of you have a history."

"We haven't kept in touch." Melanie shifted uncomfortably on the floor. "I've been on your side since the detective took you away in handcuffs. I have no regrets about choosing to believe you over Luke." The calm in her voice didn't match the unsettled vibe tapping her bones. Like anything to do with Luke, she'd learned to be neutral, to not show the emotion backing up her spine like a bad traffic jam. "You've changed. Your voice sounds happier each time you call. Let the members of the parole board see you and judge for themselves all the progress you've made. Be humble. Be smart. Talk to them like you talk to me. We don't need Luke to help you. We don't need anything from him."

Inclusions

"Getting through this life is all about taking advantage of the connections. The one man with connections happens to be the person responsible for putting me behind bars. Not ideal, I know. I'm not above reaching out and playing my part. One trip to see him is all you need to make. I'll never ask for anything again. You've been my biggest supporter and I need you one more time."

"We're not talking about making a phone call. You want me to see him." Melanie flattened her hand over her forehead. "I have no idea where he lives. I haven't kept track of him. You're taking a huge gamble he'll even listen to me in the first place. We didn't part on good terms. He sent his lawyer to break-up with me! I don't think walking into his office and outright asking for a letter of support is going to help your case. The second he sees me, he'll throw me out, and shut the door in my face. You're asking too much of me."

"I'm asking you to try. Any life I can look forward to living is better than this one. He ruined my life and he should be the one stuck behind bars. All of those false accusations, his big-time lawyers, you can't let him win again. I have one chance to do this. You have one shot at helping me. Luke won't take my calls. I've tried writing to him, calling him, nothing gets through to him." An impatient sigh escaped Mark's mouth. "I know what I'm asking of you. When I hang up the phone I won't ask you again. I won't wait for you to reconsider. It's now or never."

Caught in the middle between loyalty for her brother and her self-respect, Melanie hesitated. The thought of going to Luke and asking him for anything, let alone this huge favor, forced her to swallow more than pride. She'd have to endure watching his memorable judgmental gaze pound down on her. The details of their relationship, especially towards the end, resembled more a game of tug-of-war, than an actual romance. All of the pain of the breakup she'd put behind her. She'd finished school, inserted herself into her career, and moved on with her life. The past had healed over like new grass on a dirt bed. Eventually, she'd found happiness. The answer she gave him reflected her uncertainty. "I don't know, I don't know, I don't know."

"Luke lives outside of San Francisco in a city called Belvedere," Mark couldn't speak fast enough. "He's going to be leaving for his annual summer vacation in Maui in a few days."

"Two minutes," said a deep voice.

"Time's almost up." Mark coughed. "What's your answer?"

The sound of their sister, Jessie, the youngest of the Cahill's swept through the house. The sound of her coming through the doorway and dropping her purse on the entryway table filled the house. "Jessie's home," Melanie announced.

"I need your answer."

Strangled desperation rang in Mark's voice. They'd survived their mother divorcing their father, the first time Melanie crashed the family car, and the trial for Mark's attempted murder on the life of Luke Harrison. They could persist through another big hurdle together. Years of blame and sadness could be put to rest. Melanie could almost, almost see Mark's homecoming through their front door: a big party with a large banner hanging over the fireplace mantle and their friends and family coming back with open arms. That shining image of their family being put back together gave Melanie pause. The rest she could figure out later. "I'll leave tomorrow."

"I owe you."

"Good-bye, Mark." Fraught with unease, Melanie ended the call and remained sitting on the floor. She stared out at her bedroom wall, painted a lovely shade of light blue. Mark might as well have taken a shovel to her head. She'd actually just agreed to go see Luke. The neighbor's lawn mower rumbled up again, coming closer to Melanie's window. Closer still, until Melanie thought he'd bust through the wall and mow down her bed. Big houses built on little property: the signature of their community. The conversation with Mark hung in her room, thick as the grass churning up outside and causing an allergen catastrophe.

"What are you doing in there?" Jessie said, knocking softly on the door. "I'm going for a swim. Are you coming?"

"I'll be out in a second," Melanie said to the closed door. Jessie's footsteps moved away from the door and down the hall. Both girls still lived at their mother's house, Melanie at the age of thirty-five, and Jessie, three years younger. Along with Mark, they'd all grown up in this house. They stood at the end of the street and waited for the bus from the first day of kindergarten until they'd received their driver's licenses. The two-story, cookie cutter stucco with a tile roof and two-car garage looked identical to every other block in a hundred-mile radius in Fresno. The age of the house showed up in the semi-stained carpet, the cracked tile in the first floor bathroom, and a yard full of after burns thanks to the brutal summer sun.

Melanie tossed her phone on the bed and resumed folding her laundry despite her hollow heart and full mind. Officially, she'd be on vacation tomorrow from her job as a speech pathologist at the Growing Tree, a prestigious privately-run center for speech disorders in children ages birth through five. The entire year she'd taken no personal days and the next two weeks promised a long overdue vacation. She'd finally look for a condo. She'd made out a list of books to read and set dates with friends. Clients at her place of work had all been reassigned to substitute therapists. Vacations took planning and Melanie's diligence paid off in the form of the upcoming worry-free days and the hope of sleeping in past five a.m. That was before Mark had called. She realized she'd been refolding the same shirt over and over again and tossed it aside. Leave it to Luke to ruin her plans, again.

Jessica Cahill pulled out a carton of ice cream, a bottle of root beer and some ice, slammed the refrigerator closed and grabbed a glass. "Talking to anyone interesting on the phone?" she said to Melanie.

"Our brother called," Melanie answered; grabbing a glass for water. The selection of ingredients on the counter meant a root beer float would soon follow. "You must be finished with finals."

"The problem with med school is I'm never really done. I've got two seminars to attend tomorrow, a sign-up for internships for next year, plus a boatload of summer classes I need to attend, then there are summer internships I haven't secured and I haven't even started my final presentation on ethics." She sighed. "Ice cream seems like a logical solution for the moment." A thick scoop of vanilla slid into the tall glass. "We're out after this. Talk to me about something else besides school. How's Mark?"

"He's pretty much the same. Then again, I don't ever feel I know what the real story is with him." Melanie couldn't keep the conversation they had shared from Jessie. Plus, going to see Luke meant she needed to talk to Jessie. They told each other everything. "There's a chance the parole board will consider his case in the next few months."

Jessie's eyes flared. "You're talking for real this time? What do you know about his sources, are they credible?"

"I don't ask about his sources."

"No, no, you really can't." She pointed to her glass. "Float?"

"I'm good." Melanie folded her arms over her chest. In looking at Jessie, she saw a reflection of herself: long cheekbones and eyes a darker shade of honey. They both wore their hair past their breasts. The length of Melanie's eyelashes beat out Jessie's in length, but Melanie lost on height, standing one inch shorter than Jessie at five-foot-six. A perpetual frown formed on Jessie's lips, as she did now, lost in some equation related to medicine and the human body. Melanie pressed on, despite her sister's obvious distracted mood. "What do you know about the city of Belvedere?"

"Belvedere's affluent." Jessie poured the root beer from the bottle to her glass, waiting for the exact moment to pull the bottle away. The bubbles frothed and fizzed to the rim without going over. "The city overlooks San Francisco." A scrutinizing gaze fell over Melanie. "Why do you ask?"

"I'm thinking of taking a road trip. I finally have some time off and I want to do something different."

"You never do anything different." Jessie added a red straw to her float while keeping an eye on Melanie. "Why would you go up North?"

Melanie watched Jessie, but thought of Luke. "I have my reasons."

"Is this about a guy?"

"This isn't what you think." Melanie decided to cut to the chase. "I'm going to see Luke." No last name required.

"You're funny." The determined expression on Melanie's face caused Jessie's eyebrow to arch in concern. "Why would you go see him?"

"Mark asked me. He needs my help and I'll be fine." Jessie wasn't convinced. Melanie continued anyway, feeling her dignity shrink. "Our brother feels I have a certain pull when it comes to Luke. I'll convince Luke that Mark's a changed man, and in return, I'll get Luke to write a letter of support to the parole board."

Jessie erupted in laughter. "Luke will never agree to help you or Mark. He'll only help himself." Jessie pushed the root beer float away like some great dignitary refusing to eat. "Do you really think Mark has forgiven him? Have any of us?"

"Mark wants to come home. I don't think anything else matters." Melanie rested her palms on the counter. "I have an opportunity to help bring home our brother. I know what I'm doing."

"I'm not sure you do." Jessie pursed her lips into a thin line—the effect made her look like their mother. "I know what Luke has meant to you. You wanted to marry him and up until he ended the relationship, you thought he'd bought you a ring. Heartache like that takes a long time to get over."

Melanie prepared herself for what came next, her sister's inevitable, broken theory about how Luke still had her heart on a string.

"Don't rush up to do this one thing for Mark. You'll see Luke and come back with your heart on ice. A trip to see Luke, even for a few minutes, is a bad idea."

"I'm all out of good ideas. It's been seven years. I'm a big girl now. And I miss my brother." Melanie grew impatient. For the past five years Jessie, and her boyfriend, Carl grew more and more in love. Her sister's credentials in heartbreak didn't exactly count. "You don't have to worry about me."

"If you insist on going, then I'm coming with you." Jessie stood up, determined and straight-shouldered with bony elbows and a rigid collarbone. "Better yet, I'll see if Carl can rearrange his schedule. He's starting an internship next week at an ear, nose, and throat doctor's office. Did I tell you he won the position out of a pool of five-hundred applicants?"

The last thing Melanie wanted was for Carl to come with them, cramped in her mid-sized car, insisting they listen to alternative rock for five hours. She had nothing against Carl. She just had nothing in common with him. Their conversations tended to revolve around ear canals and sinus infections. Melanie sniffed as she always did when Carl's name came up and she swore her ear began to itch. No, she didn't want him to come along. Standing on the side of the road and getting picked up by a stranger seemed more enjoyable. "I need to go on my own, Jess," Melanie finally said, secure in her decision. "I haven't seen Luke in a long time. Somewhere inside of me there's a woman he never knew, a woman he didn't get a chance to get to know, and I want to show him I'm not affected by him anymore. I'm different now. I don't need him to love me. I don't even need him to like me."

Jessie walked over to the cupboard, took out one of the bottles of hard liquor and unscrewed the top. She reached up to the cupboard, took out two shot glasses, and poured the drink. "Well, here's to finding your courage."

Melanie couldn't find her courage if it hung around her neck like a necklace. The more time she packed, the less sure she felt about her decision to go see Luke. Jessie wasn't much help either, sitting on the bed with a righteous gaze and commenting on anything Melanie put in her bag. "That shirt's too low-cut to mean business," she said. "You need to look the part. I still think a suit would be best."

"A suit will be wrinkled and stuffy from a five-hour drive. I'll wear a t-shirt with a jacket," Melanie said. "I'm driving up tomorrow, which means I'll wear something comfortable. I'll go to his house, talk to him, turn around, and drive home. End of story. I'll lose a day-and-a-half of my vacation at most."

"What if he asks you to stay for dinner?" Jessie frowned and nodded her chin to the black cocktail dress hanging in Melanie's closet.

"He won't."

"You have to admit, it would be satisfying to have the opportunity to turn him down."

"He's not going to ask me to dinner."

"This is going to be a total disaster," she mumbled. Jessie hopped off the bed and walked over to Melanie's dresser. "I'm nervous for you. This could go twenty different ways."

"Then I'm taking a chance." Melanie zipped up her bag. "I have one change of clothes in case I need to stop in a hotel on the way back."

"I'd like to argue against Mark's logic, really I would. I also know he's right at the same time. You're the person in our family with a shot at getting him to listen. Maybe he'll agree out of guilt for what he'd done to Mark. Maybe Luke will use this as an apology for dumping you so cruelly through his lawyer. You're empathic, a good risk-taker, and you've been negotiating between Mark and me for years. You're a classic middle child and you're used to fighting to get your way. So fight. Mom will be livid I'm sure. She'll wave this off as you being on some peacemaking crusade within our family."

"I don't want Mom to know where I am. I don't want her worried." Melanie picked up the bag and put it on her nightstand, next to the address she'd written down. Turns out, Luke's address wasn't difficult to track down. The street name and address number left Melanie a little confused as to whether this was a business or a residence. By this time tomorrow, she'd know either way.

"I wish I could watch from a hidden camera and see the look on his face when he sees you." The family photo framed on the dresser showed off their family prior to the divorce and she absentmindedly smeared a layer of dust off the glass. "Luke's made something of himself. He's not the small business owner he was when he'd worked with Mark. He sells gemstones in the big league now. Luke and his brothers have all been in the news at some point. Don't you pay attention? They bring back these unheard of gemstones and sell them for a lot more money than you'll ever make. I wonder what the company would be like today, if Mark hadn't gone to prison, if they'd remained friends and business partners."

"I wouldn't know." Melanie scoffed; knowing she'd thought similar thoughts. "Personally, I'm offended you've kept track of Luke and his family."

"I looked him up while you took a shower. Maybe Luke has forgotten about Mark. Perhaps he doesn't think of us and what he's done to our family at all. Aren't you a little curious?"

"No." Melanie shot Jessie an incredulous glance.

"Mark is right to try and pursue Luke's forgiveness, even if this whole visit is one big act. Our brother can talk a good game, and you're skilled at telling people the reality of their situation. Look what you do in your job each day. You look at some scared, worried parent in the face and tell them that their child needs more testing; that their child isn't where he should be developmentally. You break down the bad news on a daily basis and they pay you to come back."

Maybe time had softened Luke's perspective on the situation and perhaps, he would be open to listening, and what if, what if, he agreed to write a letter of support without reservations? Melanie released some of the weighed down hope she'd been holding onto.

"Keep me updated, will you?" Jessie set the photo frame back down. "I won't let our mother in on the scheme." She gave Melanie a fierce hug. "Don't let him win this time."

"I'm going to bed," Melanie said, stepping out of Jessie's embrace. "You should too."

"Wake me up in the morning, before you go."

"I will."

Melanie stayed up most of the night trying to guess what Luke would look like and what he might say to her. The moon faded and the morning came, leaving Melanie tired and her stomach wound in knots tight as a springboard ready to snap. She showered, skipped breakfast, and changed four times before choosing her originally planned outfit of a t-shirt, jeans, and tailored suit jacket. Jessie's door remained closed and Melanie didn't want to wake her. The sound of the shower in her mother's room filled the hallway and Melanie got her bag and headed out to her car.

The GPS displayed the directions in a colorful map hooked onto Melanie's dashboard. Weak morning sunlight exposed the car's age, a relic in the family's line of automobile purchases. Scratches veined the hood and driver side door. A recent run-in with the shooting rocks off a gravel truck put two cracks in her windshield. It's not that she couldn't get the glass fixed. She could. There were other, better things to buy in this world than replacing her car's windshield. The rough, worn seat cushions caused Melanie to sit on a sinkhole of worn leather and any day now, she might fall through and not get back up. She'd hoped by her thirtieth birthday she would have been able to get a new car. The day had come and gone without as much as a drive by the car dealership.

All of the money she saved now went towards the purchase of her own place. The purchase of a new car would have to wait. Everything felt at a big, drawn-out standstill these days. The wait for some guy to call back. The wait for her bank account to be full enough to buy a condo and new furniture to go with it. She eyed up the higher-level positions at work and did everything she could to be on the receiving end the second one of her coworkers gave notice. She received wedding invitations almost monthly and seven weekends in her summer would be devoted to attending engagement, wedding, or baby showers, all while she waited for her life to move forward. Waiting. She turned the key in the ignition and held her breath for the car to start. The engine came to life. The soft wheel sped out under her hands as she turned the corner, entering the highway at the same moment a sharp pink sunrise broke over the rooftops.

The drive to the interstate didn't take long. She put a hundred or so miles between herself and her house until stopping for coffee and a rubbery bagel at a gas station. A warm wind whipped through the air as she filled up her car with gas and got on her way. Those nerves she'd woken up with intensified with each mile she drove closer to Luke. The little amount of food she'd eaten felt swishy in her stomach. She hadn't planned on seeing him ever again.

Chapter 2

Thirty-seven-year-old Luke Harrison leaned back in his chair, satisfied at the half cup of newly polished Axinite sitting on the table in front of him. The stones gave off a deep coffee color thanks to their rich iron mineral qualities and the room smelled of rock. They would fetch a pretty sum either sold in individual pieces or as a group. The buyers would get a hard-on at this latest find. Luke turned off the polishing machine and stood. He stretched and felt the acute strain in his shoulders and neck from sitting and leaning too long. A ring of sweat formed at his collar from the stifled air in his laboratory, which occupied the basement of his house.

Luke picked up the cup of stones and tilted the container so they fell like a waterfall from one palm to the next. The smoothness of the gemstones never felt ordinary. It never got old. A man knows when he's in the presence of something no one else has. Luke grinned. The Axinite had come from a granite deposit in France, thanks to his brother Brent. Luke returned the gemstones to the container and sealed the opening with a lid.

The full weight of his responsibility breathed exhaustion down his neck. The upcoming vacation to Maui came at a good time: three whole months with minimal interruptions from investors, retailers, and lawyers. They would find him, of course. Buyers always did. They liked to flash their cash and see what Luke and his brothers could find. There was always someone, somewhere, with their mind set on owning the next big gemstone. Business in the gemstone-hunting world was at an all-time frenzy. Beyond South America. Past South Africa. The rarer the gemstone the better. Luke's clients demanded bigger than the biggest. Purer than the purest. Brilliant. Flawless. Fewer inclusions meant more value. Diamonds are out. Rare gemstones are in. Tanzanite, Emeralds, Cambodian Sunset Rubies all topped the list of most wanted. The world had finally woken up to the fact that there are scarcer gemstones worth more than diamonds out there and Luke cashed in on this shift in demand.

Luke brought those gemstones to the market. Trace Elements, his business, now ran up against the largest corporate competitors. The term *Trace Elements* actually held a specific meaning in the gemstone world. Every stone comes with impurities. Those impurities gave a gemstone color, like iron, lithium, copper, or chromium: the natural food dyes of the earth. The color attaches a market value. Luke had devoted his entire life during college and after to create such a monster business.

Luke picked up a paper he'd set aside earlier and glanced over the recent inventory sheet for a large quantity of Swiss Blue Topaz, found deep in the spine of Brazil. The mine, recently visited by his older brother, Brent, produced a large quantity of the gemstone with a color rivaling the Caribbean ocean. Those gems sat in one of Luke's many vaults in his house now, awaiting sales.

The vault in the basement sat flush in the wall at the far end of the room. Luke walked over, past the heat treatment machines, two gemstone polisher machines, and a cutting machine, and scanned his fingerprint on the digital scanner. The small door swung open and Luke set in the cup of Axinite. He closed the door and the lock automatically sealed in his life's work.

Ding. Luke glanced at the digital box on the wall. The alarm system alerted Luke of his next meeting or if someone in the house needed him. Twice today he had interviewed two women, one older and one younger, for the position of a second nanny/personal assistant to his daughter, Vivian. The main nanny would need some help on their upcoming trip. He didn't have to look at the schedule on his phone to know the next meeting would be the third and last interview of the day.

The previous two candidates hadn't impressed him. The younger woman had a face easy on the eyes. But Luke wasn't hiring for a woman to be his lover. He preferred a lover not to be in his employment. Those situations had never ended well before. His daughter required around the clock care, since he often jetted out of the country on a moment's notice. The younger candidate seemed more interested in what Luke did for living than the actual position of working with Vivian. The other woman, the second candidate, a veteran of teaching preschoolers, had mentioned her husband. A fact of little significance, except the position required the employee to live in Maui for the next twelve weeks, and possibly more, if the person worked well with Vivian. He needed someone flexible, not attached to their home.

Luke slid the suit jacket over his arms and turned off the lights. He walked up one flight of stairs to the main level, where he worked out of his office. He'd made enough money to afford living in Belvedere and he wouldn't be chained to some office space in a corporate building.

He paused in the hallway, at one of the large windows and saw the fields of tall, curvy grass bow to the breeze. The gates in the distance remained closed, with the triangle roof of the security hut in his eyesight. A car rolled up outside the gate and he glanced at his watch, ready to get the interview over with. If none of the candidates impressed him, he'd have to wait until they returned at the end of summer.

Luke returned to his desk and adjusted the room's temperature from the small tablet sitting upright on his desk. The latest, most advanced gadgets unburdened him from the ordinary process of walking to a wall-mounted, clunky, temperature-control unit. One of his friends, an engineer in a very private technology lab in Palo Alto would ask him to try out different, emerging technologies like voice and vision-controlled electronics from time to time. One of the many perks of retaining a certain level of cliental.

"Mr. Harrison," Kendra's voice carried through the speaker on the tablet, "Ms. Gardner has arrived at the gates. Security is checking her in now. Are you ready to see her?"

"Check if she'd like a drink first, I don't like the interview being broken up for beverage orders," he responded to the automatic voice system. No need for buttons or phones anymore. He could access anyone at the command of his voice.

"I'll see to it she has her drink before she enters your office."

Interruptions in general upset Luke, who remained rigidly in-control of his business and his life. The candidate he hired must understand the expectations Luke put on his life and his daughter's well-being. Such a person existed. The right amount of salary could get anyone's attention, and Luke paid from generous pockets. He simply hoped the person he needed would walk through his doors in the next five minutes and he could get on with his plans to go to Maui.

Kendra's voice buzzed through the intercom. "Mr. Harrison, I apologize. Security says the person at the gate is not Ms. Gardner."

"Who is it?" Luke began checking his email on his phone and typed with furious fingers about a fellow gem-hunter being captured and tortured somewhere in Turkey.

"Her name is Melanie Cahill. I don't see her on our interview list. I'm certain I didn't approve her."

Luke's head shot up and he looked at his door. "What does she want?" he said sharply.

"She wants to see you."

"Send her up immediately."

Chapter 3

The bright white paint of the security booth glowed in the late afternoon light. High, wrought-iron gates held closed by an impressive gold lock at both handles prevented anyone from seeing the house beyond the gates. The security guard could double as The Hulk. Broad-shouldered, round face, no neck and wolf eyes. "You may proceed," he said, unsmiling.

"Really?" Melanie answered. She'd been certain Luke would send her away. This bothered her. It wasn't like him to be so *friendly*. Then again, maybe time had softened him. Maybe he'd regretted how he'd treated her. Melanie manually rolled up her window. The hand-me-down car had survived years of Cahill teenagers and quite possibly, was one of the last models sold without power windows and locks. She smiled and asked, "Where should I park?"

The guard pressed a button and the gates cranked open slowly, giving her a glimpse of an imposing home at the end of a long driveway.

The security guard extended his arm out of the window. "Follow the road up to the house. Drive around the circular driveway and park to the left. You'll see the vacant spots. Do me a favor: don't block the entrance. Kendra Wright, Mr. Harrison's personal assistant, will meet you at the door."

The name Kendra didn't ring a bell. Then again, Melanie didn't know anything about Luke's business or his life, including him, anymore. Melanie tempered the exertion on the gas pedal so as to make the car glide, not speed. She would ride this opportunity long as she could.

A thin cloud of dust curled behind the back of Melanie's car all the way up to the security gate. The sight of the extensive protection around his property pinned Melanie's heart and hopes under a boulder. Every reason she'd thought of on the drive up had sounded lame and she scrambled to think of a plausible reason for her showing up at Luke's residence. None came to mind and honesty in the most desperate of times seemed like a bad option. She had no idea what her next move would be. Should she jump right in and tell him about Mark? Should she make small talk?

Inclusions

The asphalt ahead looked freshly repaved. Melanie kept both hands on the steering wheel, while spying up the row of Eucalyptus trees on either side of the road. The trees formed a border on the road, like armed guards. Between the wide, tall trunks, she could see spurts of green grass extend as far as the eye could see. The house sat in grand isolation.

The offensively large house came into view with peaked rooftops touching the sky. The home sprawled across the lawn and devoured the grass, leaving behind a pristine yard of professionally-trimmed hedges. She drove the car around the driveway, parked in one of the three open spaces and sat in the car for a moment. Their situations couldn't be more different. She'd been living at her mother's house and he'd been living in a place five times the size. Bitterness tugged at her chest. He'd done well for himself. Very well.

She couldn't leave now, she'd come too far today to turn around and quit. Melanie turned off the engine and smoothed over her hair, her face, and smudged a small stain on the hem of her shirt. She took a deep breath, which did nothing to calm her nerves. The first time she'd met Luke, she remembered feeling a similar surge of nervousness. The straps of her bag affixed to her shoulder while she contemplated the first time she saw him and she got out of the car.

The fresh air and stretching her legs helped her to refocus. The front of the house boasted two large glass doors clear as air. She approached and before she could locate a doorbell, the doors slid open automatically and the interior led her to a small foyer with yet another set of doors. They opened within two steps, granting Melanie passage to a barren room full of marble floors and an arched staircase at the far end. A person's home reflected the owner. Luke's home painted a picture of large, empty, and dark.

High heels charged across the floor and Melanie looked up in time to see a woman walk towards her with her arm extended.

"Ms. Cahill," she announced; giving Melanie a firm handshake. "I'm Ms. Wright, please accept my apologies. The doors are supposed to set off a warning bell anytime someone enters the house. I don't like for any of Mr. Harrison's guests to go wandering off in his private residence."

The face smiling back at Melanie showed off smooth skin and an attentive gaze, younger than Kendra's serious voice sounded. "Nice to meet you Ms. Wright." Melanie went along with the charade of actually being there for some important reason.

Kendra held up three fingers. "New technology can be so tricky. In three years houses all across the country will have a similar type of door. Keys are so clunky, aren't they?" She gave a little laugh. "Mr. Harrison will be onto something new by the time these doors hit the mass market. You're lucky he's able to see you, with his upcoming travel."

"Upcoming travel?" Melanie asked absently, trying to take in the grandeur of the house.

"Of course you know he's spending the entire summer in Maui. Mr. Harrison is a reasonable human being and an excellent boss." Kendra gazed critically at her watch. "If there are no other questions, may I offer you something to drink? We have coffee, tea, or water."

Kendra obviously didn't know why Melanie had shown up at his house, she had the weirdest feeling, like she was here for an interview or something. "Thanks, but I'll pass." Cue taken, Melanie walked next to Kendra. Spacious archways led them down a hallway without much decoration except for antique tables on one side and windows on the other with heavy drapes pulled back by thick cords. A pink, fuzzy elephant stuck under one of the curtains caught her eye. Her heart slammed against her chest. "Does Luke have a daughter?"

Kendra stopped and followed Melanie's gaze. "Yes, of course. Vivian turned two years old last week." She continued walking. Her heels knocked with *oomph* on the floor and echoed throughout the high ceiling and she kept moving apparently without a care for what she'd just admitted.

Melanie's bag dropped to her elbow. Luke was a father. Which meant his daughter had a mother. Melanie's heart hid behind shame. At one point she'd wanted to marry this man. Now he had a family, a fact Melanie couldn't breathe in without a quick stab to her heart. Without her, he'd been doing quite well for himself, a reality she swallowed with bitterness. In a different life, this might have been hers.

Abruptly, Kendra stopped at the double doors at the end of the hallway. "This is his office. Are there any other questions?"

One question jumped to the forefront of her mind. "How's his mood?"

Kendra blinked. "Excuse me?"

"I'd like to know if he's in a good mood or bad mood. Gives me a little bit of leverage, don't you think?"

She breathed in hard. "I think he's a busy man. Don't waste his time."

Melanie's gaze steadied on the dark-wooded doors with hand-carved, ornate lines. They screamed expensive, one-of-a-kind. The nerves in her stomach bloated up her chest. She put a hand high on her stomach. The worst he could do is to kick her out of the house. The thought brought little comfort, seeing as how Luke had long, strong legs from what she remembered.

"I'll be waiting for you when you're done." Kendra rapped on the door. The glitzy silver bracelet on her wrist dropped from her wrist to inside her jacket sleeve.

Melanie felt downright sick. Facing her past had been tougher than she'd ever imagined. Her hand remained on the doorknob a second too long and sucked out all of her courage.

"He's waiting," Kendra urged and gave the door an impatient push.

Melanie saw Luke first. She held her breath. Unaware of her presence and on his cell phone, Luke sat behind his desk and glanced at his computer screen. Lean, long arms stretched out in front of him. Arms and a chest and body made for wrapping around someone and holding them close. His clean-shaven jaw took her a moment to get used to. Her lips curled in at the thought of those demanding kisses every time they were together. There used to always be some length of stubble thanks to his days and weeks spent out in the wild. The Luke in front of her wasn't rugged anymore. He'd traded his cargo shorts for black pants and a tailored suit jacket.

Luke glanced up at her with such sharpness, Melanie's hands balled into fists. She stood there, met only by a piercing, hostile gaze.

The phone slipped out of his hand onto the desk. "So. It really is you." Luke got to his feet.

"Hello, Luke," she said, staying put, and not certain her feet would actually move if they could. Any clever opening line she'd rehearsed on the drive up scattered into hiding. Words stuck to her throat. She couldn't remember where to begin. A cough fled her mouth. *Say something,* she panicked. The plot to make a grand entrance and demand support of her brother's release seemed as ridiculous as the need for automatic sliding doors in a house. "How nice it is to see you."

A caustic smile crossed Luke's lips. "I see you still begin your sentences with lies." Luke took his time walking over to Melanie; his intolerant gaze pinning her down.

The harshness in his voice ripped through her plans. Forgiveness hadn't come to his house like she'd fluffed up in fantasy. The shadow in his eyes when he looked at her told her she didn't have much time. She found her voice in the bottom of her gut. "I'm going to explain why I'm here today and then I'll leave."

"No." Luke glanced at the door. "I want you off my property."

"I drove a long way to see you. I deserve—"

"You don't deserve my time." Redness rose up through his cheeks. He pointed at the door with a hard finger. "Get out."

"You let me up here."

"You had your chance to see me. Now you can find your way out."

Tears burned her eyes. She wouldn't have a chance to walk out with strength and composure. Luke kicked her out and it hurt a lot more than she'd imagined. All she could do included flinging the door open and running down the hall.

She never said the right thing in the heat of the moment, except working with children, because they served as a very forgiving audience. And most of her clients didn't know how to string two words together. Melanie's hands trembled. Thankful for Kendra not stalking the outside of Luke's office, Melanie took hold the mess of emotions taking over and breathed out slowly. She retraced her steps back down the hallway.

It split into four different shoots. If she walked left, she'd return to the front doors. Melanie chose to go right and gave a backward glance at Luke's office. The pounding beneath her chest began to subside.

The first set of doors she came to she pushed down the brushed knuckle handle and stepped outside. She thought she'd be able to get to her car easily from the door, but instead, she'd found the back yard. Two staircases descended below to a large, rectangular swimming pool, patterned by lounge chairs, tables, and potted red hibiscus on the outside. Melanie's gaze followed an invisible line over the diving board. Beyond the gray ocean, the cluster of ghostly buildings at the helm of the San Francisco skyline came into view. Unsettled currents ran through her body like the choppy waves. The patio directly in front of her overlooked the crystal blue water in the lavish pool.

Melanie walked over to one of the five Adirondack chairs surrounding a fire pit with broken down coals and ash, and sat down. Under the circumstances, she didn't feel proud for being at Luke's residence like this. Seeing his face and knowing how much he couldn't stand her, hurt more than she'd expected. She reminded herself that they hadn't been happy at the end of their relationship. Today she'd come full circle with all those heated feelings clogging up her chest. His actions still hurt her. They had never really left. This much, she knew.

Something moved to Melanie's left and she stood up fast. A little girl peeked up at Melanie from behind one of the chairs. Those crystal brown eyes, belonged to those of her father and she could see the slight upturn of her lips matched Luke's as well. "You're Vivian," Melanie said. The girl blinked and ducked again. Melanie sat back down.

Vivian showed her face. The wind blew her wispy, thin hair over her cheeks. She fussed and came out from behind the chair.

"Hi," Melanie said, setting down her bag. The trusty, sturdy canvas tote filled with a wallet, sunglasses, hair ties, hand sanitizer, and a variety of educational toys she carted with her everywhere. The trunk of her car held more boxes, each one filled with toys and games she'd checked out of the Growing Tree in their inventory room and carted to her clients' residences. The needs of her clients changed with their progress and her boss worked at securing very generous donations to buy age-appropriate and developmentally appropriate items. Melanie selected a plastic baggie with five, small, red blocks. Children loved this little game she played with them. She didn't think twice about engaging Vivian in a quick activity. What she did question, was why Vivian had come outside alone.

Curious at the blocks, Vivian took a cautious step forward. She squinted and rubbed her cheek.

The blocks fell on the chair next to Melanie. She picked them up and stacked them. "I'm going to play with these blocks," she said and stacked three blocks. The task she repeated two times while Vivian watched. "Your turn."

Vivian walked up to the chair and instead of taking the blocks, picked up the baggie, examined the cheap plastic while giving the blocks a lazy glance. She set down the bag and picked up the blocks; hoarding them in her small hands.

"Stack," Melanie said, encouraging her. "Stack blocks."

Vivian made fleeting eye contact. She looked back at the blocks. Vivian's eyes spaced out a little and they came together again. She stared at the blocks like she looked right through them.

"Stack," Melanie repeated and showed her what to do.

Vivian took the blocks in her hands, pushed them on the chair, and attempted to stack one without success.

Again, Melanie took the blocks out of Vivian's hands, built them up, and knocked them down. The second time, Vivian knocked them down and tried to grab them before Melanie could. Vivian swatted at Melanie's hands in frustration and she shook her head.

"You want more." Melanie closed her fingers and tapped them together, making the sign for more as she said, "More." Always give a verbal cue with sign language, a golden rule of her profession. Not surprising, Vivian didn't respond in either gesturing or words.

"Vivian, say "Ba," Melanie said, making an exaggerated motion with her mouth. "Ba."

Vivian wiggled and looked away. She looked off into space and mumbled a nonsensical noise.

Intrigued, Melanie played a few minutes longer. She tried out different letters and sounds, encouraging Vivian to mimic her. Vivian did nothing in return. She kept going for the blocks and Melanie put her hand over them to prevent her from grabbing them. Speech meant more than speaking. Listening included more than hearing. Development wasn't always straightforward and she could see without much formal evaluation that possibly, something was off with little Vivian. She worked around enough children to make a pretty darn good estimated guess, although she always approached her clients objectively and with testing standards.

Of course Luke would be aware of any developmental or speech issues with his daughter. This wasn't her case and he probably already had his daughter receiving the best services. She glanced up at the house, to a row of first-floor window, and a chill ran up her spine. Somewhere in the house, she could sense those dark eyes of his watching her and she pulled back from close proximity with Vivian.

Chapter 4

The fire beneath Luke's skin hadn't been extinguished. The longer he watched from his office, the deeper the burn spread. Melanie Cahill sat in a chair on his patio and interacted with his daughter. The look on her face, serious and interested, drew out the natural confidence. The hair waved in the breeze and Luke's fingers twitched at the thought of its softness, of how it looked made to be touched. His gaze lowered to her body, to the slight curve of her hips. His gaze reverted back to her striking face. Lips that beckoned a man's notice. Wide eyes complimented by elegant, arched eyebrows. Thoughts full of forbidden ideas entered his mind. Luke caught himself. Melanie handed the blocks to Vivian and he grew doubly irritated at her on his property and the whereabouts of the nanny. "Kendra, get in here," he ordered.

He thought about his younger days when he'd started up his first company with Mark Cahill, a college roommate at UCLA and a fellow entrepreneur. They had ranked in the top of their classes in physics and organic chemistry. Their aptitude for science didn't take them on a course suited for medicine or working in some confined, biohazard waste plant like a lab rat. Both of them had stumbled into gem-hunting by accident, after one of his professors set out an announcement called "The Race to the Kashmir Sapphire." Anyone in the class who could produce such a stone would get his or her entire tuition paid for by the professor.

No one did or ever had found such a rare gemstone. Last time Luke had checked, the offer still hung on the professor's wall. Each year the story made the news. The idea of going in search of such a gemstone had intrigued Luke. He enrolled at the prestigious International Gemology Association and had become certified to appraise gems. Mark had taken a similar path, and together they set out to create their own business—a business that failed horribly within the first two years, ending in a trial, and Mark's attempted murder on Luke's life. Luke couldn't think of Mark without thinking about his sister, Melanie.

What's Melanie doing here?

He couldn't get past that one question. He could have her escorted off his property this very second. Luke continued to stare at her intently as he scratched his chin. A thought entered his mind and he toyed with the possibilities.

"Sir?" Kendra answered and slid in through the door. Questions lit up her eyes at the notable absence of the guest. "Where's Ms. Cahill?"

Luke motioned her over and stabbed the window with his finger. "What do you know about her?"

Kendra took a moment to observe the woman outside, presently dumping blocks on the ledge of the fire pit with Vivian looking on. "I feel like this is a trick question."

"There's no trick." Luke pointed at Melanie again. "You know everything about everyone who walks into my office. What is she doing here?"

Kendra's face looked cut off from oxygen. "I can either find out or call security to escort her off the property."

Luke's gaze swept back to the window at the perplexing scene. His daughter didn't warm up to people. She usually screamed and fussed at anyone getting in her space. Melanie grabbed a small plastic cup from her bag and Luke made a decision. "Get Ms. Cahill. I want to speak with her."

Confusion clouded Kendra's eyes. "Okay. I'll go get her." She left Luke at the window.

Luke continued to watch and listen with ears strained to hear the dialogue. Melanie hid the small blocks under a cup. The sound of her firm, clear voice carried to the open window. "Want turn?" she said, followed up by, "Your turn."

Vivian pushed Melanie's hands.

"More blocks?" Melanie grinned and brought the tips of her fingers together in what looked like sign language. "More," she repeated clearer and louder. "More." She reached out and took Vivian's small hands. Vivian flinched and started to turn, but Melanie gently and firmly pushed Vivian's fingers together making the same motion as she'd done a moment before. "More."

Vivian surprised even Luke. Disappointment is what he often felt in terms of his daughter's general connection towards adults, himself included. Such a short time ago she'd come to live with him and he'd been patient about giving her time to adjust to the big house and swapping out a mother for a father. The first year of her life he hadn't been around much. He'd been busy traveling all over the world at a moment's notice, waiting for the next big tip. Gem hunting proved an addicting, all-consuming activity and to this day, to this very moment, a pang of separation anxiety crossed his bones at the thought of not getting out there again. He couldn't of course, the scope of his parental responsibilities made hopping on a plane and disappearing for weeks unworkable, even with the nanny, who'd been around since Vivian's birth.

Kendra appeared at Melanie's side and instructed her to follow her back inside. The genuine, full smile Melanie had used around Vivian flipped to a frown. The gentle arch of her eyebrows drew two sharp angles. "I'll leave," Melanie said, already plopping the blocks and cup back inside the bag.

"Mr. Harrison has changed his mind. He would like to see you," Kendra quipped.

A quick press on the window and the glass closed, giving Luke a moment to return to his desk and wait for Melanie to return. Annoyance flashed through him with every second. Every instinct told Luke to send Melanie away, to punish her for her betrayal. Luke liked to gamble and today his fingers twitched to roll the dice and ignore the bad hand about to walk through his door for the second time.

Chapter 5

The walk back down the hallway to Luke's office felt like the slow march to torture. The hallway seemed longer than it had when she'd first arrived. Melanie couldn't imagine what Luke wanted with her. She should be halfway to the Golden Gate Bridge by now. Home by midnight. The possibilities all pointed to some kind of embarrassment or legal threat. She'd trespassed and she'd remained on his property, and technically, he did have the upper hand in this situation.

There wouldn't be a chance to talk about Mark and the letter. She could forget such a lofty goal. This trip had been an activity in reaching too high on a very tall shelf. The strap on her bag kept falling and her steps couldn't sync with Kendra's cheetah legs. The frown on Kendra's face and her blunt silence served as acknowledgment that she'd been duped and didn't like it one bit.

Kendra sidestepped in front of Melanie and cut her off in front of the doors to Luke's office. "What do you want with him?"

Melanie arched an eyebrow. "That's for me to know."

A low grumble emitted from Kendra's throat. Kendra clicked her heels together twice, gave the door a stern knocking, and left Melanie. She gulped and went inside.

Luke waited for her at his desk; his legs outstretched in front of him, his expression disguised as casual. Appearance-wise, there wasn't anything casual about Luke. A man with a face hard as the angles on the table either looked pissed-off or almost content and in this moment his mood wasn't close to content. Carefully, he rubbed his jaw, looking at Melanie with a grim expression. "You have a serious problem following rules," he said with a flat voice. "I asked you to leave."

"And you have a problem with your security," Melanie retorted. She closed the door and hung back. "I took a few minutes to enjoy the view. I'm not sorry for that."

Luke didn't flinch. He rubbed his eyebrow and squinted. "Why *are* you here?"

"I came to say hello."

"Bullshit." Luke snapped his fingers and knocked twice on the desk.

His gaze leveled on her big bag. "You came to cause trouble. I saw you with my daughter. What are you now—a teacher?"

"I've never been a teacher."

His eyebrows lifted. "I thought that's what you studied in college."

"That was a long time ago." Steadier than before, her hand clamped down on her strap and she stood taller. He'd remembered at one time she'd planned to be a teacher.

He let the comment fizzle and pounced on another topic. "How's Mark doing these days?"

Melanie's lips flattened into a sharp line. "He's still in prison, but something tells me this isn't news to you."

Luke leaned forward and folded his hands on his desk while sporting a cavalier grin. "Let me tell you why I think you're here."

"Okay."

"I have two theories. The first one includes you coming to me on behalf of your brother. The second one is where you have finally come around and agree with the decision the jurors made. You want to ask my forgiveness and for turning your back on me." He smirked and shifted his feet. "You've come to apologize."

Melanie gritted her teeth. "I forgot that you're a jerk." The tote bag straps dropped off her shoulder, underscoring the moment. She repositioned the straps and added proudly, "Mark is innocent. The belief I have in my brother will never waver."

"Never's a dangerous word." Luke mocked her with his gaze. Slowly, Luke stood up from his chair. "One day I'll have my apology from you." He took a step closer and said in a low whisper, "Maybe you'll give me that apology in bed."

A laugh escaped her mouth. "Your wait's going to be cold and long."

"I'm a very patient man when I want to be." Luke folded his arms over his chest. "Is there anything else you want to tell me?"

"Maybe I *am* here because of Mark." Melanie pulled the strap on her bag for support. "My brother's become a changed man."

"Has he now?" Luke shrugged. "I'll stop you right there. I'm sure you'll say anything to convince me. I'm sure the two of you came up with some ridiculous agenda on your own. I'm not interested to hear how he's changed. Although, I do commend your effort. This must have been a real stretch for you. Driving up such a long way, assuming you're still in The Valley."

"He's a different man," she tried, knowing it made no difference.

"Regardless of the actual reason, I think it's fair for me to level with you. Your brother took something from me the night he tried to kill me. Something of great value. Go run back to your brother and tell him I want my property returned."

Melanie's feet felt like someone hammered them to the floor. She stood frozen with no idea as to what property he was talking about. Luke stared at her; pressing for an answer, any answer and each second passed as if she looked at the seconds hand on a clock and it wouldn't move faster. "You'll have to go through Mark to deal with unresolved issues. I've come today for another reason."

"You know what I'm talking about. I'll remind you in case you've forgotten. You remember my old, crappy apartment."

"The one with the neighbors you could hear having sex," Melanie pointed out.

Caught off guard, Luke laughed. For a moment their guards crashed to the floor. A thousand other good times stood between them.

Luke's grin vanished and he continued, "The night in question, the one I almost lost my life, my brother Brent had brought me a bag of very rare, Paraiba Tourmalines he'd collected on a recent hunt."

"You never introduced me to anyone in your family," Melanie reminded him bitterly. "I don't remember. Is Brent the older brother or the younger one?"

"Older." Luke cocked his head as if tempted to pursue this topic, but changed his mind. "I didn't take the tourmalines to the office Mark and I had shared because I didn't trust him at this point in our business partnership. I kept the stones hidden at my apartment, in my bedroom."

"You and Mark always kept the gemstones at your office, in the safe. What made these tourmalines so special? Were you going to sell them on the side and keep the profits?"

"The blues of these stones are like nothing you've ever seen. Ten in all, cut in various shapes: triangle, pear, rectangular, and they vary in carat size from almost five carats to a half. Their high clarity is astounding, the inclusions aren't visible with the naked eye. Beautiful stones. Brent and I were already starting the plans to build our own company and these tourmalines were going to finance the entire thing."

A flush of heat whipped through Melanie's cheeks at Luke's admission of splitting off from Mark's company. She'd always suspected he'd turn his back on her brother and his disclosure on the topic riled her all the more. She tapped her foot. "You sent my brother away, and somehow, you've managed to come up with some unwarranted blame about these stones your own brother probably took, or one of your shady neighbors."

"Don't try to put this one on my brother. I trusted him more than I ever trusted you."

Melanie forgot to breathe. Her cheeks prickled with anger. "Now you're just being cruel."

"Those tourmalines are what started the argument the night he tried to kill me. Mark made them worth more than my life."

"Your theory is convenient, unfounded, and a flat-out lie. Nobody said a blessed word about these tourmalines at the trial. You must be bored to make up such a ridiculous story."

Why didn't Mark tell me about them?

Later, in private, she could confront him on the phone. Right now she needed to deal with Luke. "Stay away from my family."

"You came to see me." Luke pointed at Melanie and then at himself. "Seven years is a long time to wait to recover what's mine." His eyes narrowed. "Your brother knows where they are and I'm happy to take him to court over this and reclaim the estimated eighty-five thousand dollars they're worth."

Melanie flung out her arm. "You never quit."

"You showed up here on my doorstep. Not the other way around. What did you expect?"

"I expected someone slightly more mature." Melanie fumed. "By the way, how's your daughter? I hope she's getting the services she needs. You *do* know for a two-year-old she should be speaking sentences around you."

"Don't ever talk about Vivian." Luke stomped over to her and stopped within a foot of her.

Melanie's eyes flared. "Does she talk at all?"

"*Get out.*"

The maddened look in his eyes couldn't stop her. Not now. Not when she was finally on a roll. It felt good to have the upper hand for once. All the ethics and objectivity which she abided by with the utmost strictness in her job flew out the window. There wasn't any reason to hold back. "Does she know how to say her own name?"

This pushed Luke over the edge. He stabbed his arm out so fast that it sent a tunnel of wind past her ear. He pointed to the door behind her. His eyes did the talking. Two narrowed angry slits and an even jaw.

She felt his breath on her face. Smelled the trace of caffeine from his mouth. Melanie dared to breathe with his lips so close. She relaxed her shoulders and regained her composure. "Okay."

"Mr. Harrison?" Kendra said, intercepting the moment.

She turned and stalked out of the room and inadvertently knocked Kendra in the shoulder. "How do I get out of here?" she said.

Kendra responded with a single, sharp point of her finger to the hallway behind Melanie. "Continue straight until you reach the sliding doors. The security guard will see to it you don't come back."

Melanie made her hurried way to the front of the house and to the doors. The automatic duo opened at the pulse of her step. Half-buried in her bag, Melanie's hand ruthlessly searched for her keys, forever lost on the inside. Frustration spread through her arms and fingers as she couldn't find the thin, circle keychain, and she considered dumping her bag all over the ground to search. Today didn't go anywhere near as planned. Luke had been horrible to her and she couldn't locate her keys. Everything felt like a big mess and she held back tears as she reached the door of her car. Now she'd have to wait another seven years to put this day behind her.

"Great," she said sarcastically. A shadow fell over her bag. Instinctively, she looked up at the cause.

"You're still driving that piece of crap?" Luke commented. "I thought you'd have traded up by now."

She snapped her gaze to his. "Don't pretend to know me." The keychain met her palm and she pulled it out of the bag with excitement.

"I should have given you more credit for showing up on the same day I'm giving interviews for an assistant nanny position. I must have Mark to thank."

"Save yourself the trouble of writing a thank-you note."

"I don't have the address to the prison on hand."

Melanie contemplated Luke and gave a sigh. "Look. The reason I came to see you is because Mark has a chance at an early release from his sentence. He asked that I come speak with you and I agreed, against better judgment." Melanie took a step towards Luke with her neck craning up so her face could meet his six-foot-two frame. "I'm not sorry for breaking onto your property and I'll get out of here." She gestured to the car door. "Let's pretend this visit never happened."

Luke's hands crossed over his chest. "I want to know why you said those things about Vivian."

The question erected sympathy in his eyes and such gentleness in his voice that Melanie dropped her hand with the keys to her waist. "Because I see something in her that I see in other children who are…" her voice trailed. She really had no right to intercede.

"Who are what?"

"Delayed. It's probably nothing. Vivian's doctor would have told you if there's reason for concern."

"I asked for your opinion."

"I think she needs some help with her speech. She needs to be around other children, if she isn't already, and not stuck in a mausoleum all day." Melanie stopped talking and stepped close to him. "She's your daughter. That's between you and your wife."

"I don't have a wife." He flashed a purposeful glance at Melanie's left ring finger. "Vivian's mother lives in Los Angeles and I take care of Vivian full-time, as of recently." A warm grin softened his angled features. "What makes you think I'm married?"

Those lips had caused damage, Melanie thought, irritated by the distraction. She glanced at his left hand, as if to prove him wrong. The question trapped Melanie. Any answer she gave would give her away. He wanted her to admit she'd been keeping up with his status. "Don't flatter yourself. My sister Jessie mentioned some updates about you a few months ago." Pleased with her solid answer, she nodded. "I haven't kept track of you."

"How did you get my address?"

"Don't you know? I just drove into town and asked. You're too wealthy to be anonymous." Cornered by her lie, she jiggled her keys, waiting for his response.

"There have to be no more lies if you're going to accept." Luke grinned and shrugged his shoulders.

"Accept what?" Now he had her worried. "I've got a long drive and we have nothing else to discuss."

Luke put a hand on her arm. "Stay for dinner."

Melanie laughed. "Out of the question."

She heard and saw as Luke's phone vibrated in his hand—he glanced at the screen and read the content. The corners of his mouth tightened. "Excuse me a moment. This message is important."

The distraction gave her a chance to open her car door.

Dinner, her mind raced, *he invited you to dinner.*

She glanced up at him, reading something with intensity on his screen. Business came first, nothing new here. The wind pushed scents of dried grass and dirt through the air.

"Melanie Taylor Cahill," Luke announced. "You graduated with a Master's degree in Speech Pathology from Cal-State Sacramento. You've worked at The Children's Center for Speech & Communication Disorders for two years, with children ages from birth to five-years-old. You primarily visited clients in their home…" Luke's eyes scanned the text. "You moved onto work at the Growing Tree, a privately-funded speech center for children. Highest ranked early intervention center for children in the entire state…" Luke read a little more and then tucked his phone away in his pocket. He moved closer to her and stopped directly in her front of her and spoke to her like they were shooting the shit, "Tell me what you really think of my daughter."

The keys felt heavy in Melanie's hand. "Are you sure?"

"Absolutely."

"Do you have her working with anyone on her speech?"

"No."

"Luke, she's not where she needs to be. I'm surprised she's gotten this far without any intervention or support services. Most kids her age can say around one hundred words. She should be putting small words together. She should be communicating at a much higher level." Melanie held Luke's gaze, knowing he wouldn't want to hear the rest, but needed to, in order to understand the severity of Vivian's situation. "The lack of speech isn't her only problem. There's limited eye contact. She doesn't point or gesture. I tried to get her to mimic some animal noise. A cow says "moo" a horse says "neigh." She doesn't understand and most kids her age do. Before she can speak, she needs to make sounds. Without the sounds, she won't be able to form words, and eventually, string words together in a sentence." Melanie stopped rambling, unable to tell whether Luke had stopped listening. "It's imperative she start receiving some sort of therapy soon." She turned around and clicked up the handle. As an afterthought she added, "Good luck with everything."

Luke took one more step in her direction. He stood so close that he breathed warmth down her neck. "Come work for me."

Melanie's fingers missed the door handle. She turned around and faced him. "You're not serious."

"I am serious." He shut the door when she tried to open it. A grin crept up his lips. "You haven't heard my offer."

"I'm not looking for a new job."

"I need someone in the ring with my daughter, fighting for her."

"That's *your* job." Melanie leaned against the car, fiddling with the keys. The air in her chest felt thick as dough. "You're the parent."

"Two days from now I'll be traveling to Maui. Vivian and I will be there for three months. The person I intended to hire today would be going with us, in order to provide the nanny with additional help. I no longer want to hire for that position. I want you to come work for me, for Vivian. Help her with her speech for the duration of our vacation. You will be paid as a full-time employee."

"This isn't ethical—"

Luke bore his gaze into her eyes. "Forget the ethics. This is you and me talking. You come and work for me for the entire summer. In exchange, I'll give you that time to locate the tourmalines your brother stole from me."

A combination of impatience and fatigue ran through Melanie. It made things worse that she couldn't stop staring at him. Of course, Luke would make this about himself; about something *he* lost. "You're not even trying to be charming. You're outright bargaining with me. Those stones could be anywhere by now."

"Gem hunters always know where their stones end up. I'm confident your brother knows exactly where they are. They're probably in your mother's house under his bed. When you find them, I'll write Mark a letter of support for his release. I'll forgive him on paper and I'll tell my contacts at the parole board he's no longer a threat to society. I'll give you what you came all the way to ask me for."

The chance at securing Mark's release seemed deceptively easy. She bent her head, sighed, and felt her fingers coil at her side. The implications for this job offer ran deeper than a simple "yes" or "no" response. "This is blackmail."

"We both have something the other wants." Luke stepped back and put a little more distance between them. "We each picked our loyalties. You picked your brother. I'm giving you an opportunity to get what you want. I don't care about what happened between us in the past. I'm talking about today. I'm talking about right now. Why did you come see me?"

This might be the only way to help her brother, a point she couldn't argue with for very long. "I came to help my brother."

"Exactly; I'm asking you not to go just yet. Stay the night in town. There are several hotels nearby. I'll put you up, you think over my offer, and we can negotiate the details in the morning."

Melanie stood stock still for more than once in the hour. She didn't know what to say to him. No part of her wanted to give in and let him win and yet, could she say no? Would she look back on this and wish she'd done this for her brother? There wasn't any good way to work around Luke's sudden offer. With her hand behind her, she opened her car door. "I'm going home." The door swung wide under her fast reaction and she got into the driver's seat before she could change her mind. "Good-bye, Luke."

Chapter 6

Traffic backed up the road before Melanie drove very far. The sunlight blinded her. The lack of water and food generated a headache, grumpy stomach, and leg cramps. Today hadn't turned out at all as she'd anticipated, and although she should have been happy about Luke's offer, she admitted to herself how much the entire situation wrapped around her head more than once. She knew Luke and she'd grown up with her brother. Both men could distort the truth, but the nagging thought at the back of her head persisted.

Luke wouldn't have offered you the position if he wasn't certain Mark had the tourmalines.

The wheel jerked under Melanie's sudden movement and she veered to the exit immediately on her right. An overnight detour at a local hotel could buy her a little more time, not to mention she could have dinner and sleep. She could always leave in the morning and fight traffic on a full stomach and a night of rest. Plus, she wouldn't have given Luke the gratification of agreeing to think over his offer. She would think about this on her own terms and in her own time. She flipped on her blinker and followed the winding road.

The town of Tiburon is where she ended up for the night. The short drive from Luke's house got her off the road for the evening. Tiburon stretched out across the high cliffs like a golden belt hilted with stunning homes and green landscape. A layer of thick fog crept in the distance as if rolling in a round of applause at her decision to stay put for the evening. The first hotel she spotted she pulled into the short driveway and found a parking lot full of BMWs, Mercedes, Range Rovers, and a Tesla. As a child, her parents hadn't taken her to any of these quaint resort towns. They always did big touristy city stuff like ride the trolley and have packed lunches at Pier 39 with the sea lions barking and moaning.

Melanie took her tote bag and entered the hotel. The small lobby consisted of a counter and concierge table with pamphlets on nearby attractions. Elevator music played from above and a couple dressed in formal evening wear walked by her and exited the lobby. The check-in process took no time at all and the clerk gladly took Melanie's credit card.

Melanie followed the brightly-lit hallway to the elevator where she got on and went up to her room on the third floor. She found her room in the middle of the hallway, swiped her key card, and went inside. The air conditioner spewed off at full blast and sent chills over Melanie's skin. She walked over to the unit and turned it off at once.

The curtains had been pulled back, which gave her a view of the restless gray waters and the creeping fog, surrounding a cliff. The spacious room and eye-catching view made her feel more alone than she had in a long time. One encounter with Luke and she felt like a whirlwind had knocked her upside the head. He could still affect her. He could still turn everything she'd worked for upside down. No matter what she told herself about being hungry or tired, she stood in this hotel room because of him.

Turning away from the view, she plopped on the bed, succumbing to the layers of waves on the downy comforter. She lay down on her side, closed her eyes, and tried not to think about Luke. What a wasted effort. She thought about this job offer and the smugness on his face at making such an offer without even mentioning a salary. No, she couldn't take the job. She had a job she liked very much. She lived a full life with her family and friends. Melanie flipped to the other side and punched her pillow. This wasn't supposed to be how the day ended, with her heart stumbling over the sight of him and lying on a hotel bed actually considering his offer. Then, now, all the time in-between didn't matter, it's as if she'd been living in a glass world and he walked up and took a hammer to it.

All angles needed to be considered, including the absurdity of the story about the stolen tourmalines, a breathtaking sight in pictures alone, although she'd never seen one in the flesh, let alone ten. Not many people did. The story he'd made up about her brother and the stones had to absolutely be false. She sat up, turned on the bedside light, and called Jessie. The screen on her phone indicated her mother had called twice.

Avoid, avoid, avoid, she thought. They lived in the same house. Such a thing as too much togetherness existed. The woman who had birthed her could sniff out a lie an entire country away, let alone up the state. Her mother wouldn't understand. Luke had been accurate on this account too, Melanie couldn't lie. Her traitorous body gave her away in the form of a cracked voice, an averting gaze, or fidgety fingers, sometimes all three.

Jessie picked up on the first ring.

"I'm glad you answered," Melanie said.

"I've been keeping my phone close to me all day," Jessie answered. "How's everything going?"

"I'm not sure." Melanie dove into the events of the day, ending with, "He offered me a job."

"A job?"

"I turned him down."

"Yet, you're staying the night in the town next to his. You're considering his offer, or at least entertaining the idea of listening to the full extent of his offer, aren't you?"

"I'm tired."

"Don't take the offer."

"I'm leaving first thing in the morning. I won't have to fight traffic tonight." She paused and rubbed her temples. "What do you think about the other story Luke told me, the one about the tourmalines?"

"I think he's telling more lies. If these gems were so important, Luke wouldn't have stored them at his apartment when he had a safe at his office. Mark has never mentioned this tourmaline, which sounds like poorly named vineyard, and Luke didn't bring them up at the trial. He's kind of late in placing blame if you ask me."

"I thought the same thing."

"Exactly."

Melanie's eyes popped open. "Didn't Mark have a key to Luke's apartment? The defense attorney made that point very clear during the trial."

"That doesn't make a difference now. Keep your focus on what matters. Don't buy into Luke's story. He spreads lies. He convinced an entire jury, of mostly females, might I add. Our brother is behind bars because Luke lied about being attacked by Mark. Our family's been broken wide open and we've all struggled to redefine our family. Don't let five minutes with Luke get to you. You are above him and we can help Mark without Luke's help."

"I know." A faint beep reached Melanie's ears. She pulled the phone away from her ear and looked at the screen. "Mom's trying to call. Does she know where I am?"

"I told her you were doing some shopping in San Francisco and you'll be back tomorrow. The end of the school year is on Monday, she's too busy to nose around until then." Jessie said something to someone in the background. "Carl just arrived. We're going out to dinner."

"I'll call you tomorrow, when I'm on my way home. I have to get something to eat and then I'm crashing."

Melanie remained seated on the bed after the call while the dark clouds outside shadowed the room. Luke, the mystery of the tourmalines—she knew a reasonable person, a stronger person, would be able to let this all go. She would too, if not for the troublesome whisper of her gut telling her to dig deeper, to look closer. Mark wouldn't be able to talk tonight. She'd have to wait until the morning and put a message through or wait until he called her. They could dissect Luke's lies in seconds. The answers would have to wait.

A quick shower ate up some of her spare time. She changed her shirt, wishing she'd packed a little more, and dried her hair before leaving the hotel room. The walkway from the hotel led to the main part of town, a quaint street with charming boutiques, art galleries, and restaurants. The air smelled like mist and the wind served up a slice of evening chill.

A bistro on the corner looked inviting with pretty potted annuals on either side of the brick storefront. A chain of small bells jingled as she opened the door and stepped inside to the cozy sitting area, so warm and painted in browns and red, she swore the room gave her a hug. The hushed atmosphere of candles on tabletops and mismatched chairs with tables appealed to her. Downbeat music without words played from speakers. Her feet scuffed on the hardwood as she approached the hostess.

"Welcome," the hostess said, handing Melanie a narrow green menu. "How many people are in your party?"

"Just one," Melanie said, taking the menu.

"Sit where you like. We're a bit slow this evening." The hostess looked around the room, partially full of patrons eating their food. "Someone will be right with you."

She thanked the hostess and went towards a table in the back; her hunger amplified with each step. The table might become her dinner if she didn't eat soon. Two steps towards her table and she stopped. Luke sat in the corner table, across from the table she'd been about to sit down and order dinner. Dressed in the kind of sport coat with an insignia on the breast pocket and a shirt collar so crisp, she could cut butter with it, Luke looked in his element at a cozy bistro in an exclusive neighborhood. Upon spotting her, Luke leaned back with the faintest grin on his uneven lips. The blonde woman seated across from him, turned to see what had robbed Luke of her attention.

The decision to stay or go hung in the balance. Melanie raised her eyebrows back at Luke and made a choice. She'd rather go hungry than sit across from his table. Maybe he had decided to pull the job offer. This woman might be another coworker, or his girlfriend.

Melanie turned around and walked back to the front door. "I've changed my mind," Melanie commented to the hostess on her way out, handing the menu back to her. The bells jingled again on her way out of the bistro.

She couldn't get away from him. A stifling thought coupled with a loud protest from her stomach as she scanned the street for other dinner options. The coffee shop across the street made for a quick getaway. The pink neon sign blinked O-P-E-N and she crossed the street.

The name of the restaurant she didn't know. She opened the door and walked inside. The smell of baked goods and grease hung in the air. Instincts led her to the large glass counter full of displays of cakes, cookies, and near the back shelf, a buttery ham and cheese croissant. Along with a coffee, she paid for her dinner and found a table in the back. The coffee bar appeared to hold a different kind of clientele than the bistro she'd attempted to eat at a few minutes before. Luke wouldn't follow her into a place like this, and, for the third time today, she had interrupted his private life. The table wobbled from one of the legs being too short and Melanie's heart rate shot up. Such a silly aggravation to expect four legs to stay firmly planted on the floor. The table wasn't the real problem. She brought the roll to her lips. The table dipped and straightened again. Melanie cursed.

"I thought you'd be well on your way home by now," said the familiar, baritone voice.

The roll dropped out of her fingers at Luke's presence. She responded without looking up at him. "Don't leave your date waiting too long."

Luke ignored the comment. He removed his coat and casually swung it over the back of the chair. "Does this mean you'd like to hear more about the position?"

"No." The table dipped again.

"I'd like to point out that you didn't go home." He flashed a questionable glance at the croissant and sat down. "Let me buy you dinner. We'll have more of a formal interview if you like."

"I'm satisfied with my dinner." She took a large bite out of the croissant to prove her point.

His lips twisted into a cunning smile. "I made a few phone calls after you left my house."

"You know how to use a telephone. Good for you." Buttery flakes stuck to her palm and she wiped her hands on a napkin.

"You'll be interested to know I was talking with Linda Meyers."

Melanie's hand froze. Protectiveness bolted through her veins at the thought of anyone going behind her back. "You spoke with my boss? Why would you call her?"

"I called her to find out more about you. Apparently, you're in high demand. Your boss told me there's a waiting list of clients who want you to work with their children and you've won prestigious awards for your work in the special needs community with children and their families. You're a speech pathologist and you're also trained in cognitive development. I must say, you should learn to brag more about your qualifications."

"My job isn't some gemstone up to the highest bidder. How could you call my boss?" Melanie's phone rang. She shook her head. Luke infuriated her. The sight of her boss calling her sent her into a panic. Melanie's fingers accepted the call. Linda wouldn't call and interrupt her vacation for any reason unless an emergency.

"I'll wait." Luke leaned back in his chair; his face certain.

"Hello, Linda," Melanie answered grimly. "Is everything okay?"

A minute later, everything wasn't okay. The call ended. Melanie put her phone on the table and took a slow, calculated breath. She narrowed her eyes. "What did you do?"

"I made a phone call. I already told you that I spoke with Linda."

"How do you justify what you've done? My God, I forgot how full of yourself you can be." Melanie's raised voice garnered a few glances from the people seated at the table next to them. "Linda let me go."

"You didn't hear her then." Luke scooted his chair forward, his gaze intent upon Melanie.

She leaned forward. "This is my job and my life. You can't mess with me. I'll take you to court. I'll sue you." Melanie slammed her fist on the table. The coffee shot out of her cup and trickled down the sides. The response to blot the hot liquid, immediate and hastily, she rubbed her skin with the napkin. *What have you done?*

"I moved my name up to the top of your waiting list." Luke scooted his chair closer to Melanie's. He spoke low and strong, the confidence of someone who had already won the battle.

"Linda wouldn't fire me." Melanie blinked unbelievably. The fury in her eyes clouded her vision. She didn't feel the tears until they dripped on the backs of her hands.

"You haven't been fired. Not exactly. Didn't you listen to your boss? Think of this arrangement like a temporary loan. A new client came in and hired your services."

Melanie laughed. "Thanks for turning me into a prostitute."

Luke wasn't laughing. "I secured your services for working with my daughter until the end of August. Linda will keep your job for you until then. You're on sabbatical for all intents and purposes. There's nothing left in your way to say no."

"You are so presumptuous. I have a family. I have my own life. I refuse to work for you."

"Why?"

"We have a past. We have a complicated personal situation. You also went behind my back and recruited my boss to be on your side. I stayed the night because I didn't want to drive home. For a very brief moment, I did think about giving your offer a fair chance. This," Melanie said, making a small circle with her hand, "this is too much. You've trapped me into a corner."

"I'm making it easy for you to say yes." Luke stood up and grabbed his coat.

"You're leaving because you're not getting your way."

"It's got to be two hundred degrees in this place. Come outside with me."

"I don't want to go anywhere with you."

"Melanie, please."

She caught the same look in his eye she'd seen earlier, when they'd talked about Vivian while standing by the car. "Okay," she said simply.

They moved out of the coffee house and away from the probing gazes and whispered dialogue. The coffee, the wadded napkin, and the half-eaten roll remained on the table. Melanie let Luke go ahead while she collected her jacket and her bag, thus allowing herself a few extra seconds to think about what he'd done and consider her options, for once she stepped outside, she didn't know what to do or what to say. The decision should be easy; the direction obvious and she couldn't begin to know which way to go. Luke had reached the point where a phone call and his bank account could buy him whatever he wanted and she should have been more careful. She should have known this about him the second she'd stepped onto his property.

The street light flickered upon her stepping onto the sidewalk. Luke leaned against the street lamp with his hands in his pockets. Such a casual, sexy countenance and the very picture of a man on the verge of getting what he wanted. "All of our history aside. Give me one good reason why you won't work for me."

"Because I despise you," Melanie said to the sidewalk.

Luke's long finger lifted her chin and he forced her to meet his gaze. "This time say that to my face."

Melanie shrugged off his hand. "You have no concept of what my life has been like with Mark behind bars. Do you know what my family has gone through? I came here today to—"

"You came to ask me to write a letter in support of Mark. A letter I will never hand over simply because you showed up and you asked. I make deals, Melanie, with the worst kind of people out there. I don't give away anything for free just because you feel entitled. What you did today with Vivian is more than anyone's done for her. I can see you care about her. You're the only person who has bothered to confirm some things I've seen in her. You're diligent and you have exceptionally high expectations for yourself and your job. Those were Linda's exact words when I called her. I also knew that before she ever said any of it. I have to have you."

"I don't see how we can work together." Melanie felt herself weaken at the firmness of his voice and the determination in his eyes, he wore her down and she stood on the fragile line of confused and curious. Could she really walk away? Did she want to? The wind pushed for a fleeting moment carrying with it memories of the past and possibilities for the future. Although, what those possibilities were, she couldn't say. The choice before her tempted her interest and she played her only card. "Drop the issue of finding the tourmalines. Accept they are gone and I'll consider this position."

"No way."

"Luke, please."

"You've been loyal to your brother. Now let's see how loyal he'll be to you in return. My name alone will open doors of opportunities. My clients are some of the wealthiest in the world. They have the resources to have someone else go scatter across the globe and look for gemstones. Your boss said it herself, after you're finished working for me, you can return to your position at the Growing Tree if you choose. Or, if you want to go somewhere else, you'll be able to work anywhere in the world, at the location and company of your choosing. The tourmalines are part of my offer. Put them back in my hands and we can go our separate ways."

"Say for one crazy moment that Mark did take them. What if I can't get them back? What happens to the letter of support?"

"You will get nothing."

"Nothing?" Melanie tried to keep up with all the questions swimming around in her head. "What about my salary?"

"I'll still pay you. I'm offering to double your salary. That was the agreement I made with Linda. My lawyers have already faxed over a letter of intent. I promised to take on the financial responsibility. Your boss, I'm sorry, your ex-boss, did not agree to this until she saw in writing the donation I offered to her company to close the deal. The position I am offering you is once-in-a-lifetime. You know this. As for your brother, I'm willing to bet he'll be freed from prison only to wind up back on the inside. He's the repeat offender type."

"Watch what you say about him around me."

"The chance I'm offering you will not come your way again. Make a deal with me."

The promise of something more—the need for something darker lingered in his gaze. She felt herself cave at what else he would ask of her.

What he wanted from her and not trusting herself to say no. "What if I can't give you an answer?"

Luke's hand brushed over her hand at her side. The tip of his finger touched her thigh. "Yes or no."

Twelve weeks in Maui. More money than she'd make in the next two years. Plus, access to Luke's resources. She took his hand. Her heart hurtled. She could do this. No turning back. "Yes, we have a deal. I want this in writing."

The worry on his face vanished, swapped out by an all-business demeanor. "They are already drawn up and waiting for your signature."

Chapter 7

"What will you have?" Latonya said, wiping down the last of the pots and pans. The chef of the house insisted on handling all of her own cleaning, instead of directing a fully-staffed kitchen. Her mother had raised her to be in charge of all aspects, right down to drying a pan. The cleaning part was as important as the cooking. Latonya set the pan to the side. "I've got jumbo shrimp scampi, linguine with clams, or I could grill something for you."

"Thanks, but I've already eaten," Luke responded upon entering his kitchen, after having made the deal with Melanie. The lawyers worked at the very moment putting together Melanie's contract.

Unconvinced, she set down another pot on the composite countertop. The oversized light fixture above the island mimicked several layers of blue and green strips, like individual ocean waves. The kitchen counters shone under the blazing light. No crumb dared to show a bumpy face, no fingerprints smudged the refrigerator, and not a germ hid in the sink. "You look like you need a drink."

Luke lifted his hand as Latonya started to go the refrigerator. "I'll get my own." A tall glass of beer seemed appropriate to Luke, who drank very little, unless entertaining or out with clients. He grabbed a bottle of Sam Adams off the shelf and took the chilled glass handed to him by Latonya.

The heavyset black woman with hair neatly pulled back in a ponytail, handed Luke the bottle opener. "You want some company?"

Luke took a seat at the counter. A long sigh escaped his mouth. "You've worked for me for some time."

She hummed low. "Worst six years of my life." Latonya pulled a jar of salted mixed nuts from the pantry, poured them in a bowl, and set them in front of Luke. "You're going to need a new dishwasher soon. I'll put in the order with Kendra."

"You practically designed this space, pick out whatever you want." Luke dabbled in cooking now and again. Each time he got a little better under Latonya's mentoring. He found cooking relaxing and a good escape from appraising and selling gemstones.

She sighed heavy with her shoulders. "What's bothering you?"

"I hired a speech therapist today." An overly salted almond caught Luke's attention and he picked around for more.

Latonya began wiping down the counter around the sink. "I heard about the unexpected visitor. News travels fast around your house. Is she really—?"

"Yes. Melanie Cahill." The name rolled off his tongue familiar and strange, a name he hadn't said in a long time. Her name wasn't one he expected to say today. She'd walked through his doors and landed herself a job all in the span of the sun rising and setting.

The towel under Latonya's fingers stopped. Sharp disapproval lit up her face. "Excuse me, but why would you hire the sister of the man responsible for an attempt on your life?"

Luke took another swig of his beer. "I'm well aware of the history I share with this woman."

"You're either up to something brilliant…" she paused, and shook her head, "…or you have a death wish."

"You could be right." The woman he'd confronted tonight wasn't the dispirited, routine woman he'd known intimately. Today he'd seen something bolder in her gaze from the moment she'd walked through his doors. The effect of her irresistible face stayed with him even now. Her eyes and that body. A current ran through him at the thought of touching her. He should have sent her home right away.

"You'll find out either way." She raised two sharp eyebrows at him. The towel folded under her quick fingers and she placed it on the counter. She continued to talk while opening the refrigerator and selecting a beer. They did this sometimes, they talked like friends. "Have you kept up with Melanie?"

"We lost touch." He left it at that.

She took a seat next to Luke with her opened beer bottle. The fat gold wedding band on Latonya's ring finger showed small scratches under the light and she twirled the band out of habit, even though she'd lost her husband three years ago. "Well, what are your intentions for Ms. Cahill? Is she really capable of helping Vivian learn to talk or are you suddenly lonely?"

"So you've noticed Vivian's lack of speech too."

"I notice everything."

"Then you know that I wouldn't hire Melanie under false pretenses. Turns out, she's extremely qualified. What are the chances? I'm simply…" Luke said, stumped, "I'm curious to find out what's become of her."

I've also got business to address.

"Curiosity is a dangerous creature. It's a big black cat slinking down the street at night staying in the shadows all hissy with claws out and fangs for teeth. Be careful what you choose to sink your teeth into. You don't want to bite into something poisonous."

"I've been bitten by poisonous spiders, never a woman." Luke chuckled. "Melanie isn't her brother."

"Still, family vengeance is the worst kind. I'll be keeping my eye out for you." She raised her beer a little. "On a different topic, we're leaving for Maui soon."

"Yes, we are."

It didn't take long for Latonya to switch the topic to business. "Breakfast and dinner are covered for everyone in the house. The house guests are on their own for lunch. We'll work around the dinner parties and socials Kendra has planned. Unfortunately, you'll be getting little rest. There's an event almost every night leading up to the week of your brother's wedding. Thankfully, Damon's bride is handling everything for her side of the family. Felicity has already provided me the details of what she wants for the wedding rehearsal and wedding reception."

The label on Luke's beer bottle loosened under his finger and he pulled at the sticky wet paper. "My vacation doesn't sound much like one. I should switch places with Brent and go look for a gemstone on the other side of the world."

"You miss the chase of the hunt, I know you do."

He couldn't argue with her statement. "Make sure all the bills for Damon and Felicity's wedding come to me. I want them to have whatever they want."

"I'm surprised he's getting married at all." Latonya picked up the two used bottles, walked over to the utility door, and tossed them in the recycle bin. "I'm going to head out. You need anything else?"

"No."

She lowered the lights, removed her checkered apron, and hung it up on her hook. "I'll see you at the airport."

"Good-night, Latonya." Luke's phone began to beep. Email notifications popped up on his phone screen. Heavy footsteps grew quieter down the hall, until Latonya left through the front doors. The house settled into the noiseless night, interrupted by no one, not even Vivian's loud footsteps or shrieking laughter.

Luke rested his elbows on the counter and read through his messages, none of them urgent. The thought of Melanie sleeping a short drive away occupied his mind. Tomorrow, he reminded himself, he'd see her in the morning when she came over to sign her contract. The initial thought to hire her had been nothing serious when they'd been standing by her car. Melanie had looked too good to let go. She'd enticed him with one seductive smirk. He'd like to rediscover what those lips would feel like on his again. He would also have his work cut out. Melanie still stood by the idea of her brother's innocence. She'd get him back those tourmalines to prove a point, to get something in return. Whatever happened in between, he'd be damned to send her away for a second time.

Luke got up from the stool and left the kitchen. Moonlight gouged through the windows in the hallway where he walked to get to his bedroom. He bypassed the windows and saw the eerie, chalk-white scene of the outdoor tables and chairs. Melanie was back. Somehow, he knew he wouldn't sleep tonight.

* * * *

The following morning began on noise overload the instant Vivian hopped out of bed and ran down the hall, squealing high-pitched and announcing her presence. She slammed every door in the hallway before running downstairs. Stevie's heavy footsteps pounded after Vivian and she caught up to her in the kitchen. Luke lifted his mug of coffee to Stevie, Vivian's longtime nanny. "Good morning," he said.

Vivian flung into the kitchen, speeding and laughing. She sped up at the sight of Luke in the corner table. He put down his coffee. "There you are." He tried not to laugh at Stevie rounding the corner after her, too slow to keep up.

Halfway to Luke, Vivian tripped over her own feet and clocked her forehead on the corner of the counter. "I've got her!" Stevie yelled and caught her fall before Luke could scoot back his chair.

Deafening silence filled the room a split second before Vivian let out the loudest scream they'd ever heard. The small lips of hers quivered and tears poured from her face. Stevie held her close and ran her aged hand over Vivian's head. She whispered words of sympathy between Vivian's cries. One of the chunky blocks of quartz on Stevie's bracelet captured Vivian's attention. The tears and shuddering breath subsided as she picked at the large, pale pink stone surrounded by tiny diamonds.

Luke walked over and kneeled down in front of his daughter. He awkwardly patted her on the head and glanced up a Stevie. "Do you want me to take her?"

"I've got her." Stevie shook her wrist and the bracelet looped closer to Vivian.

The bracelet charmed Vivian and everyone breathed a sigh of relief, everyone except for Luke. Frustrated with himself, he stepped back. The daughter he'd fought for primary custody of felt more comfortable with the nanny. Vivian didn't go to him when she was hurt. Much of the time, she treated him like a stranger. He remembered what Melanie had asked him yesterday and he looked at Vivian and asked, "What's your name?"

Vivian didn't bother looking up from Stevie's bracelet.

"She's only two. Give her time," Stevie added.

"I know." Luke brushed his hand over Vivian's rosy cheek. The vacation would be a good chance to spend more time with her.

Luke stalked out of the kitchen, distracted by another round of notifications on his phone. He walked through the kitchen doorway without looking up and *smack!* The sharp edge of his jaw hit someone's forehead and his phone crashed on the ground. "Watch out," he griped.

Melanie stooped to the ground and picked up his phone. "Don't bother moving. I'll get my own bag," she snapped.

The sight of her caused Luke to grin. She looked sexy and tempting and irritated. He assumed the irritated part had something to do with him. Which gave him satisfaction. He liked knowing he could get to her. "Good morning," he said back to her, "and I'll get your bag." He bent down and picked up the large tote bag, chuckling at the heaviness. He transferred it to Melanie's waiting hand. "What do you keep in here, a dinosaur?"

"Yes. The kind that jump out and rip people to shreds. I didn't get much sleep. There's a lot to go over."

"You could have slept here," Luke said, straight-faced.

"You could have called me seven years ago." Melanie patted her bag. "I spoke with my other boss, the woman I will be returning to work for at the end of the summer, and she emailed me some materials, documents, and evaluation forms. I'll have to buy some supplies and toys once we get to Maui that will be essential for my sessions with Vivian."

"Buy whatever you want. I'm paying."

"You don't have to remind me you're footing the bill. Now, are the papers ready to sign? I'd like to get something in writing before you take anything else from me."

"You're eager to work for me. Good." He crossed his arms over his chest. The shade of rich color of her eyes, like brown zircon, drew him in. "I thought you would change your mind."

"I did, several times."

He could see she wasn't lying. "Why did you show up then?"

"I'm eager to prove you wrong about my brother."

"Let's not waste another minute then. The papers are ready and waiting for your royal signature. I told you they would be. My lawyers live for my unpredictable requests. They don't know what to do with themselves unless I have a last-minute, complicated request."

"Luke—"

"Mr. Harrison," he corrected happily and enjoyed the flash of provocation cross her face. No need to make her think she had any special privileges. She could call him Luke in bed. And she would.

"Mr. Harrison," she responded in a drawn-out voice. "Are you sure this is what you want?"

He heard the honesty in her voice and decided to be straight with her. "You are exactly what I want." Let her interpret his words anyway she wanted.

She blushed and looked to her bag. "We're talking about work."

"Always." Luke steered her by the elbow. "Let's go to my office."

They walked down the hallway to his office and found Kendra waiting outside the door. She raised a sharp eyebrow and her lips dropped to a frown. "Hello."

Inclusions

"Melanie Cahill, this is Kendra Wright, my personal assistant. The two of you met yesterday, unofficially. Ms. Wright is your contact person for everything."

Both Kendra and Melanie stepped forward at the same moment and their shoulders bumped together, bringing them to a standstill. "After you," Kendra said unhappily, and motioned Melanie inside Luke's office.

The three of them sat down at a large, rectangular table off to the side. Kendra placed several documents stapled like a booklet in front of Melanie. "These are standard hiring documents, tax forms, personnel documents you'll need to fill out first. Usually, our new hires have a few days, but we'll be leaving for Maui tomorrow morning. The details of the trip are outlined on page twenty-two. I must have everything signed, sealed, and delivered to our lawyers within two hours. I'll go over all of these documents with you."

Luke put aside his flirtatious mood and switched to a serious tone. He never joked when the topic impacted his business. "One of the core principals of all my employees is confidentiality. Gemstones are in high demand and you may hear or be told information about certain trips Brent is out following up with tips at any given moment for whatever gemstone we are looking for. We have high-end clients. We have people giving us a lot of money to find something rare. There's a level of discretion I expect from all of my employees. You must sign an agreement indicating that you understand any information relating to my company, whether personal or business is not for public knowledge. You are not allowed to talk about your work to anyone, including your brother." The stern expression on his face matched his voice when he spoke next. "Your position is highly sensitive. You'll be working closely with my daughter. I have exceedingly high expectations of your judgment when including others in conversations pertaining to Vivian. I am very protective of her."

Melanie ran her hand over the slate gray tabletop. "I've gotten to where I am because of the trust I've built with my clients and their families. I know Linda must have told you something when you stole my job. My guess is she said something to sway your decision. So you know," she said to Kendra, "Linda is faxing over my hiring information, including my background check to work with children."

"I received those forms an hour ago," Kendra replied. "I also need a brief job description, in your words. We can change the information later."

Melanie swiped a lock of hair off her forehead. "You can expect to have regular progress reports for Vivian. When I get to Maui, I'll give her a formal evaluation and I'll set goals for her, along with your input, Mr. Harrison. We will all be held accountable for helping Vivian succeed. I can help give her the push she needs to develop her language and skills, but my time with her won't produce miracles. Each adult in her life has a part to play in helping her meet her goals." Melanie flipped through the document and gave the details a cursory glance. "I see here that Vivian has a nanny."

"Stevie Burrell has been Vivian's nanny since birth," Kendra said, scribbling a few last notes. "She'll be traveling to Maui with us."

"I want to meet with Stevie today and get acquainted. The two of us will be spending a lot of time together with Vivian."

"That shouldn't be a problem." Luke folded his hands in front of him and Kendra began to review the forms with Melanie. Long, graceful fingers curled around a pen as Melanie nodded and initialed and signed each line. The forms arrived in his email early this morning and he'd reviewed every single page to make sure there were no mistakes. "I should also point out your medical and travel expenses are covered."

"I would expect nothing less."

Luke lifted an eyebrow. "Don't overstep your bounds. My generosity only goes so far."

Melanie looked up swiftly. "I'm doing this for my brother. I took the job for your daughter. I didn't sign on for your generosity."

"I've got to make a copy of your driver's license and social security card." Kendra stood up and waited for Melanie to find her wallet and pull out the identification cards. "I'll be back with these in a moment." She glanced at Luke and excused herself out of the room and left the door open.

The room fell quiet around them, enough to hear the scrape of the pen on the paper as she turned the page. Melanie turned the page without taking her gaze off the text. She raised an eyebrow and suspicion clouded her eyes. "You're giving me a five-thousand-dollar signing bonus."

"There's no time for you to go home and pack your bags. You'll need to take some time either today or when we get to Maui to get what you need."

"No strings attached, right?" she joked with an undertone of seriousness.

Luke ignored her comment. "Do you have any other questions?"

"What should I do with my car while we're gone?"

"I'll sell it for scrap metal." Luke stretched his hands behind his head and flashed her a caustic look.

The pen slipped between her fingers. Hastily, she retrieved it before it rolled off the table. "Don't touch my car."

"I won't touch your car." He grinned. "There's a parking lot on the outskirts of town. I'll have your car driven there."

She set down the booklet. "You have this all figured out, don't you?"

"Yup." Luke didn't have it all figured out. He wouldn't admit this to her.

"We're all set," Kendra said; returning to the office with a handful of more papers and Melanie's ID cards. "If you've signed everything and have no more questions, we're done here. Welcome to Trace Elements. I'd like to take Melanie around the house and introduce her to the other staff members who will be joining us in Maui. When we're all finished and you've had adequate time with Stevie and Vivian, you'll be taken back to the hotel in Tiburon. I'll have your car removed off Mr. Harrison's property and a taxi will pick you up in the morning and take you to the airport."

"Wait. I didn't see anything about the accommodations once I get to Maui. Where will I be staying?" Melanie looked from Kendra to Luke.

"You will be staying at my beach house." Luke held up his hand at her shaking head. "My core staff stays at my house. The location of my home isn't close to hotels or condos. We're somewhat isolated and this point is not negotiable. My brother is going to be married at my house and it will be easier if everyone is in one place. This way you'll have access to Vivian each day. You'll create your own schedule and will have plenty of separation, I can assure you."

"I don't like the idea of staying in the same residence as a client," Melanie protested, "not to mention how completely unethical this is."

Luke got up from his seat, content with the ease of this particular hiring process. He didn't point out the residency during the trip was outlined in the document she already put her signature to a few moments before. "You used to visit clients at their homes. How is this different?"

"I showed up at their homes in my car and left an hour later. Because this is your house..." Melanie's voice faltered as she glanced at Kendra, waiting with a hand on her hip and a sour expression. "There are ethics."

"The word 'ethics' is a bit loose in my line of work." Luke whisked by the table and walked over to his desk. "Kendra, give us a moment."

This time, Kendra shut the door when she left his office. Luke waited until Melanie wrestled with the idea of staying in his house and lost the battle. He walked over to her with every intention of putting her nerves to rest. "You shouldn't be bothered about staying at my house." Luke touched her chin with his fingers, bringing her gaze to his. "Sharing a bed with me wasn't repulsive before."

"I'm not thinking of your bed."

"I am."

Melanie's face flushed. "This trip is business, for both of us. Don't confuse the situation."

"I'm not at all confused. Neither are you. We're going to get something out of the way before we take this trip together." Luke pushed aside the papers in front of her. His mouth came down on hers with such force. The pen slipped out of her hand and rolled off the table. He breathed in her soapy, fresh scent. His tongue moved inside her mouth with urgency. His hands moved to her jaw and soaked up her creamy skin. She gasped between breaths and tried to pull away.

Luke kissed her again. The warm tongue he sought fought him at first and then opened up to him. The hesitation of her mouth gave way to her tongue screwing around his. Her entire body moved and the shift caused the chair to make a loud noise. Luke's lips parted from hers and he trailed kisses down her neck to the open spot at the top of her shirt. His ragged breath matched hers and he forced his lips back to hers and kissed her harder, deeper, and faster. His hands grabbed at her waist and he thrust her on his lap so he could feel her against his arousal. Her plush breasts pushed up against his chest and his hand flew down to skim over them. The sound of her quiet moan undid him. Melanie's hands raked down his shoulder and around, to the front of his shirt where she unbuttoned the top button.

Abruptly, Luke reined in his control. He pulled back. "No."

Melanie's face reflected surprise and disappointment. Breathless and flushed, she stared back at him. "What?"

"Now that's out of the way. We'll have no problems working together." He pointed to the door. "Kendra is waiting for you."

Chapter 8

What the hell? Melanie thought as she boarded Luke's private jet. The kiss hung on her mind like a bad idea. She didn't know what he'd been thinking. She just knew it changed the dynamics between them. The sight of the jet's gleaming interior gave her pause in the doorway. The individual leather seats, a flat screen mounted to the wall, and glossy wood tables gave the appearance of a posh restaurant and not a mode of transportation.

"Sit where you like," Stevie said, standing and rummaging through a bag; her designer sunglasses propped up on her head. Vivian sat alongside her, taking in the new surroundings.

Melanie selected one of the chairs towards the back of the cabin. A tray of cheese and crackers packaged from a farm in Napa sat on the table in front of her with a card. She picked it up and read the thank-you note from a winery owner, who wished Luke a well vacation. Stevie and Vivian settled into their seats, followed by Latonya, and Kendra. There had been no sight of Luke this morning and Melanie didn't know how she would react upon seeing him. They hadn't run into each other since he kissed her unexpectedly in his office.

The previous day she'd spent at a nearby shopping center buying new clothes for the trip. Not a dime of the bonus had been used a decision Melanie felt good about. The monetary reward for signing with Luke would be used to bulk up her bank account, and ultimately, go towards the cost of the condo she would purchase upon returning to Fresno at the end of the summer. Financially, she felt this decision to be a smart move. The money she would make almost justified her impulsive decision to join Luke and receiving the letter of support would be the ultimate win. She could tie this summer up with a tidy bow at the end.

She heard Luke's voice before he boarded the plane and she buckled her seat belt, attempting to look distracted and not at all concerned with his presence. The attempt failed the second she looked up and found his piercing gaze directed at her. The attention didn't last long. Kendra walked up behind him and handed him some papers. They sat down and began talking in low, serious voices and going over the document.

A short time later, the flight attendant closed and locked the door. The pilot, an acquaintance of Luke's, guided the plane further away from the hanger and took off down the runway into a cloudy blue sky. Melanie looked out her window at the sight of the other airplanes stationed on the runway at San Francisco International Airport. The buildings and the air traffic control grew smaller in her sight. The bay expanded out in front of them until the pilot drove the plane out west, towards the ocean.

They had been in the air for some time. Luke remained busy working with Kendra and from what Melanie could see, Vivian slept. Stevie read a magazine and Latonya read a book. Ripples and bumps met the plane high in the sky. Melanie glued her hands to the armrests. She didn't mind flying, but she preferred to be on solid ground. The conditions out of the window showed off thick clouds connected together as far as she could see. More thumps disrupted the plane and Melanie's hands flew to the seat belt buckle.

Kendra turned around and saw Melanie's death grip on the strap of her seat belt. "You shouldn't worry," she said. "Captain Miller and the co-pilot are the best at their job. All of us on this plane have flown in worse conditions."

Another bump jostled Melanie's entire body. "Do you fly a lot on this plane?"

"I fly wherever Mr. Harrison goes." She snuck her boss a sideways glance. Luke sat with his back to them and his laptop open in front of him. "He used to travel much more when he actually hunted the gems. Now that he's more business than thrill-seeker, we're on the ground more than in the air."

"What changed?"

"Vivian came home."

"I see." Melanie tried to imagine Luke turning down an opportunity to be out in the field.

"You'll get used to this life, trust me. Flying commercial is a complete downgrade once you get accustomed to this." The plane gave a hearty shake and Kendra's face paled. "I'm sure the pilots will get through this turbulence soon."

Luke looked back over his shoulder at Melanie. As quick as he looked at her, he turned back around and refocused on the laptop open in front of him. Concentration on the screen in front of him took over his expression.

"I hope so." Melanie smoothed out a wrinkle on her shirt. "How long have you worked for Mr. Harrison?"

"Three years ago, he hired me on the spot." Lowering her face and her voice, she continued, "He's a great boss, once you get to know him, or in your case, get to know him again."

Melanie pursed her lips. "Fair enough; we used to know each other."

"Then I don't need to say much more." Another round of rough air shocked the cabin. "Ugh. I think I might lose my lunch." She unbuckled her belt and got up from her seat. "Excuse me."

The moment Kendra disappeared into the restroom, Luke closed his laptop, and turned back to face Melanie. "How did your family take the news of your promotion?"

"This is not a promotion, and no, I haven't told them." She drummed her fingers on the armrest.

"You haven't told them?" Obviously intrigued by her answer, Luke cocked his head and continued, "Where do they think you're going to be for the next three months?"

"Kiss or no kiss," she whispered furiously, "my personal life is none of your concern." Boundaries needed to be set—mostly for her sake, particularly with the way Luke undressed her with his eyes. The sooner she cleared this up, the better she would feel. "I think this is an excellent time to go over the parent evaluation." She reached inside her bag and took out the bulky binder.

"What's in there, a bill to Congress?"

"I use hardcopy forms." She searched for some type of table to rest her binder upon. "I prefer them."

Luke got up, reached down by her leg, and pressed a button. A small tray table popped up. Melanie dropped her binder on the tray with a thud. Stevie looked up from her magazine and returned to it.

The top of the form Melanie had filled out with information about Vivian: name, chronological age, sex, and the name of one parent. There was some catch-up to do, which meant Melanie would have to find out about this other woman; the woman who had gotten close enough to Luke to have his child. Between Luke dumping her and today, he'd fallen for someone enough to have her child. The notion forced a bolt of jealousy within Melanie whether she liked it or not. She coughed, shook her pen, and proceeded with asking the one question she didn't want to hear the answer from. "I'd like to know about Vivian's mother."

Luke returned to his seat. "A little early for this kind of interrogation, don't you think?"

"I'm not flirting with you. I'm doing my job."

"You're sure there's no part of you sitting there that wants to know why someone else is the mother of my child." Luke grinned. "At one time, you wanted to marry me. You saw us having children together. You were that transparent."

Melanie's face turned to stone. Embarrassment crept up her cheeks. She was mortified to have him say this with Latonya and Stevie in earshot. "I have never wanted to marry you," she said flatly.

I had the organza gown with the draped bodice already picked out. So what if I had taken Jessie to the little boutique and tried on the dress to get her opinion?

"What is Vivian's mother's name?" she proceeded with professionalism in her voice. She would address the issue of Luke bringing up their past openly, without her consent, in Maui. She wouldn't be made a fool by him discussing their past again.

"Her name is Ava Sullivan." Luke scribbled something on the corner of Melanie's form.

She didn't read the message and wrote down the name. "Will Ava need to be included in reports for Vivian's progress?"

"Ava doesn't impact Vivian's life at all. She's out of the picture and I don't want her name on any of your forms."

Whew.

She continued and filled in Luke's name and other information about Vivian: address, birth weight, and the name and contact information of Vivian's pediatrician.

"Are there any other concerns you have with her speech or her development?" The pen hovered over the document.

Luke's jaw hardened. "I have no other concerns."

Melanie put down her pen. "I'll be looking at more than speech. There are six areas related to her language development I'll be considering when creating a services plan: expressive and receptive language, social and self-help skills, fine and gross motor skills. At the Growing Tree, we look at a child's deficiency in those areas. Children who meet less than twenty-five percent in one area qualify for services. In other words, if she scores above this number, she's probably close to or above how other children her age are performing, what we consider inside a normal range. The areas she scores below twenty-five percent are where I'll concentrate my time with her." Melanie picked up her pen and tapped it slowly on the table. "In the public space, children have to qualify as deficient in order to receive services; otherwise, everyone could come knocking on our door and demand services, which would take up resources intended for children who actually need them. You're paying me whether she qualifies or not, so I'll focus on the areas of her greatest needs and work in the other ones as secondary. Is she involved in any play groups or classes?"

Stevie turned around and said, "None."

Luke grew quiet in front of her and she brought the binder to her chest and spread her fingers on the back.

"There's nothing like cold, airplane water on my face to feel better," Kendra said, rejoining the group and gave Luke one of her curious, inner-circle glances. "Apparently my stomach and turbulence aren't meant to be friends." She sat down, arranging her suit jacket over her belt. "Am I interrupting?"

"No, we're finished." Luke moved his chair back around to the laptop. "I need to talk to you."

"What did you say to him?" Kendra mumbled and sat back down. "He's in a bad mood, I can tell."

"It wasn't me. He needed something and you weren't here to go fetch." Melanie released the lock on the chair and turned her back on Luke and Kendra. The look she'd seen in Luke's eyes while she'd brought up the speech therapy lecture had gotten to him. She thought she'd glimpsed something close to fear. A man who used to trot the globe and slept in the jungle wouldn't be afraid of a little evaluation for his daughter, would he? Fear wasn't in his nature.

Sweet, shy, little Vivian sat a few feet away kicking her legs. She wasn't keeping up with her peers and Luke knew it. Melanie's gaze sailed over to Luke, whom sat staring at a document on his computer screen. Somehow Vivian's development had slipped down a steep crack between her parents.

Melanie would have to dig to get the full story. She also had her work cut out for her.

She reached for the binder and pretended to go over the forms, until she found the one where Luke had written his note. A shot of heat run up her spine. Her eyes widened.

I look forward to seeing my tourmalines on your naked body.

She looked up sharply.

He stared back at her, completely full of himself.

* * * *

The blast of cool air conditioning greeted Melanie like family the second she stepped inside the Kahului Airport. A rush of travelers sped by holding onto their rolling luggage bags. Everyone in her path smiled and laughed. They had arrived in Maui. Even the caffeine smelled fresher and the vacuumed rugs seemed nicer than the ones back on the Mainland. A few feet up ahead, Luke crossed his arms over his chest, staring intently at Kendra; his mouth clipped as he spoke to her. The frown on his face stuck out in a room full of chipper grins.

Technically, they needed nothing inside the airport since they'd arrived by private jet and landed in another part of the tarmac. The detour served as a short cut to the cabs waiting for them at the front of the airport. Melanie turned around and looked for other members of their group. Latonya showed her face first, but Stevie and Vivian staggered behind, a pair already on beach time.

Latonya switched her canvas tote bag to the other shoulder. She stood next to Melanie, catching the sight of Luke and Kendra. "Business doesn't ever stop for them. Don't be fooled: this isn't a vacation for him. A man worth enough money to travel by private jet doesn't get a break." She ran her hand over her face. "Don't worry about the bags either. They'll be delivered to the house."

"I must be obvious," Melanie answered and opened the door. "I don't like other people being put in charge of my belongings."

"Uncertainty looks the same on everyone. You're new to traveling with us and you're traveling with the best. This lifestyle takes some getting used to and you will. Everything's prearranged: his luggage, our luggage, the taxi drivers, rental cars waiting for us at the house. Mr. Harrison doesn't like interruptions."

"I'm well aware."

"You keep that in mind." Latonya fanned her face. "Good Lord the air is muggy."

Kendra whisked off in another direction, holding the phone up to her ear and shouting at someone on the other end.

"Poor baby." Latonya chuckled. "She hasn't slept since she took the job. The bags under her eyes are the size of her luggage. Don't let the same happen to you when you're up late at night planning his death."

"Excuse me?" Melanie's jaw dropped.

"When you're up at night, thinking this job will be the death of you."

"That's not what you said."

"It's not what your brother said either." Latonya walked ahead with hips like a motorcade and she continued to fan herself.

The blaring beep of the luggage cart honked at Melanie and the operator yelled into the loud speaker, "Move to your left."

Melanie's feet sidestepped the cart while she contemplated Latonya's words. The passengers swallowed Melanie in their haste to get to their destinations. The rest of the way through the airport, Melanie kept to herself.

Three taxis waited for the Harrison entourage outside the airport doors. Kendra bustled from each cab, talking fast to each driver and then handing out an envelope. The sunshine offended her white skin. She circled her arm, signaling a black town car. The driver pulled ahead and parked in front of the cabs. The driver emerged, dashing to the curbside door. Luke, still talking on the phone, nodded at the driver and waited for him to open it.

"Melanie, our cab is the third one in line," Kendra barked. "The tip's already included."

Stevie ushered Vivian to the first cab. A burst of *White Linen* clogged the air as Stevie passed, holding Vivian's hand. The two of them settled in and Latonya took the second cab all to herself. They were settled in their cabs and took off, leaving the airport.

Kendra rested against the headrest. Misery covered her face and she closed her eyes and patted her stomach. "I'm already exhausted and my stomach hasn't recovered from the flight. You should make yourself comfortable. Our destination is a good distance away, on the north side of the island."

The entire forty-minute drive strained Melanie's nerves. She'd been impulsive most of her life, but this felt like stretching the limits. The attraction she felt for Luke didn't help the situation. Her body could lust after him but her mind and her heart wouldn't. She wouldn't fall for him again. She could handle this.

The cab stopped in front of the house with a squeaky brake. Melanie's eyes took a moment to adjust to the house, big and grand enough to make her feel like a speck of sand at the bottom of a large hill. The modern, angled, architectural marvel crowned the top of the hill with veins of deep green mountainside running out from underneath. The same feeling of being awe-struck charged through her bones as it had when she'd seen his home in Belvedere. The man had done beyond well for himself.

"The house is incredible," Kendra commented, flipping close the lid on her tablet. "Every now and then a network executive or the owner of a magazine asks him to open up his doors and showcase the home on television or have a writer put together an article. Mr. Harrison turns them down. He doesn't like the outside world knowing much about him."

Unable to tear her gaze off the estate, Melanie picked up her bag, noticing the banyan trees she'd read about in a magazine on board the plane. The leafy, full trees filled in the landscape. The house sat in a semi-private neighborhood with houses at least a half mile apart. The cab driver opened her door and Melanie got out, feeling odd about not tipping. The walkway up the front steps snatched Melanie's breath up the steep climb until height gave way to a flat, landscaped yard.

Breathless once they reached the top, Kendra paused and held onto the rail. "I've got to check the luggage situation. Wait in the foyer until I check on the bedrooms to make sure everything's in order." She hit her palm on the rail and shook her head. "I'm still out of breath."

Melanie dropped her trusty tote bag on the floor, out of the way of anyone entering the house. She stared at the spacious open room with a ceiling going up at least two more stories. A large stone fireplace scaled up one wall and the other, where the back of the room should have been, didn't exist. The back wall was missing entirely. The deck, a pool, and the distant view of the beach could be accessed by simply crossing over the tile floor. Nothing protected them from the weather and she began to head outside, to see what sort of trick Luke had built. Surely, the room required something in order to protect the rest of the house from rain or storms. "How do they open?" she asked aloud.

"They're called pocket doors," Luke said, sneaking up behind her.

She turned suddenly, catching him approaching her. "I didn't know you were there."

"The doors are retractable." He pointed to the side walls, where a narrow chamber ran the length of the wall on each side. "I press a button and the doors close." His hand dropped to his side. "Come with me, let me show you something."

Intrigued, Melanie walked alongside Luke. He smelled like the breeze coming off the ocean. They walked past the stone fireplace, and over to the large patio. "You actually live here. This house is all yours."

"I don't apologize for my success." Luke rocked back on his heels. "You should know that about me."

"You've come a long way from your days of scraping by." She stepped in front of him and gazed over at the pool. The circular swimming area made an optical illusion, giving the edge the appearance of spilling into the ocean. The small waterfall at the end recycled the water. Tiny white lights lit up the pool's perimeter and the sky above faded from blue to green. One step in any direction and the illusion broke, sucking the magic out of the scene. The place felt both grandiose and full of warmth and color all at once.

Luke moved up behind her; his hands dangled dangerously close to her thighs. "I'll assume by your critical gaze that you don't like my house. Most people who come over can't stop talking about the place."

"I *do* like your house." The thin watch she wore dropped down her wrist. "I'm thinking of how far you've come. I'm happy for you," she admitted sincerely. "You did everything you set out to do and you've done well."

"I could say the same about you." Luke's hands brushed against hers.

"Luke," she said with emotion, "you embarrassed me on the plane today."

Luke spun her around. The corner of his mouth tugged up. "How did I embarrass you?"

She faced him fully now. "I don't like Latonya, Kendra, and anyone else on your staff knowing what transpired between us when we were younger. You insult me every time you bring up the past, for example, on an airplane where everyone can hear us, and not think twice. I don't want our past flung around in casual conversation."

"Dully noted," he answered shortly.

"You don't know me anymore, Luke."

"I know you better than you think." His hand bumped into hers.

A pleasant, silky warmth spread through her middle and down her thighs. "Keep your theories about me to yourself. My work with Vivian will be temporary. No more kisses. No more intimacy." She really did feel offended. He had no right to make assumptions about her. She'd become someone else. She'd shed the skin of her past and liked herself much better now. She changed the subject entirely. "You should spend more time child-proofing this house than analyzing me. Look around: there are sharp edges and hazards everywhere. There are outlets with no covers." She pointed at the unprotected outlets. "There's no gate around the pool. I assume Vivian can't swim yet."

"I'm waiting to install the fence after Damon's wedding. Vivian should have an adult with her at all times anyway. There's a playroom for my daughter too. As for the other subject..." Luke's phone rang and he picked it up, narrowing his eyes at the number on the screen. "I have to take this."

"I'll go."

Luke grabbed her wrist. Whatever he'd wanted to say must have changed because his hand disengaged from her wrist and he said, "Fine; I'll see you later."

Intent on getting settled and taking a shower, Melanie crossed back to the interior side of the house. This house would be her home for the next several weeks and she worked on someone else's schedule and time, which meant, more waiting. Tonight she could relax and get to bed early. Tomorrow she would start a rigorous schedule with Vivian. A package on the table behind the couch addressed to Damon Harrison caught Melanie's attention. She ran her finger over the brown box and thought about how she'd never met Luke's family, not even his mother. She'd known his father had passed away a short time before they'd met, but Luke wouldn't speak of him and when she tried to get close to him, the topic of his family drove them apart further. How odd to think now of all times, she would finally meet his brothers. She glanced back at Luke.

He was the combination of sexy and wealthy. He exuded defiance and demanded attention. Luke stood in front of the knee-high stone wall and stared out at the beach. The beats of her heart pumped fast and loud. She couldn't look at him without her body tensing and her head thinking crazy thoughts. She told herself to not get too close. This wasn't about her. The entire purpose of getting back in Luke's good graces revolved around the need to do something with the desperate bone her brother had thrown her way. The consequences of messing up would cost her brother more time stuck behind bars; more years down the toilet, and their family forever trapped in limbo, a place between knowing and not knowing. Melanie forced herself to turn and walk away.

Chapter 9

Melanie woke up in the morning slightly jet-lagged and groggy. She showered and dressed early and made her way down to the kitchen. Anxiousness blossomed inside her at getting started on her work. She lived for her job. Down-time wasn't something she enjoyed. She liked to keep her mind active, her skills polished, and her schedule crammed from morning until night.

She thought she'd be the first in the kitchen. Turns out, she walked in last. "Good morning," she said, upon entering and spotting the feast on the counter: pineapple, Star fruit, and papayas sat cut up on the kitchen counter like a rainbow. Bagels, cream cheese, croissants glowing in butter, and scrambled eggs.

Latonya used the entire kitchen when she cooked. Pans on all four burners, plus another two on the island stove bubbling with hot water. Green onions, mushrooms, olive oil, fresh herbs, and three different kinds of cheese lined the counter. The smell of bacon and fresh-baked cookies tricked the senses. Melanie grabbed a cup for coffee, plucking one of the mugs from in between rows of spatulas and measuring cups. Not a free inch of counter space existed. The disarray didn't match Latonya's cool and collected demeanor, not a hair out of place or her deep purple nail polish chipped.

"There's coffee, juice, milk, whatever you need, you ask," Latonya said, coming up for air from below one of the counters. "This is my work space and I don't like people rifling through my cupboards."

"She really doesn't," Kendra said, from the table.

"If there's something I don't have, write it on the list on the refrigerator. I go to the market every two days, sometimes more."

Next to Vivian, Melanie found an open chair at the end of the long table. Directly in front of Vivian sat a plastic bottle full of milk. Vivian wriggled and squeezed the eggs in her fists, shoveling them in her mouth in between grunts. Melanie reached out and removed a piece of egg lodged between her gapped front teeth. "Hi," she said to Vivian and repeated, "Hi."

The bowl of lumpy oatmeal in front of Stevie steamed and she scooped

Inclusions 75

up a hearty helping. Something resembling raisins dripped down. The morning light from the kitchen windows drew the eye to a sparkling square-cut ruby around Stevie's neck. The natural course of wrinkles latticed up her neck to her cheeks, and the faintest blonde upper lip couldn't hide from the direct sunlight.

Kendra sat at the table with her head buried in the tablet. "I'll get house keys made up for everyone this afternoon," she said, not touching her plate of honey dew, cantaloupe, and pineapple parked alongside a heap of cottage cheese. "I've got a few items to add to your shopping list, Latonya."

"Add Sippy cups too," Melanie said. "Bring back a variety. Some with straws, some without, the brand doesn't matter." The thin, stretchy dough of the croissant melted in her mouth.

"We looked into some a while back," Kendra replied, "at the suggestion of Vivian's pediatrician. They're on back order."

"They're on back order?" This made zero sense to Melanie. "We are talking about the same ones found in every grocery store."

Kendra punched the screen with her finger and decided to give Melanie the time of day. "The ones I ordered have GPS tracking."

Laughter hurled out Melanie's mouth and she looked from Kendra to Stevie. "You're serious?"

Kendra squirmed. "Well, I thought, I mean, the pediatrician did tell Stevie we need to transition Vivian away from the bottle. I spent good time researching Sippy cups. The major complaints included lost cups, missing straws and lids, cost of replacing the cups. I may not have children of my own, but I'm good at averting problems down the road. I don't want there to be any problems with this transition."

"I'm sorry to hear that Mr. *Harrison* would expect something as complicated as childhood to go smoothly. You can't avoid Vivian being two. Get plastic cups with straws. This is a common sense solution. Your employer has overcomplicated the matter. He should stick to selling gemstones."

"Good morning," Luke said, strolling into the room. He leaned against the counter, crossing his arms over his chest.

"I'm sure she didn't mean to insult you," Kendra said, narrowing her gaze.

"Oh, I'm sure she did." Luke allowed the silence to fester, until Latonya dropped a pan, diverting everyone's attention. "I thought kids hung onto bottles for years. Why is this matter urgent?"

"Vivian is too old for a bottle," Melanie spoke up, when no one else would. "Sounds like Vivian's pediatrician already communicated this to you or Stevie, whoever of you is in charge. The muscles in Vivian's mouth need to be worked out and strengthened like any other muscle. Straw cups can help with this. It's a good start."

"I don't remember hearing anything about needing to strengthen Vivian's mouth muscles," Stevie said, laughing. "I've taken Vivian to almost all of her doctor's appointments since her mother wasn't responding well to motherhood. I don't see why we should be running and jumping at whatever you decide. You've only been with us a few days. My nephews didn't speak until they were three, then they never stopped talking. Children talk when they're good and ready. There's been so much change with transitioning to living with her father. I don't think one more piece of change is good for her. The travel to Maui uprooted her entire routine. She didn't go to bed until late last night. Now you want her to get rid of the bottle." Stevie turned to Luke. "Tell me I don't have to listen to her."

"The two of you need to work together." Luke swung his leg and stood up straight. "I'm sure you'll come up with a common sense approach to a solution."

"Everything I do has a purpose from this point on, whether you like it or not." Melanie grabbed her plate and her coffee cup. "I'd like to talk with Vivian's pediatrician. Will you get me authorization?"

"I'll add it to my list of jobs to complete today." Kendra smirked at Melanie. "Don't expect it today. You do realize there's a wedding taking place soon."

"Get Melanie what she needs." Luke picked up his mug of coffee. "Kendra, let's go to my office."

Melanie sipped her coffee in silence as they left the kitchen. Luke trusted her enough to not give into Stevie's way, which counted a lot to Melanie. "I don't suppose any one wants to talk about moving Vivian to a booster chair?"

Latonya sharpened her knife. "I think you've made enough changes for one morning."

Inclusions

"I haven't even really gotten started. The two of you are going to learn how to use signs to communicate with Vivian. "She can't tell you what she wants. How would *you* feel if you couldn't form a single word? We're going to stop anticipating her answers. Vivian has to work for what she wants."

Stevie pushed her bowl of oatmeal to the side. "This is nonsense. Vivian will talk when she's ready." She got up, carried her bowl to the sink, and dropped it in with a loud clank. "I'll be ready to take her back from you at lunchtime."

"Vivian, want to play?" Melanie asked, using the sign for play, a hang-loose sign while rotating her wrist. "Play."

"She'll come around," Latonya said once Stevie left the room. "Nobody's been around Vivian more than she has. She's taking this personally. She was supposed to get an assistant nanny on this trip, not a speech therapist."

"Sometimes the parents or caretakers of the clients I work with have a harder time adjusting to my work than the children." Melanie leaned forwards, holding up a finger, forcing Vivian to look at her eyes. "Play," she said, demonstrating the sign.

Melanie got Vivian down and brushed egg off her shirt. She and Vivian walked to the play room, a room at the opposite end of the house. The large room looked untouched, like they'd moved in yesterday and hadn't gotten around to unpacking. Stacked boxes lined the wall. Shelves still in their packaging crowded the corners. Toys remained wrapped in boxes with images of children laughing and playing on the front of the cardboard box. A mini guitar with two strings sat in the other corner and Vivian went right to the toy.

"Guitar," Melanie said, pointing at the instrument. "G-G-G," she mimicked the sound, unzipping her bag. The binder and stash of papers inside slid out onto the plush carpet amongst the electronic melody as Vivian banged on the guitar face.

Melanie took out her Preschool Language Scales Record Form or PLS-5 and began her evaluation. The results would determine Vivian's greatest areas of need. The beginning section of the evaluation didn't require many tools and Melanie started with the first section, noting whether or not Vivian glanced at her when being spoken to. She observed whether or not

Vivian turned her head when a burst of laughter erupted outside the hallway. Vivian didn't.

Does Vivian mouth objects?

No, she does not Melanie noted and gave her a score. Melanie tried engaging her by making silly faces and Vivian didn't smile in return, although she looked interested. Melanie placed toys in front of Vivian. Vivian went for one of the cars and Melanie said, "Stop," but Vivian continued to go for the toy, which gave her a score of zero.

Thirty minutes through the evaluation, Melanie stopped. Vivian's attention waned at the prospect of doing another task and Melanie decided to take a lunch break. The rest of the testing she could break out throughout the week, and plus, she needed to go through and gather the testing items she couldn't substitute or find in the play room.

Stevie wasn't anywhere to be found and so, Melanie left Vivian in the kitchen with Latonya, whom seemed eager to feed anybody. Melanie went out back on the patio where she heard a woman calling up to the house from the beach. The waist-high wrought iron gate granted Melanie access to a narrow staircase and she crisscrossed down the path to the sand. Pink-and-red umbrellas stuck out of the sand like giant flowers, shading the few beachgoers underneath.

"Hello?" called a high-pitched voice from the bottom step. "Girls, move aside!" One of the young girls hid behind the woman, the other, obviously a twin, jumped up on the stone fence.

The woman and the two girls ascended the staircase and met Melanie halfway. "May I help you?" Melanie asked, eyeing the identical faces of the young girls.

"You know Luke?" said the woman with legs like an ostrich and eyes like a hawk. She squinted up at Luke's house. "I live at the end of the street. We don't have direct access to the water. Ava and I are good friends," she boasted, as if this meant something to Melanie. "My name is Goldie Elliot and these are my daughters, Kari and Alyssa. We've known Luke and Ava for years. They are our local celebrities if you ask me." She smiled down at Vivian and spoke in a baby voice, "My soon-to-be-ex-husband moved out earlier this year. I'm officially a single mother. My poor girls won't remember their two-parent days. This is our first trip to the beach in months." She glanced at the house. "How do you know Luke Harrison?"

"I work for Mr. Harrison. My name is Melanie."

"Huh." Unimpressed with Melanie's connection to Luke, Goldie's smile faded, then recharged. "What exactly do you do for him? Are you one of his gem-hunters or do you do some kind of jewelry design? I dabbled in jewelry design myself, but nothing high-end level like Luke's accustomed to having." The two girls ran circles around Goldie, kicking up sand and screaming in delight. One of the girls pushed down her sister and they fell to the ground in a mess of bony limbs and curly hair, wrestling with each other.

"How old are your girls?" Melanie couldn't resist the possibility of easy access to friends for Vivian.

"Be careful girls." Goldie pointed at the sand. "A few weeks ago we had trespassers on the beach, teenagers we think, loitering and smashing beer bottles. One of our neighbors went to the hospital with cuts to her leg from the broken glass. Kari and Alyssa: get up," she ordered. "They're four-years-old, In-Vitro babies. My husband and I couldn't get pregnant on our own. They took to the womb on our third try. Ava knows the entire story. She helped me recover after their birth." Goldie lowered her sunglasses from her head to cover her eyes. "I hear there's a wedding at the house. Do you know the date or the time? June is such a busy month for me and the girls." The unsubtle hint of a potential invite hung in the air between them. "I would hate to miss Damon's big day. I'll stop by later and give my congratulations."

"I don't know much about the wedding." Melanie enjoyed being nondescript on purpose. The slightest nod and Goldie thought this a cue to continue.

"I've heard Luke's headboard is lined in jewels. Is that true?"

Laughter burst out of Melanie's mouth. The image of Luke, propped up on his elbow on some fur-lined bed with a headboard full of big gems was absurd. "I wouldn't know. I don't spend time with Luke in his bedroom."

The shrill of giggles erupted from her daughters and Goldie flung her head back. "Girls," she hissed, "stop throwing sand." Goldie snapped her fingers, as if the next idea fell from the sky. "Let's get the girls together for a play date."

Melanie couldn't say no to this. Vivian needed to be around other children. The socializing couldn't be put off any longer. "A play date sounds perfect. I don't have your phone number."

"Next Friday morning, ten o' clock, we'll come to Luke's house." Goldie grabbed Kari's hand. "Let Luke know I'll be stopping by and I want to see him." One wistful glance at the house and she smiled. "We'll see you soon."

"Melanie?" Stevie called from the patio, causing Melanie to turn around.

"I'm down here," she said back, and began walking up the stairs.

"No rush; I've got Vivian. Take a break, do what you need to get done. Vivian takes a nap after she eats."

Melanie made herself comfortable on the sofa in the main room. The paper calendar splayed out on the coffee table was next to a glass of pink lemonade Latonya made from scratch. She'd gotten so used to tasting the powder stuff that she'd forgotten how sweet and acidic fresh-squeezed lemonade tasted.

"She's tired today," Stevie said, limping down the staircase. "I'm beat between the beach and running after Vivian." She took a seat next to Melanie. "I see you have out your calendar, let's discuss our schedules."

"I'm still waiting to talk to Luke, but yes, after working with Vivian this morning, I have a minimum number of hours I'd like to work with her. We're going to do some intense work from five to seven hours a week of language-centered activities. I'd like to hold a session with her immediately following breakfast and after her nap."

Stevie leaned forward and rubbed her hands together. "What am I supposed to do while you're working with her?"

"I want you present some of the time and other times, I'll work with her one-on-one. You're around her more than anyone, so some of my job will be to train you on how to really give Vivian language with purpose, not just talking at her. She's watching you, even if you can't tell or feel that she's paying attention. The sounds you make, she'll learn to make, especially when used with repetition. Beginning tomorrow, I'd like you to start getting Vivian to point to objects. I noticed she doesn't point much to objects and

Inclusions

when she does, it's sporadic. When you mention a bird in the sky, stick out your finger. If you're reading a book, point to the pictures. Tell her to point. Physically take her finger and have her do it."

"I don't know about all this." Stevie sighed.

Melanie couldn't help but think of what Kendra had said at breakfast, at how the pediatrician had suggested the bottle transition to Stevie. "Stevie, do you really take Vivian to some of her doctor's appointments?"

"Yes."

Melanie nodded. She wondered what information about Vivian hadn't been fully communicated to Luke. Now wasn't the time to back Stevie in a corner, the woman barely accepted Melanie's presence in the house. Melanie would get the missing pieces filled in on her own.

"Stevie, try my methods and give Vivian some time. You'll see the improvement in time. Helping Vivian will be a whole-house effort—Kendra, Latonya, Mr. Harrison; all have to start expecting more from her." Melanie jotted down the play date. "Twice a week I want Vivian in some kind of play activity with other children. Take her to the park, to a library for story time, a gym for kids—you get the picture. More peer interaction and less adult interaction. I cannot emphasize this enough. Get her around other kids. Get in between them and show her how to play. Does Vivian initiate play when she's around other kids?"

"Of course she does. She gets right in there and grabs toys and becomes excited when she's around other kids."

Melanie kept her doubts hidden. The play date with Alyssa and Kari would give Melanie a more accurate assessment of Vivian's social interaction.

"Play dates, park, other children," Stevie repeated and gazed down at her hands.

Melanie thought about what Latonya had said at breakfast. She closed the calendar and said, "Stevie, this isn't personal. This isn't a reflection on you as a nanny."

"Your opinion doesn't make a difference." Stevie stood up and brushed the wrinkles out of her pants. "I forgot to tell you that Mr. Harrison is at a charity fundraiser for underprivileged teenagers. He took a plane to Oahu earlier today and will be there overnight, with Kendra. Each time we come here, he's off somewhere else, auctioning off some gemstone for a good cause."

"Are Kendra and Luke together?" Melanie asked on impulse.

"Thank you." Stevie smirked. "You just made me one-hundred dollars richer."

"How?" Melanie frowned; feeling foolish for asking in the first place.

"I bet Latonya you would ask within the first seventy-two hours if Luke is single."

"What did Latonya bet?"

"She thought you'd hold out until after the first week." Stevie pretended to fan cash in front of her face. "I do love winning and I'll tell you what you want to know for being such a good sport. Kendra and Mr. Harrison are strictly employer and employee. They spend a lot of time together but they do not cross the professional line. Kendra is pretty and ambitious, but Luke is her boss and he's too smart to get involved with one of his employees."

There wasn't any point trying to read between the lines. Melanie snatched the calendar. "Don't make any more bets on me. I'm going for a swim."

"Don't give me a reason to." Stevie laughed.

Melanie kept busy the rest of the day. She worked with Vivian and had her involved with a few language-focused activities using a plastic farm and animals. The energy of the house felt flat in Luke's absence and Melanie took the opportunity to acquaint herself with the property, respond to emails, and begin to type out some initial observations about Vivian. After Stevie retired for the evening, Melanie went up the stairs to her bedroom on the second floor and changed into her two-piece bathing suit. The reflection in the mirror showed a mid-section hidden from the sun for months. The other parts of her body: arms, neckline, below the knee, showed off a piecemeal tan. A few rolls existed in her middle, the flat stomach had left her body at sixteen and though she worked out regularly, some of the stubborn patches of flab remained on her inner thighs and waistline. Despite the slight increase in plumpness, she liked the way she looked and felt good about her body.

A quiet hush fell over the house. The soft padding of her footprints sounded as she walked across the tile and outside. The warm breeze flowed in the house, shifting the leafy green house plants. Fans with two blades churned overhead, keeping the flow of air moving in and out of the house.

The pool lights were on and the night air was warm. Nobody else in the house took advantage of such a gorgeous evening or access to the swimming. Kendra and Luke would be away until tomorrow. Latonya had

Inclusions

gone to her room and the kitchen transformed into a dark, spotless space. The thought of taking a swim invigorated Melanie, who'd grown up swimming to relax at the end of the day. Some of her best memories came from pushing, racing, and doing handstands with Jessie and Mark in their own backyard pool, a much smaller version than the one laying out before her.

Melanie poured herself a glass of wine from the outdoor wine bar. The temperature-controlled refrigerator housed wine labels she'd not seen before. Some were in another language, clearly not of the Yellow Tail variety. Upon closer inspection, she could see they weren't wine at all. They were bottles of champagne. She picked one and brought it to the light. "You're very pretty," she said to the bottle of rose-colored liquid. "Who are you Armand de Brignac?" She put the champagne back and closed the door, not willing to open something that might be worth more than her car.

The open mahogany trunk to her left showed off a stack of fluffy towels and she took one, dropping it off on a lounge chair. Melanie secured the knot on her bikini top and jumped in feet first, relishing in the water welcoming her. She stayed submerged for a moment, kicking her feet and pushing her arms, becoming deaf and blind for a moment before coming up for air. She burst through the water giddy with the thrill of having the entire pool to herself.

The water swirled under her arms and legs as she worked her way over to the fountain where lights changed color from blue to green. Physically she rested, but not mentally. Thoughts of Ava and Luke occupied her mind. Ava had staked a claim in Luke's heart and she felt caught between wanting to know the truth of their relationship and hoping to avoid the entire topic. What did Ava mean to Luke now? Would they ever reconcile? Did he love her? She could ask Stevie, but Melanie didn't trust her yet. She couldn't find out more about Luke without eventually bumping into what went wrong with them. She'd have to dig a tunnel through the past to get up to speed on the future. She gave the water a splash and a backlash of drops hit her face.

Chapter 10

The movement of the ceiling fan caught Luke's eye as he shut the door. Anxious to get back to the beach house, he'd left the charity event early. Kendra's upset stomach had given him a good reason to sneak away and get back to his house, while she remained in Oahu, vowing to fly back the moment she felt better. The event hadn't been a total waste. A four-carat, fancy yellow square-cut diamond would be auctioned off later this evening and he'd met Karen Adams, a jewelry designer he'd persuaded to work for him. The jewelry end of Luke's business did very well, until their longstanding designer left due to health issues with her family members. For weeks, he'd been looking for a replacement and the work of Karen Adams had got his attention with her skill in setting stones and engraving to antique restoration. Luke's stones sat in vaults, divided between each of his brother's houses, since they didn't have a formal office. They never liked to keep the exploits of their hunts in the same location, too tempting for anyone outside of Brent or Damon. Even with Kendra, he kept the details of the vaults in both of his houses minimal. She knew it existed, she just didn't know where.

Luke removed his jacket and placed it on the back of the sofa. In his other hand, he held onto a box of raspberry truffles he'd picked up from a chocolatier in downtown Oahu. The purchase of the chocolates wasn't his style, he liked to take a woman to the best restaurant or buy a bottle of champagne or go on a weekend getaway to somewhere private. *Chocolates,* he mused, holding the box with the thin gold bow, he hadn't bought chocolates for a woman in some time. The situation required him to tread lightly between his attraction for her and proving her wrong about her brother. The sound of water splashing caused him to turn and walk over in the direction of the pool.

He saw her at once. He recognized the long legs kicking and her arms extending out. Lounge chairs, coffee tables, and sitting chairs made from aluminum sat around the water with Melanie swimming in stride, in water turning from yellow to green. The chocolates could wait. Luke set them on the table, kicked off his shoes and removed his socks, and unbuttoned his long-sleeved shirt a couple of notches before walking over to the far end of the pool where she'd finish up her lap.

The breeze tunneled through his open shirt and he spotted the fluffy towel strewn across the chair along with Melanie's discarded clothes. He picked up the towel and stood at the edge.

Melanie bobbed up from her swim. Water streamed down her face. She wiped her closed eyes and opened them.

"Luke," she said, startled, and pushed the matted hair off her forehead. "What are *you* doing here?"

The towel opened under his fingers. "I returned early," he said, with notable edginess. "Get out of the pool."

"No."

He didn't want a battle. "Please."

She shrugged. Suspicion crossed her dark eyes and lovely frown. Her hands settled on the concrete and she lifted herself out of the water and snatched the towel out of his hand. She dried her hair, her face, rumpled her hair, and stood crossly in front him. "Don't tell me you rushed all the way back from Oahu to keep tabs on employees taking advantage of all that your property has to offer."

Luke laughed. "You're not the one taking advantage."

She frowned. "Oh."

The sight of her wet, shapely curves packed into a revealing swimsuit was what he took liberal advantage of at the moment. "Swimming's fine."

She folded the towel protectively around her chest and asked, rather accusatory, "Why are you back early then?"

"I think you know why."

"I don't."

Luke grasped the top of her towel and yanked her body to his. No hesitation. No second thoughts. Luke's lips crushed down on hers, stormy and demanding, slanting over hers and forced her lips to part under the blunt movement of his own. His tongue intruded her mouth, seeking and probing until she gave up hers and gave into his kiss. He reached around her neck and slipped his hands underneath her hair. Long, wet strands dripped water down his fingers like satin. Heat rolled off his muscles and into his quick fingers. The distance between them was too great. One tug and she collided into his body. Luke worked out the knot on her top until the towel plunged to the ground and landed on his feet. She grabbed his face and moved her slick tongue around his. The effect of her tongue on his and her wet body sticking to his clothes undid him and ripped a trail through the pit of his stomach and blazed through his loins until his manhood throbbed against her and the kiss no longer became enough. The softness of her cheek glided over his collarbone and her moist mouth trailed kisses at his neck. He needed more of her. All over him.

The strings of her bikini top loosed and detangled under his quick fingers. The fabric flopped down over her beautiful, round shoulders and exposed her breasts. Dark areolas crowned her white breasts and her perfect, stiff nipples tempted his mouth. Luke's hands skimmed over her face and reveled in touching her supple skin, smooth as hot liquid. He couldn't get enough of her. He didn't want to stop. His hands rushed down her neck, over her collarbone, and paused briefly over her heart and felt the shudder. Both hands plunged down her chest and he groaned at the bareness of her skin. He handled her there and teased her nipples until the dense flesh filled up his hands. Luke groaned at the pressure in his groin and he pushed down the rest of her bikini top so his lips could taste her. He kissed the spot just below her breasts and worked his way up.

Melanie moved her hands around and undid the clasp on her top, which unhindered them both from the last of the bathing suit, positioned near her belly button. She moved his hands down to her hips, arched her back, and gave Luke access to her. He accepted the silent solicitation and raised his lips to her nipple where he closed around her large areola and flickered over her peak with his tongue. She smelled like chlorine and tasted salty. He moved fast, working his mouth around each nipple, retracting his mouth and applying pressure according to the small cries escaping her mouth. His hands claimed her waist and he drew back, admiring the sensual glow on her face. His hands drifted down the indents of her sides and he thumbed over the hitch of her hips.

Melanie's hand found his erection and she put her hand over his shaft and began to rub up and down. Luke's lips parted in a gasp. He buried his head between her breasts. He couldn't keep up with his breath with her touching him like this. God, she made him hard. The muscles around his shaft intensified and shot off electric currents, shooting stabs of pleasure all to the tip of his arousal. Dizzy with distraction, he shook his head and cursed her name. He kissed a trail from one of her breasts to the next and this time, cupped it in his hand like a shiny, prized apple. He stroked his tongue over the taut tip of her nipple and slid his hand under her rear. The shock of cool skin hit his warm hand.

Luke dropped to his knees with his gaze on her pelvis. His hands moved around her backside to her thighs and his lips traced kisses around her triangular border, buffered only by the swimsuit bottom, the last piece of clothing physically in his way. And he would have his way. She ran her fingers through his hair and shockwaves rippled down his neck and back. With his eyes open, Luke pushed down her swimsuit bottom and ran his hand over the spine of hair between her legs. The moment he felt her modesty intrude he quipped, "I want to see you."

"What if somebody sees us?" she said, running her hands over his shoulders and keeping him close.

"They won't." Luke began to touch her private area with bold intimacy. She was already wet and ready for more than his finger, but he didn't want to rush her pleasure. He pulled her down on the lounge chair so her body covered his and her hair swept over his jaw. He reached down and began stroking her, pursuing the slippery nub between the bends in her skin and once there, circled and pushed his finger rapidly over her until her hands clenched his shoulders and he could feel her holding her breath. The muscles in his arms and legs tensed. Melanie unzipped his pants and pushed them down. Their heavy-lidded eyes met and this time—he pushed back her hips and prepared to enter her. A noise from the house caused him to look up at the same moment Stevie said, "I didn't see you!"

"Christ," he muttered. Luke sat upright. Melanie flattened against him with arms chained around his with a painful grip. He put his hand on the top of her head.

"I didn't realize you were back." Stevie's gaze landed on Melanie's back. She re-flung the towel draped over her shoulder and turned around. "Clearly, I'm interrupting."

Luke waited until Stevie left his line of vision before he breathed. "She's gone."

Melanie's warm breath released against his chest. "I'm mortified."

"I'm not."

"Of course you're not."

"This is my house. I can do what I want."

"I'm a guest and this," she said, pausing and moving her finger between them, "can't happen again."

"Because you loathe me?"

"Because there's nothing between us."

The corner of his lip turned up. "Kiss me again. Prove me wrong."

"I'm tired of proving myself to you."

The cocky grin disappeared. His eyes narrowed. "What are you talking about?"

Melanie separated her chest from his and folded her hands over her breasts. "Nothing. Never mind. You crossed the line."

"You crossed it with me. If you want me to stop, I will. Tell me now and I won't ever touch you again." Luke's hands fell down her back and hung together loosely. "You do know how much I want to see you again—naked or clothed, although, I do like you like this."

"It's getting late. I should go back to my room." Melanie's hand dipped to the concrete and she picked up the towel. "I've got work in the morning. I began this new job and I don't want to jeopardize my position."

Luke helped wrap the towel around her. "Your position's secure." He ran his finger down her arm and sensed her pulling away. The movement in her jaw caught his attention. "I want you to be comfortable with this. With me."

A nervous laughed escaped her mouth. "This wasn't supposed to happen. A few days ago, when I walked into your office, I wanted to slap you across the face."

"You should have." Luke's thumb ran over the edge of the towel. "Enemies can still be lovers. We were, once before."

"Most of our relationship we spent apart from one another and when we were together, you and my brother were obsessed with the next big hunt. Most women would find the boyfriend/gem hunter an ideal combination, and at first, I knew what I had in you. When other women hit on you in front of me, I didn't get jealous. I took you home and made love to you. Then the trips for the gems became more frequent, the distances became longer, without much contact in between. You became secretive and private. That's when I knew something wasn't right between you and Mark. I respected your trying to build a business from scratch. I knew the time commitment and personal sacrifice. The hunts were exciting to hear about in the beginning and then, I just didn't want to hear about them anymore. I wanted you to take me to dinner, or to a movie. I longed for ordinary. I wanted to go bowling."

"Bowling?" He lifted a quizzical brow.

"Don't pretend you don't know what I'm talking about. I want normalcy in a relationship. I got tired of making excuses for you as to where you were: Brazil, Sri Lanka, Tanzania, those places I kept hearing about stopped being glamorous. They were special to you, not me. Those faraway lands, all those brilliant gems, they became my competition, not other women. I wasn't insecure. I was jealous. I tuned you out because I felt left out." She lifted her arm to the house. "This ridiculous house; the champagne worth more than my wardrobe are all reminders of how different we really are. There's no way we could have worked out. There's no way we would ever want the same kind of life."

"You were jealous of my job?"

"Luke," she said, exasperated. "That's what you heard? You're missing the point and I know you're not daft. I wanted a piece of your adventure. I wanted to understand what you were doing out there. I was a warm body in a bed to you. We didn't talk about your family. We didn't look at old photos of you as a child. I didn't meet your brothers or your mother. I thought you might be ashamed of them or embarrassed, but then I realized you just didn't want to let me into your life." She let out a distressed breath. "We both ended up exactly where we're supposed to be. Not with each other."

"Melanie," he said her name like the whisper on the summer evening. "We're together now."

Melanie shifted her body off Luke's and she moved to the end of the chair. "There's a difference in hoarding your memories and letting someone in a little bit. You wouldn't give me an inch. How could I have gone through my whole life with you and not know one single thing about your family other than you have two brothers and parents unworthy of you discussing? I know you had a rough childhood and I know you don't want to talk about them."

"I don't like discussing my family or my childhood. You know this about me," he reminded her firmly. "Yet, you continue to push the subject. Why?"

"Because I love you." Melanie's hands jumped to her mouth. "I meant because I *did* love you, when we were together." She held up her finger. "I don't love you now. Anyway, I wanted to know all of you and you wouldn't let me inside. I couldn't be with someone without a past."

Something in her soft gaze betrayed her adamant voice. He let her slip-up slide, for the moment, and wondered whether or not she did, in fact, love him.

"Your family issues aside, I waited for you to invite me on one of your hunts. Mark said there wasn't any reason I couldn't come along and so I waited." Melanie brushed a chill off her leg. "I wanted to experience the thrill of the chase with you and understand what stole you away from me for days, weeks, sometimes months at a time."

Stunned, Luke pulled the towel gently to him. "I had no idea. You never once asked to come along."

"I shouldn't have had to ask. The end of our relationship is one of the best things to happen to me. I got my life back. I started my own adventures."

Chapter 11

The phone call interrupted Luke's sleep. Calls from Brent always disrupted some event in Luke's life. Luke put the phone to his ear and said with his eyes closed, "I'm going to hang up on you unless there's a solid lead."

"I have two beautiful words for you: blue garnet," Brent yelled with enthusiasm over a loud engine roaring in the background.

Luke ran his hand over his face. "Not interested."

"Did I tell you this baby is rumored to be eleven carats?"

"Holy shit." Luke threw off the covers and turned on the light. "You have my attention."

"I knew I would. My contact's solid. I've used him before."

The tips they worked on came from nothing more than a watered-down rumors stretching halfway around the world and essentially, made gamblers of them all. Luke ran a hand over his face. "Tell me where you're headed and more about this source."

"Madagascar." Another loud boom filled the phone. "My source is a friend of a friend, a guy I've worked with before, named Andry. I want you to go with me on this one. I need backup and my usual team isn't able to get here in time. What do you say?"

There had to be someone else. They operated on a team basis only. Nobody went in the field alone. A loner could wind up beaten, robbed, or dead. The very nature of gem hunting took on a life of its own, in an unsettling environment without rules. It tended to bring out the worst and most desperate of people. They always hired from a pool of shady individuals, of men with nothing to lose. They enjoyed any reason to keep a gun at their side or a knife in their pocket. Someone helped Brent with the money; another member of the team would handle logistics of keeping everyone together and safe. They hired translators when needed or influencers, usually someone local to give Brent and his men information that would help secure a deal with a mine owner, trader, or seller. Safety in numbers is the rule they went by out there. "There's nobody else?"

"We ran into a situation in Thailand. Pete came down with some nasty disease. He's in a hospital in Bangkok. The doctors think he's got malaria.

The others: Skinny and Kevin are dealing with their own personal problems at home. Rudy's wife is in labor and I don't like traveling with our second string without one of the regulars."

It wasn't wise to think about going to a remote place without back-up, without a team. They had gone rogue before, in the early days, before they could pay for someone to carry a gun and shoot at the slightest bit of trouble. "Tell me more about the mine. Is this one controlled? Will the trip be worth our time?"

"The mine owner works independently. The operation is small, outside the town of Bekily in the southern, central region. The word is he's found a vein of blue garnets. We both know these precious beauties go for thousands of dollars on the market."

"Where are you? You sound like you're in the middle of an engine exploding."

Brent laughed. "I'm at the Maui airport."

The last three months Brent had been out on his own, finding gemstones, heating them, and getting them to Luke. Their operation ran flawless as their precious gemstones. They kept quiet about their business and when opportunities like this came up, Luke knew better than to pass the chance.

"I don't want to be here. I want to get those garnets. If you want this blue bitch you're going to have to come get her yourself. I took an early flight for Damon's wedding and I got a call with a hot tip during my layover. There's no way I'm going to let this chance slide. I made some calls, got on my connecting flight, and reached out to someone who knows a source. Kendra's working on getting our flights. We can leave tonight. We'll take the jet to Honolulu; from Honolulu we'll go to New York; New York to Paris and Paris to Bekily."

Even if it came to choosing, Luke and Brent would both pick the blue garnets over their own brother's big day. Still, he said anyway, knowing his brother wouldn't change his mind, "Damon's wedding."

"We'll be back in a week. Plenty of time to show up at the altar and stand by our brother."

A quiet knock at his door got Luke out of bed. He held the phone with one hand and opened the door with the other. The thought of another hunt, his first one in almost a year, got him moving swiftly. Kendra stood on the other side and looked nowhere near ready for sleep. Luke snatched the piece of paper in her hand and said to her, "Dare I ask?"

"A copy of your travel itinerary, assuming you are talking to Brent and he's got you convinced you need this gemstone," she responded, stepping into his bedroom. "You did tell me to turn down your brother if he called me with any leads. Then he told me about the blue garnets and I know you've been waiting for this for years."

"You understand me all too well." Luke shifted the phone against his ear. Certain gemstones drove a hunter out of their bed in the middle of the night and for Luke, this one was one of the elusive conquests he'd dropped everything for once and had failed.

"I don't know much about these stones, so I did a little reading online. They're very scarce and have unordinary properties. They are a mystery even to gemstone followers. The stone changes color in the light. A purplish blue color will turn to a stunning purplish pink under the right light. They are borderline urban legend. We haven't dealt with buying or selling one before and we might not get a chance for months or years. I got flustered simply reading about this stone. I don't think you can say no to this. I'm sorry, Mr. Harrison, your vacation will have to wait."

Adrenaline coursed through his blood. He hadn't been this excited about such risk in a long time. Kendra's impromptu, self-education on the blue garnet only heightened his anxiousness to find one. A stone impressive. A stone capable of changing colors.

"What do you say?" she said.

He nodded curtly. "I'll be at the airport within the hour," Luke answered both his brother and Kendra. He tossed his phone on the bed and began to walk to the closet. Halfway there an idea occurred to him and he knew he wouldn't be able to leave such a random, jagged thought alone. It consumed him the second the idea entered his mind. He knew what he wanted to do. Right away. "Kendra, hold up. Come here."

She reappeared in the doorway. Tiredness fell over her face. "Yes?"

"I have a favor to ask you. There's something I want you to do for me…"

Kendra left his office after they discussed the logistics of his request and she understood her job. Quickly, he dressed in rugged clothes and packed his bag. The few items he packed fit in his backpack. He wouldn't need much and he'd survived out there with much less than a spare change of clothes. A smaller bag of cash he would wear around his neck. All he needed to do was get his travel gear. Brent would already have arranged all the tools they needed like canteens, food, tents, and knives to keep on their bodies for protection. Their local contact and guide, Andry, would provide them their resources and shelter and in return, he'd get paid half up front and half the money after the hunt. A bodyguard typically accompanied them, but occasionally, they went out on their own and risked their lives without the help of someone paid to carry a gun and sniff out trouble. They traveled fast and light. Luke brushed his teeth, shut the bedroom door, and went to his office.

The overhead lights switched on at the touch of Luke's finger. The door to his office closed behind him and he immediately walked over to the book shelf to the left of his desk, where a few books and artifacts took up space. A forty-gallon aquarium in the middle of the wall housed various tropical fish. They all swam around the tank among colorful plants and a solid gold treasure chest at the bottom. The shelf directly above the fish upheld two fat, silver candle holders, one of which doubled as a key. Luke tweaked the left candleholder and a square of wall popped back and a vault appeared with a finger print scanner. Luke pressed his index finger on the screen and the scan ran over his print, accepted the image, and the vault door opened.

Stacks of cash and velvet bags of gemstones greeted his line of vision. The cash he kept on hand for emergencies and the gemstones they sold and saved for interested buyers. The short list of names in his line of business all competed for the same clients and they all ran up against the larger corporations, but Luke had made a name for himself and a Harrison gemstone, like any of the ones in this vault, paid for his lifestyle. The hiring of the jewelry designer would bring even more business. The cash felt heavy in his hand and he took two-hundred-thousand dollars. The money he stuck in a brown bag, closed the vault door, and spun the lock. The candle holder released under his firm grip and the wall popped back into place, undetectable to anyone outside his office.

Before he left his office, he unlocked the closet and pulled out his ever-ready bag of supplies. A similar bag existed at his house in California. The first item he pulled out, his altimeter watch with the rugged strap went on his wrist. The other items in his bag included: a jewelry pocket scale, extra batteries, an 8-inch rock chisel, a hand-held loupe lens, a UV flashlight, and dichroscope.

Luke left his office, locked the door, and set his backpack down. He carried the bag of crisp dollar bills with him to the end of the hall, paused in front of Melanie's room, and then knocked twice before opening without her permission. A triangle of light from the hallway angled over Melanie and he went to the side of the bed where she slept. She looked peaceful and breathtaking with her hair splayed over her shoulders. "Wake up," he whispered in a rush. "Melanie."

"Luke?" she answered in a yawn. Offended by the light, she blinked open her eyelids. "What's the time?"

"It's one a.m." He sat on the bed in the room still surrounded by night. "Earlier you said you were jealous of my job. You said that you'd wanted to go with me on my adventures."

"Yes, but all of that was a long time ago," she said cautiously, staring back at him through a sleepy gaze. "I'm okay now. I don't need a big adventure."

"Brent woke me up less than an hour ago. He's at the airport in Maui. There's a hot tip on a blue garnet in a remote mine in Southern Madagascar. These gemstones are worth traveling around the world to try and bring back home. I'll never have this chance again and I'm going to go with Brent. I'm packed and I'm ready to go and meet him at the airport."

Melanie began to sit. "Two questions," she said, holding up two fingers. "Why are you telling me this and what about Damon's wedding? If you're concerned about my work with Vivian while you're gone, there's not much to worry about. You didn't need to wake me up personally."

Luke put his hand on her blanketed leg. He felt sure about what he was about to ask her. "I'm not worried about Vivian. Stevie will take care of her. She's used to my traveling."

"Then what's the problem?" Her gaze dipped to his hand on her leg.

"I want you to come with me."

Melanie's hand leapt to his. Her mouth hung open in disbelief. "You want me to come with you? I wasn't trying to be literal. I haven't gotten a chance to say those words to you before."

"I'm glad you did. You deserve to see what I was up to all that time. I want you to experience what I've experienced. I would have brought you along, before, if I'd known how much you wanted to join me. Most women aren't turned on by the idea of spending countless days in the middle of nowhere with no air conditioner, no heater, no running water, and rodents the size of your head. I kept my travels separate from you, from us, on purpose."

"I don't see how any of this is relevant today. We are not in a relationship and you don't owe me a trip to the other part of the world. You have your job and I have mine."

"I have five minutes to convince you and I've already used up three of them." Luke grabbed her hand with both of his. "This is something I have to show you. I'm giving you your chance. Say yes. Come with me."

"This isn't a good example of backing off."

A slow grin crept up his mouth. He spoke low and husky, "Come with me, Melanie."

A smile tugged at her lips. "You've already managed to get me to Maui."

Luke stood up and spoke fast, "Get dressed. Pack lightly. Don't bother with makeup and don't bring anything of value. The nights will be cold and the days will be hot. Meet me down stairs in fifteen minutes."

"Wait. Luke. I don't know if I can—"

"You can."

"No. I mean, I can't. I didn't bring my passport." Disappointment rang loud in her voice and spread over her face. "There's no way to get mine when I left it at home."

"Kendra has your passport."

"She does?" Melanie looked surprised. "How did she get my passport?"

"All my employees are required to have one on them at all times. I never know when my staff will need to travel. Given the fast nature of your being hired and our destination to Maui, I had Kendra contact your sister, Jessie, and she sent over the document to have on file. Your passport arrived this morning and has been in Kendra's safe-keeping."

"You're good."

"I'm the best. I'll see you in a few minutes." Luke left Melanie in her bed and he raced downstairs. "Is everything ready?" he asked upon seeing

Kendra.

She met him at the bottom of the staircase. "I have Ms. Cahill's passport." The small manila envelope in her hand moved to Luke's hands. "I interrupted your other brother's engagement dinner and notified him of your upcoming trip."

"What did Damon say?"

"Damon said to only contact him if either you are stuck in a prison overseas or if a firing squad has you standing in a line with a bag over your head. He's not interested in your excursion to Madagascar, since there's not much he can do for you legally if you get into trouble. He said to pack extra weapons and pray for the best."

"Damon's engagement party is more painful than where we're headed." The sight of Melanie walking down the stairs holding an armful of clothes with a toothbrush stacked on top caused him to laugh. "Are you planning on tying those clothes together so you don't lose them?"

"I don't have a backpack," she said dryly. "You said bring a backpack."

"I have a spare one." Kendra ran off down the hall. She returned before Melanie and Luke could say more than five words. "Anything not fitting into this bag stays behind."

Melanie stuffed what she could, leaving behind a bulky sweatshirt and pair of jeans next to the couch. "What about vaccinations? Don't I need some to travel?"

"You'll be fine as long as you're current on your vaccines. The usual ones like measles-mumps-rubella, tetanus, polio." Luke took her backpack, his own, and the bag of money. "You're at risk for Hepatitis A, Malaria, and Typhoid."

"You make those diseases sound like no big deal."

"We travel with our own food and water. We get our supplies when we arrive and we don't rely on outside sources for food and water. Oh, and there's also the risk of contracting yellow fever and rabies."

Melanie gulped. Her face turned white. "My skin is crawling."

"Not to worry. You won't catch yellow fever in Madagascar." Luke held out his hand. "You do realize I'm kidding? There's no way I'd let you travel with me without taking precautions. Kendra has a doctor waiting for our arrival at Maui County General Hospital. He's an infectious disease specialist. We'll get our vaccinations and medicine."

"I wasn't going to get on the plane otherwise."

"Good; let's go."

Melanie, Kendra, and Luke exited the house and made their way down the steep steps, lighted by a few lights on either side of the railing. An air of thrill hung around them and followed Luke to the cab where a driver got out and waited for them to reach the idling car. "Good evening, Mr. Harrison. You're headed to Maui General and then the airport."

"I'll double your tip if you get us to both locations in record time," Luke responded and got into the back seat after Melanie.

"I left my phone on my nightstand," Melanie said, fumbling to get her seat belt.

"You won't need one. If there's an emergency, Kendra or Damon will know how to reach us."

"You really have this all figured out." The buckle clicked under her fingers. "I forgot you've been doing this a long time."

"Your brother liked the chase in the beginning more than I did. When he went to prison, I took on the bulk of traveling until Brent came on board. Now I can't pin Brent down for trading places. A desk job would kill him." The driver sped away from the curb and away from the large home, looking more like a shadowy mountain at this early hour instead of a residence. Luke rested back his head.

"When we were kids, my brother and I used to make a competition out of everything. He once had a neighbor kid of ours hide some of Jessie and mine's favorite dolls around the street and we had to go look for them. The winner always got some obscure prize like redistributing chores for the week or handing over all of your allowance money. Mark has always liked the chase of the treasure. Jessie and I lost most of the time." She laughed a little and then sat quiet for a few minutes. "I don't like what happened to your friendship. I know the two of you understood each other."

"You understood him better than I did." Luke watched her intently, deciding whether or not to say more. He gave in, deciding he had nothing to lose by confiding in her. "At times your bond to your brother seemed stronger than our relationship."

"I won't disagree with you." Melanie turned her head and looked outside.

Inclusions

There's a first, he thought and mulled over the first slip in her trust towards her brother.

They rode in complete silence to the hospital with only the sound of the driver humming occasionally or changing the radio station. The few cars on the road blinded them with light and then disappeared. Melanie slept in the seat next to him. He longed to reach out and touch her. They were headed into a dangerous, lawless place with few certainties and high risk and for the first time, he second-guessed his decision to bring her along. It would be his job to protect her and keep her safe. If something were to happen to him, then she would be compromised. Luke grabbed the ceiling handle and clenched the bar with his fingers. He would do everything in his power to make sure no harm came to her.

Chapter 12

Doctor Gerrard Sanjay greeted Luke with a hearty handshake and large grin. "Mr. Harrison," he said, "good to see you again. How are your brothers?"

A nurse rushed by in her blue scrubs and squeaky sneakers. She handed Melanie and Luke a clipboard each with information for them to fill out and a pen. Melanie moved off to the side and tried not to listen to Luke's conversation with the doctor.

"Damon is getting married at my house and Brent is still traveling all over," Luke responded. "I appreciate you meeting us. I know you're busy."

"You're in luck that you got me on my overnight shift." The phone at the nurses' station cut through their conversation. The nurse at the station picked it up without much energy and rubbed her forehead while talking.

Melanie's gaze lifted to Luke. He cupped Doctor Sanjay's elbow and they shook hands. She scurried her gaze back to her paper when both men looked at her. She cleared her throat and continued writing her personal information.

Dr. Sanjay led them both to a private room on the other side of the nurses' station. The sound of a cart with a loose wheel grew louder and then faded, as the door to the room closed. The vacant hospital bed had been made up with a thin blanket and pillow. The open mini blinds gave way to a view out the window of the other buildings across the street.

Melanie hugged her arms. The subtle smells of cleaning products and sadness flew over her, if sadness could be considered a smell. The room felt forgotten and lonely, even with Dr. Sanjay and Luke standing inside with her. Another nurse with the nametag of Lucy, entered the room by pushing a tray with two paper cups with water and two pills.

"I'm prescribing Maxcrone. The drug is ideal, given the last minute travel. You'll take this once a day and continue to take it seven days after your trip." Dr. Sanjay stepped in front of Melanie. "I'll need to ask you some personal questions."

"Luke can stay," she responded and turned her back to him. "What do you need to know?"

"Are you pregnant?"

"No chance of that."

"You're not breastfeeding then either."

"Nope."

Dr. Sanjay seemed relieved. He stepped back and asked both Luke and Melanie a few more questions, gave them each the pill. "The medication might be rough on your stomach. If you throw up within the hour, take another dose. Call me if you have any trouble stomaching the medicine. Alright, is there anything else?"

"I appreciate your help," Luke said.

"Lucy will get you the prescription. There's a pharmacy on the second floor, and we can give you your pills before you leave." Dr. Sanjay shook Luke's hand. "I hope your trip goes well."

"I do too."

Dr. Sanjay shut the door and Luke turned to Melanie. "No chance of pregnancy?"

"No chance at all." Melanie averted his gaze.

"I forgot to ask if you're seeing anyone back at home."

"Clearly, you've assumed there's no one."

"Well?"

"There's no one."

"Good." Luke's fingers slipped under her chin. "Are you ready for this?"

She'd been waiting for forever for this. "I am."

* * * *

The jostling woke up Melanie as the cab rolled to a stop. She groaned out of a sleepy haze and realized she'd fallen asleep. Her bones protested at having to be awakened and she sat half-awake with Luke sitting next to her. A loud engine frittered away in the background. "Where are we?" she asked.

"We're at the airport," Luke said. "You fell asleep on the way over."

The seat belt unbuckled at the click of her fingers and she got out of the cab. The feeling of forgetting something overcame her. "Where's my purse?"

"You don't need one. I have your backpack." He doled out some cash for the driver, exchanged a few pleasantries and they were on their way to the tarmac, walking under a moon three-quarters full and an off-yellow color.

Melanie stifled a yawn as they approached the plane and she continually swept the hair off her face as they walked into the wind. This flight marked the first of several flights she would be on in the next couple of days and would be the first time she'd traveled anywhere remote. The one trip she'd gone on to London had been for her high school senior class trip and technically, she didn't think this counted. Madagascar seemed a distant island on another planet and in reality she knew nothing about what she'd signed up for. How typical of herself, to have wanted something so strongly and then when faced with the opportunity, she suddenly became rational and cautious.

She watched Luke head up to the staircase, waiting for them like some white blocks off an alien ship and she couldn't help but wonder why he'd decided to take her along. They weren't a couple, as she'd stated before. Why now? She wasn't naïve in thinking one kiss from her set Luke off on a romantic crusade to win her over. Why risk losing this blue garnet with a newcomer and novice at gemstone hunting? A chill ran up her arms. What was he up to? Not a blessed word had been mentioned about those tourmalines her brother supposedly stole. Surely Luke hadn't backed off from his goal of getting them returned. Either way, she was here now. Time would give her all the answers she needed. You never knew how long people would be in your life and this trip, this summer, could be the last time they had a chance to live in the moment.

The lighted steps on the plane guided Melanie up to the door and inside to a lighted cockpit and cabin. A different crew member from their ride out to Maui assisted them. A beautiful woman with a slick-backed ponytail and red lipstick greeted them. "Welcome," she said, "Feel free take any seat."

Miss Bright-eyed got out of the way, allowing Melanie to walk back and choose a seat by the window. She laid low in her seat soaking up the clean, luxurious travel of leather seats and enough space to lie down without hitting the seat in front of you. This moment of flying on a private jet would stay with her each and every time she downgraded back to coach. Unable to keep her eyes open, she closed them, and reclined her seat back.

"You're Melanie Cahill," said a rough voice.

So much for sleep, Melanie thought and opened her eyes to find the man towering over her bared an eerie, almost twin resemblance to Luke. Tall, broad shoulders, and stubble shadowed his jaw. The slight crooked hitch of his nose and bushier eyebrows separated their appearance. He stunk like a dirt road and looked deprived of soap and water. Before he ever said his name she knew his. "You must be Brent," she commented, taking in his greasy hair and bags under his eyes.

"I've waited a long time to meet you." Brent grinned the smile of a man stuck on himself and didn't waste a beat. "How's your brother these days?"

Laughter shot out of Melanie's mouth. "Interesting choice of words for our very first introduction."

"Interesting choice to get on a plane with a bunch of strangers." He grinned in a way that mimicked Luke. "I hope you don't mind sleeping with bugs the size of rats crawling all over you."

She sat up a little straighter, refusing to let Brent get to her. "I don't mind at all. I used to sleep with your brother."

"Touché."

Luke entered the cabin. The attractive stewardess welcomed him instantly with a kiss on the cheek. They stood together for a few moments and spoke quietly.

"There's my brother," Luke finally said, noticing Brent and Melanie. He clapped Brent on the shoulder. "I see you've met Melanie."

"She's charming, really." Brent shook his brother's hand. "Good to see you. Are you sure about…" He glanced at Melanie. "I thought you were kidding about bringing her."

"I asked her to come." Luke nodded solemnly at her. "You're to give her the same respect as anyone else traveling with us. She's my guest."

Relieved at Luke sticking up for her, Melanie flashed Brent a victorious smile and closed her eyes until the purr of the engine sounded in her ears and the subtle movement of the wheels gliding on the tarmac rippled under her feet. The plane took off and flew into the night and all remained quiet as Brent and Luke spoke in hushed voices and Melanie drifted off to sleep.

The rest of the flight Melanie slept. They arrived in Honolulu and she shuffled her feet like a sleepwalker to the next plane, taking in the people and airport around her, but not really fully awake. Someone looked at her ticket and ushered her through a flight gate. She followed Luke and Brent to another terminal and she kept yawning and fighting off the need to sit down and sleep more. The scent of caffeine didn't entice her tongue. The tiredness saddled onto her back onto the next plane. The cushioned seats helped her settle in and someone threw a blanket over her. Another engine rattled off…a voice came over the loudspeaker…the pilot drove the plane on the runway…Luke whispered something to her about blue garnets…one of them would be for her…and then she slept some more.

"We're in New York," Luke announced abruptly and turned on the cabin lights over her seat.

"Already?" Melanie came around and stretched her arms. The other passengers formed a line and retrieved their carry-on luggage from the compartments above the seats. They wore anxious expressions to get off the plane and get on with their lives. "I feel ten years older."

"You'll feel thirty years older by the time we're done with this trip. We have an hour layover. Brent's already off the plane."

Melanie took his advice and they parted ways after entering their terminal at JFK. She purchased toothpaste and a toothbrush from a kiosk and found a bathroom where she washed her face and brushed her teeth. When she emerged from the restroom, she found Luke holding a single cup of coffee and he did not look like somebody willing to share.

"Brent needed to make a few calls," he said and removed the tab on his coffee lid. "Do you need to call anyone?"

"Where's my cup of coffee?"

"They only had one left and I bought it for myself."

"At least you're consistent."

"So, do you need to make a call?"

"I should call my sister. My mother doesn't know I'm in Maui. I mean, in New York, or wherever we are now." Guilt stifled Melanie's good mood at the truth she'd kept hidden from her mother.

"I thought you lived with her."

"I do."

"She doesn't know you're across the country and about to be off the continent?"

"I'm sure Jessie has told her by now I'm working for you."

"She doesn't even know that I hired you?" Luke stuck out his neck and turned up his palm. "Why the hell not?"

"Because," Melanie seethed and grabbed the phone out of his hand, "my family's been through enough thanks to you. She wouldn't understand. I would rather die than having her know I'm here with you. Give me a minute, okay? Let me call my sister."

She waited until he'd gone and she called Jessie. Voicemail was such a beautiful invention in times like these, when she could outline her plans, her location, and end with a message without ever getting the backlash of their outrage at her decision. "There," she said and ended the message. Melanie handed the phone back to Luke. "Phone call handled."

Luke wasn't placated. The mood on his face read more interested than ever. "Do you ever talk to your father anymore?"

"I email with him occasionally." Melanie shrugged. "He calls on my birthday and sends me a check each year or a gift card to a store I don't shop at anymore. I'm not ungrateful for his kindness. I'm just over trying to tell him about myself. He can't get to know me through a phone call twice a year or a few emails."

"At least he's trying." Luke waved his hand at Brent walking towards them. The tanned skin and layer of dust breathed excitement in every one of his steps.

Like some enigma bearing coffee and a sexy grin, Melanie saw the way people passing by looked at Brent and then their gaze lassoed over to Luke and they tried not to stare. One of the women passing by gave Luke a long glance and then she whispered to her friend. Melanie flashed Luke a harsh glance. "Oh look. Here comes Brent. The brother I've finally met after seven years."

Luke laughed. "I bet you've been waiting all night to say that."

"Accept that I'm right about you purposefully keeping me from learning about your family."

"Should I come back later?" Brent said, handing Melanie a cup of coffee. "Sorry, I got distracted with a phone call. I put sugar in your cup. Maybe it will get rid of the perpetual frown on your face. You two look ready to get in a ring together and fight it out."

"Nonsense," Luke answered happily, "Melanie was telling me how impressed she is with you."

Brent laughed hard. "No chance in hell."

They spent the next hour drinking coffee and getting food at a sandwich shop near their gate. Luke spent most of the time on the phone, with whom, she would never know. They boarded the plane without excitement and took their seats in first class. Luke stretched out his legs and closed his eyes, which left Melanie to occupy her time with Brent. They took out their frustration on each other by playing Hangman. Melanie won seven out of ten times and I-Spy, which Brent won more than lost and when they'd grown bored of playing child games, they sat back and began talking.

Brent ordered champagne. "Would you like a glass?" he offered.

"No thank-you. Alcohol might put me to sleep again." She drew the blanket over her shoulders.

"I'm glad my brother is joining me on this trip. His face is too clean-shaven for what we do. The two of us, actually, the three of us when Damon first left home, we used to fly all over the world living out our backpacks and running from one mine to the next." Brent rested his head on the headrest. "This one time we were in Thailand looking for rubies. We'd gotten a tip. Our tips are often good leads as we give a cut to our contact. The three of us set out to get to the mine before any of the other buyers. We ended up getting to a dead-end and the mine was a trap to rob buyers. We got everything taken from us and I mean everything. They let us keep our underwear and shoes. You should have seen us when we came back to town, dehydrated, sunburnt, and wearing only underwear." Brent laughed to himself. "We consider ourselves lucky they didn't shoot us right there."

Melanie sank lower in her seat. The dangers for a woman might be far greater out there, but she didn't voice her opinion. She wanted to be on this trip. Whatever came next she could handle. Her traveling companions excelled at this business. They knew how to keep each other safe. They would watch out for her, even if she didn't trust her heart to one of them.

The pilots landed the airplane in Bekily early in the morning. The heat hit Melanie as she stepped off the plane along with dry, dusty, air that coated her skin and baked her simultaneously. They grabbed their backpacks and supplies, headed to the interior of the airport to use the restroom and buy some water.

Inclusions

Melanie and Brent waited outside on a street corner juxtaposed by traffic and a rickety fence on a small plot of sidewalk. The landscape, more modern than Melanie had expected, bustled with people going about their day. Old t-shirts covered their backs and worn jeans enclosed their legs. The women swayed rather than walked in their long skirts and dresses tied around their necks. A vendor selling spotted brown bananas waved at Melanie. The rows of buildings and houses weren't of the hut variety Melanie had imagined. Cars and people moved up the street with abundant noise. Their entire group stuck out by way of light skin color, healthy faces, and glowing white smiles. Melanie clutched the strap of her backpack, feeling protective of her belongings.

"You look out of place," Brent commented.

"At least I don't look sketchy," she quipped.

"I fit in more than you." The sly Harrison grin rode up his cheeks and he elbowed her playfully. "Don't worry too much about your safety. You're a woman in a foreign land. What could go wrong?"

Melanie tried to think of other topics. Fear rode up her spine, but she wouldn't admit this to Brent or Luke. Thankfully, the rental car appeared around the corner with Luke at the wheel. His bulky frame filled the driver's side and his shoulders hunched a little. The rusted exterior, broken door handle, and roll of paint missing on the hood elevated the status of Melanie's car back home.

She got into the back seat holding her bag while Brent took up the front seat. Luke pulled away from the street corner without much notice by the people around them. "Where are we going?" Melanie asked, once Luke drove the car back in the stream of traffic.

"The friend of a friend I told you about. His name is Andry and he's expecting us. He lives about an hour south of the airport." Brent angled his head back. "I've worked with Andry before. He'll translate for us and show us the way to the mine, unless you speak Malagasy and know your way around the southern terrain."

Melanie snapped her fingers. "I knew I should have taken Malagasy in high school."

The engine gave an unpromising gurgle and sputter. Luke's hand hit the wheel and the car settled. "You look nervous," Luke said, looking at Melanie through the rearview mirror.

"There's the observation of the year." Melanie clutched her bag close to her chest. The gaze in his eyes was enough confidence for both of them. She saw the corners of his mouth creep up to grin.

The geography unfolded the further away from the airport Luke drove. She remembered very little about the actual, physical whereabouts of gemstones from what Luke had told her so many years ago. The term Metaphoric Rock stuck out; found miles within the Earth where the pressure is too great and gemstones are borne.

But there weren't many mountains around, at least none liked she'd imagined. The city transformed into countryside consisting of bush, brush, rocks, and a landscape overlooked by no one other than God himself. The desolate place wasn't inviting even to a stray cat. An elderly woman carried a basket on a dirt road. A mangy dog chased something in the distance. Puny fences teetered over to divide property and the dirt swirled up from the road and gave everything a dusty, forgotten layer. Melanie couldn't see the potential beyond the poverty and desolation. She couldn't fathom how something worth so much money came out of this place; came out from the nothingness they drove through.

"The community Andry lives in is near the Menarandra River," Brent commented. "They are mostly farmers. They raise cattle. This is their land."

"Why aren't we meeting Andry in the city?"

"He doesn't like the city. He's a family man and he likes to stay close to his land. He'll meet us out in the country because it saves him time. Competition is fierce. We're not the first to visit this land and we won't be the last. There could be any number of our competitors out there trying to steal Andry. Someone else might offer him more money for his help."

"He's scaring you," Luke interjected. "Don't look like you just drank poison. Staying out here, looking for treasure is nothing more than high-risk and high-reward."

"If you survive," Brent joked.

Melanie saw no humor in the moment.

They traveled a bumpy dirt road that constantly knocked Melanie's knees together. The car held up, though she swore one of the tires would blow at any moment. They moved farther away from the city until she didn't see any sign of human activity. They could have been on a different planet with all the dust and wide open space.

The plateaus in the distance grew nearer after some time on the road. Shrubs appeared in bigger clusters and the dry grass became fuller and thicker closer to the road. Luke pulled off the road at a section of dried up trees and low bushes. A plastic shopping bag clung to a bush and flapped like a flag in the wind. Luke veered the car to another road, one with bigger dips and more rocks. The car bounced and sputtered before Luke came to a stop in front of the tree with the bag. Both Brent and Luke cast furtive glances through the windshield.

"We're meeting him at the plastic bag," Brent said and pointed to a large tree with a large circle etched in the tree. He looked out every window and squinted. "He'll be here."

Luke turned off the engine. "We're all getting out of the car."

The bag in Melanie's arms slid. They had arrived in the middle of nowhere, without any resources except the little food and water they'd stocked up on at the airport shops. Melanie opened the car door and caught sight of a dark-skinned man appear from behind the circle of shrubs. "Andry," she heard Brent say. "This is my brother, Luke."

"Welcome, welcome," Andry said in return and slapped Brent's hand like an old friend.

"This is Melanie," Luke said and looked around for her. "She's a friend of ours learning the gem business."

"Hello," she said and shook his hand.

Andry smiled with a mouthful of stained, overcrowded teeth. "We have much work to do."

"Tell us about this garnet," Luke got right to the point. "Is this the real deal or have we flown all this way to chase a rumor?"

"The garnet is real. We'll go there now. We take the car close to four-hundred kilometers and then walk to the entrance of the mine. The mine is too remote for a car to go."

"Then we'd better get moving." Brent slapped Luke on the back. "Daylight's burning."

"Yes, yes," Andry replied with his thick, enthusiastic accent. "We must move quickly."

They all piled back in the car with Andry sitting next to Melanie. His strong body odor filled the back seat and she could see sweat breached the fabric of his shirt collar. The kindness in him outweighed the physical nuances and they quickly began chatting about their homes.

Andry, a father of three daughters and two sons, grew up in the same farming community his family owns today. Their community had started a school a couple of years ago and up until recently they were too overcrowded for girls to attend. This year an unexpected cash flow came in the form of his brother selling a large blue garnet he'd been hiding for years and he'd used the payout from this deal to hire a second teacher for the girls. They passed the time in small talk and every time Melanie glanced out her window, everything looked the same dirt, spacious, and parched landscape.

They'd been on the road for close to the length of their trip when black smoke puffed out the engine. "No, no, no!" Brent yelled as Luke pulled the car over.

"Why did you pick this car?" Andry asked. "You should have bought bigger."

"I thought we'd be more discreet in this one." Luke turned off the engine. "Now we might get robbed regardless."

"There's nobody on this road to rob us," Melanie said, strained from the long day of travel.

"We will get robbed," Andry said, "at some point, I assume. There's a group of rebels that roam around these roads and they stay close. They like to stay hidden. They ambush your car and they take what they want. There's little you can do to prevent such an attack. There's too much land to control. Madagascar is not like your California. There's no Mickey Mouse."

Disneyland? Melanie scrutinized shrubs around her, wondering if she hadn't already seen the faint movement of someone crouching behind or in the tall, dry grass. She gulped and held her bag closer.

The hood popped up and Luke inspected the engine. He came back and stuck his head through the open window. "She's toast. We're done."

"What are we supposed to do?" Melanie said.

Andry opened the door. "We walk."

"We have to get moving," Luke said, sticking his head through the open window. "Melanie, keep your eyes open."

Inclusions

Luke's warning didn't console Melanie. She stepped out of the car and went around to the trunk where Luke and Brent worked to divide up the supplies. Andry unzipped his long, army green bag and pulled out a gun, small enough to fit into a spare back pack brought by Brent. Luke slammed the trunk closed and they got moving on foot.

The soles of her shoes wore out faster than she would have liked. Soon, she began to feel the stabs of the pebbles on her feet, the thin layer of rubber keeping her skin from touching the ground grew soft and stretchy. The path in front of her she had to watch carefully. Lizards darted out across their path; snakes slithered in the trees and around the rocks. The spiders and scorpions owned the land. There wasn't another car, person, or house in sight as far as Melanie could see. The sun beat down and drained her energy. Tired and hungry, they all sort of stopped at the same time near an area semi-protected by boulders.

"We'll stay here tonight," Luke said. "We need to rest. We'll have another couple of hours to walk tomorrow."

Two simultaneous currents of hunger and exhaustion moved through Melanie. She began to sit down, when Luke barked at her to go find twigs and leaves. The response she gave sounded like the voice of a drone instead of a human.

"Get whatever you can find," he said with edge. "Just don't go far."

She looked around and saw a plethora of scrawny branches and leaves, but when she picked them up, they held moistness not suitable for making fires. There must have been rain not long before they arrived. Wet twigs wouldn't make a fire go. She dropped the twigs and scouted out an area further away from their camp. She gathered what she could and returned to the camp, already complete with two tents, and a makeshift fire pit in the middle.

"Not bad," Brent said and took her load. He tossed the twigs in a pile and got down on his knees. The fire starter in his hand lit a flame on the pile of twigs and Brent cupped his hands around the twigs and blew careful breaths until the fire took and spread.

The rest of them gathered around the fire, useless at the end of their long day at making further conversation. Melanie ate some of the canned goods they'd brought along, but nothing tasted good and she wanted sleep more than to eat. She turned to Luke and caught sight of his intense gaze aimed at the fire. There was so much to him, such depth. She felt like reaching out and touching his cheek, but she held back. "Where am I sleeping?"

"With me," he answered without looking at her.

Melanie hesitated; unsure of whom she trusted less: Luke or herself. She got up, said good-night to Brent and Andry, and walked over to the triangle-shaped tent several feet away from the fire. She ducked into the tent where a single blanket lay on the ground.

"I call dibs on the blanket." Luke sided up next to her.

His thigh brushed against hers. She stood crouched over with her head grazing the top of the tent. "How am I supposed to stay warm?"

Luke ducked inside and stretched out best he could on the ground. "You're a smart woman, you'll figure out something."

Frustrated, she kneeled down and joined him on the cold, hard ground. The sharp nudge of pebbles on the ground hit her back. She reached up for her bag, punched the canvas material a couple of times to fluff, and she positioned herself with her back to Luke. Back-to-back, they lay there in the dark, pressed against each other like two stone pillars. The chill of the tent settled on her skin, particularly her lips, nose, and cheeks. Shivers ran through her body and her teeth began to chatter. Sounds that had been drowned out by their voices earlier in the day, came to life. The chirping, the ticking, and the strange cries and scratching in the distance made her grow uneasy and further from sleep. This place thrived more at night than during the day. She wiggled her butt up against Luke and stopped suddenly at what sounded like the faintest shuffle close to their tent. She waited with wide eyes, expecting something or someone to unzip their tent and massacre her limbs. The cool air slipped out of her mouth and her heart pounded hard like an entire marching band cutting across her chest. She flipped over and anchored herself to the one person in this remoteness.

Melanie slid her hands and arms under his shirt, like sliding into a glove. The instant heat pumped blood through her fingers and inched up her arms. Her fingers moved over his front side and flattened over the sinew of his muscles covering his torso. She molded herself against his angles. She inhaled the scent of campfire and dried sweat and pressed her lips to his back. Immediately her face thawed. The warmth from his body subsided her quivers and chased the coldness from her face. Luke's hands buckled over hers and pulled her closer. A deep sigh came out of his mouth. They remained like this for some time. The calmness of his breathing lulled her eyes closed. She'd almost fallen asleep when the blanket graced her body and he turned and swallowed her up in his embrace.

Chapter 13

The smoky smell of burning branches awakened Melanie, followed by the stiffness that had spread throughout her bones and settled during the night. She sat up on her elbows, looking at the light filtering between the tent doors and highlighting the dust particles being carried by the wind. The wind, rough and chilly, seeped in the tent. The blanket fell off her shoulders and onto the ground. Vaguely, she remembered Luke holding her. She could be wrong on that account. She opened one of the tent flaps and glimpsed Luke standing next to Andry. Together they packed up the other tent. Her gaze followed the hazy trail to the campfire, over to Brent holding a pan over the flame.

Luke turned his head to the tent. Melanie released the nylon fabric and ran her hand through her hair. "We're leaving as soon as you're ready," he said with agitation in his voice and anxiousness in his eyes.

Melanie hugged her arms with numb fingers. "Thanks for the blanket," she said.

Luke nodded to his right. "There's coffee out by the campfire."

"Luke, we've got to hurry," Andry called.

The thought of coffee or of any liquid appealed greatly to Melanie. She grabbed her backpack and headed out of the tent. She could weather Luke's indifferent mood for a little longer.

"Good morning," Brent said as Luke began to disassemble the tent. He removed the poles and the tent deflated to the ground.

The pot in his hand intrigued Melanie and she looked over his shoulder at the black goop in the pot. The semi-liquid smelled like dung and resembled tar. Her nose scrunched and she covered her mouth. "Don't tell me…"

"Gourmet wilderness coffee." Brent reached for a tin can. "Guaranteed to put hair on your chest. Do you want a cup?"

"I'd prefer to keep my chest hairless." Melanie smiled at Andry.

Brent shrugged his shoulders. "Suit yourself."

While the men drank the coffee, Melanie excused herself for some privacy. She wasn't hungry, just thirsty, and she drank half of her last bottle of water before returning to the camp.

Luke held out a small orange. The fruit might as well have been a beautiful jewel in a land of brown and gray accents. "Take it," he said.

"Thanks." The orange felt bumpy in her hand and tasted juicy and sugary on her lips.

The seven-mile hike to the mine began with an arid morning. The temperature increased steadily, along with Melanie's thirst. Each of the men in her group stalked over the arid ground with long strides and a gaze pointed at something unreachable in the distance. Unlike the lighthearted mood yesterday, where Andry talked about his children and told Melanie about his family, today he said little. Brent too seemed to knock away any attempt at picking a fight with her, and Luke, when he did speak, reminded Melanie of a set of clippers trimming down any branch in his sight. Today was all business and she understood.

The shrubs grew sparse and gave away to jagged hills and steep plateaus which they climbed. The heat attacked Melanie's body and she sweat in places she couldn't discuss in this group of men. The sun beat down on them like a punch to the face. She tried not to be overjoyed to the point of tears each time they stopped for a break. Luke increased his pace at the same time Melanie struggled to keep up with the group. She stopped to catch her breath on a steep climb and placed her hands on her knees to get some air.

"When we get to the mine," Andry said, slowing down to talk to Melanie. "Say as little as possible. Luke and Brent will talk."

Melanie caught Luke glancing back her for the first time in hours. "I understand," she answered.

"Get out of the way!" Luke yelled out of nowhere.

Andry and Melanie dove to opposite sides of the path. The sound of rocks crushing the ground rolled past her. A large boulder toppled by her, missing her by a few inches. Melanie's face dropped to her hands. Her heart pounded.

"I told you to keep your eyes open." Luke crouched down beside her. "That rock could have hurt you." Luke yanked her up by the wrist. He unzipped his backpack and handed her a bottle of water. "You're dehydrated."

Melanie gulped down what she could and handed the bottle back to Luke.

"The mine is on the other side of this ridge." Brent unscrewed the lid on his canteen. "We're close."

"Not close enough." Luke drank a sip of water and put the bottle back in his back pack.

The loose boulder woke up Melanie out of her misery. She made it a point to keep up the rest of the grueling hike. The top of the mountain provided a view of the valley full of more or less nothing than barren land all leading to another set of mountains. They hiked down, turned, turned again, and cut across a dry riverbed. The trees provided bouts of shade followed by long period of sun exposure. The question "How much longer?" scratched the tip of Melanie's tongue by the minute.

The riverbed came to life around the next corner. A pool of muddy brown water formed and they followed the path which would be upstream if there were more water. The water increased in width and height and depth with each step as they crossed to the other side of the bank. Cool water rushed up and over Melanie's knees until the toll of walking and slipping on the rocks became too much, and she, along with the others, plunged in the water and swam to the other side. Occasionally, they saw another person. Nobody acknowledged them or said hello. The distrust in their gazes sent creepy-crawlies up Melanie's back.

"This is a good sign," Brent told Melanie. "People come from miles around to follow-up on leads or work for the mine owners. They're mining."

Andry called out to one of the men in the river in his native tongue. "The mine is a quarter of mile. We're close and we're headed in the right direction."

"What will you do with the garnet?" Melanie asked.

"Don't mention gemstones," Luke said tersely. "Whatever you do, don't talk about why we're here. Say nothing. Do nothing except on my cue. Walk and don't react to anything you see. Be invisible."

She headed the warning in his voice. Melanie clamped up and kept walking. Each step she felt the tension in her muscles and her jaw refused to relax. The mood between Andry, Brent, and Luke surpassed serious. She saw the unease in their eyes and the careful way they watched their surroundings.

Inclusions

The closer they got to the base of the mountain, the more congested the river became. Miners, shirtless and wet up to their ribs, filled up the landscape. They held baskets of some sort and sifted them back and forth underneath the muddy, clay-colored earth. They were mining for a stone, garnets, Melanie assumed, but didn't dare ask. She was too afraid to speak; too fearful that a sneeze would bring too much attention to their group. A group of young boys looked up at them and their gazes shifted to Melanie. Their dark, shiny eyes kept on her and she felt clammy in her cheeks and wobbly on her knees. She didn't belong here and they knew it.

Luke led them around a steep corner and away from the river. Melanie wiped the dirty sweat off her eyes. They stung and she tried not to rub them. Her eyes began watering and stinging worse than ever. She blinked profusely and more water leaked from her eyes. She wasn't paying attention to the sight in front of her and stopped abruptly, hitting Brent square in the back with her face.

He turned around and glowered. Silently, he pointed ahead. Melanie followed his finger to the narrow opening in the mountain. A thatched roof hung over the entrance to the tunnel. Large boulders sat on either side and a pile of rocks formed a mini version of the mountain in front of them. There was dirt everywhere. A random tree provided little shade off to the right. It looked like the sort of place someone went into and didn't come out from.

"We're here," Brent said.

The mouth of the tunnel didn't look big enough for a dog to fit through let alone an actual person. Four men armed with big guns and instant suspicion stepped up to the side of the mine like living, protective doors. Melanie couldn't take her stare away from the weapons. They were bigger than her legs and full of ammunition capable of taking out every single one of them. She gulped back over the rock in her throat. A dizzy spell overcame her. The worry about what would come next ran deep inside and choked her sense of safety.

Andry approached the men with his hands in surrender position. He spoke fast and loud at the four men. They glanced at the group in front of them, rugged, tired, and very white. Very American. The guards responded in rapid fire. One of them pointed his thick finger at Luke. The other guard watched the rest of them. The third guard, and the largest of them all, went into the entrance of the mine.

Andry muttered to Luke, "He'll be back in a moment."

Melanie's throat dried out of anything worth saying and best she could, she took Andry's advice to blend in and not say anything. This wasn't the time or the place to challenge Andry on how far women had come in the world. Equality hadn't caught up in these parts and today wouldn't be that day. A small man with skin the color of the riverbed appeared at the entrance to the hut. The man spoke a flutter of words Melanie couldn't interpret.

"This is Bruno," Andry translated, "he owns this mine."

"Does he have any large blue garnets?" Luke said, taking the lead.

"Bruno says they are mining rubies, not garnets."

Luke ignored the comment. "Tell him we have cash. We're willing to pay for the right price. We want a big garnet. The biggest he has."

Melanie watched Andry repeat Luke's impatient words to Bruno. Bruno scratched his chin and spoke again. He pointed at Luke.

Andry nodded. "Come." A bead of sweat slid down the side of his face. "The others stay outside."

Luke looked sharply at Andry. "You come along." He started to walk forward to the lightless entrance of the mine and he looked back briefly at Melanie. An edgy glare in his eyes. Bruno got in her view of Luke and they each disappeared inside. The other guards stepped together and formed a human gate at the entrance, blocking all of Melanie's view.

Unease crippled Melanie. The pit in her stomach constricted. She walked over to the group of boulders to the right of the mine and took a seat. It didn't break her heart to not go into the thick of the mine. She valued her life. "What's going on?" she asked Brent.

Brent paced in front of her. He cast the guards a furious glance. "They are playing a game. The mine owner, if he has such a garnet as the one we came to find, will save it for last. He won't want to sell the stone to our group, we could be the first interested buyers or the last. We'll never know. Luke is negotiating. The owner may have what Luke wants. Could be a handful of blue garnets or the big one. Eleven carats," he said wistfully. "There's none ever been found at that weight."

"Yes, but how do you know if a gemstone is real? What if Luke's in there picking out a generic one?"

Inclusions

"Luke and I can generally tell what we're getting. We deal with gemstones in their natural form all the time. In fact, we spend less time with the final, shiny product you see in jewelry store windows. Has my brother never taught you about inclusions?"

"Not really. I know they are flaws."

"I can't get into it now. My brother did you a disservice if all you've retained is the word flaw."

Melanie didn't want to revisit the past. Certainly not with Brent. "What will happen next?"

"Luke will bring the garnet outside to get a better look. The small magnifying glass you've seen us carry around is called a loupe." Brent put his hands on his hips. He looked at the guards and back to Melanie. "I bet you feel really uncomfortable right about now."

Melanie scoffed at him. "If this miner has gems to sell, why didn't Bruno look happy at our arrival?"

"He's got something special and he knows this. Blue garnets fetch a lot of money and interest. Especially the bigger ones. They are few and far between. Old Bruno's trying to hold out for one of the bigger gemstone hunters. There could be five other groups just like ours. Word travels fast in this business. We aren't the only ones chasing after a tip. We haven't done business with these guys before. They don't know us and we don't know them. There's a catch to us being here. Bruno owns the mine. Legally, he has claim to everything inside that mine." Brent lowered his voice. "We can be considered trespassers; trespassers get shot. He can kick us off for any reason and make sure we don't return. Everything's sketchy at this point."

Melanie looked down and saw that Brent's hand shook a little. She thought she would double over from the rock in her stomach. She thought she might be sick.

Luke appeared at the mine entrance and the guards parted. They got out of his way, though stayed close to his every move. He looked immediately at Melanie, then at Brent. One quick jut of his chin and he'd communicated some message to Brent. One of the guards shifted his heavyset legs and he shifted the gun over his other shoulder. They spoke amongst themselves and glanced over at Melanie. She pressed the palm of her hand onto the rock beneath her. She worried about Luke and Brent.

The shortest of the guards began speaking lower and more rapidly. He looked at Melanie again. She grew restless and fearful about the entire situation.

Brent walked over and they exchanged hushed conversation. She saw what looked like a rock pass from Luke to Brent. Luke produced a small, hand-held tool, different from the loupe. He handed the lens to Brent; Brent raised the lens to the rock and kept turning the rock around and examining it from several angles. He returned the rock and the tool to Luke and he did the same. They talked again with the words, "color," and "carat," and "you're call," being spoken louder.

"How much?" Brent said.

Luke uttered a number and Brent nodded. The guards stepped to the side as Luke returned to the opening of the mine with his hand firm against the strap on his backpack.

Only a few minutes passed and Melanie stood at the sight of Luke emerging from the mine for the second time. This time he spared no conversation with his brother. Luke's eyes darted to Melanie and he pointed beyond her shoulder. "Go. Now."

Everything happened all at once. Andry fled out of the mine and started to walk away from the entrance without consulting anyone. Melanie followed and felt the commotion of Luke and Brent walking swiftly behind her. A swirl of anxiousness rotated around them. Nobody spoke. Their pants chaffed together from moving so fast. Their backpacks jostled. Their lips pursed to the point of being white.

Something was very wrong. Luke grabbed her elbow and picked up his pace, practically dragging her next to him. His fingers dug into her skin. They wound back down the way they'd come, past the curves of the river. The half-naked people swishing their baskets in the muddy river stared them down. All eyes were upon them. She snuck a peak at Luke's profile. A muscle jumped on his neck. He was looking ahead, but his mind was clearly somewhere else. She kept up. Her legs took on a superpower, charged by the morbid thoughts pushing her to move fast. The rapid beating of her heart and the worry expanding in her stomach helped to keep her moving. Like walking in a parking lot at night with no one else around and you know you shouldn't be there in the first place.

Inclusions 121

The view of the shallow valley and riverbed came into sight. They hiked down the ravine, away from the local miners. They swam back through the river. Even with her clothes wet and heavy, her shoes slippery. Each passing minute was like a hammer chiseling away at her stamina.

Luke let go of her elbow. "Run," he said.

Everyone followed his command. Melanie kept her focus on the back of Andry's head. Sweat drizzled down his back and got soaked up in his shirt. They sounded like a pack of dogs running and moving without stopping. Sweat streaked down her face. She thought her heart would explode from the palpitations. She didn't understand why they had left so suddenly. A heart-stopping noise exploded from somewhere nearby. The bang, like a bolt of lightning, unsettled every bone in Melanie's body. She craned her neck to the sky and then she looked to Luke.

"Gunshots," he said and put his hands on Melanie's shoulders. His gaze traveled to every member of the group. "We have to keep moving."

Melanie took off too fast and tripped on a rock. The front of her toe snagged on a low branch and sent her skidding down a short hill on her rear. The backpack bumped up and down her back. A sharp thorn ripped through her jeans and broke through her skin. The cloud of dust mushroomed around her as she came to a halt at the base with the backs of her arms scratched to blood. "Not again," she mumbled under breath.

"No time to stop." Luke helped up Melanie and then he kept going.

"Keep moving," Brent said without asking. A second round of gunshots rang out, nearer to them. "We've got to get as far away from the mine. We're open game."

"The guards are coming back for the blue garnet," Luke explained through a choppy breath. He gripped Melanie's hand.

"So you didn't buy it?"

"Oh, we bought it. I just think he wants it back, plus our money. Andry overheard Bruno saying something to the guard inside the mine, something he wasn't supposed to overhear. Bruno will wait for the next buyer and pull the same stunt."

The group stayed close to the mountainside and used the trees and brush for a natural camouflage. "Get down!" Andry yelled.

Melanie threw her body on the ground and waited while the sound of a car engine charged by them. The pause in movement led her hands to shake as she waited until Luke stood up and rolled his arm for everyone to follow.

The way they took back looked like a different path then the one they'd traveled in the morning, at least to Melanie. The surrounding vegetation all held the same shapes. The grass and the long, dry leaves made their walk feel like one big giant circle without end or beginning. She longed for a moment to feel safe, or to at least carry the illusion of being safe. Nobody was ever really safe from anything.

Calm took over Luke and he chose a campsite protected by rocks forming a natural roof, nature's version of five-star accommodations. To either side of the rocks small, shallow cave openings gave off an ominous allure and Melanie's instinct told her to stay away.

Luke tossed Melanie the water bottle. "We're running low and we need to conserve our resources for the long hike back tomorrow."

"Tomorrow," Melanie echoed, and absentmindedly pulled a thorn out of her leg. Another night out here in the wide open. She took a couple of sips of water and wanted to drink an entire lake. The shallow breaths returned to regular and the streaks of sweat dried on her face. "Where are the others?"

Luke wiped off his forehead with the back of his hand. "They're checking around. Andry thinks there might be a stream nearby and he's confident Bruno's men won't track us to the caves. These caves are too far off the path. We'll have to leave at first light to be sure. Bruno will be desperate come the morning. His guards can't look for us much longer with the sun setting soon. We should be okay for tonight."

A sudden grin spread across his face. He reached inside his pocket and pulled out a chunk of gray-brown rock. "Come, take a look," Luke said to his brother.

Brent walked over to his brother and took out the loupe from his pant pocket. Luke held up the rock to the sunlight and used the handheld lens to have a closer look. He closed one eye and looked through the loupe. He turned the rock at a different angle, at the sun, away from the sun. He said nothing and passed the rock over to Brent. They spoke a wordless exchange and Brent also took a look at the rock with the lens.

"Perfect," Luke said.

"Well done," Andry commented, and leaned in to look at their prize.

Inclusions

Melanie handed the canteen to Luke. She caught sight of the ordinary rock and frowned. "I know they look different by the time they reach the stores, but I don't even see any color. Is there a stone even in there?"

"She's in there." Luke squeezed his hand around the rock. "This baby is at least nine or ten carats. She's more valuable, more stunning than anything you'll ever see."

"Bruno wants her back," Melanie pointed out, bemused.

"My darling, half the thrill of the job is running away with the treasure." Luke removed the bag around his neck and emptied the single content. "You didn't think we'd walk up to the mine, sit down at a conference table, and shake hands, did you?"

"I didn't think I'd be running as much." She looked more closely at the rock. Close to the size of a ping pong ball with rough edges and uneven grooves sat in his hand. She swiped a bit of dirt off the exterior.

"This is worth the risk."

With an armful of twigs, Andry returned with a grim expression before Melanie could respond to his statement. "I heard a car engine," Andry said, watching everything around him. "Wait on a fire until closer to sunset."

"Are we safe?" Luke said and dropped the garnet back in the bag.

"We should be. We can't stay here for more than a few hours. We'll sleep and be up before sunrise."

The sunshine dipped behind the mountains, sending an orange glow over the plains, reflecting the kind of warmth a hundred-degree evening can bring. The temperature plummeted fast. The fire in their camp flared after Brent got it started using his fire starter. The sound of animals pattering over the dirt and scattering around the rocks soon became a constant noise. A little bit of food and some water went a long way and Melanie found herself too tired to remain awake much longer. She wanted to be alone with Luke. She wanted him to stay close to her and keep her protected. One glance in his direction and she saw him cup his hands around his mouth and breathe into them. He looked rough and hot. The glow of the fire drew out his face from the rest of his body and she decided to go to bed with this image of him in her head.

Inside the tent, Melanie stretched out and used the back pack for her pillow. The conversation outside carried on about their day. Brent got Luke caught up on his recent excursions to Turkey with fondness in his voice. Bruised, sore, and cold, Melanie drifted to sleep on the floor of the Earth.

The wind blew in through the tent and kept waking up Melanie throughout the night. Shivers ran through her body and she hugged the blanket for warmth. Then she felt his fingers and the warmth of his body touching hers and heating away her chills. His arm draped over hers and her body stilled. "Thank you," she said.

Luke responded by finding her hand and placed an object in her hand. The serrated edges and slough of mineral filled her palm and he closed her hand around the rock. "Keep this on you," he spoke warm and gentle, like a fire reducing to coals. His skin felt hot and smooth against hers. "You'll be the last person Bruno's men will think to look at when they come find us."

"You think they'll find us?" Melanie scooted closed to him.

"I know they will." Luke pulled her closer. "They'll look to Brent and me first, then Andry, and then you. Don't give them the stone, no matter what."

She gasped. "Luke, I can't."

"You don't have a choice." One of the logs on the fire fell and the sound of crackling embers filled the tent.

The rock felt heavy in her hands and she set the stone down under her back pack. "I wished I'd done this with you, before. When we were together." She took his hands and ran hers over his. "I get why you love doing this. I saw how alive you looked when you exited the mine."

"I liked seeing you on the other side." Luke moved his hand over her thighs. He angled her face to his and his mouth found hers.

She didn't fight him. She breathed in Luke's sweaty rawness. She drew in her breath and closed her lips on his. Melanie's tongue twisted around his; her parched lips parted and slanted over his. Luke's tenacious, scorching kiss set off a trail of heat throughout her middle and down her legs. Luke's tongue moved around hers. His rough hands blazed a path down her front; his fingertips plowed into her pants. She shifted underneath him. Luke's lips clung to hers and he cursed in between breaths. His stubble scratched at her face. He didn't take his time. He wasn't gentle. His hands moved with commanding pace and firmness over each part of her body. Melanie's desire matched Luke's. She didn't want him to take his time. She wanted him inside her. His finger went right to the spot she needed him to go. All the blood in her body rushed to this one spot, to the center of her pleasure.

Luke unbuttoned her jeans and pushed them down. His hand slid down and his finger worked over the place ready to explode with need. His finger swirled among the folds and her dampness and shots fired up her middle and loaded her breasts with desire. Every corner, every inch of her body swirled in a needy frenzy to experience release from this man. His lips roved over hers and his kiss demanded much, much more. "Make love to me," he ordered in a strained whisper.

Melanie gasped at the lash of pleasure crippling her thighs. She tightened her grip on the back pack, relaxed her legs, and breathed to take in the pleasure building between her legs. She bit her lip and tasted blood. Luke's fingers worked fast. They circled her nub and slipped around her and inside her.

A loud *crack* outside caused them both to jump. "What was that?" she said with a rapid heartbeat.

"I don't know." Luke's hand came up from her underwear. "Let me check."

The tent door opened and he looked outside. "I don't see anyone. There's probably an animal out there getting too close."

Instinctively, she reached for the rock under her back pack. Next, she pulled up her pants. The intimate mood faded and gave way to a seriousness she sensed without ever seeing his expression. This wasn't the time for them to make love. It was time for them to stay alert and to stay alive.

He lay down next to her with his uneven breath and put his arms around her again, but did not kiss her or touch her. He turned his back on her and said nothing more. Melanie kept her eyes open and waited for sleep. But it never came.

Chapter 14

The cool air surrounded them inside the tent. Luke woke up with a scowl. Irritable, dehydrated, and worn, he rolled over and found himself staring at Melanie's back. The evidence of their laying together all night, touching and holding each other close made him swollen and hard at the thought of waking her up and taking her to bed. He switched his thoughts to the garnet and to the day ahead, until he could walk out of the tent without a hard-on. The garnet would be safe with her, he told himself. The blanket locked around her body so that he could see the roundness of her bottom, the rectangular line of her shoulders, and her toes peeking out of the blanket. His gaze roamed back up her frame pausing at the thick paleness of her hair from days without taking a shower. Pride and fear swept through him. She could protect the stone, but could he protect her?

Early on in his life, he'd learned not to expect much from other people. Love came with conditions and expectations. If he said the wrong thing, his father started drinking; the drinking had turned into violence. Love was nothing more than a destroyed bridge that unconnected their family. His mother had loved him so long as he didn't piss off his father; his father had adored alcohol more than any of his children. His parents couldn't protect Luke or his brothers from their own selfishness.

Luke bowed his head and closed his eyes. The disappointment he'd felt from his parents. The disappointment he felt in other people. He'd sent his lawyer to break up with her because he'd expected her to choose her brother. He dumped her and made the decision easy for her. He'd been giving her a way out of their relationship and she hadn't come back to show him otherwise. Luke lifted his head and watched her sleep. What if he'd been wrong? What if, given the chance, she would have picked him? He extinguished those questions on the spot. The past was the past.

"Time to get up," he said and pulled the blanket off of her shoulders. He couldn't look at her without wanting to be inside her. "We have to get moving."

Melanie turned on her back and stared up at him. "I'm well aware. I didn't sleep at all."

He expected her to start moving. Instead, she reached out her hand. Her fingers brushed under his chin and she brought her mouth to his. Tender, warm lips brushed against his. The slow, winding tease of her tongue wrapped around his. Luke's hands cradled her face and he took his time, exploring her mouth, all-too aware of her hard nipples rubbing against his chest. Heat soared through his muscles and his arousal bulged with longing to bring them both satisfaction. She pulled back with eyes full of warmth and beauty.

"You're finally coming around to my line of thinking."

"Shut up, Luke."

He touched her face and kissed her again. He unhooked his mouth from hers. She'd undid the calmness of his body, including his now tender member. "There's going to be little time to rest today, just so you know."

"I know."

Andry and Brent began to move around the campfire. They spoke low and made just enough noise for Luke to know they had to get moving. Another sound shot Luke to his feet and he hit the tent's ceiling. Melanie sat up fast. "Car engine," they both said and exchanged fearful glances.

"Get up." Luke held out his hand with urgency. "Where's the garnet?"

"I have your treasure."

Luke and Melanie fled the tent and the campsite with Andry and Brent. Their group scattered away in a mad fury. Their belongings served as evidence of their existence, along with the gray smoke of the freshly extinguished fire.

"Stay close to the hills," Andry ordered. "The rocks will protect us and they'll go crazy thinking they keep seeing someone."

They trekked the way they'd come yesterday while staying close to the line of the mountains. Luke took the lead with Melanie behind him, and Brent and Andry stayed a few feet back. They kept their eyes open and ears strained for the slightest sound of footsteps or voices. They carried on like this for a solid hour before stopping, drinking a few sips of water, and moving on at hasty pace.

Luke's feet couldn't move fast enough. He didn't trust the lack of gunshots or car engine noises. Bruno's men knew the landscape. They'd probably been sleeping close by and they would continue to get closer. Relief wasn't an emotion he would feel until they'd gotten back to the airport and to the safety of the city.

"How much water do we have left?" Melanie asked.

"Brent has one more bottle, and then we're done. We need to stay alert and push through. I know how tired and thirsty you must be." He could see the exhaustion all over Melanie's face and in the way she tried to move fast, but in general, walked with a bit of sluggishness and hunched shoulders.

"We're still heading north," Brent called out over his shoulder and held up the compass.

The survival skills Luke had honed over the years were not lost on him, even with being back in the office. Basic human survival was one of the first rules of becoming a gem hunter. The best stones tended to be hidden in the most volatile climates and locations. The outside world was the true maker of a man. Sleeping on the ground, freezing at night, boiling water, up until this trip, Luke had forgotten his body had limitations. He stole a glance at Melanie. The moving picture of a woman transformed physically by the dirt on her hair and in her face. Pride beamed through him at how well she'd managed to keep up and at how strong she really could be when the situation demanded all of her effort.

Luke stopped for a brief moment at a familiar juncture and with one glance at Brent, read his brother's mind. Andry too nodded and they continued walking. He didn't want to alarm Melanie with the details of their new problem.

"I don't think there's much to smile about," she quipped at him. "We're thirsty, starving, and we're the hunted ones."

"Out here, everyone's hunted," Andry said, smiling. "Man, woman, animal, everyone has a predator out on my land."

"Is this how you reassure your wife?" Melanie smiled back.

"My wife does most of the hunting."

She reached back, pulled her hair up into a ponytail, and spoke to Luke. "I remember the one time you came home; I think you'd been to Tanzania looking for tanzanite. You arrived back at your apartment covered in so much dirt that I shut the door in your face because I thought you were a stranger."

Luke laughed out loud. "I remember."

Andry came up beside them and squinted at the ridge ahead of them.

Inclusions

The wind picked up, forcing the dried-up branches to scratch against each other. The faint sound of an engine could be heard. "They're getting closer."

"We must be close to the car," Melanie said.

"You didn't realize..." Brent started to say.

"We already passed the point of the car," Luke said, strained. "We kept moving without talking about it because we didn't want you worried."

"There's no car?" Melanie took a seat on a rock. "We're nowhere near the city. Nobody bothered to tell me?"

"Did you forget the car broke down? Keep going." Luke walked ahead, refusing to let her sit on this dilemma for another second.

The aches in Luke's lower back and knee took second place to the pounding headache. Worry filled his mind. He also knew Melanie was hurting, though she toughed through the hike. She'd done better out here than he'd expected. They needed to find shelter and water. Nobody would come looking for them. No one would try to find out their identities and times were different now for Luke. The sweetness of the hunt soured at the thought of Vivian back home. He had someone to answer to, and he wanted to watch his daughter grow up and be relevant to her life. The thought of being responsible for something happening to Melanie forced him to walk faster too. Maybe he shouldn't have taken such a gamble bringing her along. In trying to make up for the past, he only hoped he hadn't screwed up the future.

A narrow road appeared out of the rocks. Tire tracks indicated this road would lead them back to the city. This road turned into an even larger one; the larger road would lead them straight to town where they could barter for another car and make it back to the airport. The money left over remained safe in the bag tucked around his neck.

Without warning Andry yelled, "Get down!"

They dropped in place without hesitation. Luke looked up and saw a beat-up, discolored Jeep barrel towards them. Each small bump announced a weakness in the car, the noise alone sounded like metal ready to snap. The car stopped in front of them and four guards jumped out of the car and cocked their guns.

Automatically, Luke made unflinching eye contact with Melanie. "Don't move," he mouthed.

The leader of the group walked over to Luke. "I am Sedra. You know Bruno, yes? I know Bruno too." He grinned with malice. "Get up," he said and nudged the gun at Luke's back pack. Without asking, he began to rifle through the pack. "Watch the others, Jordan," he instructed one of the other men.

Luke and the others stood up slowly. The other guard, the one Sedra referred to as Jordan, stood next to Brent with a gun pointed at his head. They'd been in this situation before. Brent could handle a gun pointed at him, as could Andry. Luke glanced at Melanie and could see her ghost-white face and her teeth gnawing on her lower lip. Then Sedra's large head obstructed Luke's view of Melanie and he watched a fat bead of sweat bubble at the edge of his nose. Electric red veins in his eyes led to large, black pupils. "Give me all your money," Sedra ordered in thick Malagasy accent.

Luke held up his hands. "We don't have any."

"Of course you have money." He looked at one of the guards and spoke in another language, presumably his native tongue.

One of the men stepped forward and accosted Luke, checking his pockets and nudging the gun against his chest. The other hand patted down his body and any pockets on his clothes. The guard indicated for Luke to remove the bag.

Luke complied. Never had there been a more important time to remain indifferent, to act unaffected by the threat surrounding them.

The guard took over, rifling through the bag with one hand. Dried scabs decorated his jaw. The three clumps of cash worth ten thousand U.S. dollars he spotted right away, collected, and passed to Sedra.

"Tell Bruno to go to hell," Luke said with pleasure.

The guard dumped out the rest of the bag with eyes full of concentration. Luke kept his eyes upon the bag and didn't look at Melanie. Another moment passed and the guard looked up at Sedra and shook his head.

Sedra spoke to Andry. Andry yelled back and then translated, "He says you're the ones going to hell."

The other guard, the one on Andry, roughed him up. Andry put up his hands to protect his face and managed to dodge a second attack. They fought and Andry freed himself from the guard's grasp and stumbled towards Luke.

Sedra circled around Brent. "Empty your bag."

Brent also obeyed. A flashlight dumped out along with wrappers, a lighter, his compass, and a small case for his magnification tools. He shook the bag and the wrapped stack of cash came out and clunked on the ground. The guard swooped down and picked up the money.

Sedra jabbed the gun under Luke's chin hard enough to leave an imprint. A fly landed on the man's hand and he flicked away the pesky bug.

The fourth guard, the one rounding on Melanie, stopped and grabbed her arm. She yelped at the stranger's unwanted touch and tried to wrangle free. He only jerked her closer to him.

"Bruno wants his property returned," Sedra said.

"You have all our money," Luke said evenly, despite his control slipping. Now wasn't the time to budge. He stared hard at Melanie, hoping she understood this.

"Where's the garnet?"

Nobody in Luke's party spoke.

A restless, ominous energy oozed from Sedra's countenance. He tore Melanie out of the other guard's grasp. In a split second he put her in a chokehold and smashed the barrel of the gun to her temple.

Melanie screamed.

"What do you want? The girl or the garnet?" Sedra's fingers wiggled on the trigger.

"Go ahead, shoot her," Luke warned through a compressed jaw. The instruction fell deaf on her ears and he couldn't stop what happened next. Melanie screamed. Her hands rose up in surrender and then she reached inside her shirt, further into her bra, and pulled out the rock. The rock dropped out of her hands and onto the ground. Everyone watched it hit the dirt with a thud. Sedra pushed her aside and one of the guards retrieved the rock.

"Bruno thanks you for doing business," Sedra said and waved his gun in the air. "If we see you again, we will kill you." The guards and Sedra moved at lightening pace and hopped into the Jeep and took off down the road. Their tires shot out a trail of dust down the road.

The dust settled over Luke. "You never, ever give up the stone," he told Melanie, storming over to her.

Dirt spit out of her mouth as she lifted her head. "You were going to let him shoot me?" She looked pleading to Brent and Andry. She refused to let Luke help her up off the ground.

She took a loose, desperate swing at Luke, nothing strong or close enough to do any real damage. "Easy," Brent said, holding her back.

"Easy?" With a quick turn of her arms she engineered her way out of his grasp. She glared at Luke. "You told him to shoot."

"I stand by what I said."

Incredulity overcame her face.

Now wasn't the time to explain or justify his decision. He looked beyond her shoulder. Dust tinged his lips. "I wouldn't expect you to understand."

"It's not her fault," Brent interjected.

Arms spread, Andry got between them. "We're out of water, which means we have few options. We need to keep moving."

Brent started to walk. Melanie fell in line behind him. Not once did she look back.

They did keep moving, silent and tense; full of thoughts on what they'd lost. Luke in particular stewed with each step. This is what happened when other people became involved in his life. Something inevitably gets screwed up and the end result is a strong disappointment in other people. He could have fulfilled the purpose of his trip and obtained his prize if not for letting her come along and get in the way. He wished he'd never involved her.

* * * *

Exhausted and gritty from the Madagascar outback, Luke, Brent, and Melanie returned to Maui three days later. The cab ride home lacked the spirit of adventure when they'd set out days earlier. An air of defeat hung over them. Disappointment stayed around them. There would always be another hunt, another stone. But Luke didn't like to lose. He didn't like his property taken from him. He'd lost and he wasn't good at accepting a setback. Melanie looked out the window of the cab and he studied her profile. The anger from the trip still emitted from her cool gaze and set in the stubborn upturn of her jaw. The beach house came into view and Luke spotted Kendra waiting for them at the curb.

Kendra met them at the cab, paid the driver in cash, and opened the door for Luke. "Welcome back," she said and flashed Melanie a contemptuous gaze. "I'm sorry you ran into trouble."

"Where's Vivian?" Luke said and got out of the cab. Brent and Melanie mulled around the trunk waiting for it to open.

"She's with Stevie, in the playroom." Kendra stood back until everyone got out of the cab and closed the door. "I'm glad to see everyone's alive. I still haven't been feeling well. The good news is no one else seems to be getting sick."

Luke and Kendra fell into step aside each other, making their way to the house. "What have I missed?"

"Nothing major has gone on, one of our buyers, Luis Hannigan from Charlotte, contacted me with interest in obtaining an eight-carat blue sapphire. Are you interested?"

"I'll talk to Brent. If we don't have something in the vault, we'll have to go back out and find one." The loss of the blue garnet killed Luke's eagerness to rush back out for another gemstone. "I don't want to send Brent out again with the wedding being so close." Luke stopped at the front door and paused. "Have you heard from Damon?"

"No; there's been no change in his plan. Damon and Felicity are arriving in two days." Kendra opened the door and stepped inside first. "On the other subject you asked me to research, I do have some hopeful news."

"Go on." Luke flashed his gaze over at Melanie and Brent, talking and walking up the steps without hurry to the front door.

"Is Melanie okay?" Kendra said. "She doesn't look so good."

She always looks good.

Luke stopped this train of thought. "She's fine," he said, void of emotion. "Tell me your news."

"I tracked down the former owner of the apartment you had lived in while working with Mark Cahill. The man is crude and rude as they come, which worked in my favor once I mentioned I would pay him two hundred dollars for some information. The night the tourmalines were stolen, the same night Mark had tried to kill you, the manager had said he'd seen someone, a tall man, enter your apartment through the fire escape out back. He didn't see a face but said he looked familiar, like he'd seen him before."

The man in question couldn't be anyone other than Mark Cahill. Luke flashed a curious glance at Melanie. There were only three people who had been to his apartment on the West Side: Brent, Mark, and Melanie. "What else?"

"The manager didn't report anything to the detective on purpose. Something to do about paperwork or permits not being filed correctly and he didn't want to draw attention to himself or his background. He only spoke to me because I paid him and assured him I wasn't a cop trying to dig into his background. It's not much, but a lead's a lead."

Luke's fist gave a light pound on the doorframe. "Keep digging."

"Luke," she said, in a rare moment using his first name. "I also haven't found any evidence of Melanie's involvement with the tourmalines having gone missing. I used some of Damon's legal contacts to check into any bank accounts and safe deposit boxes set up in her name or her sister's name and there's nothing. If Mark took those tourmalines he might have sold them."

"He didn't know how to sell. He handled the hunts and the new clients. Mark didn't and doesn't know how to turn rock into a product."

A thoughtful expression dawned upon Kendra's face. "What makes these tourmalines so special? Why are they so rare?"

"A tourmaline in any color aside from blue has elements like iron, vanadium, manganese bringing out the vivid color. Paraiba Tourmalines are different. Copper is the reason they are set apart. It's one element not found in other tourmalines. The ratio of copper to manganese brings out a blue worth traveling around the world to find. They are mostly found in Paraiba, in Brazil and they are somewhat new to the gemstone market, within the last twenty years."

"The copper, right." Kendra contemplated what he'd told her and returned to their original conversation. "What if Mark did learn on his own? He could have learned without your knowledge."

The thought bothered Luke but he didn't see much importance in debating the credibility now. "Mark took those stones and he gave them to someone for safekeeping. He wouldn't have had the time to sell them before the police took him for questioning. Don't forget the night he tried to kill me is the same night I believe that he broke into my apartment. I think Melanie knows where they are, she's certainly got good reason to take this job and suddenly make them appear." Luke rubbed his hand at the back of his neck. The trip to Madagascar had complicated everything about his feelings towards Melanie.

Luke went into the kitchen and poured himself a drink. He sat at the kitchen table, in the dark, and let the dark liquid of the Brandy he'd chosen swirl in his glass. Unsettled thoughts ran through his mind. Something he couldn't resolve during the journey home.

The trip and all of the close calls reminded him of his position. He ran the company. He had a daughter. He couldn't afford to take these kinds of trips for much longer. Melanie could have been hurt. She could have died and Luke sucked in an irritated breath at how much he cared for her. He didn't want anything bad to happen to Melanie, ever. The decision to bring her along had been a mistake. The exacting judgment he typically used had faulted. He took another sip, stared out the window at the night, and realized with clarity why he was so annoyed. It's the first time he'd ever had to choose between his gemstone and the woman who turned over his heart.

Chapter 15

The pack of birth control pills indicated Melanie had missed too many days to get her cycle back on track. Madagascar had ruined everything, even the comfort of her hormones staying on schedule. The adventure she'd wanted so bad was over. The incident with the blue garnet turned out to be a huge rock sticking between the progress she'd made with Luke, and he treated her differently now that they were back to the beach house. She sensed a looming disappointment or mistrust every time she walked into the room. The scratches on her face, arms, and legs began to heal after access to clean water, daily showers, and a pristine environment, yet on the inside she felt sore when it came to Luke ignoring her.

She could close the door on any hope of a relationship. Not after the way he'd simply stalled and done nothing with a gun pointed to her head, scheming how to keep his gemstone. The layer of fury fuming from her heart began to grow two heads at the thought of Luke picking his gemstone over her life. Worse than his messed-up actions out there, she got the feeling he blamed her for losing the garnet. Melanie walked into the bathroom off her bedroom and grabbed her swimsuit. The two-piece hung over her shower rail, dry and crisp as toast and it smelled like mildew. She touched the bikini top, growing hot at the thought of Luke's fingers on her body. They hadn't been able to make love in Madagascar and now she knew they wouldn't. She didn't want to kid herself. Luke still hadn't shared with her anything about his family or his childhood. Aside from their heated, stolen kisses, she still hadn't learned anything new about him. What she did know, she could count with the fingers on her hand:

He would have let those men kill her.

He would never forgive her.

He would never allow her to get too close.

She'd considered quitting her job. She could see the disdain on Luke's face every time he looked at her. There wasn't the option of walking away from him, or from their agreement, at least not when she still could salvage her time here by getting to the bottom of those tourmalines and solving the mystery once and for all. Her brother wouldn't lose from Luke again. The end of the summer would bring about the end to their love story. They could both walk away happy and free of each other.

Melanie stepped outside her room, dressed and ready for the day. Fresh bouquets of Orange Anthuriums shaped like hearts with stamen sticking out their lily-pad like centers had been tied with white silk bows and graced each table next to a bedroom door. The sound of her phone ringing in her bedroom pulled her back to her room—she shut the door and took the call.

"Hello?" she answered fast.

"Where have you been?" Mark barked. "Why haven't you returned my calls?"

Melanie sat on the bed and held the phone close to her ear. "I'm in Maui."

"Yeah, I know. Jess told me. All of a sudden you're with Harrison, and what, too busy to remember me?"

"I don't want to get into it." Melanie ran her hand over her forehead. "I've been out of the country."

Silence.

"You've been out of the country with Harrison. What gemstone was he looking for? How did he talk you into going?"

"I wanted to go." Besides, how did you know?"

"It's not a far leap to make. He's out there enjoying his freedom and running his company and I'm stuck in here."

"I'm working on getting your letter of support."

"I bet you are."

Melanie felt her patience wane. "Don't get upset with me for traveling with Luke. I'm working for him. We're not a couple. We made a deal."

"You shouldn't have made a deal with Luke."

"What did you think I would do after you begged me to help you? I don't think it's fair for you to be angry with me. Why didn't you tell me about the tourmalines?"

"I don't know what you're talking about."

"Yes. You do. The same tourmalines that went missing from Luke's apartment the night the two of you got in a fight. Luke wants them back. He's so convinced you have them that he hired me, his ex-girlfriend and sister to a felon, to work with his daughter. Why would he do that?"

"He's desperate."

"He's also smart. Tell me what you know. I need something, Mark. You have to let me in on this and help me or I cannot help you."

"When Luke and I worked together, you remember our cramped office. We heard each other's conversations. I knew he'd gotten something from Brent, but I didn't know what and I didn't ask. I thought since we were partners he would have shared in his find. He didn't."

"You just dropped the subject?"

"Jesus, you're falling for him. Aren't you? Let me remind you that Luke doesn't forgive. Don't kid yourself in thinking he's falling for you. He's trying to get his way. Aren't you tired of him always getting his own way? The tourmalines are irrelevant. They are probably in some obscure hiding spot. Maybe right under your nose."

She grew suspect. "How do you know all this?"

"I have a lot of time to read. Don't focus on me. Use your brain. I'm willing to bet the tourmalines magically appear and he won't uphold his end of the bargain. You better start to think of a plan-b."

Melanie bit her lower lip. She didn't know what to think. "Did you take them?" she asked him again.

"Come on, Melanie. You're talking to me."

"I need to know before I stay one minute longer. I gave up a lot to help you. I don't want all of this to be for nothing."

"When I worked with Luke, I didn't do any of the treatment processes or actual cutting of the stones. I wouldn't know how to sell them in their natural form. I wouldn't be able to do much except pawn those tourmalines off as a bunch of rocks to the right dealer."

Melanie heard a burst of laughter down stairs. "I have to go."

"I appreciate all you're doing to help me. Be careful."

"Good-bye, Mark."

Melanie sat on her bed and felt worse than before the phone call, like her arms were stretched in opposite directions. She didn't know whether to believe Mark or Luke. She glanced around the room. The tourmalines could be anywhere. Perhaps, right under her nose as Mark had suggested.

The first time she'd met Luke, he'd come over to her house. She'd answered the door, surprised at the sight of him. He'd knocked the breath right out of her with his good looks. She'd been eighteen and ready to leave for college and had never met a guy with such transparent strength to the point of a being a repellant, a shield, a natural protectiveness about his life that he wouldn't share with anyone. Even then she'd seen the standoffishness and the drive. He wasn't like anyone else and she hadn't wanted there to be anyone else.

They didn't go on their first date until three years later. Melanie had been home from college and Luke had been at her house, waiting for Mark to arrive. He'd asked about school, as he always did. They were standing in the kitchen and she told him about a date she'd go on later that night. He crossed the kitchen, backed her up against the sink, and kissed her in way she'd not been kissed before. It was all-consuming. The kind that makes your stomach flip and shoot pleasure down your legs. The kind that erases everything else from the background.

Melanie saw him romantically for a full year after thinking she would soon walk down the aisle and into his arms. There's no way she could have predicted how quickly everything would change. The phone call her mother made on an ordinary Friday morning telling Melanie to come home. The detectives came next and brought their questions. The lawyers soon followed and invaded their lives. Luke had accused Mark of attempted murder and she'd heard the news second-hand. Then he broke up with her before ever facing her and looking her in the eye. She could have known the truth…if he'd just looked her in the eye. Time had robbed her of knowing the truth.

Dressed and hungry, Melanie went down the stairs to the kitchen. Latonya wasn't in the kitchen though her culinary footprints remained in the form of a mini-breakfast bar of scrambled eggs still steaming, bacon, and a plate of various toasts and pastries. Not even the buttery English muffin and sidekick of coffee improved her mood. There was work to be done and Melanie went straight to the playroom to find Stevie and Vivian and try to spend a full minute in the present.

"Hi, Vivian," Melanie said, entering the playroom. She took a seat next to Vivian. Vivian looked up with unfocused eyes. Melanie snapped her fingers and pointed to her own eyes. "Right here." Vivian's gaze focused at Melanie's eyes. "Hi."

Vivian broke attention for a second, curious at the big bag. The bag's zipper snagged halfway through opening. The zipper enchanted Vivian.

She scooted over to the bag and put her hand around the tiny object.

"Z-z-z, zipper," Melanie commented, not one to miss out on a verbal application. She opened the bag, took out the binder, and flipped through to halfway. "Does Vivian often have trouble transitioning between activities?" The document she looked for hid behind an Articulating Screening questionnaire, a document used to test if a child needed further assessment with regards to oral and phonological development.

"She's two; she gets upset at everything." Stevie frowned and cleared her throat. "She reminds me of her mother when she doesn't get her way." She snatched the document from Melanie and took a look at the paper.

"These are letters."

"I'm familiar with the alphabet."

Melanie tapped the paper. "These are the letter sounds we're going to work with Vivian on making first. B, p, m, and w are important for speech development. They are easy to learn. All sounds are good of course. The goal is to saturate her with language and sounds. Part of learning speech is imitating sounds and from what I've seen, there's not a lot of purposeful interaction with Vivian. I see grown-ups talking around her, over her, and she's hearing a muddle of words attached to complex sentences. The vowels and consonants aren't broken down. It's too high-level. All the words are going over her head. We need to bring our speech down to Vivian's level. Break down the letters and sounds for her."

Stevie turned the paper over and perused the back side. "You also wrote down d, n, and t."

"Those letters are good to work on as well. I've already heard her make the *d* sound. The point is also to get her to understand da-da is her daddy, I'm not sure if she understands and there's a difference."

"Vivian knows her father."

"Does she?" Warily, Melanie glanced at the open door. "I understand Luke travels quite a bit."

"There's less travel now than he used to do. You don't know our family dynamics. Luke adores Vivian."

"From a distance," Melanie added.

Stevie paused and contemplated what Melanie had said. "I won't disagree with you."

"The question is why?"

Inclusions 141

"You'll have to ask him yourself."

"I was afraid you'd say that." Melanie smiled weakly at Vivian. She sensed Stevie knew a lot more about Luke than she'd realized before and every part of Melanie wanted to push Stevie for answers. She couldn't push though. The phone call from Mark reminded Melanie to keep a distance and distance meant no prying, no caring, no doing anything other than solving the mystery of the tourmalines before Luke could and not give her the letter of support. "Make eye contact with Vivian when you speak with her or ask something of her. Try not to anticipate her needs. If she wants a ball, you make the *b* sound, say the word, and point to the object. Make her work for it. Let her make the sound. Force her to use her own words."

"Do you want me to stay during your session?" Stevie said.

This surprised Melanie. "I think Vivian would benefit."

"Alright, get started."

"Time to play." She made the sign for "play" and began the session by using the book close to Vivian's foot. Melanie pointed to a picture of a baby. "B is for baby, ba-ba-ba-by."

Uninterested in the sounds, Vivian tried to open the slider and couldn't thanks to Melanie's firm hand in the way. Vivian wiggled and grunted in response and tried to move Melanie's hand away. She blew up in a string of wails and threw herself on the floor.

Stevie picked her up and held her in her lap. "Listen to Melanie."

Melanie waited until Vivian calmed down. "Ba-ba-ba. Your turn."

Frustrated, Vivian used more force to push away Melanie's hand. The task Melanie repeated five times until Vivian made the sound. Stevie took a deep breath. "She's never done that with me."

"She will." Melanie took out her binder and pulled out the PLS-5 and began where she'd last left off. The question she started with gave Vivian a chance to identify basic body parts using a doll. "Show me the nose."

Vivian stared at Melanie.

"Point to the doll's ear." Melanie recorded a zero and continued on with, "Point to the doll's hand." She went through each item on her list and went to the next category which included identifying things a person will wear. "Point to my shoes…point to my shirt…show me socks…" Melanie finished out the category and gave her another score.

They moved onto other tasks with Stevie fully on board for the first time. "I think we're going to try something new."

The blue plastic cup from the play kitchen would work well and Melanie got out one of her red blocks. She retrieved a bag of Cheerios from her bag and put one in the cup to see if Vivian could dump out the Cheerio by turning it over. Vivian smacked the cup away.

"Tell me there's a point to this," Stevie said.

"There's always a point," Melanie said and tried the trick again.

Vivian flailed, thrashed her legs, and inadvertently, knocked over the cup again.

The session ended close to lunch time and Melanie helped Stevie clean up the toys and the books before they headed for the kitchen.

Activity overflowed in an unusually quiet and well-managed ship of a kitchen by Latonya. Bowls of cream-of-something-wonderful soup sat on the counter, with a little wildflower placed lovingly on each plate, along with a soup spoon and napkin. The pans on the stove bubbled with what sounded like water. Fresh greens, tomatoes, and red onions garnished the countertop. Melanie reached out to touch the plate holding the soup bowl.

"Don't touch," Latonya said. "Mr. Harrison and his guest are dining outside in a few moments. I have lunch for Vivian over here and you're on your own. There's sandwich bread in the pantry and cold cuts in the refrigerator. Help yourself and make it yourself."

The soup smelled divine, like cream, butter, and leeks. A dry turkey sandwich would have to do and she said unhappily, "I'll put Vivian in the high chair."

A movement at the far end of the kitchen caught Melanie's attention and she saw Luke pacing outside and talking on the phone. Tanned and rugged, he took over the room with the sheer force of his handsome face and muscled body. Melanie gulped and stood there speechless. Damn, he looked good. It wasn't fair.

"Who are his guests?" Melanie asked, not daring to raise her voice too high and be heard. Thankfully, the stone columns made the separation from the inside to the outside much better than the main room.

"Well, there's Brent, and then some of Luke's friends."

Melanie kept her gaze on the buckle of Vivian's chair. A violent thwack of Vivian's foot hit Melanie in the thigh. She shook out her finger and tugged at Vivian's strap until she settled in securely. The steaming pan of mac-and-cheese on the burner made its way over to Vivian's bowl thanks to Latonya.

Melanie blew off the steam before offering the plate to Vivian. The time Luke spent in the background talking on his phone or speaking to Latonya irritated Melanie. Stevie should have returned by now, which only boosted Melanie's impatience to get away from him. Melanie leaned her head to her hand, while Vivian kept playing with her food. She'd never wanted an apology from him more than any other time.

"Hello," Luke said, suddenly behind her. "I hope you've recovered from the trip."

The warmth of his presence radiated over her, making her anger and confusion towards him dissipate with frightening ease. The slump of her shoulders straightened out and she commented nonchalantly, "If one can get over a gun being pointed at one's head, then no, I'm not recovered."

He shrugged. The cavalier attitude got under Melanie's skin. Blood simmered beneath the surface. She glanced up at Latonya, doing her best to mind her own business and not doing a very good job. Melanie couldn't put the subject to rest. "I would have thought someone capable of letting another human die right in front of them would have had something more prophetic to say, like an apology."

He shrugged, done with the topic. "I've been in situations like the one with Sedra before. It's all one big bluffing game. A negotiation, if you will. We hadn't even gotten to the part where I would have offered Sedra more money when you up and dropped the rock."

"You gambled with my life." She scooped up the cheesy noodles and offered them to Vivian. Vivian smacked the spoon away.

An intimate chuckle escaped his mouth. "Don't pretend you didn't get a little satisfaction in letting Sedra take back the rock."

Melanie's gaze widened. The aloof attitude, his growing agitation towards her made sense now and she wanted to slap him across the face. "You think I let the garnet go on purpose?"

"Did you?"

Melanie slowly rose up to her feet. The chill in his eyes clashed with the fire in hers. The indifference on his face drove her mad. She dropped the spoon. "You should have your lawyer to tell me this. That's how you communicate your insults to me."

The comment stumbled Luke's response. "What do you mean?"

Cognoscente of Vivian, she lowered her voice and carried her rage through a whisper. "I've waited years to tell you what a jerk you were for sending your lawyer. You owed me an explanation and you were too chicken to come tell me you didn't want to be with me. Your accusations of me giving up the garnet on purpose is seven years ago all over again. You have no idea how your cruelty affects me and how hurtful you can be."

Luke's hand slammed on the table. They stared at each other eye-to-eye. "What did you expect me to do? Your brother had tried to kill me."

"And you would have let me die out there in the desert. What's the difference?" Melanie shook her head. "You invited me on your trip, and then when it didn't work out your way, you blamed me. Now you accuse me of losing the garnet on purpose. You put your precious blue garnet above my own life. Congrats, Luke, because every time I get too close you; every time I think we're good, you find some way to push back. Well, congratulations, you've achieved your goal. Go. Be alone and miserable. Live your life in that cold shell you've created for yourself. I'm leaving at the end of the summer and I will never see you again."

She walked out of the room and didn't look back. Not surprisingly, Luke didn't follow. She closed the door of her bedroom and fell into the pillow. The bedspread felt cool on her skin and she rolled onto her side. The people in the house moved and talked below—someone dropped a pot in the kitchen. The conversation with Luke swam around her. She turned over on her back, stared up the ceiling. The time had come to put him behind her in a way she never had before: totally, completely, inside and out. They could have no future together. Not when he'd find ways to push her away. She couldn't spend her life waiting to find out if the next morning he would wake up and go away. It's what he did. It's why he chose gem-hunting as a career whether he would admit this or not. He'd picked a job that gave him an out-clause, the second he needed a break. From this moment forward, she would get down to the business of finding those tourmalines; assist her brother with getting out of prison, and get on with her life.

Chapter 16

The intimate dinner party took place later in the evening. The guest list consisted of friends of Luke's, along with Goldie and her two daughters. The laughter and noise of the party injected life into the house. Melanie hung out with Vivian in the playroom using her job as an excuse to keep busy.

"Dinner is going to be served," Kendra said and peered into the playroom, "and time for you to come out of hiding."

"I'm not hiding," Melanie retorted and continued putting books back on the shelf. "I'm busy."

"Hiding from Luke after a fight is the worst thing you can do." She put her hand on her hip and smiled. "Don't let him think you're weak now."

"I don't recall asking for your advice." She wedged a book in the last possible space.

"All I know is with you around, Luke has been in the worst mood of his life. He must care for you."

"Luke only cares about himself." Melanie paused and glanced at Vivian. "I shouldn't have said that in front of you." She would be more careful in the future. Kendra and Luke played on the same team. Melanie didn't want her words in the mix of their conversations.

"I think you're wrong." Kendra straightened and held out her hand to Vivian. "I think you get to him in a way nobody else can. In any case, I came to tell you Kari and Alyssa have arrived. Dinner is ready and Stevie needs your help with the children."

The unusually pale color on Kendra's face led Melanie to ask, "Are you feeling okay?"

"I can't shake this bug. Whatever I eat doesn't agree with me."

Melanie actually thought Kendra looked beyond sick. She looked terrible. "You make standing look painful."

"Let's not exaggerate." Kendra's poised smile remained on her lips. "I don't have time to be sick and we're going to be late."

Vivian took Kendra's hand and Melanie walked alongside them down the hall to the sound of boisterous people talking. Melanie glanced up the stairs, in the direction of Luke's office. "Kendra, where does Luke keep the gemstones he needs to sell?"

The lighthearted mood disappeared. "Why do you want to know?"

"When we were in Madagascar, it occurred to me Luke doesn't have an office in the traditional sense. He works out of his home and so do his brothers. They have to keep the gemstones somewhere. I'm curious, nothing more."

"I don't know where they are kept. There are certain aspects of his job I'm not allowed to know about. My guess is as good as yours."

* * * *

The small gathering of guests interacted with familiarity towards each other. Aside from Goldie, Melanie knew no one outside Luke's immediate circle. Goldie and the other women dressed similarly, wearing silky, bright-colored tops and lots of gold, the official color of summer. They all wore a tan like an accessory and their hair down to their waist. The women walked out by the pool, carrying their drinks with them. Melanie felt a longing to be home with Jessie. They both reveled in spending their summer evenings wearing fun dresses and attending parties. Even if they didn't know anyone else at the party, they had each other.

Melanie spotted Luke instantly, and to a fault. Taller and leaner than the other men, he stood in the middle with his back to her. The wind fluttered through his hair as his hand extended, talking presumably about the property and the ocean view.

A gaggle of giggles came from outside and Melanie saw Kari and Alyssa darting around the trio of men. "Girls, no running inside," Goldie chastised, breaking through her protective ring of men. She flashed an apologetic smile to her admirers. "My regular babysitter is home sick. Or so she says. I happen to know she's the mistress of a well-known attorney from Seattle, who always spends the month of June at his beach house in Lahaina."

Melanie stood back in the early-evening shadow and waited until Kendra had handed Vivian off to Stevie. She backed up to the stairs, turned around halfway up, and quickly moved up the steps and down to Luke's hallway. One quick peek at his office couldn't hurt. Whether or not Kendra knew the whereabouts of the gemstones didn't make a difference. Melanie couldn't rely on anyone else to help her. She assumed he kept his gems either in a bank or a private vault. The vault made more sense, given the easier access. She glanced on either side of the hallway to make sure nobody saw her, and then she entered.

The early evening sunset deepened the hues of the office. The space suited him, Melanie concluded. Elegance and boldness tapered with the slightest touch of warmth, just like Luke. The water in the aquarium bubbled and gurgled from the filter and she walked over to the tank and squinted at the thick, gold coins at the bottom of the tank. She wondered if they were real or not.

The shelves on the wall gave her nothing to go on in terms of hidden spots. She touched a few of the spines and pushed them, laughing at herself for watching too many mysteries. The bookcase is one of those places perfect for building access to a secret room, a vault, or a keypad. The books on Luke's shelf, mostly dictionaries or old fiction, didn't give way to anything. A cloud moved over the sun outside at the same moment her gaze met the silver candleholders. They didn't fit with Luke's taste or the rest of the décor. They looked cheap, maybe even plastic or another special material she didn't know about. "Where are you?" she said, and reached out to touch one.

"The better question is why you're in my office?" Luke said with a shrewd voice.

Melanie spun around and met his biting gaze. "Luke."

"I saw you go up the stairs and turn in this direction." He crossed his arms over his chest and lifted an eyebrow. "Answer my question."

"I'm picking out a book." She hated herself for the lame, last-minute comment. He would eat her alive.

"I don't think so."

"I wanted to see the fish."

Ugh. Even worse!

"Stevie told me you have fish and I thought Vivian would like to see them. Has she seen them? Fish can be therapeutic for some children."

Luke walked over to her. "You're snooping and you shouldn't be in my office."

"You know what? You're right." Melanie walked by Luke. "There's nothing in your office I want anyway."

He whisked her against him with one grasp. "Do not come in here again. For any reason."

Unable to decode his new attitude towards her, she laughed off the warning, knowing how silly she must sound. "I have to get back to the party."

The anger in Luke's voice directed at her stuck with Melanie as she walked out of the room and down the hallway. He had no right to be mad at her for being in his office or letting go of the blue garnet. She, on the other hand, had a full list of reasons why she could hate him.

"We've been over this," Stevie said at the bottom of the stairs; flustered and red-faced and in the middle of arguing with Goldie.

Melanie slowed her walk down the stairs and heard Luke not far behind.

"Kari is a gentle soul. She wouldn't hit Vivian on purpose." Goldie's lips coiled into a smile. Kari said something to her mother quiet enough for only Goldie to hear. "There's no need to—Luke, I'm glad you're back. Stevie thinks my little Kari hit your darling Vivian on purpose."

"She did, I saw her." Stevie pursed her lips and Vivian went over to Luke.

He picked her up. "I think we should all eat dinner."

Stevie and Melanie walked outside and over to the kids' table and Stevie sliced up strawberries for Vivian. "I know what I saw," she muttered.

Melanie glanced over at Goldie. "I know you did."

"Anyway, where have you been?" Stevie paused at her with an accusatory look.

"I went to the restroom." Melanie didn't dare tell Stevie about getting caught in Luke's office. She'd try again, of course. Next time she'd wait until Luke wasn't home. She turned her attention to Vivian. "Want to eat?" Melanie brought the tips of her fingers to her mouth, making the sign for *eat*.

"Ah, more signs again. Nonsense, all trendy, useless, nonsense, you're going to see. Vivian will talk when she's good and ready." Stevie helped Vivian up from the ground and put her in the high-chair.

The table for adults gleamed beautifully with silver chargers and aquamarine plates on top. Beachwood infused with crystals and candles stretched the length of the table. Small flames rose up out of the candles and the dinner guests took their seats. The sky turned into a giant emerald.

A waiter, unrecognizable to Melanie, poured from a bottle of wine for each of the guests. "Where should I sit?" Melanie asked.

"You're sitting with me," Stevie said, tapping Melanie on the shoulder. "Right here."

Melanie gaze stretched over the table in front of them. Vivian sat strapped into her high chair at another, smaller table. Alyssa and Kari mocked making a toast and sipped their juice. "The kids' table," Melanie replied sorely.

"You've already caught the attention of one of Luke's business acquaintances, Mr. Coats." She nodded to the gentleman sitting next to Goldie. "The evening will get awkward if he knows you skinny-dip in the pool with Luke."

Melanie snorted laughter. "You should mind your own business."

"I have no other business. I'm too old." Stevie circled her glass so the ice chunks clapped together. "I must say, since you came here, the entertainment value in this house has gone up a notch."

"Find yourself a sugar daddy and get your own life."

"Who says I don't already have one?" Stevie sipped her drink with a clever smile.

"I was wondering where you get all those diamonds and rubies from." She pinned her gaze down on one such a bracelet dangling on Stevie's wrist.

Alyssa yanked on Melanie's dress. "I have to go potty," she announced.

"Where's your mother?" Melanie craned her neck over to the big kids' table. Goldie laughed, knee-deep in Brent's lap.

"You have to take me. You're the babysitter." Alyssa stuck out her tongue and she whined, "I have to go *now*."

Stevie leaned in and whispered, "Give up on Goldie taking them. She's trying to secure an evening with Brent. Her daughters might as well be invisible."

The trip to the bathroom took place without fuss. Melanie didn't think Goldie had even noticed her daughter wasn't at the table. They returned and resumed their meal. The evening wore on Melanie in the way exhaustion of keeping-up-appearance does. It took more strength to not look over at Luke than it did to look in his eyes and bear the brunt of his mood.

Pretending to be distracted didn't work too well either, considering the company at the table of three little girls and an overbearing grandma-type. Melanie cleaned up the bits of red sauce off Vivian, wiped down her sticky hands, and unclipped her buckle. The other girls got up and gravitated towards their mother and were promptly shooed away. They began chasing each other at the other end of the pool, much to Goldie's irritation. She looked over at Melanie every ten seconds with raised eyebrows and big eyes as if to say, "Do something about them, will you?"

Vivian wiggled out of her seat and ran over to Alyssa and Kari. The sister duo ran circles around Vivian, screaming and laughing, playing tag. The adults occasionally took a moment to check out the kids and promptly returned to their conversation.

Melanie kept strict watch on the children. The loud laughter and shrieking girls faded for a moment. The rosy, serene moment passed in a heartbeat. Luke's ardent gaze switched abruptly to horror. The girls, including Vivian were on the opposite side of the pool. Melanie turned in time to see Kari's hands extend and push Vivian in the chest. Vivian lost her balance, falling straight to the water. The splash of clear water burst over her head along with a back-breaking scream. Melanie bolted from the table and jumped into the pool without pause. She swam to Vivian, grabbed her, and gasped with water running down her face, all to the beat of her fast-pounding heart.

Everyone had moved from table to the pool. Someone grabbed Vivian. The adults hovered around and shouted at once. The pool water stung her eyes as she blinked and tried to assess the situation. Brent pulled Melanie out of the water. The dress she wore glued to her skin and she stood there. "Get her a towel," Brent roared.

Stevie appeared a moment later with a towel. She wrapped it around Melanie and guided her over to one of the lounge chairs. Goldie sat down on the chair next to Melanie's and sobbed into Alyssa's head. "How terrifying, how scary…my girls."

"Everyone's okay," Stevie reassured and draped a second towel around Melanie's shoulders. "Go inside and get dry, Luke and I will be with Vivian."

"She's okay?" Melanie finally asked.

"Thanks to you, she's okay."

Inclusions

Melanie left the scene and made her way up to her room. The commotion subsided altogether by the time she walked into her bedroom. She went over to her dresser and pulled out a new set of clothes.

The hot shower warmed up Melanie and calmed her nerves. She worried for Vivian. She dried her skin, applied lotion to her legs, and settled into the comfort of her firm bed. She wouldn't return to the party. Those people meant nothing to her. Vivian's condition was all she cared about in the moment. She thought about checking in on Vivian and changed her mind, knowing the more adults in the mix made the situation more uneasy for children.

The doorknob on Melanie's door began to turn and she jumped up and grabbed the knob, expecting to see Kendra or Stevie. Instead, she found Luke standing in her doorway. The moonlight from one of the windows in the hallway shed light on him, outlining his broad shoulders and half-lit face. A profile she'd know anywhere. "Thank you," he said with genuine affection. "Vivian's doing fine. I ended the dinner party and Stevie put her to bed. I think appropriate, considering the events of the night. May I come in?"

"Yes," she said and allowed him to walk through. She closed the door. "I'm glad to hear she's okay. I saw the whole thing happen."

"I don't want to discuss what happened right now." Luke ran his hand down his jaw, like a man running all the doubts out of his mind and off his chin. "I owe you an explanation."

"You'll have to be a little more specific."

Luke dropped his hand to his side. "I owe you a personal explanation about why I sent a lawyer to break off our relationship."

This wasn't what she had expected. She hugged her arms closer to her chest. "I thought you must have despised me to send your lawyer."

"I didn't despise you. I simply didn't see how we could have continued with everything going on with the trial. I thought a quick, painless ending would be best."

"How could you think such a thing? You sent *your lawyer* to my house. Do you know how hurt I was to find him at my front door? He stood outside my door and told me you had sent him. You humiliated me at the worst possible time."

"All of the reasons I can think of for doing that at the time are pointless. I was lazy. I thought shutting you out would be easier. I didn't have the balls to go to you myself. You deserved a man with enough integrity to look you in the eyes and tell you it's not going to work out anymore."

Melanie reached out and put her hand over his. Her heart felt light. Flutters flapped through her stomach. "You don't know how much I've needed to hear you say that."

"I think I do." He brought his hands underneath hers and made their fingers intertwine. "I didn't think we would have been able to survive the outcome and I didn't want you to get hurt."

"I know because I felt the same way. Don't you think I stayed up at night trying to figure out how we could continue? I don't think we would have lasted. Not how we were back then. We were both different people living different lives."

Luke kissed her forehead. "I'm sorry."

Melanie gave in. "Why do you act like you can't stand me?" Tears began to form, she could feel them ping the backs of her eyes and cling to her eyelids. One blink and they'd slide down her cheeks. She could see how much he felt for her, but she couldn't pull it out of him. The barrier in his gaze was too big for her to extract.

"On the contrary, you're on my mind all the time." Luke put his hands on her waist. He put his forehead to hers and for a moment, they did nothing. Their breaths swirled in the same space.

She expected Luke to kiss her; to drag his fingers down her arms and lower, to wherever his fingers led him. The tip of her finger touched his chest in an offer to explore her body the way he had in the dumpy tent in the middle of nowhere. The breath rolling off her lips in heated waves blew into his neck.

Luke did the opposite of what she needed him to do. He lifted his head and stepped back. "There's nothing else. I came here to thank you for saving Vivian and to apologize to you." Without further explanation, Luke opened the door and walked away.

Chapter 17

Luke returned to his bedroom after seeing Melanie. Thankful for her quick action back at the party and jumping in the pool, he owed her more than a thank you. The long, overdue apology is what she deserved and he gave her the explanation. He could have kissed her. He could have taken her right there on the bed, if not for the lines he'd drawn between them after coming home from their flight.

He had no idea what do now about Melanie. He did want much, much more from her. Maybe just a moment. Maybe a lifetime. All of these thoughts rushed from his heart to his head at the exact moment he knew the truth. He couldn't touch her. Their past proved to be a bigger problem than he'd anticipated. When he'd found her in his office earlier, he knew she'd been scoping out the room, looking for the tourmalines, which meant she clung to the past. She didn't fully trust him. He couldn't convince her of her brother's guilt and he couldn't be with her until she saw him as innocent. He couldn't make love to her knowing she saw him as a liar. He tossed his suit jacket and shirt in the laundry bin and walked half-naked over to his bathroom.

* * * *

The next morning Luke found the breakfast table abandoned and Latonya mulling over a tray of prawns. A fishy smell hung in the air and Luke grabbed a mug for his coffee and began pouring.

"How's Vivian?" Latonya said, peeling back one of the shells. "I've been worried about her all night."

"Stevie updated me this morning. Vivian's getting up now, and she's doing well." A spear of anxiety shot through him at the thought of how ignorant and careless he'd been about the pool. "All those adults sitting and standing around the pool and she still fell in the water."

"Children are quick." She removed another tail and lopped another prawn in the bowl, adding to the pyramid of translucent shells. "I saw Goldie's girl push Vivian, in case you're interested in my point of view."

"Your point of view always merits value." Luke spoke the truth. "I'm planning on speaking with Goldie later this morning."

"Thank goodness Melanie acted fast." Latonya dumped the stack of shells in the garbage, tapped the metal bowl to make sure all of the unused prawn bits made their way to the trash, and continued, "I'm glad to see her watching after your daughter."

"You complimented my judgment." Luke put down the coffee pot.

Latonya wiped down the counter using her muscles and eradicating every possible crumb unfortunate enough to be in her path. "Don't underestimate her. I heard she's been asking Kendra about where you keep your gemstones."

Luke narrowed his gaze. "What?"

"During the party last night. Kendra said she approached her and asked." The towel slopped into the sink and she washed her hands. "I don't know what happened out there in Madagascar, but I also know you've never come back from a hunt so distracted. Don't go giving her too much space."

Loathing coursed through Luke's veins at the thought of Melanie asking Kendra such a question. He brought his coffee mug to his lips. The ache in his jaw strained down his neck and to his shoulders from whatever Melanie was now doing behind his back. "I'll see you later."

Luke drank his coffee outside in solitude. The distrust he felt for Melanie tripled and ate away what was left of his relaxed mood. Golf with Brent ranked high on his list today of activities and the dry, breezy air made for a great day to get outside and to get away from his own house; to get away from Melanie. The waves of the ocean rolled in and out. Some of the neighbor children appeared in the distance on the beach with towels in hand, coolers, and large bags slung over their shoulders.

Brent and Damon meant everything to him and their friendship ran beyond genetics. They had created allies out of each other out of necessity, with each brother emerging out of a home broken beyond recognition, by a father who told Luke every day he was stupid, useless, and worthless. Luke could see his father now, a sallow face and looming eyes, a man fluent in derogatory and high on belligerence. Empty beer cans decorated the countertops as he would sit in his recliner and toss one at Luke or his mother.

Luke touched his jaw. The bruises had healed, but the memories had not. Brutality sticks with a person forever. He could see himself, stepping in front of Damon, taking a blow or a stream of foul language. Brent ran away from home the day he had turned seventeen, followed by Luke less than two years later. They had survived a bully of a father and a mother living in constant fear for her life.

Even in paradise, Luke couldn't completely escape his past. Sometimes he felt he stayed away from Vivian on purpose. He would never hurt her the way his father had him; he would never touch her except in loving, respectful ways. Luke blinked back the tainted image of his father. The mind was a bitch and memories were the accomplice. A shuffle behind him caused him to turn. "Vivian," he said, eager to hold her in his arms.

"I didn't mean to startle you," Melanie said, studying his face. She held Vivian's small hand in her own. The two of them made for quite a pair.

"Hello," Luke said, standing straight looking down at Vivian like some tall tower.

Vivian let go of Melanie's hand and started playing with the ruffle on her swimsuit. He gazed up at Melanie, also covered by a swim robe, with her hair pulled back and a numb expression. "Don't tell me she's going back in the pool."

"We're both going in together. An introduction to swimming will be good for her. I don't want her to be afraid of the water. Babies have been shown to be able to float on their own. Obviously, she won't swim without supervision for several years. Stevie's bringing some floaties and extra towels. You're welcome to try and teach her yourself."

"I'm busy." Luke suddenly wanted to ditch Brent and be in the pool with Vivian. He couldn't be with her though, or near Melanie.

"I thought as much." Melanie glanced disdainfully at the coffee mug in Luke's hand. "We'll get started then."

Stevie bustled through to the pool with the inflatable arm rings and more towels. "Goldie's at the door, Luke. She'd like to see you."

"I'll go talk to her."

Luke found Goldie seated on his couch with a skirt stretched around her thighs. The large breasts Sid had purchased for her tumbled out of her shirt. "Luke," she said, sniffling with puffy eyes. "I'm so sorry about yesterday." She sat up and reached across the coffee table, pulling a tissue out of the box. "The girls and I are having a terrible time without Sid around. Summer is supposed to be a fun, wild time for kids and Kari and Alyssa are miserable. We all are without Sid." Sheepishly, she looked up at him. "I've been meaning to ask how Sid is these days. He only communicates with me through lawyers. We haven't had a real conversation since he left us last summer. I'm alone in my big house and all of our friends have turned on me. They chose him over me because he had all the money before we got married. I'm an outcast. No one will give me updates." She honked into the tissue and wiped her eyes. "You two work in the same circles. I thought you might be able to help me."

"I can't help you." Luke knew a great deal about the life and whereabouts of Sidney, her ex-husband. None of which he would tell her about. "I don't keep up with him and we don't work in the same circles. You already know this."

Unsatisfied, she pushed more. "You haven't heard from one of your lawyers or associates if he's seeing anyone?"

"I don't know. What I do know is that your daughter pushed Vivian into my pool."

"Kari is deeply upset about what happened and I hope this doesn't change anything between us. My girls are so young, a year older than Vivian, and we're all getting through this terrible toddler phase together, aren't we?" She tried to add more humor, poked his arm, and said, "We should commiserate together."

Luke set the coffee mug on the table and sighed, knowing Goldie wasn't going to go away. "Keep an eye on your daughter when you're around Vivian. Now, if you'll excuse me, I've got to get going."

She released a sigh, traced away the last of her tears, and flipped her hair. "You're an amazing man." This time she threw her arms around him. "I knew you'd understand. I don't want to do anything to jeopardize my welcome, with the wedding coming up and all I don't know if I'm invited…"

Luke got out of Goldie's emotionally charged embraced. "Damon and Felicity know their guest list."

"I'm thinking more along the lines of being invited as someone's date," Goldie clarified. "I thought we could go together."

"No."

"What about Brent?"

"You'll have to ask him."

The prospect set off fireworks in her eyes. Idly, she touched one of the thin chains around her neck, "could you put in a good word for me?" All smiles, she got up from the couch and fixed her dress. "I don't want to seem pushy."

Brent came downstairs hurriedly and at the sight of Goldie he halted and began taking slow steps back up the stairs, trying to go unnoticed. Luke suppressed his laughter.

"Hi there, Brent," Goldie called out and walked right up to him. "I've been meaning to talk to you."

"I'll see you in a few minutes," Luke said to Brent and left his brother to deal with Goldie's hunt for a date for the wedding.

Chapter 18

Dinner time came around and Melanie couldn't eat much, waterlogged and deliciously tired from swimming, then holding a session with Vivian, and more swimming afterwards. She glided through the day on Luke's apology and knew they'd reached a turning point in their friendship, if one could call their complicated interactions a friendship. He didn't kiss her last night, but that didn't matter. He'd been sincere and real. Luke and Brent hadn't returned all day and she washed her plate, following Latonya's written rules about cleanup, and decided to read the notes sent over from Vivian's pediatrician. Melanie stretched out on the couch and opened the bulky envelope and scanned the handwritten note with both Luke's and the doctor's signature in releasing the files to Melanie. At the Growing Tree, the doctors on staff usually met with Melanie and they discussed individual cases. Normally, Melanie wouldn't need to ask for such a report, but she couldn't put her finger on something. Vivian's behavior went beyond her struggles with speech. The tantrums, the intermittent eye contact, and the zoning out during her sessions all concerned Melanie.

The first questionnaire she read, *Ages and Stages*, gave Melanie an indication of the milestones Vivian had reached. She flipped through the questionnaire, a tool designed for doctors and parents to assess their child's strengths and struggles at an early age, and she almost threw the packet across the floor. Whoever had filled out this report had lied. They'd indicated Vivian could speak more than fifty words, she could string together simple sentences like "No thanks," and she could mimic facial expressions. The date of the exam was also recent, within the last three months. The space for the name of the person filling out this form had been left blank. Melanie didn't understand and her stomach knotted. She checked the time on her phone and called the number on the doctor's cover letter.

The receptionist took Melanie's name and phone number and let her know the doctor would be out of the office until next week. "Thank you," Melanie responded and ended the call. They'd have to get this sorted out another day.

Inclusions

The second half of the questionnaire dealt with fine and gross motor skills and Melanie tried to think about what she'd seen Vivian do. The answer on the questionnaire indicated Vivian could string together beaded items, which she couldn't, and could she dump out a Cheerio from a cup? No, no, and more no's which summed up a bunch of answers on the questionnaire contradicting Vivian's capabilities. The answers made no sense and Melanie tried not to overthink the crux of the communication problem between Stevie, Luke, and the doctor, but like everything else in her life, she couldn't let it go either.

"She's exhausted," Stevie said, walking down the stairs. "Vivian will sleep the night away. Kendra and I are going to eat on the patio, care to join us?"

"I already ate," Melanie said, closing the packet and stuffing the papers back in the folder. "I've got some work to prepare for my next session."

"You're a hard worker." Stevie paused behind the couch. "I don't understand what you do with Vivian sometimes." The tone she used sounded like someone punctured a hole in her pride.

"I'm trying to figure out how to help her. You've got to trust me on this. I'm not in competition with you for time with Vivian and I'm not going to take your job."

Stevie patted Melanie on the shoulder. "I know."

The front door swung open, followed by Brent and Luke's hearty laughter and easy strides. Stevie slipped out of the room just as Brent saw Melanie sitting on the couch. He plopped himself next to her and her nose fought back the strong odor of sweat and grass.

"What are you doing?" he asked, suddenly nosey.

Melanie hugged the binder to her chest. "I'm reading."

"You really know how break loose, don't you?"

Luke took the chair opposite the couch, his face tanned and red marks on the bridge of his nose from wearing sunglasses. He looked sexy and dirty, like a man, and he made her blush without even trying. "Back already."

"Luke won by cheating." Brent stretched out his legs, placing his shoes on the coffee table. The grin on his lips spelled trouble. "So. Have you recovered from our excursion to Madagascar?"

"I have," Melanie said cautiously, and set down the binder. "I must say that I prefer a mattress to the ground."

"You get used to the ground. I don't like mattresses much anymore." Brent uncrossed his legs and hung out on the couch without regard for his burly body. "You shouldn't feel too bad about losing our one-of-a-kind blue garnet."

"I don't feel bad," Melanie clarified, sensing Luke staring at her. "I value my life over some gemstone."

"You should know I heard from a friend that one of our competitors paid three times as much as we did and there's talk that it went up for auction for close to a half a hundred-thousand dollars by some royal. You didn't need Luke to buy you the garnet, I'm sure you have other gemstones he bought you when you were together."

Luke's face flushed red. "Enough," he said.

"The garnet wasn't for me." At least, Luke hadn't done or said anything to imply such a thing. Melanie looked Brent in the eye. "And Luke never bought me any gemstones."

The genuine surprise on Brent's face couldn't be faked. He looked at his brother. "Never?"

"You heard her," Luke added, uncomfortably.

"Huh." Brent scratched his jaw. "A gemstone could have smoothed over the fact that you had to put with my brother. Melanie," he said with a grin, "What kind of stones would you have wanted?"

"A bag of Paraiba Tourmalines," Melanie answered dryly. "Know where I might find some?"

"You tell us," Luke fired back. He got up and walked over to the fireplace.

"At least tell me why these gemstones mean so much to the both of you."

Melanie's steadfast gaze shifted to Luke. "I don't think 'gem-hunter' is on anyone's top list of sustainable jobs and yet, the two of you act as if there's no other job in the world you'd rather do."

"When we were kids, we didn't spend much time indoors on purpose. We got lost for hours on the weekends. There were these housing developments a few blocks away for these big homes. Lots of wood, stone, and building materials ready to build houses. We'd pretend to be treasure hunters. We turned rocks into diamonds, trash into money. We'd spend an entire Saturday with nothing to eat but a bag of Doritos and soda and we'd be out all day, digging and going through the piles of dirt. Our father—"

"Our father has nothing to do with our choices," Luke cut in rudely. "I can assure you, the details of what led us to this life will bore you. We didn't become treasure hunters because of some dirt hole a block away. My brothers and I are good at chemistry. We understand geography. We liked the subject. We found a career that suits us. There. I've given you a synopsis."

Melanie cleared her throat. She could see how much he didn't want her to know. The tension on his face told her to stop prying, and she did. Luke couldn't be pushed into sharing about his childhood or else he would close down. He'd become an expert at dodging his past and she could see this moment wasn't the right one to keep going. Deep in her own thoughts, Melanie realized Brent had continued talking.

"Gemstones are actually ordinary-looking in their original form. You saw the blue garnet. Nothing exciting, right? Nothing more than a rock. Rocks come from the mountains; they're hidden in the rivers. All matter belongs to a species. Sapphires, for example, are in the species corundum; corundum is derived from the chemical composition aluminum oxide. This chemical changes the formation of a crystal. Crystals form gemstones. Add heat; add cold, throw in some wicked pressure and your crystal changes into a precious stone."

"She's about to nod off to sleep," Luke said. "Sorry about Brent. He gets more excited about aluminum oxide than a naked woman."

Melanie seriously doubted that. Brent might be a nerd at heart, but he gave off the brawny, muscled image of man more accustomed to spending time outdoors than indoors. She liked him. She appreciated him. He wasn't as guarded or sullen as Luke. "What about you, Brent, have you bought any of your girlfriends a huge diamond?"

"I don't like white diamonds in general. They are a fine species on their own, don't get me wrong. One of my ex-girlfriends was disappointed when I gave her a seven carat citrine. She only wanted a diamond. She'd rather have a puny half carat than a stone with fire, with bold color. Sure, a citrine isn't worth what a diamond is, I understand the market. There's so many gemstones beyond diamonds."

"I don't know much about diamonds beyond the four C's."

"Ah, yes. The four C's of the carat world: cut, color, clarity, and carat."

Melanie could see the ring she'd picked out for herself in a magazine advertising for Tiffany's. The round cut with the diamond band. She chose not to share this fact with either Luke or Brent, for obvious reasons.

"Cut refers to the shape of the stone," Brent continued. Color gives a hue, a visual intensity. When you hear the word 'carat' you often think of a size. *Her ring is two carats. The earrings are one carat each.* A carat is nothing more than a unit of measurement like ounce, yard, meter. A carat describes the weight. Not all gemstones are created equal. Two emeralds of the same carat weight are completely different in terms of their value. There are other factors that go into play. Now clarity," his voice grew excited, "is the most important aspect when I consider buying a rock. Clarity shows me the true nature of a stone. There's the scale used for grading diamonds, one you might have heard about, beginning with FL or flawless. I use this scale to grade the inclusions, which become more visible the further down the scale you go. There's several levels to this scale, VVS1, VVS2, all the way down to I3. With gemstones they vary so greatly, we classify them into 3 different types and use a similar scale to that of diamond grading, except we look for how the light passes through. Is the stone transparent and light can travel through? Or is the stone Opaque and light does not pass through?"

"I've head of those letters and numbers, I didn't know what they meant."

"You should always know what you're getting in a diamond or a gemstone. The flaws, the nicks and the indentations are important. I look beyond the image and determine whether the substance is real or fake; lab created or treated. I know if I want the stone immediately. More important, I know if Luke will want to sell it."

"You mention the term "inclusions" a lot. Back in Madagascar you asked me if I knew much about them."

Luke came away from the fireplace. The edge in his face remained rigid.

Brent looked at his brother. "Yes, a subject you haven't properly educated Melanie about."

"I think she's good at finding out information on her own."

Melanie looked at him. "What's that supposed to mean?"

"Doesn't sound like much of a compliment," Brent said.

Melanie gave him a look of death. Brent looked over at his brother. "Are you going to tell her or should I?"

Luke gave a small shrug. "Inclusions are no different than our cells or our DNA. They're the good with the bad. Inclusions mark the past and give the gemstone a future, a home, and a value." Luke glanced bluntly at Melanie. "Once I see the clarity, I know if I want it in my future."

Melanie couldn't tell if they were still talking about gemstones. She wished Brent would rush in and say something idiotic to break up the moment. She looked to Brent to get him talking.

"Personally, I'd like to get my hands on some black opals, sapphires, or maybe a red diamond." He looked to the ceiling and pressed his lips together. "Definitely a red diamond."

"I think my expectations have been too low." Melanie smiled. "I think I'll demand a red diamond when the time comes for me to get engaged."

Luke lifted an eyebrow. "Are you suddenly in a relationship?"

"I'm talking about at the end of the summer, once I go home. I'll start dating again." Her answer clearly exacerbated Luke's mood. Melanie sank her shoulders and back into the couch and her smile slipped away like the sinking sun. The attraction she felt for Luke followed her everywhere. She couldn't even get away with sitting on a couch with a table between them. What she wouldn't give to go back and un-spool the thread of time, back to when they had first unraveled and lost their grip on each other. Would she have seen him as a liar? Would she think him capable of harming her brother? She saw a quick tread of softness in Luke's eyes as he looked at her and she felt a switch flip in her stomach.

What if I'm wrong about you?

The thought brought Melanie to her feet with abruptness. She reached for her binder and refused to make eye contact with Luke. "All of this talk about precious stones is very romantic. Thank you for teaching me," she said to Brent. "However, I'm afraid those topics have nothing to do with Vivian and I do have to ask Luke a few questions. I have to get on with my work."

"Oh, sure," he responded with a hitch of disappointment. "I've got to check my messages anyway. I'll see you both later." Brent made a quick exit up the stairs without looking back.

Luke sat down across from Melanie. "What do you want to know?" he said, sliding his hands over his legs.

Melanie sat back down and hid behind a face of indifference. Diamonds, thoughts of an engagement ring, all brought shame to Melanie. She gave the past a solid kick and refocused on the present. "I've had a look at the forms filled out for the pediatrician at Vivian's eighteen month check-up. Did Stevie fill these out?"

"Yes."

"She indicated that Vivian speaks more than fifty words."

"Vivian does speak."

"Really? What words does she say?" Melanie got the pen ready to write this down, already knowing he wouldn't be able to give her the answers.

Luke sat stumped. "I've heard Vivian say Da-da along with some other sounds."

"You should know the sounds a child makes are important. I want to know Vivian associates the word Da-da with you." Melanie moved her fingers around the pen. "I'm not sure she does."

"I don't see your point."

No, he wouldn't. Melanie asked a more personal question. "Would Stevie have any reason to lie to you about these questionnaires?"

Luke's gaze turned cold. "I trust Stevie's judgment entirely where Vivian is concerned. She's been around Vivian since her birth."

"I know Stevie loves Vivian like a daughter and I'm not trying to get her in trouble. The problem is Stevie answered the questionnaire wrong. Lots of parents fib. Nobody wants their child to need help. Has the pediatrician contacted you at all? It's just odd that a doctor would examine Vivian's physical and mental development at her check-up and not recommend services like speech for Vivian." Melanie paused and let Luke take in her words. He couldn't get out of this one.

"Vivian will talk because I've hired you to help her learn. You're supposed to be good at your job."

"I *am* good at my job. But you didn't seek out a speech therapist."

"You have no idea about the demands of my work." Luke spoke with such unprecedented arrogance that Melanie's jaw dropped.

She wasn't going to back down. Melanie put down her pen with force.

"I don't care about your job. She's your daughter. Look her in the eye when you talk to her for God's sake. Make your words count. When you say 'Da-da,' point to your chest. Make her understand, because she's having trouble understanding. There's a good amount of adults in this house talking over her." Heat pulsed through her veins and up to her cheeks. "You're in; you're out, you bend down and pat her on the head and then you're gone."

"I bet you're enjoying this. You get to throw my faults in my face."

Melanie diffused the moment with a quick, "According to you, you have no faults."

Luke laughed. "I'm not used to someone being so blunt about Vivian."

"I know. I can imagine having her has been tough. I'm on your side with this Luke." She ran her hand over her hair. "Look, there's no real incentive for her to feel like she gets anything out of communication. She fusses and someone picks her up. A crying fit happens and she gets treats or a drink. Approach this like you do your business. Be aggressive about getting her to form words. I'll help you. I care about her too."

Luke's gaze softened at this admission. "I know you do."

"I'm wrapping up my evaluation with Vivian and I'll have the results soon, tomorrow. The testing has taken longer with leaving town abruptly." Melanie searched his eyes for an opening. She saw one and took a chance, using a softer voice. "Connect with her. Make silly sounds. Vivian doesn't care if you get the details right. She loves the sound of your voice. Don't run away from your daughter or else you'll never catch up to her." She collected the binder and left Luke to his brooding. "I don't know what else to say, except you should try more than you are."

A little shaken by her conversation with Luke, Melanie walked into the kitchen. The place to get answers started with Latonya, and last night she hadn't been able to talk to her because of the incident at the pool.

"I'm glad you're awake," she said to the house chef. The kitchen smelled like an oven burning off sugar. "I thought we could have a chat."

The heavy-set woman didn't break eye contact from the recipe card in front of her. The bowl on her right held flour and the one on her left, a mix of apple and pear slices. "My asking price is one hundred dollars."

"I'll grace you with my company, instead."

Latonya didn't look amused. "Sit down."

Bricks of butter stacked up next to a bowl of sugar at the end of the counter dazzled Melanie's eyes. Butter and sugar: a perfect, timeless pair. "What are you making?"

"I'm using a recipe from my grandmother's recipe box. She was the equivalent of a ghost-writer back in the forties for the wife of a Hollywood movie producer. In my grandmother's will, she left the royalties to me. Each time the publisher puts out a new edition or some writer uses one of her recipes in an article, I get paid."

"No kidding." Melanie pulled up a stool and admired the bottles of cinnamon, nutmeg, and heap of almonds in front of her. "I always wished I had a cool family secret."

"Your brother's in prison. I'm not going to state the obvious."

"I said cool, not disgraceful." The interest in this pastry outweighed Melanie's questions at the moment and she asked, "Do you need a taste-tester?"

"You're too skinny to taste-test. You think I got this big by denying myself real food?" Latonya broke from her concentration and eyed up Melanie. "You aren't going to leave, are you?"

"Do you mean am I going to stick out the summer? Yes, I am." She posed the next sentence carefully. "I want to know about Luke and Ava."

"Oh Lord." Latonya rolled her eyes. "Why do you want to know about them?"

"I don't hear Luke say much about her." The unease in her bones began to spread. Answered questions could either be a blessing or a curse. "I'm less interested in the details of Luke and Ava and more curious about how Vivian ended up living with him full-time."

The oven beeped at them and a faint smell of smoke fizzled in the air. "What makes you think I know the answer?"

"I thought you knew everything around this place." Melanie laid on the charm thick. "If you're not the right person, I'd be happy to ask Stevie."

This seemed to agitate the chef. Latonya poured a bowl of beaten eggs in with the sugar and stirred steady and slow.

Melanie broke into a smile and batted her eyes. "I know you want to do this out of the kindness of your heart."

"I'm serious about the money. I take cash only."

"Deal, but I would have held out for more if I were you."

Latonya pursed her lips. "Answer my question. What business do you have snooping around behind his back like some school-aged gossip?"

"I've been out of Luke's life for some time." The prospect of handing Latonya her reasons felt strange to Melanie, like a stranger telling you they'd been diagnosed with cancer. The eggs and sugar folded under Latonya's careful blending. Melanie laughed without confidence. "I'm mad with envy when I think about how Ava Sullivan gave birth to his child. I'm frustrated about the whereabouts of those tourmalines, and I'm questioning everything I have ever thought about my brother. Do you know what it's like to try to turnover a lie? It's messy and exhausting. It causes all sorts of self-doubt and uncertainty and a huge pile of crap I don't want to use energy sifting through. I feel like I'm standing in the middle of some big universe spinning around and around and I don't know what to do."

"Lies aren't messy, my dear. The truth is." Latonya squinted and cocked her head at Melanie. "Have you told Luke any of this?"

"How could I?"

She put down the whisk, wiped her hands on her apron, and came around the counter to pull up a seat aside Melanie. "You're going to have to try."

They each faced forward, staring at the line of appliances on the opposite wall. A creak in the oven sounded louder in the stillness of their thoughts. "You think I'm crazy," Melanie said.

"Doesn't matter what I think. Problems are often solved by going back to the starting line. Why *did* you come to Maui in the first place?"

"I came as a favor to my brother."

"Try again."

"I wanted to work with Vivian."

"No. You're going to have to do better."

"I felt betrayed by Luke and I wanted to show how well I've done without him."

"You're getting warmer. Keep going."

"When Luke and I were together, I thought the world of him: the adventure, the gemstones, and the ruggedness. Like he just didn't care about what anyone thought him. I was young and in college, and he was…something unique; someone no one else had. In his personal life, he shined; in the business world, he made a name for himself. He's got the sort of confidence that makes him stand out in a crowd. I've been trying my whole life to get the certainty he feels about his existence each day." Melanie shrugged and talked more to herself than to Latonya. "Luke hasn't thought about me since the day he ended our relationship. I always felt he used the trial as an excuse. I always thought I came up short in his eyes, like I was someone he tolerated. I wanted to make something of myself so if he ever came looking for me, I could show him I'd done great on my own."

"You couldn't be more wrong," Luke said, causing Melanie and Latonya to jump.

Melanie spun around on the stool. Tightness spread through her middle. Judging from the look on his face, he'd heard more than she'd like.

"Don't sneak up on me." Latonya breathed fast, holding her hand over her heart. Quickly, she got off the stool and returned to her baking. She began fluffing the eggs with the whisk and without glancing up she commented under her breath, "Go on you two. Take this outside."

The skin on Melanie's cheeks burned and embarrassment shot down to her toes. She went outside first with Luke on her heels. She picked one of the lounge chairs and took a seat. "Tell me you didn't hear everything."

"I heard everything." He pulled up a chair and sat across from her and added thoughtfully, "I also saw the way you said it." Their knees touched; their gazes unavoidable.

"I should begin by telling you I'd dated Ava for less than a year when she got pregnant. She thought a baby would land her a future husband and she couldn't have been more wrong. I didn't propose and marriage to her didn't cross my mind after I had decided we weren't right together. I speak to her because of Vivian and our conversations are focused on our daughter. I don't entertain the idea of having her be anything else in my life other than Vivian's mother."

"Where does she live?"

"She lives in Los Angeles, off family money. The only job she has is to keep up a lifestyle that doesn't include motherhood. She's the most selfish, spoiled woman I've ever known. Soon after Vivian was born, I grew concerned about the stories I'd heard from Stevie regarding Ava's late nights, new boyfriends, use of prescription pills. My ex-girlfriend runs in a tough crowd and I didn't trust her to raise Vivian. I took swift action and won full custody."

Melanie finally understood about how unprepared he'd been for his daughter to invade his life. She regarded him with warm respect. "You weren't anticipating Vivian would ever live with you."

"No, I did not."

"About the other things I said…" Melanie said, picking up her bravery off the ground.

"How could you think I haven't thought of you? I have thought about you. I do think about you." Luke put his hands on either side of her knees. "I've wondered how you're doing and what you're doing."

"Why didn't you reach out, after the trial? I'm not talking about the break-up either. I'm talking long after, once Mark had gone to prison."

"We both picked our sides. I thought better to leave you alone. You've always seen me as the bad guy."

The backs of her arms prickled and her cheeks flushed. Luke slid his hands off of her legs. She looked in his eyes and the troublesome thought returned to her mind for the second time within the hour: *How could he ever have hurt your brother? How could he hurt anyone? He loved you too much to take away someone important to your life.* Try as she may, Melanie couldn't answer those questions.

A slight incline of her hand and she ran her fingers over his knee. For a second, she thought he'd return the gesture, but he did not. He withdrew and got up from the chair. "I'd appreciate if you'd stop wasting my employees' time with questions you can ask me directly."

"Luke, I didn't mean to—"

"Good-night, Melanie."

He walked away, leaving her alone on the lounge chair.

Chapter 19

"They're early," Kendra said, and simultaneously tripped over her own feet and knocked down a plate of bananas and mangos. One of her hands caught the corner of the counter and the other sent her tablet flying across the air. It flipped like a pancake and landed on the floor. The entire scene brought Latonya, Stevie, and Melanie to a halt.

"My fruit!" Latonya bellowed, running to the scattered victims of fruit and a broken plate on the tile. Steadily, she pinched up a mango triangle. "You ruined the platter."

Vivian laughed from her chair. "Oh-oh-oh."

"What's wrong with Kendra?" Melanie uttered to Stevie from behind her coffee mug. "I haven't seen her like this."

"Some people live for the stress of the surprise. Kendra is one of those people. She wouldn't know what to do with a vacation day except organize her chaos."

"I gathered as much." Melanie had to admit, she got a little gratification of watching Kendra act so human.

"Please come back to me, please come back to me." Kendra grabbed her tablet and hastily opened the case and began touching the screen with her finger. "You're okay," she purred, as if holding an infant. "My phone fell into the swimming pool two days ago. I haven't had a chance to get a new one. I don't know what I would do if I lost you."

Stevie leaned into Melanie. "It's no wonder she's single. The woman is in love with her computer."

Latonya picked up the broken plate and began tossing the fruit in the trash. "I do have other meals to prepare for besides this breakfast club. Now tell me who's coming early."

Kendra set down her computer and helped Latonya clean up the mess, except Latonya shooed her away.

"Damon and Felicity are flying in today," Kendra said. "They are arriving early. The house isn't ready. Damon's room is full of boxes since Luke didn't use the space last year and I can't find Brent."

"Did you misplace him?" Melanie laughed, despite her mood, and despite the emotionally-charged conversation with Luke the night before.

He'd left her outside by the pool, shortly after she'd begun to ask herself all those questions about him, as if he'd known she needed time to think. The thoughts did her little good, and she found herself awake most of the night with her stomach in a bunch.

Stevie laughed. "You should give him the GPS Sippy cups you bought for Vivian."

"This isn't funny. Brent hasn't been fitted for his tuxedo." Kendra ran her hands through her hair, over her chin, and stared at her tablet in the desperate sort of way a drug addict looks for the next fix. She shook out her hand. "I swear he better be on this island. Never mind him. The cleaning crew won't come until Friday. Mr. Harrison is expected in Kauai tomorrow. I've got my regular job to do, plus arrange his flight with the pilot, plus make his hotel reservations, and figure out my list of wedding details to go over with Felicity."

Latonya smacked her plastic spatula on the counter. "Get a grip."

"Didn't you try his bedroom?" Melanie stated the obvious. "I saw him last night. Luke and Brent had come back from a day of golfing."

"Well, Brent's not in his room now. I checked." She drummed her hands on the counter. "I'm losing it, aren't I?"

Vivian pounded the table with her spoon, as if she too, agreed with this observation. Stevie shook her head at Vivian. Melanie could see the stress on Kendra's face. She didn't look she'd gotten much sleep and the word "haggard" came to mind.

"I've got work to do." Kendra grabbed her tablet, a cup of coffee, and rushed out the door to the patio.

Melanie picked up her breakfast plate and put it in the dishwasher. She'd gotten in a routine of having a second cup of coffee outside on the deck after breakfast. The outside view of the ocean and sky leveled her antsy mood. She took her cup of coffee, told Stevie she'd see Vivian in a little bit, and walked outside.

Today she wasn't the only person seeking solace in the early morning scene. Near the edge of the pool, Melanie found Kendra pacing and mumbling to herself. The gray clouds in the sky looked as uninviting as Kendra's body language. Melanie walked around to her.

She didn't say anything to Kendra. She sensed Kendra would vent on her own. Melanie sipped her coffee and stood next to her. "I think it might rain today," she said.

Kendra flashed a detestable glance at Melanie. "I don't care about the weather."

"Is everything okay?" Melanie kept looking at the ocean.

"I'm pregnant." Kendra sat down, placed her cup of coffee and tablet on the ground, and brought her foot up on the lounge chair.

"Congratulations?" The news didn't sound good to even Melanie.

Kendra spoke in heated breaths. "I needed to tell someone and I don't trust those two in there." She gave a quick glance in the direction of the kitchen. "I'm thirteen weeks along and due in December. I'm stuck here for the summer and I can't talk to anyone."

"Luke doesn't know."

Kendra glanced up at Melanie and drew in a long breath. "He'll be the last to know."

"What about your family, can you tell them? Or the father, does he know?" Melanie's gaze dropped briefly to Kendra's mid-section and found no evidence of the slightest baby bump.

The suggestions sent Kendra into a tizzy. "My family won't understand. They flipped out a few years ago when I moved in with a boyfriend. They're really traditional. They go to church every Sunday and take off Good Friday every year. They wouldn't understand how I could get pregnant without being someone's wife." She shivered. "I don't want to talk about the father of this baby."

Melanie tried a different route. "Does he know?"

"I just said I don't want to talk about the father." She pressed her hand to her forehead and closed her eyes for a moment. "Our relationship began as a work thing: meet-ups in hotels, late dinners; behind-the-office-door-kind of thing. People would get hurt if they knew we'd been seeing each other."

"You're having an affair."

"I was having an affair. He wasn't married, but he did have a girlfriend—a woman I know. A woman I respect. I wasn't planning on getting pregnant. My body gave me a parting gift I didn't want. He doesn't live in California. I met him on a work trip. The last time he was in town, I texted him as I always do. He shot a message back to me letting me know he's engaged and won't see me anymore."

Inclusions 173

"Ouch."

Kendra's hand flew to Melanie's wrist. "Luke cannot know. The demands of my work are high. They come with lots of travel and late nights. This child will bake my reputation. A woman with a child in this field is at the end of her career."

A group of birds swarmed and squawked through the sky over the water at something brown and slick bobbing in the water. They swooped low and began to pick at the seaweed and fought over the same dead rope of ocean slime. Melanie tried to find something useful to say. "When's your next doctor's appointment?"

"I have to go back in three weeks. I found out before coming on this trip and the receptionist at my doctor's office gave me a list of doctors in this area. I have an appointment scheduled." She inhaled a long, slow breath as if she'd been taking a drag of a cigarette. She moved her hand over her flat belly. "Felicity's wedding will keep me busy."

"You don't have to quit your job today, or ever maybe. You don't know how Luke will react when he finds out about the baby."

Kendra cut her off with one look. "You've seen the way Luke is around Vivian. He barely knows what to do with his own child."

Melanie couldn't disagree there. "I won't tell anyone," Melanie promised.

"Kendra," Stevie said, raising her voice and coming towards them. "Luke said Felicity's plans have changed again. She's flying separate from Damon and is arriving on a red-eye tonight. A last-minute emergency at the office forced her to push back her flight and she's going to go straight to her hotel. She'll come by first thing tomorrow to see Damon and the house, and meet with you."

"Why can't anything ever go as planned?" Kendra griped.

"Lower your expectations." Stevie squeezed her arm affectionately. The necklace dangling at her throat caught sunlight and sparkled. "Learn to duck when someone throws a punch. Luke's in his office."

"I'll see the two of you later." She picked up her cup of coffee and headed inside.

Melanie tried not to stare at the cross hanging around Stevie's neck. Gold embedded with square-cut emeralds the color of lush plants after a fierce rain. "You're necklace is incredible."

"Emeralds outlast a husband." She slipped her hand under the cross and laughed. "This was a gift from someone in my family. Not my husband," she added. "The man I married didn't have the best taste in jewelry, bless his heart."

"Your children must have good taste then."

"I don't have children. My husband and I weren't able to expand our family beyond the two of us. Now my immediate family is down to me." She glanced at Melanie as though a bad thought entered her mind. She asked, "Do you have children?"

"No children and no husband." Melanie grinned feeling awkward whenever someone asked her about her life. Despite how far women had come in the last thirty years, she still felt lacking without a family of her very own, like her life couldn't be good unless she could answer this one question in the positive. Her life felt full as it could be, but even Melanie knew there could be so much more to her world.

The cross fell back against Stevie's chest. "What about your family, are you close?"

"I live at home with my mother and my younger sister," Melanie admitted with a pinch of pain. "I'd been in the process of starting to look for a condo before I took the job for Luke."

Stevie's hands jumped to her mouth. "At your age?"

"I moved back home after graduate school to save money. I don't talk to my father much and I have a brother I see once a year."

"Why do you only see your brother once a year?" Stevie blinked disbelievingly. "Is he married to a woman no one can stand? I've been fortunate in my life to not have experienced having either a mother-in-law or sister-in-law. I've heard both can be dreadful."

Melanie let out a nervous laugh. "No, my brother Mark isn't married. He's ah…" Melanie cleared her throat. A natural reaction any time someone she didn't know asked her about Mark. "He's serving a sentence in federal prison."

Stevie's hand flew to her mouth. "What did he do?"

The insinuation of her brother being at fault irked Melanie. She glared. "My brother got involved in a business with a friend, a start-up company, much like what Luke does except on a smaller scale. The business partner and my brother had a falling out over the finances." The explanation rolled off her tongue in swift, practiced verse. The story of her brother had been whittled down to a few concise sentences. "The other business partner claimed my brother tried to shoot him. The case went to trial. The business partner got a sympathetic vote from the jury." Melanie uncrossed her arms. "End of story."

"Nonsense; the end of the story is never the final chapter. I'm sorry for you and the situation for your family." Stevie headed for one of the lounge chairs, stopped and turned with hands wiggling at her sides. "May I ask another question? This business partner of your brother's that you spoke about. The one claiming your brother had tried to kill him. Were you ever in touch with him after the trial?"

"Not until recently." A ripple of hair blew up her neck. Melanie pushed down the irksome strands. "His story hasn't wavered."

"Do you think he's lying?" The wind stopped blowing as if to also hear the answer. "Do you think he's capable of causing such pain in your life with no good reason?"

Melanie bit her lip. "I honestly don't know anymore."

Chapter 20

Melanie fluffed out the striped beach towel and parked herself on the beach. The sunblock on her skin created a thick layer of oil and gave off a heavy coconut scent, sweet enough to want to taste. The morning off from work, thanks to Stevie taking Vivian to the park, gave Melanie a chance to unwind and soak up the warm, blissful rays with the scents of saltwater and sunblock, pure magic. She could spend the rest of her life under the hot sun, nestled on a bed of towels with her heels crisping and sand sticking to her skin. The waves shushed out the noise of neighborly beachgoers and small kids, screaming and laughing, with their mothers yelling at them to be careful.

"Oh good; I thought I recognized you," Goldie crooned and walked up to Melanie just as she'd settled on her stomach. A large woven basket hung from Goldie's arm and under the other, a beach towel.

Melanie propped herself up on her elbows. The need to be polite stopped on the end of Melanie's tongue. Goldie could talk the waves into retreating. The less Melanie spoke, the better. Otherwise, she'd never get to finish her peaceful afternoon.

"Sid's taking me to court, again. This time he's trying to get his lawyer to lower the alimony payments when we go through with this divorce. We're going to court in two months." She ran her fingers through her tangled, wind-blown hair. "Over a million dollars in his bank account and he's playing the cheap card. What about the welfare of his daughters? Doesn't he care about them?"

A sympathetic smile crossed Melanie's lips. Still, she said nothing.

Goldie's gaze strolled up to the water, to a group of shirtless men. She paused at them and continued watching with the intensity of picking out her next husband. "I'm disappointed to see Luke's not out enjoying this gorgeous weather. For a man on vacation, he doesn't take advantage of his access. Do you think he'll come down this morning?"

Melanie's sucked in her lips and answered with a smack. "I have no idea."

"I should go up and convince him to join me. I owe him for the way he comforted me yesterday with such discretion. Sid discounted all of my emotions. Ugh. I'm such a wreck these days." The bag in her hand plopped on the sand. "I'm so embarrassed about earlier and the scene I made at the house."

"It looked like the two of you resolved the problems." Melanie eyed the bag with spite and held her breath for Goldie to pick any other spot to enjoy.

Goldie pushed the aviator sunglasses up her nose. "Luke must think I'm a silly girl the way I cried to him." She put her hand on her forehead like a visor, like she'd really seen Melanie for the first time. "You work with Luke. What do you think?"

"I've no idea what Luke thinks about." Impatience trundled out with every breath Melanie took. She could say with certainty that joining Goldie on the beach wasn't on his priority list for today.

"Of course you don't." Goldie removed her sunglasses and stared down Melanie like a bull coming out of the gates. "Ava would know. She and Luke were close. It's a shame they couldn't work out their problems, given that they have a child together. Did I tell you I'm going to attend Damon's wedding? Brent invited me. I'm getting fitted for a gown later today." She glanced up at some other activity on the beach. "Oh look, I see the Swansons. I do have to get going. We'll chat soon, okay? Tell Luke I said hello."

Melanie wouldn't do anything of the sort. She waited while Goldie moved away from her and chose a spot a good distance away near the shirtless men throwing around a football. Melanie folded her elbows and rested her head on the towel. She closed her eyes and got lost in her own thoughts. That unforgettable face of Luke's appeared behind her closed lids and she groaned. There would be no escaping him. She thought he would look past their differences long enough to make love to her, but that was before their trip. Even if things had gone better on their trip, she didn't see how Luke would have made anything meaningful of their relationship beyond a few weeks. Not when she didn't accept the guilt he placed on her brother. Why was this idea so difficult to give into? Melanie sighed. She contemplated for a moment what it would feel like to look at her brother's story from another angle. It scared her to her bones. What was the point of all those years of being loyal to Mark? What would be the point if they would never be a mended family? She shook her head and tried to erase the questions pounding on her heart.

The plans to spend the morning doing nothing and thinking about nothing fell away fast. "Oh, this is useless," she finally said. She sat up and crammed her belongings back in her beach bag, slung the massive canvas over her shoulder, and did a half-run/jump back up to the house, fleeing from the scorching sand.

The placement of her foot she wasn't watching. A sharp object pierced the bottom of her foot. "Crap!" she exclaimed and fell flat on her rear. The bag and all of the contents hit the ground. She brought up her foot, examining the cause of such pain and cursed at the sole of her foot. "You've got to be kidding me."

A piece of glass, not a shell, stuck out of her skin at a sharp angle among a ring of sand and blood sticking together. The dirt beneath her fingernails assaulted the small wound each time she tried to pry the glass out, gasping with each breath at the pain spearing skin to ankle to toe. The same moment she pulled at the glass, she looked up to the sound of footsteps coming her way. Luke ran down the steps, coming towards her on powerful legs and quick feet.

"I saw you fall," he shouted, coming through the gate. The latch banged against the lock, shaking the entire gate. Luke knelt down, pressing his hand to her ankle. He took in the scope of her cut with a testy expression. "Stop touching your foot."

"I almost have the glass out." Her toes automatically curled as she reached out her hand. "Let me try again."

"Not a chance." Luke held her foot in his hands, leaning into her naked legs. The sand brushed off on his pants. "You need to go to a hospital."

"I can get out the glass."

Luke pointed at her foot. "You're not getting out of a trip to the hospital. We're going." He stuck his thumb to his chest. "I'm driving."

"Everything okay?" called down a male voice, on a face Melanie didn't recognize. "We've got to go."

"You have to go." Melanie looked up in the direction of the voice, but was unable to get a good glimpse.

"I'm not going to make dinner," Luke yelled back. "I'll join you for drinks later."

"I'll get Kendra to drive me to the hospital."

Luke scowled. "We both know you won't do that. You'll go up to your room and try to remove the glass and douse your foot in hydrogen peroxide." He held out his hand. "Either you take my hand, or I'll carry you."

"I'll die of embarrassment if you carry me. I'd like to try to walk." She uncurled her knee, placing her toe down first, already feeling the tinge of pain. The warm skin of her sole hit the sand, rolling farther until she couldn't avoid the shock of the glass dredging into her raw skin, exacting up a pure, unfiltered cry from the well of her chest. Luke caught her fall and placed his solid hand around her waist.

"You're beautiful for trying," he added in a whisper and dug his fingers into the flesh of her bare waist. Luke helped Melanie up the stairs, and his lean body didn't fold against her jarring frame.

The freshly showered scent on Luke's skin drove her senses mad. She groaned and glimpsed the other two men at the top steps, each with a beer bottle in hand. She recognized Brent with a face wider than the younger version of Luke standing next to him. "Great. I must be suffering an aftershock of some sort. I see three of you."

"You already know Brent and this other guy is my brother, Damon." Luke paused and Melanie stopped hobbling. "Damon, this is Melanie Cahill."

Damon summarized his reaction with a cold smile. She didn't like his eyes, black as his jacket. She pulled away from Luke, instantly regretting the choice.

"I'm taking her to the hospital." Luke assisted Melanie in sitting on the stone wall. "I'll join you later."

"Ms. Cahill," Damon said, and finished the last of his beer. "I've heard so much about you."

The tone of his voice didn't sound complimentary. She sat down on the stone wall. The sun touched her face and the breeze blew back her hair. For a tiny moment, she ignored the shooting stabs up her foot, knowing the smallest wiggle of her toe could bring her to her knees with pain. "I've heard nothing about you."

Damon lifted his eyebrows. "My brother talks only about his family to those who mean something to him."

Luke flashed a glance heavy with warning. "Damon, if you'll excuse us," he said. "You both should get going. I'll meet up with you later."

Upon his command, they collected their drinks and returned to the house. Luke turned back to Melanie. "Why is my past so important to you?"

"The past is a piece of you. Besides, I want to know. I want to know all about you."

He sighed. "What do you want to know?"

"Where are your parents?" The agitated nerve-endings in her foot spiked. The pain she would put off. She wanted to hear this. She'd waited for forever to hear the answer to this question.

"My father used his fists to communicate to my mother and his punches weren't far behind for any of us." He bowed his head to hers. His breath played off her lips. "If I don't talk about my father, then he doesn't exist. He isn't real."

Melanie put her fingers through his hair. "I'm sorry."

"I've never regretted the decision to leave home," he continued without prompting. "One night I decided I'd had enough, and I left. I packed a bag and walked out the front door in the middle of the night." He looked up at her, continuing to talk with distance in his voice, "I slept on a relative's couch for a few weeks and then I began college. I wanted to start college with a clean slate. My father's reputation ran deep in our community. The outbursts, the hair-trigger temper."

She shuddered at the thought of his pain.

"This one time, Brent and I stole a bag of chips from a convenience store. My father had locked up all our food in the cabinets because we didn't clean our rooms. We hadn't eaten in two days and we tried to find food wherever we could. Our aunt who lived behind us was out of town and my father held the key, even though she'd left it for us, because she knew what he was like."

Melanie's fingers drifted down his neck and shoulders. "I had no idea."

"The convenience store owner knew us and when he caught us, he didn't call the cops. He did worse: he called our father. My dad came down to pick us up and I knew. I knew by the smirk on his face and his extra polite voice that we were going to pay. He took us home and beat us until we couldn't sit down." Luke rubbed his chin. "I haven't been back to the house since I left."

Melanie's stomach turned. "What about your mother?" Melanie feared the worst, thinking back now to the stark absence in reference to his mother.

"She's alive. She moved to Scottsdale after he died. I don't stay in contact with her. She's not really all there. She's fragile, she's afraid of her own reflection. The damage my father did to her made her someone else—someone who can't come back from where she'd started in life. She lives in a facility. My aunt lived behind us growing up and we spent all our time there, as much as our father would allow until he needed a punching bag." Luke ran his fingers through Melanie's hair; then down around her sides and gripped her thighs. "My aunt visits her once a year, but I don't ask about my mother. She died to me the day she chose my father over protecting us." Luke's voice hitched with emotion. He kicked the stone wall. "There, now you know."

Melanie took both of his hands, splaying her palms over his. "Thank you for telling me," she said. "I've been trying to understand why you've kept this from me."

Luke removed his hands abruptly. "I don't owe you any other explanations."

"Luke, don't do this."

"What do you want me say? You want me to tell you how I didn't attend his funeral? How I'm afraid Vivian will look at me like I looked at my father one day?"

Her heart broke for him. The aura of bad memories hung in the iris of his eyes, still visible to anyone willing to look past his appearance. "I see the way you're gentle with Vivian. You care for her so much. You're not anything like the monster you described." Forgetting all about her foot, she locked her feet around him and jumped up as if she'd stepped on hot coals. Luke's quick strong hand caught her before she fell back off the wall.

"I'm taking you to the hospital," he ordered.

"I'm not going in my bathing suit," she protested. "Spare me a little self-respect, will you?"

"Stay here and don't touch your foot. I'll get your clothes and be back in a moment."

****

The doctor gave Melanie twelve stitches in her foot and as a parting gift, a tetanus shot. The nurse sent her home with instructions on how to care for her foot over the next few days and a prescription for antibiotics. The stitches would fall out on their own within seven days. Luke enjoyed watching Melanie's stubbornness unfold around the doctor and each time she tried to get out of some instruction, Luke pointed at the bag of bandages, pills, and cleanser he'd picked up at the drug store.

They drove back to the house and Luke parked the car in the driveway where he went to her side of the car and helped her out, despite her unwillingness to take his help. "I'll help you to your room," he said. "Then you're on your own. I'm meeting my brothers for drinks."

He put his arm around her waist and helped her up the long flight of stairs. Luke opened the door and his hand slid off her waist. He switched on the light in the foyer.

"I can make it to my bedroom." Melanie glanced at the stairs. "There's nothing more you can do. Besides, Stevie and Kendra are here if I need help. You know they both live for this kind of excitement." Melanie laughed a little and Luke didn't. She dropped the laugh and said, "Thank you for taking me to the hospital."

"What was that?" he smirked and touched his ear.

"You heard me."

****

Luke's patience stretched thin. The resolute streak in her prevented him from carrying her up to her bed. The bedroom is after all, where he wanted to take her. Her hair hung loose and messy around her face and her eyes looked alive with the same sort of stirring he felt on the inside. The pink hue of her lips against her creamy, oily skin created an intoxicating effect on him. He'd like her lips roaming around his body, while his hands groped her lush, sun-tan covered skin. Pent-up heat erected in his loins at the thought of taking this further. He wouldn't, of course. He'd stand by his decision to remain neutral around her, even if such a feat seemed impossible. "We're going to have to be able to get along for the rest of the summer."

"I know."

His hand fell to his side and he caught himself staring at her and the space of skin above her neckline. He took in a long, frustrated breath. "I won't check on you later."

"All I want is to sleep."

"See you tomorrow." Luke left her and returned to his car.

He drove without concern for the speed. The open road wound in front of him and he accelerated. He would find some other woman to fill his bed tonight. Disgusted with himself, Luke stopped that train of thought. Another woman wouldn't take Melanie's place. She wasn't out of his system. The wheel moved under his fingers and he stepped on the gas.

The obscure bar, Riptide's, sat off the beaten path. Obscure, crowded, and with an interior unchanged in the last thirty years. Literally, a living time capsule stuck in a decade of hard rock with some of the original dust probably on the ceiling fans. Luke liked this bar the best on the island. He found his brothers inside with drinks in their hand and surrounded by a semi-circle of tanned women. The women on the island were beautiful: bright white teeth, jet black hair, and bodies meant for showing off skin. Luke laughed at the crowd they'd attracted, flipped his keys, and approached them.

Brent looked up from his conversation with a brunette first and grinned when he spotted Luke. "I didn't think you'd show," he said and laughed.

The brunette turned around and smiled wide at Luke. The blue eyes and red lips accentuated her pretty face. "You're the third brother?" she said. "I told Brent I'd buy you a drink, if you decided to show up tonight. He seemed to think you wouldn't."

Luke accepted the drink and sat on the barstool next to Brent. The brunette leaned over the bar counter and wore a suggestive grin. "Let me guess: you like your drink stiff and without ice, like your brother."

"You guessed correct," he responded without emotion. The light-hearted mood of the crowd in the bar didn't match Luke's impatience—impatience further complicated every time he ran into Melanie.

"How's the patient?" Brent passed him the whiskey. "Did they need to amputate?"

The blonde took her place next to Luke, ensuring he enjoyed the drink. "Whose body are we talking about?"

Luke ignored the blonde. "The glass is out and the patient is doing well. A few stitches and some rest is all she needs."

"How is Melanie these days, still the martyr for her beloved brother?" Damon inserted himself in the conversation. The youngest Harrison, he leaned on the counter with a grin glossed over from too many drinks—he looked like their father a few moments before slipping into some alcohol-induced zone and becoming unpredictable. "You know she's always going to see him as blameless."

"We'll see about that." Luke gulped the rest of his drink and invoked the right to keep his relationship with Melanie to himself. It occurred to him he could make love to her and just not care about what happened. They could come to some sort of an agreement. No, he shook his head. He was through making agreements with her. She was in Maui. She lived under his roof. They couldn't be together and he wouldn't give any more than take in the physical aspect of their relationship. He didn't need to give her anything more.

"The brunette that bought you the drink is a ten," Damon egged on Luke. "She's much better looking than Melanie." His gaze moved down her shoulder to her rear. "Better body too."

Luke clenched the glass. He didn't want to provoke Damon and get into it in a bar. The one thing about having a father who hits is you learn to fight back, whether you want to or not.

"Melanie cost us a blue garnet," Damon said louder at the same moment someone turned up the music.

"No, she didn't," Brent said, leaning over. "We'll get another one. It's what we do. We keep looking and we'll find something better."

Luke mulled this over. The varnish on the mahogany wood of the counter showed scratches and nicks as far as the eye could see. The bartender slid Luke his drink, not a splash jumped out of the glass. "Drink's on me, Harrison," said Curt, the owner of the bar.

Luke nodded to Curt and accepted the drink. The dim lights made this an ideal place to get lost for a few hours and re-emerge after hours. The brothers mulled over their drinks in silence while the women around them grew restless for their attention.

Damon gave in and began chatting with the blonde. She'd grown tired of waiting for Luke to bite her bait. "What's your name sweetheart?"

"Tasha," she responded with all the eagerness of a student on her first day of school. She wedged her way next to Damon, blocking him out of view of his brothers.

"Are we sure he's getting married?" Brent said, shaking his head.

"There's still time for Felicity to wake up to the reality that our brother is a perpetual bachelor." Luke clicked glasses with his brother's.

"Curt, get Tasha a drink!" Damon shouted. "Get everyone in the bar a drink. I'm getting married." The entire bar erupted in loud cheers and pounded on the tabletop. The women stood around Damon and gravitated to him, vying for his attention more now that they'd learned he was taken. Luke watched Damon reel in one woman after another, using the same moves he'd used for years. All a woman really wanted was to be heard and Damon excelled at the art of cocking his head a little to the side when interested, looking around the bar when he wasn't. Luke drank on and on, until he'd grown tired of sitting. The more he drank, the more he thought of Melanie.

"I'm worried Damon's on a downward spiral," Brent confided to Luke. "I need someone reliable to handle our legal transactions and I'm worried his priorities have changed."

"Damon is distracted, but he's also loyal. He's always handled our legal problems aggressively and swiftly."

"He's becoming unreliable in his personal life." Brent took a moment to watch his youngest brother lean over and kiss the blonde. "I hope her boyfriend isn't nearby."

"Forget about Damon, he's our brother and he's invested in us. Our business is successful because all three of us play our part. We've been operating this way since we were children, long before we established our business. Our business back then was to watch each other's back."

"If our disaster-of-a-father taught us anything, it's to look out for one another." Brent laughed carelessly at the blonde moving over to sit on Damon's lap.

The door swung open and in walked a group of men with thick necks and arms covered in tattoos. The one standing in front nodded at Curt and the bartender got busy grabbing shot glasses and a bottle of Tequila. The muscles on his arms were twice the size of Luke's arms and Brent's biceps. "Here we go," Luke said, feeling in the mood to blow off some steam.

Brent cracked his knuckles and smiled like the devil. "I hope he's the blonde's boyfriend." He swiveled around in his chair, ordered another drink, and turned back around to find Damon lip-deep with Tasha. "We'll soon find out."

They didn't have to wait. The hulk standing in the doorway took his shot of Tequila, wiped his mouth like a barbarian, and stomped over to Tasha. Luke and Brent jumped to their feet. The entire bar froze. A woman seated at the table next to Damon and Tasha took out her phone, and got ready to get footage.

"Tasha, what are you doing?" the man in the doorway said, walking over to her with purposeful, powerful steps.

She sidled up to Damon, and smirked. "I dumped you a week ago."

"You're a slut." He laughed from his belly and turned to gesture to his friends. "You're pathetic."

"He's a lawyer." She talked about Damon like a trophy. "Get lost, Sam."

"You'll regret this." Sam reduced his gaze to two slits and hurled expletives at Damon. "The second you step out of this place, I'm going to smash your face in."

"You can't touch me," Damon said back with a sneer. He wrapped his arm closer around Tasha. "Where were we?"

Sam lunged at Damon at the same time Luke and Brent jumped out of their seats. Luke got to Sam first. The patrons in the bar responded in disorderly hoots and by pounding their tables. Someone shouted for the men to take it outside. Curt ran over trying to hold back the impending fight without success.

Sam swung first. Luke ducked and moved with agility and strength. His closed fist hit Sam square in the jaw. The result shocked Sam still for a single moment; he blinked, hit back, and his fist got Luke in the side of his face. The punch hurt like hell and Luke staggered backwards into a wooden beam. Luke got back on his feet in time to dodge Sam's next attack.

Brent had been busy taking on Sam's three friends. The exchange of near misses and knuckles swinging in the air got the crowd more involved. They cheered and yelled. Damon did nothing except sit and watch with pleasure as Tasha fell all over him.

Curt ran over and put himself between Luke and Sam. "Get out!" he screamed at Luke and the instigator. "Tasha, go home. This is the second time you've brought trouble here this week. Next time I see you or Sam at my bar, I'll call the cops. Leave." A thick vein on his forehead pulsed.

Tasha clung to Damon's hand. "We're leaving together."

"I'm engaged," he said, suddenly the face of fidelity.

"If your last name is Harrison," Curt continued, "I want you out of this bar."

Luke dropped a wad of cash on the counter and nodded at a visibly upset Curt. "We're going," Luke said. Already he could feel the stiffness in the right side of his jaw.

Luke and Brent waited in the parking lot for Damon to say good-bye to Tasha. They exchanged phone numbers, to Luke's annoyance, and Damon sauntered over to Luke's car. "You're an asshole," Luke said.

"So are you," Damon bit back. "Is anyone else in the mood to go have another drink?"

"No," Luke and Brent replied together.

Luke drove home, having only had a few drinks. The fight had pummeled any buzz he'd felt. Alert and awake, he drove his brothers back home safely. They arrived to a house lit by the lights on either side of the stairs.

Damon proved to be the biggest problem. Their brother was a sloppy, wet drunk without much coordination. He rambled too. Luke and Brent laughed and cursed their brother at the same time, trying their best to get Damon up the stairs without falling down and breaking his back. "Don't tell Felicity," Damon slurred near the top of the step. The stench of alcohol stained his breath. "I can't lose her. She'll leave me when she finds out."

"When have we ever tattled on you?" Brent said, taking a heaving breath and helping Damon up the last step.

"She won't forgive me." Damon's head bobbed and he snapped open his eyes like he remembered he should be awake.

Luke shook his head. "I have no idea what he's talking about."

"Hey, buddy," Brent said to Damon, "you bought the girl a drink. Don't call her and you can clear your conscience."

They got Damon up the stairs and into his bedroom on the third floor. Damon fell into the bed with the clothes on his back and the shoes on his feet. Loud snores echoed in the room as Luke closed the door.

"I'll see you tomorrow," Luke said to Brent.

The fight in the bar left Luke nowhere close to sleep. He decided to go to his office. Inside, he flipped up the light switch, closed and locked the door, and walked over to the shelf with the two candle holders above the fish tank. The fish swam up to the glass and nosed the pane hoping for an extra meal. The left candle holder Luke moved to approximately ninety degrees and the vault opened like clockwork. The stacks of cash lined up the right side and he reached past them to the back, to the stashes of velvet bags.

The one bag, bigger than the others, he felt around for and pulled back. He untethered the small cord and opened his palm. A green sapphire fell into his palm. Five carats, emerald cut, and with a green sheen bright enough to wink at him in the light. This particular stone, product of a corundum mineral variety rich with aluminum oxide and iron, had been sitting in his vault for years. The first stone he'd ever got on his own. Long before Melanie, before he'd formed a company with Mark, he'd been stranded in another part of the world in danger and scared—afraid for his own mortality the first time in his life. There had been a lot of running, a lot of hiding, and eventually, a trip to an out-of-the way mine. Luke held the stone up to the light and admired the brilliant depth of green not comparable to anything else in nature. This was the first and last stone Luke had ever stolen. He'd escaped out of Burma with his life, without money, and the gemstone in his pocket. When he'd returned back home weeks later, hungry and ten pounds lighter, he decided this stone would be the cornerstone of his future. He'd build his own company.

Then he met Melanie. Right away he knew he wanted her to have this stone someday. They'd gone their separate ways and the sapphire remained. He was a businessman with a sentimental secret. He couldn't give it up. Luke returned the stone to the vault. To hell with all of the reasons for holding back from Melanie. He could have what he wanted, without the emotions. They could be lovers without the attachment. She could think him guilty and he could be physically satisfied.

Chapter 21

The morning brought a sky of gray clouds and drizzly rain. Melanie got up earlier than usual. She awakened feeling rested. The bottom of her foot hurt no more than a deep scratch. She sat up, unwound the bandage, and checked the small, uneven line of sutures. The first hurdle of the morning would be the shower and mastering not getting her foot wet. The second hurdle would be figuring out how to be around Luke.

The water made everything worse and she slipped in the shower, catching herself on one of the clear bars in the bath with her foot sticking up and out, away from the shower spray. The stitches ripped open and she cried out and laughed at the same moment, much like hitting her funny bone. The pain in the affected area subsided as her hair became drenched and water turned pink from the blood oozing out of the cut. She turned off the water, got herself out of the tub, dried off the skin, and rewrapped the cut.

Once dressed, she shuffled out to the hall and found Luke leaving his bedroom at the same time. "Good morning," her voice faded the instant she could see his face. A red-blue bruise amplified his right eye, spread to the top of his jaw, and reached his ear. "What happened to your face?"

"Bar fight," he explained and added with a wolfish grin, "and you actually seem worried about me."

"I'm not." She shifted her weight onto her good leg. Did he care that she worried about him? Better to avoid the topic entirely. She straightened and answered, "You got into a bar fight. How noble. You defended some girl's honor."

"Maybe."

Melanie looked at his bedroom with scrutiny, as if expecting to see another woman standing in his doorway. Much to her relief, she saw no one. There could have been another woman in the bar last night and her phone number could be in the pocket of Luke's pants as they spoke. She glanced to his pocket.

He followed her gaze. "Is there something of interest to you?"

She snapped her gaze to meet his. Charged anticipation jolted through her. "Nope."

A wry frown spread across his lips. "We'll have to see about that."

She folded her arms over her chest, all too aware of the proximity of his body and his heavy-lidded gaze. Melanie reached out and put her hand on his arm. Luke's greedy, wicked gaze didn't bend. Melanie's gaze swept over his indulgent grin. She took a step forward.

Luke moved faster. In one long step he grabbed Melanie's face. His mouth came crashing down on hers. Melanie started to stumble backwards and stopped. Luke kissed her with such possessive intent that she struggled to keep up with the demands of his mouth. Her tongue wrapped around his as he shifted the kiss to deeper territory. She didn't want to fight the kiss. She didn't want to fight him. Luke's hands glided down her sides and brushed over her breasts. His hands moved lower and rounded over her bottom. He took what he could in his hands and squeezed her flesh; he lifted up her rear and pushed her against him so she could feel his swollen manhood.

Aware of their location, standing in the hallway, Melanie started to break away. "Don't," Luke commanded. With one fell swoop he picked her up and carried her over to his bedroom. He opened the door, kicked it closed with his foot, and placed her on the unmade bed.

She waited on her back amongst the rumpled sheets and strewn bedcover with her shoulders and knees up. Her hair swept down her back. She stared up at him. The curtains remained closed and only a hint of light seeped through the crack in the curtains. She watched Luke take off his clothes. The evidence of what she did to his strong, naked body standing before her. Unashamed of his enlarged member, she rode her gaze up his body. The muscles in his chest covered by a smattering of hair beckoned for her to touch. She forgot to breathe. All of the power in the room she held, knowing the response her body could get out of his. Luke put his hands on her ankles and slid them down, over the sides of her feet.

"I don't want to hurt you," he said, pausing at the foot with the cut.

"You won't," she responded, eager to have his mouth on her body and his hands all over her.

Luke undressed her. He undid in a few seconds what had taken her an hour to do. The clothes he took off her fell to the floor unceremoniously. He slid his hands up her legs, over her womanhood, and paused there, pressing his hand against her. His hands moved away and up, over her stomach and up to her breasts. He spread his fingers over her breasts and parted her legs with his knee. He came towards her and as his mouth closed around her nipple, she took in the sight of his broad and strong shoulders, creased with the definition of muscles. The arousal she'd set off rubbed against her. Melanie watched and let go. She wanted to see him. She didn't want to hide.

The swift reaction she felt engulfed her thoughts and dragged her mind to another planet. Luke's tongue teased her nipple. The temperature of her skin swelled at his mouth working over her breast. He paused for a moment to invade her mouth. His tongue sifted around her mouth. Sweat clung to their lips and to their skin. Melanie's chest stuck to his. Intensity ripped through her mid-section and dampness spread between her legs. Luke reached down and slid his hands under her bottom. He grabbed on and squeezed her hard up to him. The hardness of his impressive manhood swiped the gap between her legs. She moaned in anticipation. His kiss tore at her lips with forceful, voracious movement. The sharp inhale of his aftershave blasted euphoria down her muscles. A bead of sweat hit her neck. She reveled in his strong body hot over top hers.

Melanie gripped his shoulders and kissed him back. Her tongue controlled his; her legs wrapped around his waist, rousing the core of her womanhood. The bones and muscle and blood beneath her skin throbbed with crazy need. This is everything she wanted. Right here. Right now. "Melanie," she heard him whisper her name.

Luke's lips trailed down her neck and her shoulders. He kissed the right one and then the left one. He groped her thighs. His lips grazed her breasts. Melanie spread her legs out a little wider and welcomed his fingers, adeptly touching her most private area. His touch scorched her skin and he moved his fingers everywhere without favoring any one part. He cupped her bare butt and spread his hands open, his thumbs touching the tuft of hair between her legs and the rest of his fingers nestled on her inner thighs. She arched her back, pushing her chest forward, and opened up for him. Hands locked behind his head and her shoulder blades dug into his chest. His incredible shaft rammed up against her lower back and she pushed her chest forward even further.

Tough and determined fingers swept over the creases between her legs. The intentional touch ran up and down the dampness between her thighs.

He came back again, harder and faster and breached her opening. The breath in her chest imploded. She twisted around. Luke's fingers followed her lead. She rummaged his hair with her hands, pushing her lips onto his, slipping her tongue inside his mouth and let her lips contour to his. Her body, gloriously naked and exposed, slid over his bulky erection. Her body felt like silk against him.

Luke's hand returned to her private part with more force and the other held down her leg. He stroked the nub, brought everything about its power to life. He touched her there and she climbed up, breathless and foggy with the sinful pleasure of loving his touch too much. Pleasure blasted through her. It consumed her body. The movements of his finger quickened. He slipped a finger inside her. The erotic march of his finger heightened her sensitive area. His finger returned to her nub and the pressure rocked her desire. The tiniest wrong movement and she would lose everything that swelled inside of her. His shaft rubbed against her with deliberate, greedy movement.

She kept her gaze on his, even when her eyelids threatened to close, she watched his gaze grow dense, like he too was somewhere else for a moment. More pressure on his fingers and he elevated her up, her rear ready to leap off the ground and the rest of her body fizzling, reeling, sitting on the edge and ready to soar. Melanie turned and straddled him.

He entered her and she leaned forward. Her nipples hung over his mouth; and an uneven grin set on his lips. Luke's body moved with hers. His hardness filled her up and ran along the ridge of her own arousal, pushing and drawing out the pleasure with each movement. His hands settled on her waist, keeping her tight and close to his body. She lowered her body so her breasts slopped up and down his chest. She experienced all of him: the sweat, the hair, the grain of sand lost on a lean body. The pressure of his manhood inside her built and built until she cried out for him to finish her off.

Luke uncurled his hands from her waist and took her breasts in his hands, pushing them and teasing the nipples with his unsmooth fingers. She rounded her seat over him, faced the sky, and let her mouth open at the rush of hot liquid pouring out of his body and mixing with the unleashing of explosions rocking her body. She held on, riding him in jagged, selfish movements. She couldn't see straight; she heard nothing.

Her body felt only his. Melanie's head tilted back and her eyes closed. She rode the release, once, twice, more times than she could count. She felt him release inside her and their bodies kept moving, kept riding, and kept going until she had nothing left inside to give. Luke's movements built and climbed until he rammed one last perfect time inside of her. She gripped his chest with all her strength, arched her back, and soared.

Slack-bodied and fulfilled, Melanie rolled off him, naked and unashamed, and lay next to him in the twisted sheets. The rise and fall of their erratic breath filled her ears. The sticky warmth of their love-making stayed on her skin and the sweet air masked their syrupy scent. The noise of the house resumed, or maybe she'd blocked out all the other voices and sounds going on. The beats of their hearts slowed to normal. Luke put his arm underneath her head. To lie in this moment without time or schedules or demands would be bliss.

Melanie started to sit. Luke put a hand on her back. "We don't have to go downstairs this second."

Melanie wished she could turn off the voice in her head trying to think ten steps ahead of her heart. They would have to go out of this room soon. Luke tugged her close to him. He wrapped his arms around her and rested his lips on her shoulder. She felt every inch of him. They lay there quiet and contented and she gave in to having fallen for him completely, newly, wholly, all over again.

"I want to see you again," he said.

What a fantastic morning this was turning out to be. "Tonight," she said.

Luke lowered his lips to hers. A slightest graze of air passed through over her lips. "I want you like this every morning, in my bed."

"I want to be with you every morning," she commented and nuzzled against his wide chest.

Melanie stayed in his bed for a moment longer. She watched his back as he moved to the bathroom. The defined muscles on his back stretched down to a long torso and his lean, bare buttocks. He was a beautiful specimen.

Their lovemaking stayed with Melanie after she'd taken her second shower of the morning. She walked downstairs with pride moving through her. She walked through the kitchen door, later than she had every other morning.

Latonya's stern face and arched eyebrow met Melanie's eyes. "Good-morning," she said, trying to remain casual.

"You're up late," she said, fully charged. Latonya's gaze darted to Melanie's foot. "Your foot looks fine to me."

"She is fine," Stevie balked from the table. "She has a little scratch."

"Where's Kendra?" Melanie asked, skipping the topic altogether. The intimacy of the morning trundled through her stomach. It's all she could think about.

"Kendra's at Felicity's hotel. The bride has officially arrived and this wedding is going ahead full-steam."

Melanie took a seat at the table. The sight of a Sippy cup sitting in front of Vivian gave her an inward smile. Change is sometimes best taken in small doses. "Such a big girl," she said.

Stevie took a small bottle of cinnamon and sprinkled the spice on her oatmeal. "The wedding is going to be the event of the island. Everyone's talking about Damon and Felicity."

Vivian picked up her plate of scrambled eggs, hung it in a vertical hold and ceremoniously dumped the food on the floor. "Ba!" she screamed to Melanie. "Bababa."

"I didn't know they were well known."

"Luke is well known and Felicity Banks comes from a family orbiting in the upper echelon of Chicago society. Half of Damon's law firm owns houses or condos on one of these Hawaiian Islands. The Harrison name's known and respected and Damon's smart. He wouldn't ask anyone less than perfect to become his family." Stevie turned to Melanie. "Is Goldie still coming over to seduce…I mean…bring her daughters over for a playdate?"

"She's coming over." Melanie glanced at the clock on the wall. "The motives she has for coming over are not my business."

"Keep the playdate confined to the playroom. I don't want her prowling around the house waiting for opportunities to pounce on Luke."

"Good morning ladies," Luke said, striding into the kitchen. "I don't know if I told you, Stevie, that Brent has asked Goldie to be his date for the wedding."

Stevie's hand flopped over her heart. "Don't scare me."

"I speak the truth." Luke enjoyed teasing her. "She might be Brent's wife someday."

"My heart suddenly doesn't feel well." She bent over the table.

The topic of Goldie and Brent outweighed the intimate moment. Luke glanced at Melanie with the same shared secret of their morning. "I thought we'd let the girls play in the playroom and if the rain holds, we can take them for a walk or get out a soccer ball. I noticed there are some bikes that haven't been put together in the closet. I'll get those assembled this afternoon."

"You can take the lead on the bikes." Stevie unstrapped Vivian out of the booster seat and wiped down her hands and face. "I won't pretend to be of much help with those."

Luke occupied the spot next to the coffee maker and Melanie had no choice other than to stand close to him to refill her coffee. Their arms touched and she could smell the caffeine from his mug and the soap on his skin. It made pouring the coffee a distracted task. How would she ever get through the morning? He reached over her, grabbed one of the spoons sticking out of a cup, and whispered, "You make me hard."

A heat wave rushed up Melanie's cheeks. She could feel everyone else in the kitchen staring down the back of her neck. "I hope you slept well," she answered, to avoid any speculation if people were listening, which, knowing Stevie and Latonya, they were. She held her breath until Luke walked away.

"The cocktail party's at seven o'clock tonight," Latonya called out after Luke.

"Kendra won't let me forget." He walked over to Vivian and kissed her on the forehead, talked to her for a moment, though she said nothing back, and left the women to process the news of Goldie and Brent attending the wedding together.

The kitchen gossip bored Melanie compared to what had gone on in Luke's bedroom earlier and she withdrew from the conversation and left the kitchen. She decided to start assembling the bikes. A task requiring physical and mental concentration would get her mind off of Luke.

She had her work cut out for her. There wouldn't be time to finish putting together one tricycle, a scooter, two plastic play bikes, and a play car with a roof and wheels. The closet in the playroom also held toddler-size roller skates, unopened. Helmets in three different sizes, also unopened and a basketball hoop for kids. A tool box on the top shelf gave her the supplies she needed to start and she picked out the tricycle and one of the play bikes. Gross motor coordination like peddling a bike would help develop Vivian's leg muscles and help her build other skills and Melanie chose the tricycle to put together first.

Melanie got to work, taking out instructions, ripping open the bags of screws and parts, working on what she could before Goldie arrived. A half-hour after her planned playdate time, Goldie arrived, along with Kari and Alyssa, parading in whines all the way to the playroom. "Hello," Goldie said in a high-pitched voice. "My girls and I got sidetracked." She led with a pink bakery box and walked over to Melanie. "These are for the girls."

Kari and Alyssa rushed inside, hitting the shelf of toys with fast hands. They began pulling out, yanking down, and emptying drawers of organized toys.

Melanie set down the screwdriver and paused to look in the box. The most fluffy, beautiful cupcakes iced in pink commanded the attention of her salivary glands. She felt her tongue twitch in response to the spoonful of sugar needed to make such a fine creation.

Goldie snapped closed the box. "We'll have them a little later. What a charming little room Vivian has. I recently changed the theme in my girls' playroom. They have a gourmet kitchen built into the side of the room with a working refrigerator, a mini theater stage complete with curtains and a chalk board wall for roll call. You simply must see their sofa. I had the fabric made from a special blend of silk and cotton."

The sofa sounded like a place for a whore to have sex, but Melanie kept her mouth shut. "Sounds like a great space for your daughters."

Goldie's hand hit Melanie's arm. "I can't wait for the wedding."

"You got an invitation?" Melanie asked while clearing her throat. She glanced at Vivian, who was not at all interested in the other girls. The natural reaction for Melanie should have been to go and show Vivian how to play with Kari and Alyssa; teach her how to sit side-by-side with them, pass toys, share, try to point or interact. The entire point today was to observe and give Vivian little guidance as possible.

"Brent invited me. He's such a man, I mean in the most physical way. Have you seen his arms? I want to run my hands over his muscles." She caught Kari looking over at her, confused. "I'm all stressed now about what to wear. I can't throw on any of the dresses in my closet. Sid bought me every single one of them and I won't show up in clothes reeking of our bad luck." She could tell Melanie wasn't listening and followed her gaze over to Vivian, looking lost in her own world. "Vivian's not much of a talker, is she?"

The comment about Vivian instantly drew up Melanie's protective shield. "She will be."

"Kari and Alyssa spoke full sentences at Vivian's age. My little project managers run my house and already talk back to me. Little girls are so demanding."

Melanie grinned. "They tend to imitate whomever they are around."

Goldie smiled and quickly frowned. "I imagine Vivian doesn't have to say much around Luke. He doesn't say much. All his thoughts are locked up in that handsome head of his." Kari came over and shoved a doll in Goldie's face. "Comb her hair!"

"Mommy isn't playing right now." Goldie pushed back the doll. "I'm talking to Vivian's speech therapist."

Not at all impressed with Melanie's title, Kari threw the doll up in the air and dropped to the floor, flailing around. "I want you to play with me. Play with me! PLAY WITH ME!"

Alyssa came over, pounced on Kari, and the two them rolled over and began to fight and giggle and forget about their mother. "Have you met Felicity yet? I haven't personally met her. I should wait until I can bring over a fine bottle of wine and some flowers."

"I know she got to her hotel late last night and I don't know anything more."

"I'm disappointed! You're staying in Luke's house. Think. Use your brain and get some information out of these people." She laughed and squirmed in her seat, the result of a joke for Melanie to take either way. "Tell me all about Luke's friends. Are any of them single? I'm kidding, of course."

"I don't know his friends." Melanie picked up one of the plastic baggies with leftover screws.

Goldie laughed nervously. "I see."

Melanie got up and walked over to Vivian, and talked to her, pointing at the other girls, showing her they were present. She took out a dollhouse with miniature life-like people and pretended to act a scene with the mom washing dishes and the little children playing in the backyard. Kari and Alyssa gravitated over to Melanie with interested countenances, and sat down cross-legged with hands eager to play. Goldie opened the box of cupcakes, picked out the fattest one, and began to eat by herself in the corner and check her phone.

Chapter 22

Felicity Banks stole the attention of every male in the room with her striking black hair, cool green eyes, and swab of freckles over her nose and cheeks. The simple nod of her head and some eager man brought her a drink. The men in the room, fellow lawyer friends of Damon's in town for the wedding, stopped by the house on their way to the private beach, courtesy of Luke. They inclined their gazes to her like cold hands to a hot fire, most of all Damon, who stood beside her, holding a stake for anyone giving off the slightest scent of flirtation.

The bride dictated the day's activities and she stood by her decision to go see and swim in the freshwater pools at 'Ohe'o in the Haleakala National Park. One quick call to the park office and Kendra confirmed ideal conditions for such a day out where guests could choose between hiking, swimming, or both.

Latonya set Damon's friends up with a basket of food and a cooler of ice, cans of soda, and bottles of water and they were on their way to enjoy a day under a blue sky and even bluer waves. The fifteen-seat passenger van awaited them outside and everyone began grabbing bags all at once.

Melanie found a seat in the row second to the back and scooted all the way down so she could see out the window. They didn't sleep together last night. Damon and Brent corralled Luke into going out for drinks and dinner. She half-expected Luke to have come to her bed last night, but he didn't. The entire day had been planned out and Melanie looked forward to seeing more of Maui. She hadn't been out of the beach house much, except for a few quick trips to the markets, and of course, the ER.

Everyone convened at the van in front of the house. The driver waited outside on the curb, in front of the van with Kendra giving him presumably some sort of instruction. Vivian sat in a car seat in the back row with Stevie on one side and Kendra on the other, while the rest of the party got in the van and chose a seat.

Luke took the seat next to Melanie's. "You'll like where we're going today," he said, with casual ease. "When I first bought this house, I did a lot of hiking up in Haleakala. There are decent trails and the scenery is unlike anything you've seen: pristine, quiet, grand."

"I bet you didn't think I'd ever see this place with you." At least she could make fun of their past.

He grew serious for a moment, responding with, "No, I didn't think I would ever bring you here."

Kendra tapped Luke on the shoulder. "Excuse me," she said, coming between them. "Everything's set for our lunch. When we get to the pools, we'll eat first, and then the guests can swim or go for a hike to see the waterfalls. We'll have three hours to see the area and we can split up or stay as a group, as long as we're all back at the van by three p.m. sharp. Will there be anything else in the meantime?"

"Take a break, Kendra. Have a glass of wine when we arrive. You've earned a day off."

"Sir?" she asked in a modulated voice.

"Enjoy yourself. There won't be any problems. We're less than an hour away from the park." He paused and laughed quietly. "There's no crisis to solve. Be social. Have fun."

"Be social," she repeated like an android. "Have fun."

Kendra leaned back as the driver started the car and drove them away from the house. The pregnancy wasn't yet showing, a fact Kendra couldn't hide much longer, especially after the summer. The thought of "after the summer" sat heavy on Melanie's heart. Where would she be? Could she go back and live at home and work at the Growing Tree? Could life ever be the same from this massive interruption? She'd want to be with Luke. She knew herself very well and she knew she'd want to be with him. Melanie snuck a glance at Luke. For all she knew, he thought differently. Maybe this would be a P.S., thanks for the summer come the end of August. Melanie watched through the window. The scene rolled by, and she wondered for the second time, if she should have clarified the things standing in their way of being together.

Luke's hand brushed across hers and his finger drew an invisible line down her palm. The blood rushed to her midsection as it always did when Luke touched her. She removed her hand from under his. The rest of the way to the park she remained aloof to him. It was too much to be this close to him, in a car with other people, and not be able to be with him.

The driver accelerated the car up the winding road and handled the curves with care. They passed through the park entrance and the driver continued driving until they reached their destination, a parking area at the far end of the lot. The last ones to get out of the van, Kendra and Melanie each carried bags and blankets up the quarter-mile hike and then down further to the pools where they joined the rest of the group at the mouth of the 'Ohe'o Gulch.

The rocky foot of the shoreline made the walk down to the water slippery and dangerous. Trees, thick and dense, filled the land and created a natural barrier to the trails and road. Melanie looked up in the direction of the *whoosh* sound and saw the staggered waterfalls with crisp white water pouring out of the mouths of the cliffs. They couldn't see or hear any other people and selected a site. Brent cleared some of the rocks and Kendra and Melanie threw down the blankets.

"You've been quiet," Melanie said to Kendra with the others in the distance, putting on sunscreen and taking off socks and shoes.

"Damon's marrying her because she's somebody."

Melanie looked over in the direction of Felicity and Damon, laughing and talking. "I don't understand."

Kendra shot a green-eyed glance at the engaged couple. "Felicity is somebody. She's from the right zip code. Her family is from the Lakeshore area of the city. Do you think he would marry her if say, she came from a working-class family with a father on disability and a manager of a Laundromat for a mother?"

"I think you've got enough to worry about than Damon's choice in a bride. He might not come from much, but he's built a successful life, more than most people." Melanie helped Kendra smooth out the blanket and continued, "Have you thought more about contacting the father?"

"Not a chance." Kendra laughed hard. "He broke up with me for another woman. I doubt he's going to insist involvement financially or otherwise, in this child's life."

"You don't think there's a chance he'll choose you?" Melanie helped Kendra pick up the sandwiches and put them in another bag.

"I know you're not stupid. You know as well as I do that there's no point holding second place in a man's heart. You either occupy the first seat or you don't. I know where I stand and it's not even close to first place."

"Don't you think he deserves to know? Maybe he'll agree to be financially responsible. Kendra, don't be bullheaded. A baby isn't like planning Luke's schedule. You've got to be prepared for the major disruption and you've got to plan for whatever you and your baby need."

She remained unyielding. "I don't need anything from him."

Melanie dropped the topic like a cannon ball in water. She stole a glance at Luke, shirtless in his black bathing suit shorts that hung low off his waist, exposing his defined abs and smattering of light brown chest hair.

Pressing her feet into the cool water, Melanie waited for the sting of her cut to pass before she moved on to find a flatter bottom of land. The best she could, she kept off the foot and trudged through the water, wincing at a random sharp branch or slick rock. She waved at Stevie and Vivian sitting a ways up on other blankets with hats and snacks.

The intensity in Luke's gaze told her what he wanted. "Now?" she whispered.

Luke responded with a reckless grin and grabbed her hand. "No one will miss us. They think we're going to see more of the falls."

A trifecta of queasy, brilliant, ecstasy, hit her middle. Melanie grabbed her flip-flops and a towel.

"They're a short hike away." Luke wore his towel like a mantle over his shoulders.

They slipped away without much notice and walked up to the road. Luke led the way, crossing the road and finding a narrow, muddier trail in the heart of the humid forest with water drops clinging to the leaves on the trees. The shrieks and giggles of Damon and Felicity faded at a rush of water soon after. The flip-flops Melanie wore slipped under her feet, causing shooting pains from the center of the cut and pulled at the stitches. Luke put his arm around her and helped her over a patch of rocks.

The jut in one of the paths extended in two directions and Luke took the one leading to the left. Their elbows cut through the trees that closed like a curtain behind them as they stepped out on the small balcony of land. Natural breaks in the rocks formed a semi-circle at the edge, which overlooked the forest, more waterfalls, and the ocean in the distance.

Luke squinted ahead at the bend in the shoreline. "I thought you'd like this." Luke put his hands on her waist and drew her against him. "I'm not talking strictly about the park, but Maui too. You do like it here, don't you?"

Words failed to articulate the source of this comment. The well in her stomach grew with each slide of his fingers over her shirt. "I'll remember this summer forever."

"There can be more summers spent here." Luke's finger rounded under her chin. "This can work out."

"You make this feel so easy." A flutter of relief escaped her mouth at the knowledge he'd been thinking similar thoughts. "I take it you've come around to my point of view. We can be together, despite our differences in opinion on the subject of my brother. What a relief to know I can be supportive to him and be in love with you." Immediately she felt his body go tense.

"No." Exasperated, Luke dropped his head. He lifted her chin and forced their eyes to meet. "You can't have this both ways."

Melanie pulled away. "What are you talking about? What about yesterday morning in your bedroom?"

"I've been talking about us being lovers. You know how I feel about the subject of your brother and where your allegiance stands."

"I don't want to be your lover," Melanie cried, with anger rising in her throat. "We've been over this before. Didn't you just ask about spending more summers here?"

"This can work out."

"Under your rules, right? Mark is my family. Do you have any idea how it feels to think, even for a split second that my brother might have attempted murder?" She clenched her jaw. "No. All you care about is yourself. This is always about what you want." Melanie shoved her feet in the flip-flops too hard and the sole swiped the cut. She winced and looked up at Luke. "Looks like you got what you wanted."

"You're angry because you know I'm right. Stop fighting the truth." Luke held out his hand. "I want us to be together. I won't wait for you forever, Melanie. You've had seven years to figure out the truth. You know every time you look in the mirror that you're wrong."

Melanie didn't know what to say. She stood there numb and frustrated with a single tear rolling down her cheek. "I hate you."

"Good; it will make it easier for us to be around each other." Luke started to walk back and didn't wait for Melanie to catch up to him. She took her time and kept within distance. The rounded muscles of his shoulders and the ridge of his back stayed in her eyesight until he put his shirt back on and led them back to the pools.

The unyielding silence continued from Luke the rest of the afternoon. Brent and Damon occupied time by swimming and telling stories from their early days of gem-hunting; stories Melanie had heard before. The cut on her foot festered and she knew she'd have to get home to clean out the dirt. The trip to Madagascar she'd survived, only to have this stupid, small cut blow up the pain in her foot. Vivian sat in her lap and rested against her. Together they sat there until Kendra announced for them to head back to the van.

They returned to the house in a van full of sun-kissed, exhausted, contented riders. Brent fell asleep with his mouth hanging open and Damon woke him up by yelling in his ear. The driver eased the van up the driveway and came to a stop. Everyone moved with unhurried steps and yawns. Luke hadn't spoken to Melanie after they'd fought, not one single word. Not even an "Excuse me," or "I'll see you later." She'd become immune to his on-and-off switch and decided to let him be angry. She wouldn't throw away her relationship with her brother because he wanted her to—even if she wanted to be with Luke. Knowing that gave her power.

Stevie reached across to the red button on Vivian's car seat and unbuckled her. "Luke looked happy this morning, when we arrived at 'Ohe'o. However, after your hike, he looked miserable. What happened?"

"I do mind," Melanie quipped. "We discussed my job. The rest isn't your business."

"He only looks that upset when he's lost something extremely valuable." She pulled a sleepy-eyed Vivian out of the car seat. "Help me with this one."

Vivian didn't budge when Melanie took her, which gave Stevie a chance to get out of the back row and out of the van. She transferred the child back to Stevie. "I'll get the car seat."

She wedged herself into the back. She hunched over to try and get the car seat unlatched. The clips to unlock the seat wouldn't move and her fingers grew sore from hitting against the metal latches. The day, the last three weeks, even the seven years had all been too much. Melanie shook the car seat and started to cry. Tears rolled down her cheeks and dripped to her bare arms. "Damn you, Luke," she whispered in a worked-up haze and wiped away the tears with her hand.

The driver leaned over the seat next to her and said, "I got this."

"Thanks," she said and grabbed her bag before he could see her cry.

Melanie gave herself a minute before heading up to the house. She didn't know how the rest of this would go. Luke wouldn't wait for her forever and although she didn't have an answer, she didn't want to be around him either.

She walked up the stairs and met Kendra at the front door. "I need to borrow a car."

"I need to get out of here," Kendra said, glancing at the brothers gathered at the fireplace. "Where do you need to go?"

"I want to get some more bandages and antibiotic cream for my foot." Melanie also looked over at the brothers all standing and laughing. "Give me fifteen minutes to rinse off my foot and I'll meet you out front."

"Make it five."

Melanie changed her clothes and took the quickest shower of her life, enough to wash the dirt off her body and clean her foot. She returned to meet Kendra at the front of the house and found Luke and his brothers had moved out to the patio and sat around the table facing the pool and the ocean with Latonya hovering with a pitcher of what looked like iced tea.

"I'm ready," Melanie said to Kendra.

They left the house together without anyone's notice.

Kendra drove fast. The isolation of Luke's home gave way to a more populated area of the island full of houses and businesses. "I'm starving. Would you mind if I got a bite to eat?"

Melanie's stomach growled. "I haven't eaten much today."

"I'm going to this place called The Fish Head. Great local food, might I add. I love everything on the menu." At the red light she glanced at her appearance in the rearview mirror and wiped underneath her eyes. "All of my friends who have had children swear pregnancy is this awesome experience where I'm supposed to look stunning and glowing. I have to tell you," she said, pausing and continuing to drive at the green light, "I don't sleep, I throw up twice a day, and my skin has broken out more than when I went through adolescence and these bags under my eyes have multiplied."

A jealous flutter hit Melanie. "I'm sure you'll have better days."

"Here we are." Kendra pulled the car into a parallel parking spot effortlessly.

They walked across the street to the quaint, corner storefront on a row of pale buildings and sporadic, hanging baskets of pansies. Plastic tables and chairs sat outside, though no one sat in them. Paper menus stuffed in wall-hanging boxes adorned the right side of the door and both Melanie and Kendra took one.

Melanie stepped inside the overly cold restaurant with fans circulating above. The corner table by the front window was free and Melanie sat down. Their sandwiches and sodas arrived and they ate too fast to talk.

Within ten minutes they sat laughing at the wadded up paper and a stray, broken French fry on Melanie's tray. "I'm stuffed."

"I could eat another order." Kendra ran her hand over her belly. "This baby is already taking my nutrients. Now she wants my fries."

Melanie sipped her soda. "I owe you an apology for bringing up the father. I shouldn't have pushed the subject."

"While I agree with you, I also don't want an apology. I'll handle my own situation. I don't need your advice." She blew out a long breath. "Except for…"

"Except for what?" Melanie could see she wanted to tell her something.

"It's just…" she looked up at the ceiling. "Nothing; I'm going to order another round of fries. Do you want anything?"

"I'm good."

Kendra got up from the table with slow movements and she made her way to the counter, ordered another basket of fries, and returned a few moments later. She squeezed a blob of ketchup inside the basket and dipped a fat fry. "I'm surprised Luke asked you to go on a hunt with him."

"I am too. Unfinished business, I guess." The straw slurped up the last of the drink and she shook the cup full of ice.

"I don't know much about your relationship with him. Why did you end things?"

"He ended our relationship," Melanie cleared up this misconception at once, "because we didn't share the same opinion about a sensitive family topic."

"I've seen when he loses something he wants. There's nothing worse than when I know a negotiation is involved and he's bidding for a stone up against bigger bidders. I get the silent treatment for three days and then he'll only communicate by e-mail or text. Eventually though, he gets over whatever is upsetting him and everything goes back to normal. Luke and his brothers aren't used to the imperfections of the rest of us and not one of them has an ounce of forgiveness inside them."

"He offered me a job. This has to mean some sort of forgiveness."

"I thought the gesture was unlike him. I've never seen Luke apologize or take pity on anyone, especially someone from his past. He's very hush-hush about his personal life before he began Trace Elements. The information I gathered is from the Internet, so I know he put your brother behind bars. What else does he want from you?"

"More like what I want from him. I need his help to secure my brother's early release." Melanie gave her the details and offered only a little bit of her history with Luke.

"I overheard Luke talking to Brent about those tourmalines."

Melanie lurched forward. "Do you know where they are? How can I get them? I need them, Kendra. I don't think Luke and I are headed in a good direction and I'm afraid he'll change his mind about me working with Vivian. If he sends me home, then I've failed. The other possibility is he's trying to get under my brother's skin by using me."

The fry in Kendra's hand dropped. "You think he's using you?"

"I don't know, maybe." A family group of five slow-walked by their window and stopped. The mom of the group wearing a neon visor and tank top with an air-brushed image of a muscled-woman's body on the shirt peered into the window and shook her head. The family kept walking, apparently deciding to search out other food options.

"Luke's a businessman. He sticks out his agreements and doesn't back out because of a personal hitch in the contract. You signed something legal about this agreement between the two of you."

"You were present."

"You don't have to worry. What's your back-up plan if you don't have anything to show him or tell him about by the end of the summer?"

"I don't have a plan. What's worse is I have no leads. I tried checking out his office, my brother suggested Luke always keeps a vault in his office, at least they did when they were in business together."

Kendra's eyes bulged. "You snooped around in his office?"

"He caught me."

"Well, you still have a job. Consider yourself fortunate." Kendra wiped her hand on a napkin. "That's why you asked me where he keeps his gemstones."

"Yes." Melanie closed her eyes and breathed a long breath. She was going to be okay. This news gave her brother a fighting chance. The summer would be worth the sacrifices.

"I'll also tell you that I know more than I was willing to admit a few minutes ago."

"Are you going to tell me what you know?"

"If I've learned anything from Luke, it's to never give anything away for free. I need to ask you a favor in return."

"What sort of favor?"

"I need you to arrange a meeting with someone. I'll tell you his name in a moment. I want this particular person, a man, to meet me one-half mile down from Luke's beach, heading North, at midnight tonight. I don't care how you get him there. You'll have to find a way and you cannot tell him I want to see him. Tell him someone wants to meet with him."

Melanie leaned in and listened, she didn't let her emotions betray her facial expression when Kendra slipped her the name. "When will I get my information?"

"After I meet with him, have breakfast with me tomorrow on the patio and I'll tell you what you want to know over coffee."

"We have a deal."

The French fries disappeared a few moments later as Kendra woofed them down. They returned to the car and she drove them back to the house. The sheer exhaustion of the day left Melanie feeling like she'd been hit with a two by four. Achy muscles, too much sun, the nerves of doing a last minute favor which would bring her closer to getting Mark's release overwhelmed Melanie when she just wanted to sleep.

The task at hand wouldn't be easy. The player in question: Damon. Kendra wanted to get Damon alone, on the beach, at midnight. The specifications didn't seem difficult at first. Then she realized how hard this would actually be to get him to agree. She didn't know him. She couldn't very well walk up to him and give the instruction.

The house wasn't quiet when they walked through the door. Luke, Brent, and Damon occupied the pool with Goldie and Felicity chatting and sipping a drink at one end. An unpleasant gurgle moved through Melanie's stomach and she wondered how on earth she'd be able to pull off this favor. She couldn't approach him with Luke, Brent, or Felicity nearby and what would she do if they remained in the pool for the next several hours? Melanie put her hand on her stomach and went to her bedroom until she could figure out what to do.

* * * *

The detached sound of a phone rang. Bleary and weak, Melanie lifted the covers off her head and stared at the nightstand, a heavy-wooded object she could make out in the room. She must have fallen asleep and somewhere in the back of her mind this was a bad thing. The phone continued to ring and she grappled for the thin object on the nightstand. "Hello?" she answered.

"You're a difficult person to reach," Mark's voice bit from the other end. "You aren't answering your phone much these days."

"Mark." Melanie sat up. "You know I would call if anything changed."

"I'm worried about you."

"You're worried about yourself."

Melanie flipped on the light. The light struck her eyes and she closed her lids to adjust. "I'm tired of being in the middle." She glanced at the clock a second time. Ten-thirty p.m. the numbers read. "Shit." The phone slipped out of her hand. She needed to find Damon. "Mark, I really want to talk, but I have to go. I have a lead on something that will help your case."

"What are you saying? Luke's going to write the letter?"

The desperation in his voice broke Melanie's heart. "I might have a reliable tip on the whereabouts of those tourmalines."

"Forget about them. I told you—"

"I have to go!" She hung up on him without feeling remorse and flew out of bed. The bottom of her foot hit the floor too hard and she covered her mouth as she screamed as the stitches ripped open. She dropped to her rear and held her foot until the flash of white-hot pain subsided.

* * * *

Slowly this time, she stood up, and took great care when putting on her shoes. She threw on a thin, long-sleeved shirt and opened the door. The hallway, lit by the moonlight and one night light guided her to the stairs. A creak in the floor sounded like wood breaking and she stopped and held her breath. The other doors on the hallway remained closed, including Luke's, and she didn't hear any movement behind them.

The pool party outside didn't exist anymore. No trace of Felicity and Damon or the others remained outside. The night felt later than the hour and she tried to think of where Damon might be at this point in time. If he went back to Felicity's hotel then Melanie could forget Kendra's deal and she'd be left to finding out the information on her own. The task seemed small, compared to what she had to lose. She'd already lost Luke. He would never give in on the subject of her brother. She knew this now and accepted her own stupidity and excitement of being with him.

The possibility of waking up Stevie came to mind. She couldn't trust Stevie to understand the situation and quickly realized she couldn't tell her. The sordid details would be all over the breakfast table the next morning. Melanie scratched this idea off her list. Brent came to mind and she knew that would be the dumbest of all choices. They didn't know each other well enough for her to go asking after the younger brother without raising a few eyebrows.

Melanie started to get up when a movement caught her eye. A body took shape coming down the stairs and she squinted to try to see through the darkness. Luke appeared, shirtless and in his swim shorts. The trail of hair began at his chest and streamlined to the top of his shorts. He caught sight of her at the end of the pool and stopped. His hand tugged on the towel. He waited a moment before coming around to the end of the pool. Melanie slipped back into the house and up the stairs.

Chapter 23

Conflict tormented Luke. He thought himself strong enough to resist her. He'd been too tempted by the sight of her today to stay away, yet he'd triggered more emotion in her than he'd anticipated. She *did* love him. A fact he could see whether she told him or not. He wanted her to love him and he hadn't anticipated how quickly she'd hurl her hurt at him. Luke turned over in the pool so he lay with his back on the water, holding his breath in spurts and being still. He stayed like this for a few minutes longer, thinking about what to do. The thought of firing her crossed his mind.

Luke got out of the pool and dried off. They couldn't talk about the subject any more. It was dead in the ground. Halfway up the stairs he stopped and looked up. Two people spoke fast and low on the third floor and he slowly took a step back and listened.

"You're insane," Damon said. "What do I get in return?"

"You get me. All of me," Melanie said. "I see the way you look at me. I'm dying to find out if you're a good kisser."

Luke gritted his teeth at the sound of Melanie's voice. He kept listening, despite the wrath growing inside. They stood so close, he saw their heads touch. He leaned closer.

"I don't want to go on the beach," Damon said.

"Nobody can see us," Melanie pleaded.

"Alright; I hear you. Give me a second."

Luke's fists curled. His veins pumped hot blood up his cheeks. Their footsteps pushed him to run up the stairs and wait in the shadows so he could see the traitorous, lying, woman he'd made love to. The moment of her deceit was his last undoing. Now she'd hurt him beyond repair. He could make out their bodies, two shadows sneaking down the stairs. He saw Melanie leave with Damon with his own eyes.

Chapter 24

Every part of sneaking out with Damon felt wrong. She kept looking over her shoulder, fearful that Luke might be watching from somewhere. He'd left the pool, which brought her more angst.

She did her best to not encourage Damon. She walked best she could and kept her distance slightly in front of him. The signal from Kendra, a flashlight, should be showing any second. Damon actually thought they were going to make love! A revolting thought as Melanie didn't think he would go for such a plan, given his upcoming marriage. When she roused him out of bed, it took a shorter time than she'd ever imagined and she convinced him without much effort.

"Let's do this," Damon said and reached for the back of her shirt.

"Not yet," Melanie said and tried to keep walking. Lights on houses in the distance blinked in the wind. She kept a vigilant gaze up ahead. They had to be close. The waves pounded to the right of her and she didn't like the darkness, the water, or the situation one bit.

"There's no one around." Damon grabbed her hand and yanked her over to him. "You can have me. I know how you want me." He leaned into kiss her and Melanie kicked his shin.

"Ouch!" he yelled. "What's wrong with you?"

A flash of light, then another, and Melanie brought her hands to her chest and shook excitedly. "I'm not going to sleep with you."

"You're not? Then why did you bring me out here?"

"Do you see the flashlight up ahead?"

Exasperation sounded in his breath. "Yes."

"Someone wants to meet with you. I can't tell you her name. You'll have to go find out for yourself."

"I'm not going to meet anyone. I'm going back to the house and telling my brother how you threw yourself at me. He won't like his little pet making a move on me. I'll get him to throw you out."

She could almost see the sneer.

"You won't get her thrown out," Kendra said, out of breath.

"I told you I will not talk to you," Damon exploded.

"Melanie, leave us alone. I'll see you at breakfast in the morning."

Inclusions 213

She didn't want to leave them alone, or more concerning, leave Kendra alone with Damon. The moment she tried to stay, Kendra barked at her to go back or she wouldn't hold up her end of the bargain. Melanie left them alone. She could hear their heated conversation as she turned away and went back to the house.

* * * *

Breakfast came and went without a sign from Kendra, Damon, or Luke. Melanie drank her coffee with jitters. She kept looking at the door leading to the family room. Worry, not personal motive, occupied Melanie's thoughts. She hoped nothing bad had happened on the beach. She also couldn't suppress the idea that Luke had somehow seen Melanie taking Damon down there.

Melanie had no option other than to start work with Vivian. The evaluation was complete. Another wave of bad feelings coursed through Melanie. She'd have to tell Luke the outcomes. Vivian was deficient in every area: personal-social, adaptive, motor skills, communication, and cognitive ability and in each of the categories, Vivian was behind anywhere from eight to ten months below her peers. A curtain closed around her heart at having to tell him.

Melanie and Vivian sat in the play room, the quietest room in the house, and got started on their session. Today Melanie took out a ball, a cup with a lid, and keys on a key ring. They would work on Vivian making sounds and learning to follow directions. "Watch me." Melanie put the ball in the cup.

Vivian sat up straight and reached out with both hands to the cup.

"Say, my turn."

Vivian babbled and reached for the cup again. Melanie rewarded her with the cup and the ball. "Good."

She watched Vivian examine the ball first and then the cup. They repeated this and Melanie integrated the cup with the lid and the keys. "Good. Do it again," she said and made the sign for "again."

"I'm sorry to interrupt," Stevie said and stuck her head in the play room. "Luke wants to see you in his office, he said it's urgent." She walked over to Vivian. "I'll keep an eye on her."

"I'm glad he wants to see me, I have the results of Vivian's evaluation. I haven't seen Kendra today, is she by chance around?"

"Kendra's at the hotel with Felicity. The bride asked for her to be there by seven o'clock. I know because Vivian was awake and we bumped into each other in the kitchen."

"Oh good, I'll catch her later." Kendra should have at least texted Melanie about heading over to Felicity's hotel, but Melanie wouldn't read too much into the situation. She'd gotten Damon over to Kendra and she'd upheld her part of the bargain.

Melanie walked the length of the hall thinking about Luke and their closeness last night out by the pool. Absentmindedly she moved her hand up the banister. Nerves ran through her at the thought of talking to Luke for the first time after their fight.

She knocked on Luke's door and entered before he responded. "Luke?" she said and stopped at the sight of him, at the sheer disgust on his face. She took a tentative step forward. "Stevie said you wanted to see me. Is this a bad time?"

Luke cocked his head. "With you, the timing's always bad."

"I know we can't figure this out between us…" her voice stalled at Luke's face, like he loathed her.

Luke sat on the edge of his desk and rubbed his chin. "Did you sleep well last night?"

"I did." She didn't trust the hitch in his voice.

"You slept with my brother," he said without flinching.

"You're wrong." There had to be another way to make him understand the mistake. "Please, give me time to explain."

Luke pointed at his chest. "I overheard you and Damon talking about your night ahead." The once-over he gave her hurled cheapness at her. "I also saw you leave together to go to the beach."

"There's more going on in this house than Damon's wedding." She took another step forward, refusing to let him win this match. "You honestly think I would be interested in sleeping with Damon?"

"You already did." Luke stood up, suddenly looking bored, and walked around his desk.

"I didn't sleep with Damon."

"Then why were the two of you making out on the third floor? I know what I heard. You didn't even have the decency to wait until I'd gone to bed."

"I didn't kiss Damon."

"I don't care."

Her heart broke. She could change everything by telling him about Kendra, about the baby, and about Damon. The other half of the story caused her to squirm in place, because she would have to take a leap of faith and give up the possibility of helping her brother. Her brother or Luke, she had to choose one. Right this second, and Melanie balled her fists at her sides. She took a deep breath. One little leap of faith... "You have a right to know the truth."

"You're fired," he cut her off before she could say another word.

This wasn't expected. Melanie's jaw dropped. She regrouped and tried again. "Listen to me."

"I'm not interested in anything you have to say. I want you off my property."

"You won't even hear what I have to tell you."

Luke rounded the desk. His arm shot out and he pointed to the door. "Get out or I'll throw you out."

Tears stormed out before she knew they were coming. "I'm trying to tell you what happened."

"I don't want to know," he shouted at her.

Tears flooded her face. The air in her chest felt thick, like she couldn't get in a full breath. She'd lost. Melanie started for the door with defeat hanging her shoulders down.

"By the way," he said in a cocky voice, "I won't be writing your brother any sort of support letter. Our contract is void. You forfeited your right to that bonus because I terminated you. It's all there in your contract."

She didn't say anything. She walked out of Luke's office in a smog of her own failure. She wasn't welcome in his office or under this roof and the stretch of hallway between Luke's office and her bedroom seemed to span ten miles away.

"Melanie, hello," Stevie said, meeting her at the top of the stairs and holding Vivian's hand. "Vivian's going to take a morning nap. She started to fall asleep on the floor. I—what happened? You're crying." She snuck a glance in the direction of Luke's door.

"He fired me. I'm going home."

"Fired you, why?" She put her hand on Melanie's shoulder. "Why would he let you go?"

"I don't want to say."

"Perhaps I could talk to him."

"No. There's nothing anyone can say. I'll say good-bye once I'm packed and headed to the airport. Have you seen Kendra yet? I really need to talk to her."

"I don't know when she'll be back. I know Felicity has a gown fitting this morning and then they are meeting with the woman in charge of the decorations and flowers. They could be gone all day." Stevie continued to guide Vivian over to her bedroom and they moved out of Melanie's sight.

Alone in the hallway, Melanie looked around. The fresh flowers, the open space with closed doors and muffled voices. A sense of hollowness seeped through at leaving this place. Everything felt like one big disaster and now, there was nothing left to stay for. No hope to ride on until the end of the summer. She could call Kendra, but it wouldn't make a difference. The information from Kendra wouldn't change anything. Twice now, she'd lost Luke over her brother, and at least this time, he gave her the courtesy of telling her to get out of his life himself. She opened the door to her bedroom with an arduous hand. She'd go home.

* * * *

The plane took off and Melanie watched through the window at her gate. She brought her knees to her chest, took the last drink of green tea out of the large to-go cup, and glanced at the clock again, noting little change in time. The ring of emptiness around her heart squeezed in a little more with each breath and a sharp pain behind her ribs made waiting even more miserable.

A woman with a cheery voice announced over the PA that the flight to Los Angeles would be delayed another hour. One more hour spent stuck in a place she didn't want to be. She wiped away a tear.

Jessie's number blazed through on the phone and Melanie picked it up on the first ring, relieved to talk to someone incapable of hurting her further. "Hi Jessie," she said. "I miss you so much."

"I got your text. You're at the airport?" she sounded hurried. "What's wrong?"

"Luke fired me and I'm waiting for my flight." A family of four took the seats across from her, spreading out their luggage and bags of McDonald's. The little girl kicked her brother and the mom shushed her and pushed a box of fries in her face. "Will you pick me up tonight?"

"Yes, yes, of course, I'll be there. I'm so sorry you're heading home upset. We don't have to go into the details this second. Give me your flight number and we'll figure it out. Mom will be glad to see you. She's been worried about you and so have I. You've been out of touch lately."

"I'll be home soon." Melanie passed on her flight number and provided Jessie with a general timeframe. "Have you heard from Mark by chance?"

"I have. He called yesterday and sounded really upset. What did you say to him?"

"I've been trying to figure out if I'm missing something about the night he got into a fight with Luke." Melanie stopped herself cold. It didn't matter anymore. "I've done what I could for Mark and there's nothing more I can do to help him. He'll have to rely on himself to get out early. Luke will not be writing Mark the letter. It's done. It's over."

"Mark understands this, really. I'm proud of you. We all are. I don't know if I could have done what you've done. I'm not talking only about going to Maui, but everything. You've been Mark's biggest supporter. You did a difficult thing, what you did for our brother. I think you should give yourself some credit for leaving your job, your family, and trying. Not many people would do the same."

The swamp of homesickness swallowed her up whole in the middle of the airport and Melanie began to cry. "I fell in love with him again."

"I know you did."

She sniffled loud. "Going home like this hurts more than I ever thought it could."

"You'll be home soon, hang in there."

Melanie did hang in there, for the next several hours, three different flights, and a sky full of turbulence. The pilot landed the plane at the Fresno Airport, known as FAT, late in the evening thirteen hours later. The warm, dry evening hit Melanie's skin and her body felt at home and she felt years away from Luke and Maui. The flight zapped her of her energy and she barreled into Jessie's arms and hugged her sister in the baggage claim.

The drive home, Melanie got caught up on Jessie's life. The boyfriend,

Carl, still hung around. Jessie crammed in her summer so far in a twenty-minute conversation leaving Melanie to think nothing much had changed while she was gone.

Jessie drove the car up the driveway and turned off the engine. She didn't unlock the door or take off her seat belt. "I haven't told Mark about your coming home. I thought you should be the one to tell him."

"I will tell him. I'm planning to call the prison in the morning and try to get him on the phone. My guess is he'll call soon, regardless."

"Don't forget that we know Mark better than anyone, better than Luke thinks he knows him. He looked out for us. He's been there for us, through the divorce, jerks in high school, disloyal friends. He paid for my last two semesters of school and helped me get out of student loan debt, before the lawyers sucked up every last dime."

"Where are you going with this?" Melanie circled her head and felt the pull of stiff muscles from the airline seats. She pinched the tension at her temples.

Jessie pulled the keys out of the ignition. The large, faux diamond-studded J on her keychain dangled and swung in her grasp. "I'm not going anywhere. We haven't spoken much while you were in Maui. I didn't know if, maybe, you've changed your mind about Mark's innocence. What happened to the mystery of the tourmalines anyway? Did you find them?"

"I don't ever want to talk about gemstones again." Melanie checked her phone and saw a missed call. "Let me check this," she said, and dialed her voicemail.

"Melanie, where are you? It's Kendra. What on earth is going on? I came back from Felicity's bridal gown appointment to find you'd been let go and on your way home. I have to talk to you. I owe you information for what you did and I hope I didn't get you fired. Please call me back as soon you get this message."

Melanie slid her phone closed.

"Who was that?" Jessie unlocked the door.

"Luke's assistant. It's nothing, she owed me some information." There wasn't any point in calling her back. Luke wouldn't give her the letter of support. She couldn't care less about what Kendra had to say. She deleted the message.

Chapter 25

"Do you have what I think you have?" Brent said to Luke, standing in the middle of the foyer.

"Arrived this morning," Luke answered. The timing couldn't have been worse with Melanie leaving yesterday and the rock he'd planned to give her arriving less than twenty-four hours later. Already, the house felt dull without her, but she'd made the choice easy for him and later, when he'd approached Damon, he didn't deny Melanie's attempts to sleep with him.

"Let me see that beauty." Brent and Luke stood close as Luke reached into his pocket and took out the blue garnet, still in rock form, as if the darn thing had been plucked out of the mine an hour ago. "How did you find her?"

"Andry contacted me. This gem has created a lot of activity around his hometown. He followed up on a couple of leads and found out that Bruno's men sold the stone to Chadwick's of London."

"The biggest owner of diamond mines in the world. I can only imagine what they wanted for her. Usually this type of stone goes up for auction. She doesn't come around very often."

"I got in touch with our contact at Chadwick's and negotiated a good deal. I also offered them something no one else could." Luke grinned at the forthcoming reaction from his brother.

Distracted by the stone, Brent held their prize up to the light. "Extraordinary. What did you promise them?"

"You. I signed a deal for you to do contract work for three months outside of Turkey. They own a hefty section of Grossular mines and they need someone with a certain set of skills to be on staff and oversee the quality of the gems once they're found."

"I don't like Turkey." Brent handed the garnet back to Luke. "All the gem-hunters are flocking there. It's too overcrowded for my taste. What are you going to do with this garnet anyway? Send her to auction?"

"I'm going to treat the rock myself, over at Seal's. The owner has the equipment to cut and polish and has agreed to let me use his shop this afternoon. Karen Adams is drawing up sketches and we'll show our garnet off in the form of a necklace." Luke left out the fact that he'd planned to give this to Melanie. He'd wanted this garnet more than anything and now it was in his hands, he couldn't get rid of it fast enough.

"There you are," Damon said, strutting into the main living area. "Why aren't the two of you on the beach, with the rest of us? Goldie won't shut up about you. Go down there before I tell her you're sleeping with Sid's girlfriend."

Brent rolled his eyes. "I'll be down in a minute. You should see what our brother scored."

"Depends what we're talking about. What do you have?" Damon folded his sunglasses and hung them on the front of his shirt.

"I have a blue garnet from Madagascar." He opened his hand and showed off the chunky, rough rock.

"Look at this," he marveled and whistled. Damon eyeballed the rock. "How much you want for it?"

Luke knew where he was going with this and he closed his palm. "She's not for sale."

"I've been waiting on the right stone to give to Felicity as a wedding present. I want this one. I'll pay full price. Have Karen make this a ring more stunning than Felicity's engagement ring. I want it big, flashy, and every one of her friends to be jealous when they see this on her finger."

Luke scratched the back of his neck. The idea of this ring going to Felicity by way of Damon irritated Luke. He stalled and gave Brent a momentary look of help-me-out-here. "What do you think?"

"What do *you* think? Luke, I'm your brother. You don't need Brent's input or approval. You run the company. This is your choice." Damon's gaze scanned the rock. "We'll discuss price after she's had a makeover."

Brent shrugged his shoulders. "Your call."

"Wait a minute." Damon held up his hand. "Why don't you want to sell this to me?"

"There's no reason." Luke didn't know why he wouldn't sell to Damon. Or, maybe he did. Maybe he couldn't stand the thought of Damon getting this ring after kissing Melanie.

"You're still mad at me for what Melanie did."

Brent's gaze slowly moved from Damon to Luke. "What. Did. Melanie. Do?"

"She threw herself at me."

A sharp, booming laugh ran out of Brent's mouth and echoed in the rafters. "Melanie and you? This is the most ridiculous thing I've ever heard." He caught sight of Luke's compressed lips and he stopped laughing. "Did she sleep with you?"

"Luke knows the story." Damon looked away, bored.

"Why would she? I don't know what to say. I now understand why she's no longer working for you."

The conversation plummeted from there with the angry stares between Damon and Luke. As a businessman, he couldn't turn down this deal and Damon could have his way. The goal was to get rid of the stone and to get this piece of rock far away from his life. "I'll sell you the stone."

"I'll take your deal." Damon slapped him on his back. "I want the ring ready by the wedding. The cut doesn't matter. She'll be happy with whatever I give her."

They all parted ways a few moments later with Damon and Brent heading to the beach and Luke going to Seal's to spend the afternoon transforming rock to value. The winding road of the highway shaved off some of his tension. Melanie stayed in his thoughts more than he would have liked. Each time he thought of the alluring voice she'd used to speak to Damon curdled his insides. He might have given her the benefit of the doubt, if Damon's story hadn't matched what he had seen with his own eyes.

Luke drove to Lahaina, to the touristy section with shops and restaurants. A cruise ship hovered in the horizon as one always did, every part of the year. The Surf's Up surf shop on the left sat next to Seal's, a small shop with overpriced gold necklaces, earrings, and bracelets. The latest charms hung in the window: Plumeria-shaped rings, a necklace with a whale's tail, and mini gold flip-flop earrings. Garrett Mugby, the owner, sold out of these items all the time and he greeted Luke with a smile.

"Mr. Harrison, a pleasure to see you again," he said and pumped Luke's hand. Garrett's short height forced him to look up at Luke. "I wasn't clear if you want me to do the cutting or if you preferred to do this yourself. You are a master at your art."

"I'm going to do this one myself. I have a blue garnet."

Garrett's eyes grew big. The age spots on his forehead rode up with his eyebrows. "Impressive. Only you could find such a stone. It's good to see you again."

A couple walked through the door and an electronic bell dinged. The woman removed her sunglasses and twisted a fashion ring on her right finger while the guy swept an uninterested gaze over the jewelry counters. "Do you have any of those gold flip-flops in a necklace?" she said to Garrett but settled her gaze on Luke. She stood up straight and put the tip of her sunglasses in her mouth.

"I do have the flip-flops in a necklace, over at this counter." Garrett showed them to the space displaying the necklace in sterling silver and gold. "I only use twenty-four carat gold," he said to them.

They proceeded to peruse the counters, and, eventually left without buying. "I'll show you to the back."

The short walk to the back revealed a small, disheveled office with an open door, a unisex restroom with a sign *For Customers Only*, and the back room, a slightly larger room with inventory stacked in boxes and locked in heavy cases. The row of machines on the back wall Luke recognized at once. The gem cutter and the gem polisher both appeared more like saws. They sat side-by-side and to the right, a station with tubes or flames, and a heat treatment machine for stones like rubies and sapphires, ones that required more heat.

The electronic bell dinged again and Garrett looked to the door. "Do you need assistance?"

"I've got this." He sat down at the bench and turned on the desk lamp. "I'll come get you if I need anything."

"Excellent. Take your time."

Garnets in general didn't require much heat treatment, if any. They posed a natural rarity of being unspoiled on their own. They didn't require countless hours of changing their color or their brilliancy. Once he got them out of the rock, they shone with minimal touch-ups.

Luke took the rock out of his pocket and tumbled it in his hand a few times. He located one of the tools, a pair of pliers on Garrett's tool board and hand-chipped away the rock with steady hands. The rock wouldn't take much abuse and needed to be dealt with gently and with care. If he pushed too hard, the inclusions could expand and shatter the stone.

The room grew hot without air conditioning by the time Luke removed

Inclusions 223

what he could of the rock. Some of the edges would need to be shaved down. He swung his leg over the crate he sat on and shifted over to the tubes providing the flames for heat. This garnet would need a small amount of heat treatment. He wouldn't use the machine. Old-school fire would do the trick. He could control the outcome better using this method. There was such a thing as overheating gemstones, a mistake he'd made too many times in the past.

Luke got lost in his work. The slightest flame burned away the remains of the outer rock, leaving with him an uneven cube of the actual garnet. Satisfied with his work, he stepped over to the machine used to cut the stone. He shook out his hands, turned on the machine and let the roar fill up the room. A bead of sweat dripped off his forehead and he held his breath. One shot is all he had to get this cut the correct way. Luke leaned into the machine. He kept the stone at the end of his fingers, which brought them dangerously close to getting amputated with the slightest error.

Luke worked the stone up against the saw until the pointed edges rounded and the surface changed to flat. He breathed a long breath and switched off the machine. "Almost there," he said, and moved onto the polishing machine.

When he finished, Luke held the stone up to the light. He took the loupe out of his pocket, turned the light up on the only lamp in the room, and inspected his work. A faint scratch-like mark appeared on the face of the gem. Luke put the gem on the small scale next to the polishing machine. Five-point-twenty-three carats, round cut transparent blue color. Next, he used the millimeter gauge to get the dimensions and copied down the width and length. The other details he recorded included the size, clarity, and the country of origin. The work was done. The stone sat in the palm of his hand and he admired the outcome.

Any of the mess he made, he cleaned up and returned to how Garrett had everything arranged. Luke put the stone in a velvet bag he'd brought with him, and returned to the front of the store, where Garrett talked with an elderly woman waffling over a multi-colored palm tree charm for her necklace.

"Is everything okay, Mr. Harrison?" Garrett said.

"I owe you one," Luke responded. "Let me know if there's anything I can do for you."

Garrett smiled and returned his attention to the woman in front of him. "This would make an excellent gift for your sister…"

The afternoon sun beat down on Luke as the door closed behind him. Tempted as he was, he didn't take the stone out and look at the finished product in the light. Throngs of sun-burnt and slow-walking tourists moved about him. A little girl took a lick of her ice cream cone and the entire scoop fell on the ground. The girl screamed. Her mother picked up the girl in a huff and walked away fast.

* * * *

Not until Luke sat with a glass of wine and watched the sun go down, did he take out the garnet. Luke admired his work and for some reason, fought the urge to keep this one. This was the gem he'd been after. The one intended for Melanie.

"You're back already," Stevie said, joining him out on the patio with Vivian a few steps behind.

Vivian walked over to Luke and climbed on his lap. The sight of the garnet beheld all of her toddler interest. Her little jaw parted and she reached out for the shiny object. "Da-da," she said.

Luke grinned at the sight of Vivian's fingers pulling on his in an attempt to get the garnet. "You can't have this."

"I'm sorry to see Melanie's left us," Stevie said after a long pause. "I know that absolutely this is none of my business. I know you'll remind me of that. I know I'm not your mother and I'm not Vivian's grandmother. But I know you, Luke. I know there's nothing about you capable of bending from your decisions. You're a powerful, focused man. It saddens me to think that you might be missing out on the biggest adventure of your life." She paused and looked at Vivian. "Your own stubbornness keeps you from forming a family."

"Don't use your status in our family to cross the line. Yes, you raised my brothers and I," Luke held his hand higher and kept Vivian's digging fingers out of his reach. "This one has a mean grasp on her."

"I will admit: I didn't like the idea of you hiring Melanie at first. Call it job security, or whatever. I didn't want Vivian to struggle. Melanie has shown me otherwise and I think it's time you paid more attention to your daughter."

Inclusions

"Suddenly you're Melanie's biggest fan?"

"I'm certainly on her side. I see what she sees. I see how Vivian acts compared to other kids her age. I've been to the park with her several times since coming to Maui and I understand now. She doesn't interact with other kids. She's afraid of everything: slides, swings, the fun little sea turtle kids fight over to climb on and ride. Other children tried to talk to her and she stared off to the sky. I've been struggling to interact with her. I didn't want there to be a problem. I want her to be normal. I keep thinking if she has more time. If she starts to do and say what she's supposed to then we won't have to worry."

"You don't think I look at my daughter and don't have the same concerns?" Luke dropped his fist with the garnet. He could see the remorse in Stevie's eyes.

"I lied to Vivian's doctor at her fifteen month check-up. I also wasn't completely honest at her eighteen-month appointment either."

Luke felt his hands sit up Vivian in slow motion. The beat of his heart shot up and his head spun. "You've been lying to me. I've put you in charge of my daughter."

"I thought what I did was harmless. I filled out a questionnaire on behalf of you, like I always do. Some of the questions needed my input. The doctor wanted to know small, unimportant findings like if Vivian feeds herself with a spoon or if she engages in pretend play. I answered questions about her speech, about all aspects of her life. I thought she would grow into these abilities. I thought I could teach her. I lied to the pediatrician and I lied to you and I'm terribly sorry."

"How can you tell me this?" Luke's nostrils flared at Stevie. He put down Vivian. "You're my family. I rely on you to help raise my daughter. I trusted you."

"I thought I could help Vivian. I thought she would catch up in her own time and I resented Melanie from the moment you hired her. Melanie has shown me that I didn't have a clue about what I was doing. I can't help Vivian."

Luke took a shaky breath; his arms and legs tightened. "How many other times did you lie to Vivian's doctor?"

"You tell one lie and you have to keep up with all of them." She cast her gaze away from Luke and gazed sorrowfully at Vivian. "I didn't think you would take well to knowing your daughter isn't like other children, that there's something different about her interactions with other people."

"She's my daughter," Luke blasted. "You're my aunt. Do you not know I'd do anything for her? Do you not think I wouldn't want to know and give her the best services?"

"You took Vivian out of her mother's house and replaced her surroundings with nothing more than a big house with an absent parent. You're no better than Vivian's mother. You don't know what your daughter can do. You're partially invested in her upbringing and you see her for a half hour each day. Your first love is your job. It's the biggest *inclusion* in your life."

"Telling me the truth is what's best for her. You had no right."

Stevie's hands trembled. "My intentions weren't meant to hurt you or come between us. You deserve more than what I've been entrusted to do. I love Vivian like I love you and I made a big mistake."

"I won't forgive you for this." Luke picked up Vivian and carried her close, as if he alone could protect her.

Chapter 26

The pile of clothes on the floor smelled like coconut lotion, like her sunblock. One whiff and Melanie's mind saw Luke's house, and she could feel the softness of her sheets, and she could see the magnificent view of the ocean from his patio. The image beat out the pale walls and rickety ceiling fan from her room at her mother's house. Four full days she'd been home and she unzipped her suitcase, ready to get on with her life.

She sat down on the floor and sorted out the clothes between colors and whites without much focus and when she finished unloading her clothes, she stared at the empty suitcase. She missed him. She ached for him from the bottom of her soul. She took in the smell of his scent on her clothes and it filled her up with a sadness she couldn't pinpoint, a constant drum of loss, missed opportunities, and mistakes beat across her heart.

The second time around she completed the division of laundry with accuracy, put the first batch in the laundry basket, and went to the washing machine down the hallway. The laundry room in the house looked more like a dump for abandoned clothes and she walked around the leaning stacks of towels, t-shirts, pants, and shorts. Jugs of detergent sat on the dryer, their measuring caps long gone, lost to the jaws of the laundry room, a vicious beast that had claimed the lives of matching socks, shirts, even jeans. Melanie kicked a pile of shorts and tops belonging to Jessie, all bright colors and flowery feminine prints, and lifted up the lid on the washer.

The house felt quiet and strange. Jessie slept in and her mother ran errands and had promised to bring back donuts. Melanie put in her laundry, got the cycle going, and headed over to the kitchen. Coffee sat in the coffee pot and Melanie grabbed a cup. She took a seat at the table and contemplated what she would do today.

Yesterday, she'd called her boss at the Growing Tree and had been told to call back in a month, no guarantees. The person working in her place happened to be working out quite well and her boss couldn't bring on anyone else at the moment. She thought about contacting Luke and pushed the thought aside. He wouldn't talk to her ever again. The garage door cranked open with the sound of wood splitting and Melanie got up to open the door for her mother.

"You're up early," her mother said, getting out of the car. She passed Melanie a box with a clear lid showing off a dozen donuts creamed in chocolate icing. "Couldn't sleep in?"

"I haven't slept in since high school." Melanie lifted the box out of her mother's hands.

"What are your plans for today?" Leslie Cahill followed Melanie inside the house and pressed the garage door button. The garage clunked a slow march back down.

"I have none. Maybe I'll lay out by the pool or see what Jessie's doing." She set the box on the counter with a subdued attitude. "The possibilities are endless."

Leslie put her hands on her hips and looked like an older version of her daughters when she did this. "You're becoming the poster child for moping. Are you ready to open up and talk to me?"

"I don't know. Have you forgiven me for leaving?"

"I was never really upset with you."

Jessie shuffled into the kitchen yawning. Her nose picked up the sweet, sticky donut scent from a hallway away. "Hey," she said, eyeing up the white box on the counter.

Leslie passed out a napkin to each of her girls and moved the box of donuts from the counter to the center of the table. "We're talking about what's bothering Melanie."

"He's gone. Get over him." Jessie grabbed a donut and dusted off a few loose sprinkles. "I want to set you up with one of Carl's friends. He's a doctor."

Melanie feigned interest. "What kind of a doctor?"

"A podiatrist," she responded enthusiastically and sat down.

"No thank you."

"I don't see why you're hung up on Luke. You're stuck in a rut and you think he's the only one right for you. Well, you're wrong. There are tons of better men out there."

"How would you know?"

"Girls, girls," Leslie broke through their arguing, "you do nothing but argue these days. Jessie, let your sister work through the breakup. She finally had gotten over Luke and what happened? He came right back into her life." One quick gaze reprimanded Jessie and Leslie turned to face her other daughter.

"So you're on my side." Melanie straightened a little.

"I wouldn't go that far. This family's been shredded by Luke. You quit your job and ran off to Maui, even after everything we've gone through. I don't think I'll ever understand, but you're back and that's all I care about."

Melanie got up, grabbed a donut, and sat back down. She hid behind taking a large bite of her donut and said with a full mouth, "For the record: I did not quit my job. I got offered a better deal."

"I'm sure Luke got the better end of that deal," Jessie retorted.

"Stop, Jess."

"I told you Luke would never help Mark." Jessie shrugged. "I wouldn't have dropped everything."

"I also can't remember the last time you've been truly happy." Melanie bit her lower lip and glowered.

Leslie took a seat in the middle of the table holding a mug full of coffee. "I do want you to know, Melanie, that I can't have you fighting every one of Mark's battles. Nor you, Jessie. Mark has survived this long and he'll come home to us eventually. There's nothing more we can say or do to change this fact." A loaded glance passed from Leslie to Jessie.

Melanie caught the glance. The one her mother used when trying to keep a secret. She put down her donut. "What am I missing?"

"Nothing," Leslie said fast. "Let me get you another donut."

"Forget the donut. You're keeping something from me." She glanced at Jessie; Jessie avoided eye contact.

Leslie's tone turned remorseful. "You're right. I am keeping something from you."

Jessie's head flew up. "No, Mom."

Leslie put up a hand to her daughter. "I'm tired of all the lies. This is probably how we got here in the first place. Sitting around the kitchen table, each one of us protecting our own interests. Melanie, you can't begin to understand what defines a mother. Neither can you, Jessie. Not until you are one can you truly know what self-sacrifice means. I know you know how to be a sister and from the beginning, you and Mark palled around together. Melanie, you've always been close to your brother in a way Jessie has never been. You have the right to think you alone can help him, but that's not the case. I can't let you continue to protect him."

Melanie's eyebrows wrinkled. "Is there a point to this?"

Leslie set down her cup and sighed. "Mark *did* try to kill Luke. The jury got that right. There wasn't ever a mistake in their judgment or their punishment."

Immediately, Melanie turned to unhelpful Jessie. The confirmation painted a clear picture on her sister's face and the air plunged out of Melanie's chest. Somewhere not to deep inside Melanie she felt the release of a lost battle. She also felt sick to her stomach. "You already know?"

"Mark mentioned to me first the possibility of his leaving the business. The decision didn't bother me so much as what he looked like when he told me. I can still see the red, alert gaze and his lips looked they'd been gnawed on by some animal. Stress eventually shows up in the face and I realized something else had been going wrong in his life." She folded over her hands. "I feared for him. I knew something wasn't right. I didn't know what though and he wouldn't say. To this day he hasn't told me, but I think he managed to ring up a lot of debt. A friend of mine's son worked in an underground gambling ring and she'd mentioned her son had spoken of seeing Mark."

"You think he owed money? How? He didn't have any. The gem company he worked for wasn't making much. It's a crap business to begin with unless you're an appraiser or a dealer. All risk and little reward."

"You don't have to have money to get into debt. I think he met some shady characters and I think he got himself into trouble. Three days later I was at home grading papers and the detective showed up on our doorstep. I went down to the police station, as you know, and I saw your brother. There are scratches on his face and there was the bad cut under his right eye. When I asked him what had happened to Luke he said Luke had tried to kill him. I knew right away this was untrue. Luke never had any reason to want Mark to end up with a face like a bloody roast. I know my son and I knew when he was bullshitting me. I'm an expert on whenever the three of you try to hide something."

Melanie leaned in the table with her fists curled at her sides. "You're seriously choosing to tell me this now?"

"I told Mark to tell me the truth. I pledged my loyalty to him as a mother, as the woman who brought him in this world. I would be with him every step of the way from the trial to the jury's decision. But I wouldn't be made a fool. He either told me what really happened or he'd lose my support. Nobody else would stick up for him and I'd put on the best poker face you've ever seen. I'd go to the ends of the earth for any one of you. I refused to be one of those mothers or fathers out there speaking into the camera and putting on a poor act of convincing the media and the nation they know their child couldn't have done something so terrible. I told him to tell me the truth. I told him I'd be with him every step of the way, but I wouldn't be a fool. If he wanted my support, he had to confess to me and the matter would stay between us. I stood up for him and I've been standing by him." She sat up self-righteously and added with finality, "That is what defines a mother, loving a child through their biggest mistakes."

"He confessed to you?" Melanie's voice sounded like the tail end of an echo. Her head swam. The whirr of the refrigerator sounded loud in a room muzzled with heavy thoughts. "What about you, Jessie, how long have you known?"

Jessie cleared her throat. "Halfway through the trial, I overheard Mom talking to one of his lawyers. The comments she had made didn't sit well with me and I grew suspicious."

"You let me fight for him." Melanie pounded her fist on the table. The strain of her breathing and the dizziness in her head overcame her. "You allowed me to defend him."

"Nobody else could know, not your aunts, your father, even the pastor. I sheltered you from having to face other people eager to judge you and treat you like an outcast. To know what Mark almost did is an awful weight to carry. I've had to live with this."

Mouth agape, Melanie got up from her chair. "Luke's been right. About everything. I—I have to get out of this house."

"Where are you going?" Leslie stood up and tried to get in Melanie's way.

Melanie sidestepped her mother and warned, "Don't follow me."

Straight to her bedroom she went. The small room boxed her in as she grappled with the revelations of the morning. The room confined her and she felt claustrophobic. She changed out of her pajamas with her mind speeding faster than she could keep up and she re-opened the suitcase she hadn't yet put away and began loading clothes inside.

Jessie opened the door and stood in Melanie's room with tears streaking down her face. "Listen to what I have to say."

"No." Melanie continued packing and zipped her bag. "You could have stopped me from going to Maui." She lifted the bag off the floor. "Get out of my way." Melanie pushed by Jessie and nicked her shoulders.

Three feet down the hallway, a disturbing thought entered her mind and she turned back around. "Where are the tourmalines?"

"I don't know, really," she said like a child.

"You're lying."

"I don't know what you're talking about." Jessie flattened against the wall. "I honestly don't have a clue."

"Mark stole them, didn't he? What did he do with them?"

"I don't know."

Melanie dropped her purse and rushed over to Jessie's room. Jessie stepped back and missed Melanie's body by an inch. Melanie plowed into the room. She opened drawers. She tossed out clothes. Jessie yelled at her to stop, but Melanie didn't hear. She moved to the desk and rattled out the drawers. Nothing but papers and pens and flash drives.

"Stop it!" Jessie shouted.

"I'll search this entire house if I must." Melanie kept digging and rooting through Jessie's belongings. She looked under the bed, in the nightstand, in the closet. The clothes fell off the hangers into colorful piles on the floor. "You're willing to lose me as a sister over one more lie. Where do the lies start? Where do they end? I resent the way you and Mom handled everything. Don't you think I'd struggled to ignore the evidence against Mark? Don't you think I felt the doubts? That I heard the conflicting pieces of Mark's story versus Luke's? Thanks to the two of you feeding me bad information and false hope, I kept those opinions to myself." Melanie stumbled backwards out of the closet, tripped on a shoe box and landed on her rear with her heart in her throat. She breathed heavy. She fought back tears.

Leslie stood in the doorway. "No more, Melanie."

She looked up to her mother. "Do you know about the bag of tourmalines?"

"I don't know anything about them." Leslie shook her head and glanced at Jessie. "Do you know?"

Inclusions

Jessie closed her eyes and pursed her lips. "I promised Mark I'd keep them safe." The lie crumbled at her feet and tears rolled fast down her eyes and over her cheeks. "Mark broke into Luke's apartment and he stole them. He asked me to pick them up from his apartment and I did. I got there before the cops arrived and I took them home. He asked me to keep them for safe-keeping, for a financial boost if he should go to prison. He didn't know if he could trust you, given your involvement with Luke. He asked me. He'd never asked anything of me and I wanted to do this one thing for him."

A suitcase on the top shelf in the closet tumbled down. Melanie flinched. It missed her by inches. "They don't belong to you."

"Jessie, give them up," her mother said. "Enough is enough."

Jessie's indigent expression reached her eyes. She took a long breath, stepped over the suitcase, and into the closet. She reached up to a boring beige shoebox and pulled it down. She sat down next to Melanie and took off the lid. A mesh of tissue paper covered the navy velvety bag she pulled out.

"I only looked at these on the night Mark gave them to me. I've never touched them since." She undid the string on the bag. "Hold out your hands."

Melanie's palms came together. She held her breath. "Okay."

Jessie poured them out. A cascade of Paraiba Tourmalines the color of paradise poured into Melanie's hands. The color alone transfixed Melanie and dulled everything else around her. The sunlight played off the electric blues. They flickered with each small movement of her hands. A soft grin rode up Melanie's lips. They were here, in her hands, and they humbled her beyond words. Luke had been right. These couldn't be anything other than unforgettable.

Melanie put them back in the bag and closed the drawstring. She stood up and walked around her sister only to meet her mother's teary eyes and red face in the hallway. "I'm not coming back for a long time."

"I know," Leslie cried.

Melanie squeezed the bag full of gemstones. They would remain with her until they could be returned to their rightful owner. "I have to get my suitcase." She walked out of the room, grabbed her bags, picked up her purse, and walked out of the house.

The front door closed behind Melanie and she didn't look back. She called a cab and waited close to an hour to be picked up and taken to the airport. While she waited, she did so without one thought of going inside. They couldn't change her mind. They couldn't apologize their way out of this. The blue-and-white cab pulled up to the curb and Melanie swore she heard the front door open a little. She wouldn't ever know.

The familiar smell of cleaning detergent hit Melanie's senses upon entering the airport. The sound of her footsteps squeaked all the way to the ticket counter where she bought a ticket back to Maui. Nerves washed through her at the possibility of Luke turning her away, but she needed to see him and tell him in person all that her mother and Jessie had been keeping from her. If he told her to get lost, she'd get lost. She'd take the next flight to anywhere and start a new life, without her family, without him, and one day she might come home to collect the rest of her belongings. No family is better than a lying, betraying one.

The short check-out lines made getting through security a breeze. Whenever she wasn't in a hurry to get some place, she found herself with more time than she knew what do with. It's not like she could buy a book or read a magazine, not with the conversations she replayed in her mind.

She took a seat on one of the connected chair benches and took out her phone. She toyed with the idea of calling Luke. The possibility of him not picking up and not calling her back felt too big a risk to take. She put her phone down, only to have the screen light up with an incoming call. The sight of the phone number twisted Melanie's stomach around. She glanced around at the chairs, empty except for a businessman typing fast and eroding away the keyboard on his laptop. Indecision plagued Melanie and her hand rested on the phone. She took a deep breath and answered with all the warmth of a drill sergeant, "Hello, Mark."

"Hi, Mel," he answered.

She said nothing.

"I feel bad about how we left our last call. I want to see if we're okay. Are you…are you busy?"

"I'm busy."

"Can you talk?"

"Can you live with yourself?"

"Excuse me?"

Melanie crowed. "You heard me. Tell me how you can live with yourself for dragging me through your crime. You exploited my loyalty. You took advantage of me. I've been fighting for you for way too long. I'm done."

"I don't know what line Luke's feeding you. I know how convincing he can be. Don't fall for his persuasive tactics."

"You assaulted the man I fell in love with. You were going to wipe him from this earth." Melanie caught the businessman staring at her and he quickly lowered his head and went back to typing. "I won't help you anymore. I'll write to the parole board myself and beg them not to let you free and if you do get out, don't call me. Don't ever talk to me again." She ended the call with a shaky finger. "You're on your own," she said to no one.

The crew member standing behind the airline counter picked up the phone and announced boarding would begin in a few minutes. Melanie got in line and boarded the plane. The seat she occupied by the window captured the colorless buildings and aged palm trees surrounding the airport. Smaller planes sat off to the side on the runway and she closed the shade on her window and closed her eyes. Whatever the future held, she would face it with her eyes wide open.

Chapter 27

The weather on the morning of the wedding became a bride's worst nightmare. Lightning struck outside and the lights flickered above. The weatherman promised a clear afternoon and evening, despite the current choppy conditions.

"I can't remember if rain is a good or bad omen for the wedding," Brent said and pointed at the barrel of thunder rolling through the gray sky.

"Are you going to give me the necklace or do I have to call my lawyer?" Damon joked and reached at the garnet dangling from the white gold chain.

Karen Adams had worked fast and got the necklace to meet Luke's exact criteria. Damon had wanted a ring, but Luke thought a necklace showed off the stone much better. "When are you going to give this to Felicity?" Luke said, handing over the final product.

"After the ceremony, while we're on our honeymoon. We leave tomorrow morning for Portugal." Damon whistled. "I still think this should have been a ring."

The reluctance Luke felt in handing it over stemmed from somewhere inside of him. A glimpse of the future he'd wanted with Melanie. The necklace should have been hers. A stone like this deserved to sit on her graceful neck, not in some showcase window in his house or on another woman's body. He tried not to think about all that. She was gone. Luke let go of the necklace. "I don't want this."

Kendra came over to him at the moment Damon made an excuse and left them. She motioned to the tables leaning against the wall. "Has Damon thought of an alternate plan if the rain doesn't clear?"

"We'll have to have the ceremony inside and set up for the reception after. The interior of this house will be fitting for Felicity and up to her standards. I don't want the weather to ruin her day, even if my brother is going to ruin her life."

Kendra's mouth opened slowly and she shook her head. "How will he ruin her life?"

"You know how my brother acts. Damon has trouble making it past a mirror some mornings." Luke scratched his chin and angled his face. He decided to confide in Kendra. "The other night I caught Damon and Melanie sneaking out of the house."

Her eyes widened. "You did?"

"Never mind. I think we should talk about finding a replacement speech therapist for Vivian. I already have an appointment set up with her pediatrician late next week."

"They weren't sneaking out."

Luke's gaze riveted on Kendra. "I'm talking about Vivian."

"I don't think…I mean…you're the one Melanie wants. She's in love with you. Don't you know? Can't you tell?"

"I don't want to hear Melanie's name mentioned again. Now, about Vivian—"

"I don't think you should be so quick to hold that against her. Maybe she needed to talk to Damon. They might have had business."

"*Kendra.* Don't make excuses for her or my brother. The only reason I haven't thrown him out is because of Felicity." Luke shifted on his feet. The persistence in her eyes drew out an impatient sigh in him. "What?"

The commotion outside the front caused them both to turn their heads. "That should be the setup crew." The doorbell rang and Kendra didn't move. "I talked to Stevie, is Vivian okay?"

"She'll be fine. I'm going to be taking a more active role in her care. Stevie's not going to be her nanny any more. She's family, so she'll help out, but the lines haven't been clear on what gets communicated back to me. The situation is too close for her to be objective with me." The doorbell rang a second time. "Focus on the wedding, nothing else."

Luke left Kendra at the bottom of the stairs and went up to his office. Tomorrow he'd brief Kendra on his plans to leave immediately and return to Belvedere. The summer vacation would end early. Without Melanie, without Stevie capable as a nanny, and Brent heading off to his temporary work for Chadwick's, Luke didn't see much incentive to stick around. Luke slid his hand up the banister and knocked twice at the end. Home is where he needed to be. The place he'd continue to run the company, raise his daughter, and keep his life settled and managed, the way he'd always done.

He entered the office and turned on his lights. Kendra's discussion of Melanie riled up Luke all over again. The thought of her disloyalty roared through his mind and he sat down, opened his laptop, and began sifting through his work, when Brent knocked on his open door.

"Hey," Brent said. "You're not in the mood for the pre-wedding festivities?"

"No," Luke quipped.

Brent walked in the room and took a seat. "I overheard Damon flirting with the wedding coordinator. A shame Felicity will have to put up with him. She's actually a decent human."

Luke's gaze shot up to Brent. "I'm not in the business of getting involved in Damon's personal disaster. I only care about if he does his job for us. He's old enough to deal with the consequences of his decisions, and trust me when I say that I would not want to deal with Felicity on the day she finds out about his interest in other women."

"I've been doing some thinking. This deal you made for me, working for one of the biggest diamond and gemstone mine corporations, have you given any thought to selling Trace to them and getting back out there in the field as a contract miner? I know you miss the hunts."

"I have Vivian and I cannot be away from her for weeks or months at a time." The chair swiveled slightly under Luke.

Brent lifted his eyebrows, causing wrinkles to appear on his forehead from long days in the sun. "About Melanie—I think we should talk about her."

Luke's fist hit the desk. "No!" The storm raged outside and blew over potted plants on the deck. It matched the maddening thoughts related to topics involving Melanie. Luke rubbed his hands together, powerless to undo the image that would forever have changed his mind about the woman he'd loved. And he *had* loved her.

He still loved her.

"I'm going to go downstairs." Brent interrupted Luke's thoughts. "Have a beer with me when you come down."

Luke stayed in his office for some time after Brent left. The isolation and down time didn't improve his mood. He'd rather be down at Seal's and changing some rock into a gemstone. The lab at his home in Belvedere served as his outlet when he needed to get away from his thoughts.

The storm blew over by the early afternoon and left a scene of bold colors in the aftermath. The green in the plants shone deep like green sapphires. The brown of the dirt looked like fresh chocolate, and the shade

Inclusions

of blue in the ocean emulated the sky. Luke drank a beer on his balcony and watched the wedding preparation from a distance. The crew of men walked the chairs and tables over to the patio and another crew hammered the trellis together off to the side of the pool.

"Mr. Harrison," Kendra said behind him.

Luke turned.

"Isn't someone down there looking for you?" The anxiety in Kendra's eyes worried him. She never showed her softer, personal side aside from being mad at someone. "What is it?" he said impatiently.

"I'm fully prepared to accept my resignation."

Luke set down his beer and folded his arms over his chest. "What are you talking about?"

The sound of a saw cutting wood ripped through the air. "I'm pregnant."

"Pregnant?" Luke's gaze drifted to her belly.

"I'm going to have a baby." She patted her belly. "I'm entering my second trimester. If I didn't tell you now, you'd find out soon enough on your own."

"I'm sure we can work out something with your job." He rolled his head. "You don't need to quit today. Six months is a long time to come to a solution." He wouldn't tell her the baby would compromise her roll, but he had other, more stationary and less-demanding positions she could work at and remain in his company. "I've been looking for someone to work with Damon and follow his paperwork with more care. I don't want you to worry. There'll be a job for you, okay?"

"I won't work with or for Damon." Her head fell to her hands. Her shoulders moved up with her sigh. "I can't work for your brother."

"I'll find you something else then." Luke took her shoulders and she lifted her head and sniffled. "I thought you didn't cry. Are you going to tell me what's got you upset, aside from the pregnancy?"

Her face turned white. "You should know you're wrong about Melanie."

Luke's teeth grinded. "*Enough* about Melanie."

"She didn't try to seduce Damon."

"I don't care." An impatient hand ran over Luke's eye. His teeth set on edge.

"You *should* care. I sent her there to talk to Damon."

"Why would you do such a thing?"

"Because Damon's the father of my baby," she blurted.

Luke's eyes flared. *"What?"* The men hammering the trellis chose this moment to pound louder and with more force than at any other time. Luke couldn't think straight. "Tell me all of it. Now."

"Damon hasn't given me the time of day since he arrived. He refused to see me and he won't talk to me. I had some information about the tourmalines and I made a deal with Melanie that I'd tell her if she could get Damon to meet me on the beach. I had to meet with him away from the house so no one would see us." She snorted and wiped away a tear. "Of course you happened to be awake and misconstrued the entire plot. I wasn't going to tell you, but I couldn't stand the thought of Melanie being punished for something she didn't do. Your grudge isn't something I would wish on anyone. She deserves more and you need to know the truth."

"How long have you been seeing my brother?"

"Longer than we should admit to, a little over a year. It started out innocently during a business trip to finalize the acquisition of those three pink diamonds Brent purchased. You remember, the owner of the diamond mine claimed Brent trespassed."

"I remember." Luke nodded. "What about Felicity?"

"I've always been Damon's other woman. I'm not proud about becoming pregnant by a man about to marry another woman. But I want to clear Melanie's name. I did meet your brother on the beach. I asked her to get him there for me. Damon wouldn't have shown up otherwise. What you overheard was Melanie coaxing Damon out of bed and playing to his weaknesses, nothing more."

Luke cringed at the entire proof of his accusations. The thought of Melanie taking the brunt of Kendra and Damon's problems blazed through his body. He put his hands on the back of the chair. "Did you meet Damon on the beach?"

"I did." She ran her hand through her hair. "I told him about the baby and he refused to take responsibility. He wants nothing to do with this child."

"What are your plans for this child?"

"I'll have this baby and raise the child as a single mother. I won't ask or demand Damon of anything. It's the way our relationship has always worked. I understand if the circumstances around my job have changed. I won't lie to you and tell you I haven't been concerned about if and when you'll allow me to work for you. This baby comprises our working relationship."

"Kendra, three days ago I had my staff entirely in place: a nanny for my daughter, a speech-therapist, and a personal assistant all at my disposal. You've put me a position to have to completely start over with a team I trusted and respected."

"What about Damon? Where's his blame?" She approached Luke with white knuckles. "If you want me to quit I'll quit."

Luke raked his hands through his hair. "Do your job. We'll figure out the rest after the wedding."

"I can live with that for today." Kendra turned and walked out. "We'll talk later."

Luke walked back into his office. He reached for his phone and dialed Melanie's number. Before she could answer he hung up and decided to do something else first. He'd go and find Damon.

The door to Damon's room was locked. Luke jiggled the handle and pounded on the door. "Unlock the door. I need to talk to you," he shouted.

A curse word hurled through the air, and finally, Damon turned the lock and opened the door. "What do you want?" he said rudely, yawned, and scratched his cheek.

"You got Kendra pregnant?" Luke grabbed the collar of his shirt and yanked him towards him. "What were you thinking?"

"She hasn't proven this baby is mine." He grinned with pride. "I'm an evidence man, let's not forget."

Luke and Damon wrestled back against the wall. Their limbs hurled punches. The lamp on the nightstand crashed to the floor. "You got her pregnant," Luke repeated.

"She wanted to get pregnant. She did it on purpose." Damon ducked and hit Luke in the side.

"Hey!" Brent yelled and rushed through the open door. "Hey!" He threw his own punch and put his fist between the two of them. "Back off.

Back off." His body jammed between them and they were forced to step back.

Damon straightened his shirt and cracked his neck. "He's attacking me on my wedding day."

"Shut-up, Damon," Brent said and stretched out his arms to keep them from going at each other. "What's going on?"

"Ask him," Luke said, wiping off his cheek. A small leak of blood came off his lip.

"Kendra's pregnant." Damon worked out a kink in his neck. "I'm the father."

Luke backed away. "Don't go through with this wedding."

"I'm going to marry Felicity. There's no reason she has to know."

"There's every reason," Luke roared. "You've grown sloppy. You're pathetic."

A low whistle ran through Damon's lips. "I respect my future wife and I won't have another woman be a menace to the life we're going to build. Kendra's all yours. Fire her, keep her on, it doesn't matter to me. I'm the one who's a partner in our company. I'll put up a much bigger fight if you try to make this legal."

Luke primed his fists. Cramps formed from curling them so tight. Brent adjusted his arms. "Don't even think about swinging."

"That's what I thought." Damon wiped his mouth and walked out of the room. "I'm getting married this afternoon."

"We can deal with this tomorrow," Brent said.

"This changes everything." Luke straightened his sleeve and stalked past Brent.

The doorbell rang and signified the continuation of more wedding activities. Luke returned to the main floor and found the trellis in place. Two sheer swaths of fabric pulled to each side and held in place by pale peach, pink, and white roses already huge in their bloom. Large pots of the same roses trimmed into circles took up space on either side of the trellis and chairs draped in bows the color of pale skin created an aisle down the center. Felicity stood up at the front, she spoke fast and loud to a woman with hair the color of the bows on the chairs. The bride looked up at Luke, frowned, and cut off her conversation with the woman.

Inclusions

The catering staff, led by Latonya, cooked up something smelling rich and sweet, and making Luke's mouth water. Both unopened and opened boxes took up space on the floor. A group of workers from the event planning company set up tables near the door. The house transformed into a warm, idyllic scene for a wedding. Amongst the setup and organization, Luke glimpsed the day through a different lens now. The scene in front of him was wasted on his brother and his unsuspecting bride. For a brief moment, he imagined this in a different light, as if it were his own wedding, and if only Melanie could be here to stand at the trellis, with the wind roughing up her hair and her cherry-red lips grinning back at him unevenly.

"Have you seen Kendra?" Felicity said. The lines under her eyes spelled stress and the tone of her voice mimicked all-out panic. "I don't know what I'll do if I can't find her in the next five minutes. My stylist is stuck in traffic behind a tour bus with a blown-out tire, and my makeup lady hasn't been heard from. The wedding cake's the wrong flavor and the florist sent me roses when I ordered Freesias. My one-and-only hasn't responded to any of my texts either." She finally released her breath. "Is Damon at least awake?"

"Damon's awake." Luke didn't want her reading into anything he said.

"I don't want to see Damon before the wedding. Kendra is our buffer."

Luke laughed. "I wouldn't say she's a buffer."

"If you see her, tell her I'm looking for her."

"I will." Luke sidestepped Felicity and dodged tripping over a box of programs. He grabbed his phone and checked his messages. He knew she wouldn't have called him. Luke ran up the stairs and waited in his office until he could get what he needed out of Damon's bedroom.

Chapter 28

The custom-made suit fit the contours of Luke's lean body. Damon stayed holed up in the first floor bedroom while Luke and Brent greeted guests and ushered them to their seats. A music trio dressed in tuxedos sat off to the side playing classical music with a cello, violin, and a flutist. The boxes were packed away, the champagne chilled, and an army of caterers led by Latonya waited with baited breath from behind the kitchen door. Luke stood off to the side of the trellis with his hands resting at his sides and his mind nowhere near the wedding about to take place. A mutual friend of the bride and groom led Felicity's mother down the aisle, followed by Brent, holding up his arm for Felicity's older, pregnant sister. He took his position next to Luke.

The smiles on the faces of the guests sparked electricity into the room. Luke's eyes raked over the guests. Excitement brewed in the air. People spoke with energy and looked on with a mix of covetous pleasure. Vivian squirmed on Stevie's lap in the front row. Her bare feet stuck out from under her dress and the big bow on her head sat askew. She slid down Stevie's lap and Stevie put her back up. His heart filled with such love for his daughter. He would find a way to help her; to really *see* her.

He glanced away from her and spotted Kendra, at the back of the room. He couldn't see the exact expression on her face. He kept looking at her and he squinted, feeling a rush of unsettled nerves down his back. Kendra moved back and rang her hands. He grew annoyed at her constant fidgeting and then he realized with alarm that Kendra paced, not walked. The look on her face—apprehensive—reminded him of the way she looked in the middle of a meeting and tried to convey to him that there was trouble.

Damon walked down the aisle with full swagger and a devilish grin to match. He wore smugness like an offensive cologne. Luke's fists tightened at his sides. The doubts about Damon's trustworthiness multiplied and expanded. Family members were supposed to know limits. Damon should know his boundaries. Instead, his brother picked himself over the interests of their business. Damon ignored the sensitive, professional relationship Luke had crafted with Kendra. She handled everything: travel, booking, employees, research and Damon was willing to throw her position away, her efforts at making the company more successful for some stolen nights. The thought of Damon lying to him about Melanie and about why he went with her to the beach brought white-hot pain to his knuckles. He opened his fingers and could feel the blood rush back to his fingertips.

The music stopped in the timeless, breath-holding moment. Like this one perfect pause in time could be stretched out forever. The poised and eye-catching bride stood at the entrance to the aisle. The musicians played *Glasgow Love Theme* and the bride took her first step while holding in her hands a bouquet of blush roses centered at her middle.

Luke fought the urge to check his watch. The plane awaited him. His forever waited after that. His gaze moved away from Felicity and over the other guests. Felicity's mother dabbed her eyes in the front row. The pregnant sister and her husband leaned into each other. An elderly woman craned her neck and another couple spoke softly to each other. Goldie dabbed her eyes with a tissue.

The guests listened and sat holding up faces of happy anticipation and Luke looked back to the bride, then to the last row, until his gazed stalled at the sight of familiar, warm eyes. The grin came into view next. That familiar, private way only she reserved for him. The music swelled and took over.

Luke took a step forward and broke away from the line of groomsmen. Brent's discreet hand prevented Luke from moving. "Looks like you have a visitor," he said through wired lips.

"Indeed, I do," Luke responded without taking his eyes off her.

Felicity reached the end of the aisle and handed her bouquet to her mother and hugged her. She gazed at Damon with newlywed eyes all the way to him, not breaking eye contact for one second. All of the guests looked to the bride and groom, but Luke looked to Melanie.

The Officiate presiding over the ceremony thanked everyone for joining Felicity and Damon on their special day. "Today you will leave your individual lives and become a union and a family," he said and continued in a voice loud enough to carry into the house. "Today you become something more than yourself. You are creating a future, a home, and a commitment to each other…"

The words spoken about love and commitment grazed Luke's ears, and he looked at Melanie as if making some silent union with her.

"The rings, please," said The Officiate.

Brent reached into his breast pocket and pulled out two white gold bands, one for his brother and the other for Felicity. He handed them to The Officiate without joke or remark.

"This ring signifies a never-ending circle of hope, love, and faith. Damon, do you take Felicity as your wife, to honor and love her, in good times and bad? If you do, say so, and place the ring on her finger."

"I do," Damon said and slid the band on her finger.

The Officiate turned to Felicity. "Do you take Damon as your husband, to honor and love him, in good times and bad? If you do, say so by placing the ring on his finger."

Felicity turned back to her mother, then at Kendra, who appeared to be standing at the back of the room, and returned her gaze to Damon. "I don't."

Damon's head jilted forward; his eyes unbelieving. "What?"

The Officiate's eyes popped. "Felicity, do you take Damon as your husband?" he tried again.

"You heard me. I said no. I don't want to marry you," she blared like a megaphone. The lace-covered shoulders shrugged up and down. "I won't marry you in this lifetime."

"What do you mean?" Damon grabbed her hand and yanked her forward. He put his face up in hers. "Everyone's watching. All of our friends and our family, this is my brother's house," he seethed.

"You slept with another woman while we were dating." Felicity turned to her guests. "He slept with another woman our entire engagement. He got her pregnant." Felicity's mother half stood up, remained stooped. A murmur skidded through the audience like skipping stones, each reaction becoming stronger and more pronounced. "My fiancé is going to be a father and I'm not anywhere close to becoming pregnant." She shoved the bouquet to his chest, picked up her slender skirt, and walked away, talking as she went. "This man is a cheater. He's a liar and in case you're going to try and weasel your way out of this, let me be clear: I'm leaving you at the altar!"

The guests sat dumbstruck. They didn't speak or move. A couple of them hid their cell phones after recording the entire scene. Damon charged down the aisle after Felicity. The infamous brother known for his suave legal skills and connected to a family of gem-hunters ran after his bride.

Luke acted fast. He stepped forward and addressed the guests, "I thank everyone for coming today. I know many of you traveled a long way. I apologize, but there will be no wedding today. I ask everyone to leave us alone and give my brother and our family some privacy."

Felicity's mother shot up from her chair and stomped her foot. "I'm going after my daughter," she blasted to another guest and left her chair, knocking over the empty one next to her. She ran down the aisle as fast as her legs would carry her.

The other guests followed Felicity's mother without protest or comment. Nobody dared to say a single word. They settled for knowing, scandalous glances to one another.

"I'll go find our brother," Brent said, slapped Luke's arm, and walked off.

Luke lingered near the trellis until every last guest departed. Nothing but empty chairs and floor vases of roses lined the aisle. A slight breeze flared up their petals and the silky ribbons tied around the vases. A cluster of people remained at the far end of the house, near the front door, and the catering staff began talking amongst themselves, waiting for direction. Melanie too had disappeared in the wake of everyone scattering out of the wedding ceremony.

Luke turned his back to the rows of chairs. He crossed his arms over his chest and stared out thoughtfully at the ocean. A thin mist of longing for Melanie stirred beneath his skin. He'd been so quick to judge her. To dismiss her. She'd done everything he'd asked of her…she'd come to Maui on a whim with an insane offer. She'd taken all the risk. She'd worn the burden he'd placed on her to take a leap of faith and trust him. But what had he ever really, truly, risked for her? Nothing. Not one thing. She showed up, sitting in the back row, not standing next to him at the altar, because he'd pushed her away, again. He hung his head in shame.

Luke turned around. His heart crashed into his chest. She stood there in the middle of the aisle breathtaking and radiant. The flowers and ribbons of the decorations flapped in a sudden gust of wind and flared up her shirt and her hair. She looked soft and supple and he wanted to reach out and touch her face. "Hello," he said, too afraid to move for fear that he would do or say the wrong thing. He was defenseless against this moment and not even he would try to take control.

"I went to find Kendra," she said.

He remembered to breathe. "When did you get here?"

"Just in time to see your brother get what he deserved." She bit back a smile. "What about the groomsman, is he okay?"

"I am now." Luke broke out of the trance and walked over to her. He slid his hand up her cheek and drew her close. "I know what happened the night you tried to get Damon on the beach. I know about Kendra's baby. I owe you a huge apology."

"There seems to be a lot of confusion surrounding each of us whenever we're together and I won't allow that to continue. I don't want an apology. I want us to be even. I know what my brother tried to do to you. I know he's guilty of the horrible act you accused of him of doing. I won't let him come between us again. Enough time has been lost because of him. You and I, we've both been wrong. We've both disappointed each other. We're also back in front of each other, despite everything. There's nothing left except how I feel about you."

The corner of his lip pulled up. "How do you feel about me?"

"I love you."

He yanked her into his body and slid his hands down her back. "I am in love with you, Melanie. There's no one else in the way. Not our past, not the people in our lives. This is how I want you. Close to me."

She laughed softly. "I agree."

"Melanie?" Stevie said, surprised. "I thought you'd left for the Mainland."

Melanie separated from Luke. "I did. I've returned after two delayed flights and bad weather. I'm late, but I'm here."

Stevie shook her head at all the empty chairs. Her gaze moved up the aisle to the trellis. The curtains and flowers attached to the wood swayed in the breeze. "What a waste of a beautiful day. That poor girl. I wish I'd known about Damon. I would have flown to Chicago and set him straight. I can't imagine what Kendra is going through."

Luke unbuttoned his jacket and the button at the collar of his shirt. "She knows we'll help her in whatever way we can."

Stevie turned to Melanie. "I owe you an apology for how I've acted to you. I was wrong about you."

"Thank you, but an apology isn't necessary. I'd like for all this to move forward." Melanie swirled her hand in the air.

"Stevie is going to be taking some much needed time for herself once we return to Belvedere," Luke explained.

"I'm looking forward to having more free time," Stevie added with a contented grin.

"Are you still going to be Vivian's nanny?" Melanie said.

"No, not in the day-to-day sense. I wouldn't dare miss out on Vivian's childhood."

"Sounds like the two of you have everything worked out." Melanie put her hand in Luke's.

Stevie's head inclined forward. "Don't leave us hanging. *Will* there be a wedding today?"

Luke watched Melanie blush. He cleared his throat and squeezed her hand. "Not today, but someday soon."

Stevie patted Melanie lovingly on the shoulder. "It's good to see you. If you'll excuse me, I'm going to join Vivian in the kitchen. There's enough food to feed this entire neighborhood. Make sure you get something to eat." She smiled at Luke and padded back down the aisle.

Melanie's gaze moved up to Luke's. "There's something I brought for you." She reached in her purse and withdrew the velvet bag.

Luke's lips parted slow. A look of peace washed over his eyes. He reached out and touched the bag. "I haven't seen this in a long time."

"My sister has been their keeper. Mark gave them to her to watch over and hold until he got out. She finally gave them to me."

Luke picked up the bag and set it on a chair. He ran his finger over the string. A strange, unassuming expression crossed his face.

"Don't you want to see them?" Melanie's mouth formed a weak smile. "I didn't know about them. I didn't know how much they tied my brother to that awful day."

Luke looked at Melanie with stark gentleness. "I think they've caused enough problems between the two of us. We can look at them later, together. Right now, I don't want to destroy this moment with talk about your brother. You are here. That's all I care about." Luke removed his jacket and reached into his pocket. A black, velvet box appeared in his hand and he laid the jacket on the back of the chair. "Don't let this get stolen." He smirked when he spoke, knowing how sensitive she would be about the content inside. "I can't get this back a second time." He opened the box.

Melanie peered inside. Her hand jumped to her heart. "Oh my gosh…" she said, speechless.

"This is the blue garnet. The one Bruno and his men got off you." He took it out and placed it around her neck. He fastened it there and admired the way it dangled against her glowing skin. The stone gave off a deep blue hue with the storm clouds moving in overhead and before their eyes, began to darken.

"How did you ever get this back?" She ran her finger over the stone.

"Gemstones have a way of returning." Luke lowered his face to her and kissed her. He encircled his hands around her waist. The heat from his body matched hers and he whispered, "There's more where that came from."

She slid her hands down his thighs. "Are we talking about gems or something more?"

"Definitely something more."

Epilogue

Speech therapist Gabby wrapped up her session with Vivian. She sat and manually held Vivian's hand, showing her how to put the toys back in the pink crate. Melanie got up, walked over to Vivian and took a seat next to her. "How did she do?" she asked.

"Vivian's doing very well. Her vocabulary's expanding every day. Soon, she'll be putting sentences together." Gabby tucked away her educational tools in her bag and zipped up the sides. "I can tell everyone involved in Vivian's life is working hard at getting her to make those vowel sounds. She's also able to make the sounds of a sheep, cow, and very close to a horse. This is good. This is progress. The therapy helps them move forward. I get concerned when I don't see progress and that's not the case here. We're also getting ready for our next sixth-month evaluation of Vivian. Put in," she said directly to Vivian and held eye contact with her. "In," she repeated and moved Vivian's hand with the toy hammer into the crate.

Melanie scooted the pile of puzzles and toys closer to Vivian. "Put in," she echoed.

Gabby waited until all of the toys had been returned and the floor clear of all the items from their session. She turned to Vivian and waved. "Bye-bye."

Vivian held up her hand and attempted, "Buh-bye."

Melanie reached out to touch Vivian's hand. She took it and Vivian meshed her fingers around Melanie's. They walked Gabby out of the playroom and down the hallway, past the rows of windows with the curtains pulled back. The sun shone with glaring brightness on the floor and showed off the faintest scuff mark. The gooey, sweet smell of melting chocolate wafted through the hallway and Melanie's stomach fluttered.

Vivian broke free and ran ahead to the front of the house. The automatic door opened and Vivian giggled and pointed and flapped her hands. She ran into it to get the door to open again and squealed with delight.

Gabby passed a knowing glance to Melanie. "I hope everything goes well tomorrow."

Melanie ran her hand over her burgeoning belly. "We'll let you know how the appointment goes."

Gabby walked through the open doors and left them to their house. Melanie took Vivian's hand more firmly than usual and turned a protesting Vivian around. Vivian started to scream and Melanie redirected her upset stepdaughter. "Want a cookie?" she said, following the scent of what could only be hot chocolate chip cookies.

Vivian broke free of her hand and ran into the kitchen. A very pregnant Melanie walked in a moment later. Her eyes shooting fireworks at the trays of cookies with steam still coming off their tops on the counter.

"Gabby's all done?" Latonya said, turning her head to the side to glance at Melanie and Vivian. She looked back to the oven and pulled out another tray using oversized pot holders.

"She's gone. Cookie?" she said to Vivian.

Vivian nodded like she hadn't eaten in hours. She understood "cookie" without confusion or needing an additional prompt. Vivian ran to the table and chairs, climbed up, and hit her hands against the table like some Viking waiting for a plate full of meat.

The house in Belvedere felt like home. The chill of winter faded a few weeks ago giving way to blossoms on the trees and too much grass on all of their acreage. Melanie sat down at the table, next to Vivian. In a few weeks Vivian would have two sisters. Luke would have three daughters.

Melanie's pregnancy had been rough at first. The morning sickness eventually faded and she'd had an overall easy time, except for the gaping hole in her support system. Her mother and Jessie hadn't been involved with the pregnancy at all. So all the highs, like the first kick and first sonogram, she shared with Luke, Stevie, and Latonya. It panged Melanie to go through this without her family, but the vacancy of their fallout remained. She couldn't speak to them without her heart turning black and her words still unkind towards them.

She nibbled on a cookie and thought about them now. One day she would forgive them. Not today. She'd get there on her own. A tree branch moved outside and Melanie caught sight of Luke talking on his phone and pacing. He'd returned from a trip to Thailand with Brent two days before and would be out of the field until the summer. He didn't travel much, and when he did, Melanie didn't hold him back. So long as he came home to her. She wiggled her ring finger, the one usually showing off one of the many gems he had made for her.

She got up out of the chair. "I'm going outside. Will you keep an eye on Vivian?"

"I've got cookies, she's going nowhere," she said to Vivian and smiled at Melanie. "Go on."

Melanie walked out the side door. Luke saw her and ended his call. "Hi," he said. "These weeks will be the last time it's ever quiet again in this house."

"I know," Melanie said, laughing. "Are you ready?"

"I've already got a gift for the girls."

Luke reached into his pocket and pulled out a burgundy velvet bag with a silky rope drawstring. "Open your hand."

Melanie's palm opened under his and out of the bag dropped two aquamarine gemstones the size of a quarter. "These girls are starting out spoiled."

"They're their birthstones," he said proudly. "They're only ten carats each."

"You're unbelievable."

"I bought Vivian one. You should see the emerald I have tucked away for her in my vault. I've never treated it. It's untouched. Close to five carats." Luke wrapped his arms around Melanie. He held her like this for a long moment. "Tell me she'll be okay."

She heard the concern in his voice. "She'll be okay. She's a bright girl and she works so hard at her speech. The development specialist we're seeing tomorrow will give us direction. We both know whatever she says won't matter. Vivian's come a long way. She's happy, she's healthy, and she's making such good progress." Melanie breathed in his familiar scent. The outdoors stayed with him for days after he got home and it reminded her of the night they shared the tent in Madagascar. "Let's not think too far ahead about the future."

He kissed the top of her head. "The moment you came to this house, unannounced, is the moment I knew."

"What did you know?" Melanie gazed up at him. A tiny foot kicked against her ribs and she put her hand up high on her belly.

"I knew you'd be standing here one day, with me."

"What a relief that you offered me a job." Another odd sensation, swiped across the lower part of her belly, a heel maybe.

Luke chuckled. "We both know I was offering you much, much more." He reached into his pocket and took out his phone. "It's Brent, let me take this."

Melanie stepped aside and watched Luke's eyes light up. She knew that look. He was receiving a tip. She laughed out loud.

Luke snapped up his gaze to hers. "Your source is for real?" He paused and nodded with a knowing grin. "You're sure this red diamond is over eight carats?"

"Go get it," Melanie mouthed.

He wrapped his arm around her chest and held her close. "I'm already where I want to be."

About the Author

Emily Duvall graduated from Sonoma State University and The University of Colorado, Colorado Springs with a Master's degree in Sociology. She worked in the field of social and educational research for several years before taking up writing. She lives in Maryland with her husband and two children. Find out more information about Emily's writing at www.emilyduvall.com.

For your reading pleasure, we invite you to visit our web bookstore

WHISKEY CREEK PRESS

www.whiskeycreekpress.com

Made in the USA
Middletown, DE
28 May 2015